T0300785

The
Politician

ALSO BY TIM SULLIVAN

The Dentist
The Cyclist
The Patient

The
Politician

TIM
A **DS CROSS** THRILLER
SULLIVAN

HEAD
of ZEUS

An Aries Book

First published in the UK in 2022 by Head of Zeus
This paperback edition first published in 2023 by Head of Zeus,
part of Bloomsbury Publishing Plc

Copyright © Tim Sullivan, 2022

The moral right of Tim Sullivan to be identified as the author
of this work has been asserted in accordance with the
Copyright, Designs and Patents Act of 1988.

All rights reserved. No part of this publication may be
reproduced, stored in a retrieval system, or transmitted in any form
or by any means, electronic, mechanical, photocopying, recording,
or otherwise, without the prior permission of both the copyright
owner and the above publisher of this book.

This is a work of fiction. All characters, organisations,
and events portrayed in this novel are either products of
the author's imagination or are used fictitiously.

9 7 5 3 1 2 4 6 8

A catalogue record for this book is available from
the British Library.

ISBN (PB): 9781801107792
ISBN (E): 9781801107815

Cover design: Ben Prior

Typeset by Divaddict Publishing Solutions

Printed and bound in Great Britain by
CPI Group (UK) Ltd, Croydon CR0 4YY

MIX
Paper | Supporting
responsible forestry
FSC
www.fsc.org
FSC® C171272

Head of Zeus Ltd
First Floor East
5–8 Hardwick Street
London EC1R 4RG

WWW.HEADOFZEUS.COM

For Derek Granger

Mentor and friend

Virtute et Industria

I

A cup or mug for drinking tea wasn't even a question for DS George Cross. A cup. Obviously. Bone china, preferably. It maintained the temperature of the tea perfectly, and the thinness of the rim meant that the drinker's lips weren't forced too far apart, enabling them to sip rather than gulp. A sip opens the palate to the complexities of the leaf. A gulp does not. The thin cup also gave the tea maximum exposure over the mouth's tastebuds, giving the drinker a more complete experience.

He was thinking this as he stood outside Peggy Frampton's bedroom, looking at her dead body. An objective observer might have found the sight of Cross dressed head to toe in a white paper forensic suit, delicately sipping his tea, strange, if not disrespectful in the circumstances. But he and his partner DS Josie Ottey had accepted the offer of refreshment from Peggy's neighbour, Joanne, as they waited for the forensic team to arrive. They had been invited in together with the deceased's distraught, and slightly hysterical, cleaning lady Marina, who had discovered her employer's body. The house itself was now a crime scene and Cross had been quick to usher everyone outside. He had accepted the offer of tea, unusual for him, as he had quickly ascertained that the

I

neighbour took her tea seriously. She not only used leaves but was going to serve it in bone china.

Detective Sergeant George Cross didn't look much like a policeman underneath the forensic suit. He was in his early forties, balding and of medium height. This is why he generally had to produce his warrant card more often than his colleagues to prove his identity. Members of the public frequently didn't believe the eccentric man in front of them was a DS from the Avon and Somerset police. With his fluorescent bicycle clips permanently attached to his ankles, drab raincoat with shirt and tie just visible under a V-neck sweater, he looked more like a downtrodden door-to-door salesman from the 1960s than a murder detective.

He had come back to the murder scene, now that forensics had arrived. He felt there wasn't much to gain from talking to the cleaner at this point. She had found the body. That was all she had to offer currently, and he would talk to her more about her employer and family later.

'DS Cross?' Cross turned to see a tall, unfamiliar young man in a white forensics suit walking up the stairs. 'I'm Michael Swift, forensic scientist, or crime scene investigator – whichever you prefer.'

Cross was taken aback by the man's height. 'Well, which is it?' he said, ignoring the proffered hand, which seemed to come down out of the sky towards him.

'Both, as it happens. Primarily forensic scientist but also CSI as I like to get out of the lab occasionally. Well, that's slightly inaccurate as this is my first crime scene. Julia's in court.'

'You're late. The rest of your team is already here.'

'Late how?'

'By not being on time,' Cross informed him.

'I came here as soon as I was assigned,' said the bemused young man.

'How tall are you?' Cross asked, ignoring his answer.

'Six foot eight. How tall are you?'

'Five foot ten.'

'Good, well I'm glad we got that out of the way. Where's the body?'

'In there.'

Cross then watched him work. He was thorough and methodical, giving the scene considered attention. Trying to ascertain where it had things to say. After half an hour Swift reappeared at the bedroom door.

'Has anyone been in the bedroom this morning?' he asked.

'The cleaner who discovered the body.'

'And where is she now?'

'Next door.'

'Anyone else been in?'

'Just DS Ottey to confirm the victim was deceased.'

'Anyone else?'

'Obviously not. It's a crime scene with a deep pile carpet, which we didn't want to disturb,' added Cross.

'Excellent,' replied Swift. 'Could you take me to the cleaning lady?'

Cross was about to object, when he realised that he wasn't actually doing anything at that precise moment, so didn't really have a valid reason to say no.

'Were you here yesterday?' Swift asked Marina.

'I come every day.'

'Did you vacuum the bedroom?'

'Yes.'

'Was anyone in the house?'

'No, Mr Frampton is in London. Mrs Frampton had left and was going to be late. She had a big day.'

'Great. Are those the shoes you were wearing when you discovered Mrs Frampton?'

'Yes,' replied Marina nervously.

'Could I take a photograph of the soles?' he asked, then immediately noticed she was apprehensive. 'It's just so I can exclude them from the other prints on the carpet.' She took off her shoes and gave them to him. He photographed them with his large camera which had a white circle around the lens. It emitted a blinding flash when he took a picture. What happened next told Cross a lot about the young man. Instead of just giving her back the shoes, Swift knelt down and put them back on Marina's feet. He then left. Ottey looked at Cross.

'How tall do you think he is?' she asked.

'He's six foot eight,' he replied authoritatively.

'Oh, you didn't.'

'What?'

'Ask.'

'I did.'

'Was that the first thing you asked?'

'No, the second,' he said, as if proud of the fact that he had avoided that mistake. 'My first question was to ask why he was late.'

Swift had detected a lot of foot traffic on the bedroom carpet and was being very careful not to disturb it. On first glance this looked like a burglary gone wrong. The point of entry was crude. A pane of glass in the back door which led directly into the kitchen had been smashed. The key had been left in the door by the homeowner, making entry easy. The intruder was then disturbed, hit out at the owner of the house and killed her, possibly unintentionally. The chest of drawers and the wardrobes had been disturbed. Things would undoubtedly be missing. First impressions of a crime scene often proved to be correct, but just as often didn't. So, he tried to view the room objectively, putting his first assumption aside. He walked around the edge of the room, then closed the curtains. He positioned a light close to the floor, and switched it on. The footsteps were immediately more visible. A pattern all over the room. He began to photograph them systematically.

Cross decided to look at the other upstairs rooms. There were four other bedrooms. Two of them appeared to be spare rooms. The other two, young people's bedrooms. A daughter and a son, Cross inferred from various photographs and posters. Children who had left home some time ago, he deduced from a calendar on a wall and an old-model Mac desktop computer in the other. Cross looked out of the bedroom window. It had an enviable view of the Clifton Suspension Bridge. The house was at the top of a hill that ran parallel to the gorge. Victorian homes descended the hill in an orderly, genteel manner, wrought-iron railings adorning their balconies.

When Cross returned to the door of the master bedroom, Swift had moved into the bathroom. He looked up at Cross. With his long angular face he could have been the love child of Will Self and Pete Townsend from The Who.

'Please don't come in,' he said.

'I have no intention of doing so, until you're finished,' Cross replied.

'I didn't mean to be rude, it's just that you've lost one of your shoe coverings.' Cross looked down at the offending shoe protruding from his white suit.

'So I have,' he replied, determining at the same time that there was no more for him to do there. He would analyse the young man's findings later. He did note, however, that there was no aspirated blood on the carpet next to the victim's mouth, which probably meant that death was fairly instantaneous. Swift threw him another pair of fresh shoe coverings. He put one on the offending shoe.

He would always see the deceased's body in situ if possible, and this he'd done. He hadn't come to any conclusions at this point. He never did. Cross was driven by evidence and facts, not impressions and assumptions. This way of working was partly down to his being on the spectrum but also because he had seen other detectives, as he was growing up in the force, waste huge amounts of time pursuing hunches and assumptions that, in the end, proved to be fruitless. This, in turn, led to him having an extraordinarily high success rate of conversion – arrest to conviction.

'Cause of death probably blunt-force trauma to the head. But I haven't come across a murder weapon yet,' Swift said.

'Are you also a forensic pathologist?' Cross asked.

'I am not.'

'Then perhaps you should keep your observations within the parameters of your field. There is a collection of glass paperweights on the table over there organised in a symmetrical pattern. One of them is missing.'

'Good call,' said Swift enthusiastically. 'There are two sets of footprints. One barefoot, presumably the victim's. The other individual looks like he was wearing shoe coverings.'

'He?' Cross asked.

'Yes, I'm pretty sure. Unless it was a woman with enormously large feet,' Swift replied.

Cross turned to leave as Ottey appeared. She looked at Swift who was now processing the bathroom, taking swabs from the sink.

'What makes you think the intruder went into the bathroom?' she asked.

'What makes you think he didn't?' came the reply.

'Not much to steal in there, I would've thought. Anyway, she ran a bath which tells you the burglar can't have been in there,' Ottey went on.

'Do we know that she turned the bath taps off?' Swift asked.

'We do not,' she replied.

'So my first point would be that if she didn't, then he must've done as the bath didn't cause a flood. My second would be: how do we know he didn't use the bathroom?'

'Forty-nine per cent of burglars use a lavatory in the premises they are burgling,' said Cross, joining in.

'So nature doesn't call for fifty-one per cent of them,' countered Ottey.

'Not entirely true,' replied Swift before Cross finished for him.

'Fourteen per cent defecate on the bed. Often mistaken as a deliberately antagonistic gesture, but more often than not done out of sheer fear, panic in an attempt to make no noise and for ease of wiping.'

Ottey grimaced.

'What Mr Swift is trying to say is that we don't as yet know whether our burglar is one of the remaining thirty-seven per cent who have full control of their bowels,' said Cross.

'You two are a marriage made in heaven,' said Ottey.

'Firstly, as you are well aware, I am heterosexual, though I cannot of course speak for him.'

'Michael,' said Swift.

'And as I have no belief in heaven, the likelihood of his and my partnering anywhere seems minimal, if not impossible,' replied Cross who seemed to be staring at the victim's face. He hadn't actually taken what she'd said literally, he was simply quibbling with her use of the expression. Ottey wanted to make a pithy rejoinder as this was her first encounter with Swift. She didn't want to be left on the back foot. Swift obviously sensed this too and waited for it. But it wasn't forthcoming.

'I look forward to your report,' she finally said. The look between them silently acknowledged that her parting shot was not really up to snuff. She decided to leave before making herself look even more ridiculous. Cross took out his phone and took a photograph of Peggy's head. After examining the photograph, particularly the area of carpet in front of her mouth, he left the room. Swift, meanwhile, examined the bathroom taps more carefully. There were prints. Likely to be the victim's, but he immediately set about retrieving them.

2

Marina Rodriguez was a diminutive woman in her mid-fifties. Originally from Spain, she had dark brown eyes and thick black hair tied back tightly in a ponytail. She had worked for the Frampton family for decades – since she'd first come to England. She was a family friend and had even been on holiday with them when the children were small. The way she talked about them you could be forgiven for thinking that she had no family of her own, but she did; a husband and three boys. When Cross and Ottey finally sat down to talk with her, she had progressed from hysterical, blood-draining shock to the kind of numb state imposed on the body by the brain – as if it were taking charge of the situation. She was still shaking, though.

'How many children do the Framptons have?' Ottey began.

'Two,' she replied. 'Justin and Sasha.'

'How old?' Ottey went on.

'Justin is thirty-two, Sasha twenty-nine,' Marina replied.

'Do they still live locally?'

'Justin does, Sasha lives in Cheltenham.'

'And what do they do?'

'Justin is an entrepreneur. Sasha is a GP.'

'Does Justin work for a company?'

Cross noticed the slightest of hesitations on Marina's part. 'He's in antiques.'

'What about Mr and Mrs Frampton? What do they do?' Ottey asked.

'Peggy is an influencer now and a writer. She used to be the mayor a few years ago. He is a lawyer,' she replied. Cross noted the use of Peggy's first name and the pronoun for the husband. Mayor? He thought the name had sounded familiar.

'*The* Peggy Frampton?' asked Ottey.

'Yes,' Marina replied quietly. Was Ottey referring to her being well-known for being a past mayor, or a social media influencer? Cross looked at his partner for further explanation, but she didn't oblige.

'Where is the husband at the moment?' Ottey asked.

'On his way back from London. He was on a big case up there.'

'He's a barrister?' said Ottey.

'Yes.'

'Did you see Mrs Frampton yesterday?'

'Yes, I make her tea every morning.'

'How was she?' Ottey continued.

'Fine. I'm not sure why, but yesterday was a big day for her,' Marina continued. Her accent still held onto its Spanish roots, but some Bristol intonations and inflections had worked their way in.

'She was the Mayor of Bristol who had lately become something of an online phenom,' Ottey explained to Cross. He sighed at her linguistic truncation. 'She blogged about personal problems. Like an online agony aunt. She had millions of followers.'

'Three and a half million on Instagram alone. Five million across all platforms,' Marina informed them.

'How was their marriage?' Cross asked.

'Excuse me?' she said, a little affronted at either the question itself or Cross's tone.

'They'd been married a long time. Sometimes that can lead to difficulties,' said Ottey.

'I'm the cleaner. I don't know about such things.'

'What things?' Cross responded quickly.

'Like their marriage.'

'But you said you are a family friend.'

'Doesn't mean I'm a busybody,' she retorted.

'Quite so,' said Ottey smiling.

'Are you familiar with Mrs Frampton's jewellery?' Cross asked.

'You think I'm a thief?'

'That I don't know.'

'I'm not a thief!'

'DS Cross isn't suggesting that. I think what he was about to ask was whether you're familiar enough to have a look at where she keeps her jewellery, and see whether you think anything is missing,' said Ottey.

'Yes, but do I have to go up there again?' she asked, obviously terrified by the prospect.

'Not until the corpse has been removed,' said Cross by way of what he thought was assurance. In fact he was about to look at Ottey for her approval when Marina burst into a flood of tears at his brusque reference to her employer's body. This perplexed him. He was making such a determined effort to be more tactful in these situations. Clearly his efforts still had a lot further to go.

'It's something we can leave till tomorrow,' Ottey reassured the devastated woman. She then looked at Cross to impress upon him silently that this conversation was over.

Luke Frampton arrived an hour later, unfortunately at the exact moment the coroners were removing his wife's body from the house in a bag. However delicately and considerately done, the sight of this is always shocking for relatives. Normally everything is done to prevent them from witnessing their loved one leaving their home for the last time, never to be seen again, in a body bag. It underlines the finality, confirms the cruel reality of what has happened in an irrevocable way. The idea that the person you so recently kissed, hugged, laughed with, has been zipped up into a black plastic bag, is inconceivable.

He had arrived in a black Mercedes and was wearing a black pinstripe suit with an open shirt. The driver was dressed in a grey suit. A private car from London, Cross imagined. The driver stood back as his passenger refused any help with his luggage – a suitcase and a large barrister's briefcase. He looked drained; the driver, that was. It must've been a long, probably silent, journey. Cross wondered if they talked about anything or whether Luke Frampton had told the driver the reason for his sudden rush back to Bristol, and the driver had left him alone with his thoughts. It was a fare he wouldn't forget in a hurry. A good one nevertheless, but memorable for all the wrong reasons.

As Luke saw his wife's body being removed from their house and gently loaded into the grey private ambulance – essentially a nondescript van which would pass by unnoticed in the street, except for the discreet lettering whispering its morbid purpose – he dropped his luggage and sank to his knees on the pavement in disbelief. Ottey and Cross observed this from the kitchen window which overlooked the road. They had been drawn to the window by the loud animal wail that came from the widowed barrister's mouth. Marina had remained rooted to the spot in the kitchen, not wanting to witness the distressing scene outside.

DC Nish Parminder, the family liaison officer who had been assigned to the case earlier that morning, emerged from the house and walked slowly over to the kneeling man. She helped him up gently and took him to Joanne the neighbour's house, explaining that he could go back into his house after forensics had finished. Another uniform appeared, went over and picked up Luke's luggage. They waited respectfully as he watched the ambulance drive off, then walked back into the house.

Cross stayed where he was and watched Michael Swift go back into the Frampton house having retrieved some equipment from his van across the road. He had hung back as Luke and the two uniformed officers went into the neighbour's house, keeping out of view as if he knew from experience that the sight of him dressed in a white forensics suit would only exacerbate Luke's fragile state. When the coast was clear he went back to the bedroom, to carry on with his meticulous search for forensic clues.

When Luke came into the neighbour's house, Joanne immediately took him in her arms and held him.

'Luke, I'm so, so sorry.'

'Why are we in your house?' he asked, having not heard a word the FLO had said to him.

'Your property is now a crime scene,' said Cross.

'We'll try and open it up as soon as possible. But it could take a few days. Is there somewhere else you can stay?' asked Ottey.

'You know you're more than welcome to stay here,' offered Joanne.

'I think I'll check into a hotel if that's all right with you?'

'Of course. Whatever you want. You know Roger and I are here for anything you need.'

Luke now noticed Marina for the first time and turned towards her. She stood up and bowed her head slightly. Cross wondered whether this was subservient or just respectful in the circumstances. Luke walked across to her and took her in his arms.

'Marina, you poor thing. You found her. How dreadful for you. Are you all right?'

'Yes, I'm okay. Poor Peggy.' And she started sobbing again.

'Would you like some tea?' Joanne asked Luke.

'Any chance of a coffee?'

'Yes, of course, or would you prefer a brandy?'

'A little early, I think.'

'Sure. I was just thinking for the shock. I'll make you a coffee.'

Luke now turned to the detectives as if it was the first time he'd become aware of them.

'I'm DS Ottey and this is my colleague DS Cross. We're so sorry for your loss.'

'Thank you.' He turned to Cross to receive his condolences.

'You're much shorter than your wife,' was all he got.

'I beg your pardon?' Luke spluttered.

'Your wife was much taller than you. She was quite a tall

woman,' Cross went on. Luke looked at Ottey for some sort of help. She was wondering what it was with Cross and people's height that morning. He often did this. Got something in his head which he became obsessed with for a while, not able to let it go.

'I'm sorry, my colleague tends to immerse himself so fully in an investigation, he often forgets the need for social niceties. Shall we sit down?'

'Murder? I thought it was a burglary,' Luke said a few minutes later in Joanne's sitting room.

'Why did you think that?' asked Cross.

'Someone told me.'

'Who?'

'I can't remember. But it has to be a burglary. Why else would someone do this?' Luke protested.

'Do you know why anyone would want to hurt her?' asked Ottey.

'Not like this.'

'Then, like what?' asked Cross.

'What?' asked a puzzled Luke.

'Did she have any enemies?' Ottey butted in.

'She did while she was in politics, but not to the extent that someone would consider murdering her,' Luke said.

'What about online?'

'No. She was an agony aunt, for heaven's sake. Though she hated that expression. Recently she'd become something of a silver influencer. I believe that's the term.'

'She was also an antiques expert?' asked Cross.

'In a manner of speaking.' Luke laughed quietly.

'Silver influencer, as in the older generation,' Ottey attempted to explain. Cross was still at a loss, but would follow up with her later.

'What about you? What area of the Bar do you practise in?' Ottey asked.

'I'm a criminal barrister. Look, could we do this later? Maybe tomorrow? I could come to you, if you like.'

'Of course.'

Then something suddenly occurred to him. The blood drained from his face. 'The children. I have to tell the children. They don't know.' He thought about it for a moment then looked up at Joanne. 'How do I do that? How do you tell your child that their mother's been murdered?'

'We could send officers to Sasha if you like? She's in Cheltenham, yes?'

'Would that be better, do you think?' Then he answered his own question: 'No, better I do it. I'll call Sash, I have no choice but call. I'll go over to Justin... what am I talking about? He's away. A short break. He'll have to come back, of course.'

'George, you have to express your condolences to the bereaved before you start to talk,' Ottey said to Cross as they walked to the car. She'd lost count of the number of times they'd had this conversation, but she wasn't going to give up.

'But you did it for us,' Cross remonstrated.

'That's not enough. You have to reiterate. Not comment on how much shorter than his wife the man is. It means something to people. You're expressing sympathy as a person, not as a policeman. It shows them you have empathy, which I know is something you struggle with. But please try.'

'I have written it down,' he said, holding up his notebook.

'No, try now,' she said.

'What do you mean?' he asked, puzzled.

'Do it to me.'

'But you're not bereaved,' he protested.

'George. Now. Do it,' she commanded.

He thought about it for a moment. She was completely serious, so the probability was that they weren't going anywhere till he did what she wanted.

'I'm sorry for your loss,' he muttered.

'So sorry. Put a "so" in there.'

'I'm so sorry for your loss.'

'But look at me. In the eyes.'

'I'm so sorry for your loss,' he repeated.

'We're getting there. But be a bit more, I don't know. Strong.'

'I'm so sorry for your loss,' he said. It wasn't perfect but at least he was trying.

'Just like that. Again.'

'No.'

3

'Burglary gone wrong,' announced DCI Ben Carson the following morning, with an authoritative tone which seemed to imply that no one else had thought of this. He was with Ottey, Cross and the staff officer Alice Mackenzie. Ottey found herself thinking how quickly this investigation had reverted to form, with Carson stating the obvious. The fact that she happened to agree with him was neither here nor there. Carson had a unique way of annoying her and getting under her skin.

'I'm going to take the lead on this one,' Carson continued.

Ottey didn't say anything for two reasons. Firstly, the fact that the case would undoubtedly be of interest to the media and her instinct was that an officer senior to Carson would be drafted in to run the investigation. Secondly, she had no need to with her partner beside her. He could never let such statements just lie.

'What makes you think that?' Cross asked.

'Well, it's up to me how I assign personnel on cases, George, as you well know,' came the reply.

'That it was a burglary gone wrong,' Cross continued.

'It's obvious, isn't it?' said Carson, immediately regretting the use of the 'o' word with Cross. Ottey grinned.

'Could you be more specific?'

'The bedroom was ransacked.'

'The chest of drawers had one drawer open,' Cross corrected him.

'And several items are missing,' said Carson with the absolute certainty of someone who is used to making things up on the hoof and, on the whole, getting away with it. Cross made no reply. 'Are they not?'

'We haven't ascertained that as yet.'

'Sure, but we can assume…' There he goes again, thought Ottey. The two magic words guaranteed to provoke Cross within a couple of minutes of each other. Would this man never learn? Carson now pretended that his phone had buzzed and he looked at an imaginary text.

'Right. I have to go. I'll pull together a team and we'll meet first thing tomorrow,' he said as he left, looking positively thrilled at the prospect. Ottey knew he saw this case as just another career opportunity.

Alice Mackenzie had figured out by now that the beginning of an investigation was a crucial time for her. It was the point at which she, as a police staff officer, needed to make her mark. If she wanted to be involved in the case with Cross and Ottey she had to act fast. Find a role, a job to do.

'I think he's wrong,' she commented having followed Cross and Ottey into his office. 'I've had a look at Peggy Frampton online. She was very opinionated. I mean, she could start a fight in an empty online forum. Some people really didn't like her advice. It was quite funny. Some of the things she said to people even became memes.'

'How could she do that if it was empty?' asked Cross.

'That's her point, George. Should we study her traffic?' Cross looked puzzled. 'Online,' she explained.

'Yes. But Marina said she had a following of millions,' he commented.

'That's right,' said Mackenzie.

'She must have had someone helping her,' he went on.

'A virtual assistant,' Mackenzie suggested.

'No, a real person,' Cross replied.

'They are real people. They're called Virtual Assistants.'

'Start by finding her,' Cross instructed.

'Hundred per cent,' said Mackenzie, leaving quickly before they changed their minds. Mission accomplished.

Which was a shame for her as she missed Cross turning to Ottey and saying, 'Peggy Frampton was deliberately murdered. I'm sure of it.'

'Shouldn't you have just shared that with Carson?' Ottey asked.

'I will. When I have absolute proof.'

'So, you want to treat it as murder on the QT?' Cross looked at her blankly. 'Without telling anyone,' she explained.

'Yes.'

'What did I miss at the scene?' she asked. 'The carpet,' he said, and left to make himself a cup of tea.

4

Luke Frampton didn't look anywhere near as authoritative and commanding in real life as in the picture on his chambers' website. Ottey didn't think the short, slightly built man would inspire much confidence in her, were she a client. Having said that, his wife had just died the day before, so she felt a little guilty making that judgement. From the website it seemed he was a relatively successful criminal barrister and had taken part in a number of high-profile cases at the Old Bailey. He had worked on murder, rape, assault. He was described as being empathetic with his clients and having a firm grasp on detail. Unshowy, he delivered a punch in court when it was needed. The website gave the impression that, while unremarkable, he was a reliable brief.

He was staying in a hotel in the centre of town. Cross and Ottey met him in reception.

'Why are you staying in a hotel?' Cross asked.

'Because I can't get into my home.'

'Why not stay with your daughter? More comfortable and comforting, surely?'

'My daughter's here. She'll be down in a minute. She wants me to go home with her. But she lives in Cheltenham, which isn't really convenient.'

'And your son's still away?'

'He's travelling back from Portugal as we speak. To be absolutely honest with you, I'd rather be on my own right now. Although, having said that, I've had a succession of visitors from chambers and the council.'

'She was a popular woman,' offered Ottey.

'She was a local politician for a long time. Loved by some, hated by others.'

'"Hated"?' asked Cross, immediately picking up on it.

'Too strong a word and to answer your next question – no, I still have no idea who would want to harm her.'

Cross looked at his notepad. 'That wasn't my next question. Where were you the night before last? The seventh?'

'I was in London on a case.'

'Name of the case?'

'*R. v. Swinton*. On the night in question, I was having dinner in my club, The Garrick.'

'Were you dining alone?'

'I was. But the club can, doubtless, confirm my presence there. I can also find a receipt, as it was a travelling expense.' Cross liked the furnishing of all the facts in a thorough, calm way. But the man was a barrister, after all, and this wasn't anything new to him. Just new in its personal connection.

'Is this a murder enquiry?'

'Not as yet, no,' replied Ottey. 'We haven't had an official cause of death from the pathologist or any of their findings as yet. So we can't say.'

'Then the purpose of this visit?' Frampton asked politely.

'We just need to build a fuller picture of you and your wife while we wait,' Ottey replied.

'But in all likelihood it's a burglary which she interrupted, with tragic results,' he said almost hopefully. It was as if the alternative was too ghastly to contemplate.

'It's possible, but as yet, we can't say definitively.'

A woman in her late twenties now arrived at their table. She was smartly dressed, in a conservative way, that was also possibly a little old for her age.

'Here she is. This is Sasha, my daughter. Sasha, these are the detectives looking into Mum's death,' said Frampton. The woman smiled politely.

'How did you sleep, Dad?'

'As well as can be expected, I suppose.'

'Have you had breakfast?'

'Haven't had the chance.'

'Do you need anything else?' she asked, turning her attention to the two detectives.

'No, we're fine. We just wanted to check up on your father. Make sure everything was okay. How long are you staying in Bristol?' asked Ottey.

'I'm leaving this afternoon. I have surgery tomorrow and we're already one doctor down, but I'll take him with me if I can persuade him.'

'We do actually need Mr Frampton to come to the house and see if he can ascertain what's been stolen. Maybe you could do that before you leave?'

'Of course. Just let us know when suits. Come on, Dad, let's get you fed.'

Cross noticed how Sasha had taken immediate control of the situation. He wondered if she were like her mother, as she seemed a lot more dynamic than the father.

'One more thing, before you go,' Cross said. 'The night of your wife's murder. Where had she been?'

'City Hall,' replied Sasha.

'Why?'

'A planning meeting. She was campaigning against a development in the harbour.'

'It'd been going on for years. From the time she was mayor. She was very passionate about it,' added Frampton.

'That's the tragic irony,' said Sasha. 'She won a crucial vote that night. She'd basically won.'

'That's right,' Frampton agreed, quietly.

That afternoon they returned to the Frampton house with Luke and his daughter. It was still a sealed crime scene with a uniformed PC stationed at the front door. Ottey gave Luke a pair of shoe covers, Cross had brought his own. Only Cross and Luke were going in. Sasha had insisted on coming along for moral support. She came over as confident, organised. Someone who always took control whether or not she needed to. Bluestocking came to Cross's mind, at the same time as the thought that one didn't hear that expression used so often these days.

Luke seemed hesitant to enter the bedroom.

'There is nothing alarming for you to see, Mr Frampton. I just need you to look at the disturbed drawer and ascertain what, if anything, is missing.'

'No, of course. It's just…' He didn't feel the need to explain any further and walked into the room. A room that would never be the same to him again. A room it was possible he would never even sleep in again. Many families of the deceased would sell their house and move on if a loved one had been killed inside. Avoid a road if someone's body had been found in it. Even an entire city.

The bloodstained carpet where Peggy had been found was covered up. They walked on the plastic elevated squares that Swift had left as carefully as if they were steppingstones in a piranha-infested pond. Luke examined the drawer. It was an untidy collection of jewellery, hair ties, make-up, free perfume samples and silk scarves. It looked like it had been rummaged through. A couple of things from the drawer were on the floor.

'It's hard to say. I think some things have gone missing. Someone's definitely been through it, as it's never this messy. But I can't be specific, I'm afraid.'

'Take a little more time and try harder,' Cross replied. Luke looked at him, surprised at the insistent tone of his request. He, nonetheless, took a further look, with the silent reluctance of a child being asked by a parent to look again, for something they knew they'd definitely lost.

'This was really her everyday stuff. I think maybe there's a diamond bracelet and a pearl necklace missing.'

Cross checked his folder then produced a couple of photographs. 'This diamond bracelet?'

Frampton looked at the photograph. There was a sharp intake of breath as he saw his wife's lifeless wrist.

'Yes,' he managed to stutter.

'And this pearl necklace?' Another photograph. At the sight of his wife's neck Luke Frampton broke down.

'Yes,' he wept.

'Anything else you can think of that might have gone?' Cross continued. He was aware the man was upset, but was unable to adjust his tone to be noticeably sympathetic.

'Possibly. I'm sure, yes. I just can't be specific right now.'

* * *

They went outside, where Sasha was still waiting. Cross noticed the alarm box on the front of the building. 'Do we know if the alarm went off?' he asked Ottey.

'No. Mr Frampton, does your alarm have central monitoring or a link to the police?'

'It does. Yes. That's a good point. It didn't go off, as far as I'm aware. I get notified by text and the police come to the property.'

'And it was definitely on?'

'It should've been,' Frampton said, thinking for a moment. His shoulders slumped as he realised something.

'Marina. She sometimes forgets. We've talked about it in the past. It's so annoying. She would've been the last person in the house.'

'We should ask her.'

'Oh, she'll feel terrible if she did.'

'Do you have her number?' Ottey asked.

'What day is it?' Frampton asked in reply.

'Wednesday.'

'She should be next door. She works for Joanna on Wednesdays and Fridays.'

The sight of Sasha made Marina immediately burst into tears on Joanna's doorstep. Sasha rushed forward and scooped the cleaning lady into her arms. When they released each other, Cross was about to speak, but Luke Frampton got in first.

'Marina, I need to ask you a question, and I want you to be honest,' he said, implying that she might be tempted to lie from the get-go.

'Okay,' she replied, picking up on this, thinking that it inevitably heralded that something bad was coming her way.

'I want you to be completely truthful,' he reiterated.

She looked a little hurt. 'I'm always truthful.'

'Of course you are,' he reassured her. 'But these are difficult circumstances, so I would understand.'

'What? That I would lie? Why would I lie?' She looked at Sasha for help.

'I'm not suggesting that at all. But the day before yesterday, when you finished work and left – did you set the alarm?'

'Yes, I always set the alarm.'

'Are you sure?'

'Completely.'

'Because it's something we've talked about in the past, isn't it?' She looked at the detectives, trying to ascertain if she was in trouble. 'Marina?'

'Yes.'

'Because you forgot a few times. Isn't that right?'

'Yes, but not after.'

'Except that we did have to talk about it on a few occasions, didn't we? You're not in any trouble, it's just important, if we're to find out what happened to Peggy, that we know all the details.' He was softly spoken and gentle in his questioning. There was no hint of censure or reprimand.

'Yes.'

'So, is it possible you forgot?'

She hesitated for just a second. 'No.'

'It's not possible?' Frampton persisted.

'No.'

'We all forget things, Marina. I arrived in court one day last week, and after I changed in the robing room, I suddenly had to check I had my briefcase with me. I was sure I did but I didn't remember actually picking it up because it's something I do automatically. But I'd forgotten it.'

'I think it's pretty clear she set the alarm, Dad.'

'Marina, I want you to take me through exactly what happened when you left the house the day before yesterday.'

As his daughter had pointed out, Marina had answered the question several times already, but he continued to probe quietly, and contrived to sound entirely reasonable. His way of asking politely almost made it seem as though she was being unhelpful. This must be what he was like in court, Cross thought. Quiet, well-mannered and persistent, until he got an answer he was satisfied with.

'I washed my teacup – I always have a cup. Mrs Frampton said it was okay. I left it on the side. Got my coat and scarf from the cloakroom, set the alarm and left.'

'What about your handbag? Where was that?'

'I picked it up with my coat.'

'Why did you leave that out?'

'I don't know. I forgot.'

'You forgot. It's so easy, isn't it? To forget something that's part of your daily routine. It becomes so automatic you can forget.'

'I suppose.'

'So, are you completely sure, one hundred per cent certain, you set the alarm? Can you specifically remember doing it?'

She hesitated, trying to picture it in her mind.

'I think so. I'm not sure.'

'You're not sure?'

'I can't remember exactly. It's something I do automatically. I think I did.'

Frampton paused, as if in court, waiting for this to sink in with the jury. 'You think you did, which means it's possible you didn't. I don't think you did, Marina, and that's okay. But it explains why the alarm didn't go off.'

'I'm so sorry.'

'It's all right. You weren't to know.'

'But if I didn't then Mrs Frampton...' She broke down as the idea of this all being her fault weighed down on her.

'I think if I was in court I'd like him to be my lawyer,' said Ottey on their way back to the Major Crime Unit.

'Why would you be in court?' Cross asked.

'It's just an observation, George.'

'But he's a criminal barrister so what on earth would you be doing with him in court as your defence barrister?'

'He's like the tortoise in the tortoise and the hare,' she said, ignoring him. 'Slowly convincing the jury, without them realising it, and getting the right verdict for his client.'

'Why isn't he a QC, do you suppose?' asked Cross.

'Maybe he didn't want it,' she replied.

'Every barrister wants to be a Queen's Counsel. Whether they admit it is another thing altogether.'

'Not necessarily.'

'It raises their fees. They can wear silk in court. It's a status thing.'

'A lot of them struggle at the beginning. They outprice themselves.'

'I did a little research into Luke Frampton,' he went on.

'Well, if you knew the answer already, why did you ask?' she said, irritated. She hated it when he did this. It always felt like a little test. Cross reached into his pocket for his trusty notebook.

'It was a rhetorical question,' he replied.

'I thought we'd banned those,' she said.

'We did? When?'

'Oh never mind.'

'Very well, I looked into various legal journals at the time you might have thought he would apply for silk. He said he thought that it was an outdated notion, mostly political, unnecessarily hierarchical and not at all meritocratic. He said, and I quote, "It's a game I've chosen not to play."'

'Good for him,' said Ottey.

'It was a view widely derided by some.'

'Those who were QCs, presumably,' she volunteered.

'Quite so, and those who wished to be, I suppose. But many went along with it. It was welcomed in many corners of the legal world, including by many QCs and judges, who felt that the image of the law, and some of the ways it worked, needed overhauling in the modern world. "I'm not a star barrister," Frampton went on to say. "But I think I'm thorough and passionate about what I do. Thoroughly passionate, if you like. I think justice is such a fundamental pillar of our society that is often undervalued and taken for granted. I will fight for it at any given opportunity. To see justice prevail. I'm not in it for personal gain or achieving any self-serving ambitions, I am in it to serve, not to be served."'

'I would've thought you'd approve, George.'

'Oh, I do in principle. But it's one thing to say it, quite another to actually go through with it.'

5

'DS Cross,' he announced customarily, holding up his warrant card for all to see as he marched into the mortuary the next morning.

'Clare Hawkins, pathologist,' came the reply, scalpel held high as a further mark of identification, should there be any doubt.

'I know who you are,' he retorted, surprised.

'Likewise.'

'Likewise, what?'

'I know who you are.'

'I'm required to identify myself.'

'Every time you come here? Says who?'

This had him stumped. The truth was he wasn't sure who required it in these circumstances, or even if it were required at all. It had just become part of his routine. So, he changed the subject as quickly and in as businesslike a manner as possible.

'Have you ascertained a cause of death?'

'Not conclusively.'

'The blow to the head?'

'Possibly.'

'Caused by?'

'Heavyish, round, probably smooth, object.'

'Such as a fairly weighty glass paperweight?'

She thought for a second. 'Yes, that would do it.'

'Anything else?' he asked.

'Not yet, but the likelihood is that she was murdered,' she said, immediately regretting it.

'I have no use for likelihood,' Cross said, and left.

Clare watched him leave and said to her assistant, 'Just as you're sure you've reached a point where it's possible to like him, he does that.'

'What?'

'Pisses you off in a way that only he can.'

Cross then walked straight back into the room. Clare wondered whether he'd heard her. But instead of saying anything he proffered his phone.

'I'd like your opinion,' he said. She looked at it. It was displaying the photograph he'd taken of Peggy Frampton's head at the murder scene. 'What do you notice about this photograph?'

Clare studied it carefully. She hated these kinds of situations with Cross because his asking meant he already had the answer. So, she was desperate to come up with it.

'I suspect you're looking for something present in the photograph, but it would be more helpful if you looked for something that's missing,' Cross said.

She knew he wasn't teasing. It was something he didn't do. For some unknown reason he actually wanted her to find it for herself, rather than him just telling her what it was. Although a more thin-skinned person might have found it a little patronising, she was used to him and indeed took it as encouragement. She looked closer. Then she spotted it. Or, rather, the lack of it.

'There's no aspirated blood on the carpet from the victim's nose or mouth,' she said.

'Precisely.'

'I'll need to check there's blood in the trachea and nasal passages, which is what I'd expect,' she went on, thinking out loud.

'And if there isn't any?' Cross posed.

'It'll mean she was prevented from breathing immediately after she'd been struck,' she replied.

'The question is, how?' he said, taking back his phone and leaving again. She thought for a moment then looked at her assistant.

'And that is why we put up with him and, if I'm being completely honest, love him – just a little bit, despite ourselves.'

6

Ottey practically gasped when she walked into the department and saw the size of the team that had been put together. She couldn't believe how many people were in the room – definitely over forty. How could this be, after all the struggles they'd had with manpower on other cases over the last few months? The excuse always being 'staff shortages'. It would, though, make things so much easier. She noticed Cross wasn't there, which annoyed her, as she didn't know where he was and he was never late. This generally meant he was somewhere he'd either forgotten to ask her along to or, more likely, deliberately hadn't asked her. It was like a game between them sometimes, and today he'd already made the first move and was at an advantage.

Carson didn't look at all happy as he came into the room. Chief Constable Simon Pringle entered behind him, followed by a woman in her late thirties, with black hair flowing in an envious abundance over her shoulders. Ottey had no idea who she was. Probably from the PR department. There were going to be a lot of eyes on this one. Everyone stood as the Chief came into the room.

'As you were,' he began. 'Peggy Frampton, sixty-two, wife, mother of two and former Mayor of Bristol. She devoted her life to this city and more recently to people far and beyond on the internet. I knew her quite well. She was a friend to the force and always supportive. She was on the police commission for several years. She gave her best and so will we in return, to find out who killed her. I'd like to think it's no more than we give to all our cases. But I won't have people thinking they can get away with doing this to one of ours. Because that is what she was to me. One of ours. I'd like us to spend a minute's quiet reflection on a life well spent, before we track this bastard down.'

This was certainly new. Alice was impressed that the Chief was taking such an interest before they got down to the business of the investigation. Ottey was still trying to figure out who the woman to the chief's left was. Was she the reason DCI Carson was looking so bereft? Had she taken away a case in which he had had the chance not just to be in the Chief's peripheral vision, but right in the main beam of his headlights?

'I'd like to introduce you to Chief Superintendent Heather Matthews who will be the senior investigating officer in this case. This is in no way a reflection on DCI Carson.' Which of course made everyone in the room immediately think it was exactly that. 'It's simply that he already has a huge caseload here at Major Crimes to get through. He will act as Deputy SIO on the Frampton case. Heather has worked across several departments: vice, child protection, drugs and major crimes. She's originally from Manchester, but we won't hold that against her. We are lucky she found herself in Bristol after attending university here and decided to join the force.'

So Ottey's instinct had been right. The higher-ups had thought the case of sufficient importance to supersede Carson and put a senior ranking officer in charge. She knew nothing of Matthews, but she must have done something right to be as senior as she was at such a relatively young age. Also, to have anyone other than Carson leading this investigation was a result, whichever way you looked at it. She now castigated herself for making the initial assumption that, as a woman, Matthews had to have been from the press department.

When Cross finally arrived, his heart sank. He hated large teams. He would keep his head down on this one. Do the work, but in his own particular way. He would've tried to jump onto another case had he not been to the crime scene the day before. For someone who struggled to make relationships with the living, he had no such problems doing so with the dead. Once he'd seen a corpse, someone whose life had been ended prematurely, more often than not violently, he developed an immediate sense of loyalty, duty almost, to them. It was something he simply couldn't walk away from, until justice had been done. So, having spent time with Peggy Frampton the day before, he was now her detective, large team or not. He grabbed a chair and placed it at the back of the room next to the door, as Matthews began to address the team.

'Good morning. Now I'm not going to waste your time going through what we already know about the case. I'm assuming you've all talked through it. If you're not up to speed ask someone.' She had the residual tones of a Mancunian accent, tempered slightly by so many years in the south-west. 'I've drawn out an initial plan of action for the next two days. Mostly door-to-door, it has to be said.' This would normally be greeted by a universal low groan but the self-censoring presence of the Chief in their midst prevented this. 'DCI Carson has a folder of actions for you. We'll regroup tomorrow and start being more specific.' She looked at Carson as a cue for him to hand out the sheets. Ottey detected a slight reluctance, as if he were either unhappy to be instructed in such a way, or just thought that the task was beneath someone of his rank. But he dutifully went round the room, handing out the pages. Ottey reached out her hand to take one, but Carson walked straight past her. Cross wasn't given one either.

'There will inevitably be a lot of media attention on this one, so please exercise discretion. All media statements, press conferences, will be made personally by the Chief. Okay, let's get to it.'

Everyone started to get up, put chairs back where they found them and discussed their assignments with each other.

'DS Cross and DS Ottey, my office,' Matthews announced.

Carson looked up, slightly puzzled. 'Um, you don't actually have an office as yet.'

'Then yours will have to do, until you find me one of my own.' He was about to say something when he noticed the Chief smiling at him, in a way that told him this wasn't going to be a problem.

'Yes, of course. This way,' Carson muttered.

'I'm sure Cross and Ottey can show me the way. Why don't you make sure the troops are happy?'

Ottey looked over at Cross, but he was already halfway across the room without even waiting for Matthews and the Chief. This was annoying as it meant she couldn't indulge in a few moments of second-guessing and speculating as to why they'd been summoned before the beak. Cross wasn't one for such trivia, unlike her previous partners, and it was something she missed.

★ ★ ★

'George, and Josie, isn't it?'

'Yes, Chief. Good memory, sir,' Ottey replied, thinking he'd been well briefed.

'This is Chief Superintendent Matthews.'

Matthews held out her hand for Cross to shake which was ignored. Ottey stepped across and offered hers. Matthews didn't seem at all put out.

'What are your first impressions, George?' she asked.

'Um, well organised, efficient, quite young for your rank which means you're either politically very adept or simply good at your job, which hasn't gone unnoticed.'

Matthews smiled. 'I meant about the case.'

'Oh. Woman murdered in her bedroom.'

Ottey looked at him. She thought they weren't sharing that opinion. Then she remembered he could never conceal the truth. But Matthews obviously took 'murdered' to mean 'killed'. She wasn't aware of how exact Cross was when it came to his use of words.

'Home invasion gone wrong?'

'I couldn't say.'

'What does your gut tell you?'

The Chief interposed. 'George doesn't work that way. No instincts. No assumptions. No feelings about a case, or certainly none that he shares. He just deals with the evidence in front of him. Doggedly.'

'Understood. So as you two were the first detectives on the scene, I want you to take the lead in this case. I've heard a lot about you, DS Cross.' Cross didn't reply.

'All good, I hope,' Ottey interjected to fill the silence.

'Mostly,' she replied enigmatically. 'From what I've seen in the crime reports I've managed to read I think you probably work better with a certain amount of independence. I've also been told that you're not so great with large teams.'

Again, as no question had been asked, Cross made no response.

'Having said that, I will expect a report from you at the end of each day.' This was directed at Ottey.

'Of course.'

'Does that strike you as a sensible way of working, DS Cross?' Ah, she was a quick learner, thought Ottey. At last, a direct question for George, name included to dispel any possible confusion.

'We can't work entirely separately from the team. That would be counterproductive. We'll need to work in tandem,' he replied.

'Which is the purpose of your briefing me on a daily basis. Obviously we need to prevent duplication of any sort. I just don't want you to feel you have to run all your actions by me, or ask for approval. You are free to do what you like, when you like, how you like. It would also help avoid duplication if you attended the daily briefings. Finding out what everyone else is across, at the same time as letting them know what you're doing.'

'Can we make use of the team?' asked Ottey.

'Of course, and I fully expect you to. The point is that your time isn't taken up organising the wider investigation or being dictated to by it.'

'Presumably we'd need to ask DCI Carson for resources,' Ottey continued.

'Is that a problem?'

'Not a problem, exactly. It can just be a little time-consuming, that's all. He always needs some sort of justification for whatever is being asked for.'

'Which is his job by the way. But fine. Come to me.'

'Thank you.' Ottey liked this woman. She was fairly sure this plan of action was the Chief's, who knew Cross well, and had a kind of soft spot for him; born entirely out of results, of course. Matthews had probably known nothing about Cross, but she seemed to have taken it all in her stride, with no hint of resentment, or seeing his 'favoured' status as an affront to her authority. She was obviously sure enough of herself, confident in her own abilities, not to feel that her authority was being questioned. Carson would doubtless have felt his ego pricked if this had happened to him. Mind you, he looked like he'd been completely deflated this morning, this investigation being given to a senior officer, and a woman at that.

'I also want to make it clear that this is an equal partnership between the two of you. DS Cross is not the lead and will not exclusively decide on the direction the investigation takes.'

Ottey now liked her even more. 'We'll figure it out in our usual way,' she said.

'Are we dismissed?' Cross asked.

'You are.' And he was gone. Ottey felt the need to excuse his behaviour.

'George—'

'No explanation needed, DS Ottey. I've been fully briefed about DS Cross and I look forward to working with you both.'

Carson made a beeline for them the moment they walked back into the open area. From the resentful looks of the other detectives preparing to go on their wretched door-to-door canvass, it was clear to Ottey that Carson must have told them about her and Cross taking the lead. Cross wasn't a universally popular figure. Some people, those who hadn't bothered to get to know him at all, just plain didn't like him. Others felt he received special treatment from their superiors and was a beneficiary of selective favouritism. The rest were just outright jealous of his success rate, which was something they couldn't simply ignore, or pretend didn't exist.

'How did it go?' Carson asked, unable to mask his eager curiosity.

'Good. All good,' came Ottey's non-committal reply.

'Good,' he said, accompanied by a deep intake of breath carefully engineered to imply that no thought had gone into his next suggestion. That it was an almost effortlessly spontaneous, off-the-cuff thought. 'So, I think it's best if we keep the lines of communication the same as usual.'

'How do you mean?'

'Well, keeping me in the loop as per. Run everything by me so I can make sure it's okay. If that's okay,' he said hesitantly.

'Detective Superintendent Matthews wants us to report directly to her,' said Cross.

'Yes, of course. But there's no point in breaking up the A team, is there? We've got such a good track record,' Carson continued. Ottey refrained from saying, 'We?'

'Matthews was very specific. We are to report directly to her and no one else,' Cross informed Carson.

'Are you sure? I am the Deputy SIO.'

'Definitely. She said it after DS Ottey informed her that reporting to you was often time-wasting and led to unnecessary delays.'

'I said no such thing,' Ottey protested. Cross looked at her, confused, for a moment and then realised what she was getting at.

'Forgive me. She's quite right. She said time-consuming, not wasting.'

Ottey was in two minds whether to say anything as she followed Cross into his office. She had pointed out his lack of tact and social awareness on so many occasions recently that she wondered whether it was having any effect at all on the way he behaved. He seemed to have learnt some things over the last couple of years, but she'd come to the conclusion that his thoughtlessness had to be innate. Particularly in the heat of the moment or in normal conversation. This was when he normally slipped up. She had also come to realise what a strain it must be, to be acutely conscious of what you're saying all the time. She'd find it a nightmare and was grateful she didn't have to do it. But was he actually improving? Were the conversational faux pas becoming less frequent? She wasn't entirely sure. She decided to say something about his comments to Carson for her sake, whether it had any impact on him at all. She knew if she didn't, her frustration would hang over her, like an irritating dark cloud that threatened to rain, never did, but all the same made you think about the possibility all day.

'Were you deliberately trying to upset Carson just now?' she asked, closing the door, as she could see Mackenzie approaching in her peripheral vision.

'No, of course not. You do ask the most peculiar questions on occasion.'

'Okay then, were you just trying to put me in the shit?'

'What on earth do you mean?'

'With Carson?'

'No!'

'Do you genuinely not understand what just happened?'

'When?'

'In your conversation with Carson.'

'Of course I do. I told him how the chain of command, and therein the reporting structure, was going to work on this case, with the involvement of Detective Superintendent Matthews. I then underlined my certainty about this by putting it in the context of your comment to Matthews about Carson.'

'Okay,' Ottey replied, desperately conscious of not being condescending. 'So, listen to me. Carson is upset enough as it is, because they brought in a senior officer to run this case.'

'He is? Isn't it normal protocol in a case like this?'

'That's irrelevant when it comes to him. But he took what you said I said to Matthews as critical and offensive.'

'Why?'

'Because they were both of those things, George! You have to pay attention to what you say and make a judgement of the context in which you say it. You have to be more considerate of these things.'

Cross was a little slow to respond as he was busy noting down what she was saying in his notebook.

'You think I'm inconsiderate?' he said finally.

'Not intentionally.'

'You think I'm unintentionally inconsiderate?'

'I do.'

'I see. I find it confusing that you're so considerate of Carson's feelings when you dislike him so much.'

'I don't dislike him. I just find him... annoying.'

'But you care about his feelings?'

TIM SULLIVAN

'Only in as much as they will impact on me, and right now his state of being pissed off has just been multiplied by a factor of George Cross.' She wanted to ask him where he'd been to make him late. She had her suspicions. He'd been to see Clare, the pathologist – or more accurately Peggy Frampton's body. But she didn't say anything. She'd just pulled him up on his tactlessness with Carson and didn't want to remind him about teamwork. She'd do that later. There were times she felt like a primary school teacher with him, and this was one of them.

7

Mackenzie had been putting in long hours for the last three days, doing Peggy Frampton's victimology. She was particularly incentivised by the fact that Ottey had told her of Cross's confidential conviction that they were dealing with murder here. She revelled in the idea that no one else in the unit knew at this point. It was taking her longer than usual to put together a report, simply because of the sheer volume of material. She enjoyed this kind of work, though. She found it interesting and, after a few cases, had learned how essential it often was to an investigation. Truth was, she hadn't thought of it as proper police work to start with, but did now. She even referred to herself as a digital detective to her friends.

Peggy came across as a benevolent, kindly woman, albeit with a core of steel. She'd let her hair, which was still enviously thick, go naturally grey and, although it had an ageing effect, it also gave an air of gravitas and reassurance. She had steel-blue eyes which Alice imagined could have been put to cold, determined use when needed. She looked like a young grandmother who would be completely overindulgent with her grandchildren. She had been a councillor for many years before finally becoming Lord Mayor – she wouldn't countenance 'Lady Mayoress' as she felt it sounded less 'businesslike'. Way ahead of her time, thought Mackenzie. Before such gender descriptive job titles became generally derided. She had obvious passions as a local politician. Homelessness was one of them. She pioneered several schemes to try and reduce it in Bristol, not just at Christmas, but throughout the year. She was keen on the heritage and history of Bristol and had been one of the first people to address the city's historic links to slavery. She was no advocate of rewriting history and erasing past figures who were important to the city because they or their family had made their fortunes from slavery. She had been an early campaigner for there to be a museum of slavery which would archive and present the city's links to such an abhorrent trade. It would also have been a place to put vilified statues such as Edward Colston. She was a champion of affordable housing in the city and had enforced many a developer to include a portion of such housing in any development in Bristol.

Peggy's online presence was quite a challenge to get through. It was after Peggy retired from the public eye that her life became a little more colourful and varied. She started a blog about retirement and also her views on various local issues in Bristol; including of an ongoing harbourside development controversy she was involved with. As more and more people commented on her blog, so the topics broadened. She started discussing and advising on family problems, relationships, health issues. She replied unfailingly to all comments and so her number of followers ballooned. After a couple of years, she had become something of an internet sensation. A digital agony aunt for the twenty-first century. Alice discovered she'd branched out onto Instagram then started making videos of the subjects in people's letters. She began doing live streams and Q&As. She had a following of over five million worldwide across all platforms by the time she was murdered and had attracted so much traffic it felt like a bottomless pit. It was going to take Alice some time to trawl through it all, weeks perhaps. Peggy came across, at times, as quite opinionated, and had little truck when her advice was ignored. She didn't use the kid glove approach of many agony columnists. One thing was clear – she didn't shy away from giving advice she knew might be unpopular. She was forever reminding people that their getting in touch with her didn't guarantee that she would always take their side. She tried to be objective and look at both sides in any given problem or dispute, often finding a solution in the middle ground – 'I know I sound like a politician. Oh, wait a minute, I was one!' was a frequent remark. Mackenzie wondered if this was part of her appeal. All her posts attracted thousands of likes and hundreds of comments.

She also had advertisers on her site. Mackenzie would look into how much she earned from that. It wasn't necessarily relevant, but it was the kind of thing Cross often liked to know. He had made it quite clear early on that he would rather have file upon file of material that turned out to be irrelevant, than her gatekeep what he should and shouldn't see. It risked something slipping through.

'At this early stage,' he'd told her on a previous case, 'none of us know what is vital and what is trivial. So, I'd like to see everything.'

But she wasn't prepared for the vicious and violent and abusive trolling Peggy was subjected to. If you actually believed what people had written about her, the list of suspects would number into their hundreds. It was appalling and quite sickening what some people were emboldened to write in the knowledge that they were anonymous. Death threats, threats of violence to her and her family were hurled in her direction, together with cancer and other terminal illnesses being graphically wished upon her. Mackenzie was in danger of being swamped by Peggy's online life and it was obviously beginning to show.

'Do you need help, Alice?' Ottey asked her on day three of the investigation. 'I'm sure we could get you some.' She looked at the number of people in the open area as if to prove her point.

'No,' Mackenzie replied a little too quickly. Partly because she didn't want to be perceived as incapable of her job, but also because she was proprietorial. This was her turf, and she didn't want any unnecessary interlopers leaving their footprints or marking it with their scent. The fact was, though, that she could really have done with a helping hand. So, it was with a sense of relief when she tracked down Peggy's assistant, a young woman called Polly Jenkins, and organised her to come in and talk to them.

'She's quite new, so I'm not exactly sure how much use she'll be,' she said to Cross on their way to the Voluntary Assistance suite.

'How long had she been working for Mrs Frampton?' he asked.

'Three months.'

'Did she have an assistant before then?'

'Yes, Janette Coombes, she'd been with her since she was mayor, actually. Sort of semi-retired when Peggy left local politics, and then, as the internet stuff took off, she started working for her again. Part time at first and then as it grew it became a full-time job.'

'Do we know why she left?' Ottey asked.

'How could we?' answered Cross. 'This is the first we've heard of her.'

Polly turned out to be quite a shy young woman. Her dress sense was bohemian, with a long flowing floral skirt, a plain lace shirt, and cardigan. Her red hair was drawn back into a pair of plaits, close to her head. She was so quietly spoken that Cross had to ask her to speak up on a couple of occasions. She was a graduate student at the university doing a PhD in social sciences. Her job with Peggy was to supplement the income she got from teaching undergraduates. They met in the VA suite. Ottey went to make them tea, despite Mackenzie's offer, as she wanted her to kick off the conversation.

'Miss Mackenzie is not a police officer,' Cross insisted on informing her pedantically. 'But she has been going through Mrs Frampton's digital presence and so knows more than either myself or DS Ottey.'

'Gosh, no wonder you look tired,' the young woman said to Mackenzie.

'I do?' came the worried response.

'I'm sorry, I didn't mean it like that. It was a feeble attempt at a joke. Bad joke.'

'Don't worry,' replied Mackenzie.

Mackenzie was about to speak when Cross continued, which annoyed her.

'How did the job come about?'

'Through a colleague at work. At the university, who knew her.'

'Why the vacancy?'

'I don't understand.'

'There was an assistant before you. Janette Coombes?' Mackenzie explained.

'Oh, I see. Yes, she'd decided to have what Peggy described as a "senior gap year". She's coming back. Well, was, sorry. There's obviously no need now.' Her voice faltered.

'Did she warn you of any trouble Peggy might be having online?' Cross asked.

'Oh no. We never met. She'd left by the time I joined Peggy.'

'Her husband is coming in this afternoon,' Mackenzie interjected, determined to wrest the conversation back from Cross.

'Any trouble?' Cross repeated, ignoring Mackenzie.

'Not a lot. But some, yes. I thought you might ask, so I made a list of some of the Peggy haters – her words, not mine. There are just over twenty.' She handed Mackenzie a sheet of paper.

'Thanks. Wow, quite a few,' said Mackenzie.

'Not really, when you consider she had over five million followers. I mean that's like—' Polly began.

'Approximately 0.0004 of a per cent. I can't be more accurate with an unspecific number like that,' interjected Cross. Mackenzie and Polly looked at each other for a moment.

'Yeah, he does that,' said Ottey, who had come in with tea for her and the two women.

'I've put an asterisk beside those I thought were the most threatening,' said Polly.

Mackenzie scanned the list. 'Yes, some of those are on my radar too. Did anything go beyond internet hyperbole and bravado with any of them? I was really shocked by how outrageously vile people can be.'

'Hiding under the internet's duvet of anonymity, Peggy called it. There were a couple. She had two stalkers who actually came to Bristol. One of them from the States, can you believe? The other was British. She had to take out restraining orders against them.'

'When was this?' asked Cross. Ottey knew immediately he would be annoyed they weren't already aware of it.

'It was before I worked for her. I think a year or so ago? She told me about it but didn't seem at all worried. She didn't take the threats seriously. But everyone knew where she lived. So, she should've done. I once joked she needed a bodyguard more than an assistant.' She smiled weakly.

'A rather unfortunate joke in the circumstances,' Cross pointed out needlessly.

'Is the British stalker on the list?'

'They both are. The English one kept harassing her under different internet names. His IP address was blacklisted, but then he started logging in with different accounts at internet cafés and such. We could always tell it was him, though. He would give it away at some point, either stylistically – he didn't seem to have a great vocabulary – or by referring to things that could only be him. He was quite easy to spot. He lives in Portsmouth. His name is Michael Ribble.'

'So, he was consistent?' asked Ottey.

'Oh, very.'

'What was the source of his beef with her?' asked Mackenzie.

'He originally asked her for help proposing to his girlfriend. He had problems with her, which Peggy tried to help with. Then it was back to engagement planning. It became quite a notorious exchange, after a while, as Peggy's forum was a public one. That was the whole point. "Problems out in the open. Nothing behind closed doors."'

'Her log line,' Mackenzie explained to Cross, who was none the wiser for it.

'Truth is, it became a bit of a running joke for people watching it progress. Peggy tried to stop it, for his sake, but then he complained that she was shutting him down, because she couldn't help, and it was harming her reputation. Anyway, in the end he proposed and the girlfriend turned him down.'

'Doesn't sound like much of a surprise,' said Ottey.

'He blamed Peggy for the rejection. Said she'd made him a worldwide laughing stock, and his girlfriend wanted nothing more to do with him. She tried to point out that proposing on one knee, in the reptile house at Marwell zoo, with a twelve-foot python coiled round his neck, might not be everyone's idea of romance. That seemed to tip him over the edge, and he was outside her house a week later.'

'"Worldwide laughing stock" suggests self-aggrandisement,' Cross commented.

'He's very unpleasant. He even posted, after her death, that she had it coming.'

'Did she keep a note of his harassment?' asked Cross.

'Yes. Luke told her she had to, in case it came to court. It'll be on her laptop.'

'I'll find it,' said Mackenzie before Cross had the chance to tell her to.

'I know he's weird, but he doesn't look like the type to…' Polly's voice faltered.

'They very rarely do,' said Ottey. 'You'd be amazed.'

★ ★ ★

Janette's husband, Mark Coombes, was in his late forties, dressed in jeans and a polo shirt with a blue open fleece on top. It had a small company logo on the left-hand side where a pocket might normally be. He carried a bit more weight than his doctor would probably have liked. His hair was cropped and looked like it was thinning on top. He had a carefully curated, sharply trimmed two millimetre beard growth over his face. He cared about his appearance. His complexion was quite ruddy. He either worked out of doors or had a healthy appetite for alcohol; possibly a mix of the two, Cross surmised. He had an open face. The kind that seemed to be habitually smiling even when in neutral. The sides of his mouth curved upwards, as did the crow's feet at the sides of his eyes. He was probably a smoker who smoked while he worked, keeping the cigarette perched between his lips, wreathing his face in a constant funnel of smoke. He also had bright blue eyes, that immediately drew an onlooker's attention to them. Ottey and Cross met him in the VA suite.

'Mr Coombes—' Ottey began.

'Mark, please,' came the reply.

'Thanks for coming in,' she said.

'No problem. I just can't believe why I'm here. It's awful.'

'Does your wife know about Peggy?' Ottey asked.

'Yes, she's obviously devastated. Not the sort of news you want to get in an email. She told me she was going to come straight back but I said that wouldn't be what Peggy wanted. So, she's going to keep travelling. But she wanted me to ask if there was anything she could do to help.'

'She didn't know before you told her?' asked Cross.

'No, she's pretty much out of reach. She's travelling through the Golden Triangle in South-East Asia at the moment. We only talk about once a month, through choice. Well, her choice. She said there was no point in her doing this if we were going to be talking every couple of days, the point was to have a break.'

'From the marriage?' asked Cross. Coombes was taken aback by the directness of the question.

'Well yes, from everything really. Marriage, work, responsibilities. That's what she needed. A clean break.'

'It would certainly be useful to talk to her,' said Ottey.

'Of course,' Coombes replied. 'It's a little tricky but we can definitely fix something up.'

'How long is she away for?' asked Ottey.

'The idea is a year. A gap year, if you like. Senior gap year,' he laughed.

'Wow, long time.'

'She needed a change. A break, like I said. We have no children – couldn't, but it is what it is. She'd been working that hard and she wanted a bit of "me" time, you know? I'm hoping to join her in Australia towards the end.'

'Did you know Peggy Frampton?' Cross asked.

'Yes, of course. I used to joke there were three of us in our marriage.'

'Did you get on with her?' Cross continued.

'Absolutely. She was very good to us; well, particularly J. She was very supportive of her wanting a break. Actively encouraged her.'

'Why did Janette decide to leave?' Cross asked.

'She hasn't left so much as taken a sabbatical, as Peggy called it. Mind you,' he said, sadness creasing his face, 'that's all changed now, of course.'

'Did Janette enjoy working for her?' asked Ottey.

'Yeah, I mean it was hard work. Peggy was quite full on, as you probably know, and if she was working on something at ten at night, she'd think nothing of calling Janette, and we had to stop whatever it was we were doing.'

'Did Janette have any issue with that?'

'No, it came with the territory, you know. It was normally when one of her clients, as she called them, were having some sort of mental crisis. It was always a kind of emergency. Made me realise how lucky I was, to be honest.'

'So, you didn't have a problem with it either?' asked Cross. Coombes laughed.

'Yeah, definitely at times. I called it "Peggy time", like Fergie time,' he replied.

'Fergie time was the amount of extra time Sir Alex Ferguson seemed to get at the end of a game when he needed it and his side invariably scored,' Ottey explained to Cross who just looked at her.

'I can't believe you're mansplaining that to him,' Coombes laughed again. 'Or should it be womansplaining? It's hard to know these days, isn't it?'

'What he said,' Cross directed at Ottey, who laughed. Coombes's happy demeanour was obviously infectious. Cross had made a joke. Kind of.

'She'd always manage to call right when we were sitting down to eat. Or during a TV show we were watching, but right at the important bit of the plot. How did she do that? It was like she knew the most inconvenient time to call. No, I'm only kidding. But I did say to J that if you added it all up, I'd definitely spent at least a whole day staring at a paused programme, while Peggy was on the phone with her over the last year.'

'Do you have any thoughts about Peggy's murder?' Ottey asked.

'Well, it's tragic. Bloody awful. What were they after?'

'I meant in terms of anyone who meant to cause her harm?'

'I thought it was a burglary gone wrong?'

'No,' Ottey replied.

'You mean it's what? Out-and-out murder?' He looked shocked at the prospect of this.

'Yes.'

'Well, Janette and I did talk about that, obviously. But couldn't really think of anyone,' Coombes replied quietly.

'Why did you discuss it, if you thought it was an interrupted burglary?' asked Cross.

'You just do, don't you? You speculate, that's the word, isn't it? You cover all bases, have all kinds of ideas about something.'

'Any theories?' Ottey asked.

'Not really. We couldn't figure out for the life of us who would want to kill her. Even now it sounds weird just hearing myself say it out loud.'

He looked down at the ground. It was as if he hadn't really thought through the reason for his talking to the police and the enormity of the fact that they were discussing someone's murder was just beginning to weigh down on him.

'What do you do for a living, Mr Coombes?' asked Ottey, changing the subject.

'I work for a conservatory company. Used to build them, but then suffered a back injury a couple of years ago. I do all the surveying for potential clients now.'

'I've always wanted a conservatory,' said Ottey.

'Really? Well, I could come and have a look for you if you like,' Coombes said, his face lighting up in cheerful disbelief that he might get a sale out of this meeting.

8

Ottey and Cross met early on Saturday morning to drive down to Portsmouth and interview Michael Ribble. As well as manpower, overtime had been sanctioned in the initial stages of this investigation. Ottey's mother had as usual come to the rescue with childcare. (Ottey would've felt guilty if she didn't know how much her mother really loved being with her granddaughters. Having said that she'd been completely taken aback by the vehemence of her mother's refusal to move in with them when she'd suggested it.) It hadn't taken Mackenzie long to track him down. This was despite his numerous online usernames designed to disguise his actual identity and make him difficult to trace. As Polly told them, he'd had a restraining order against him, taken out by Peggy. This meant his home address was on file. They were barely out of the car park when they received a call from Luke Frampton. Portsmouth would have to wait till another day.

'Peggy had some family jewellery, really quite valuable. Last time they were valued for insurance it was over three hundred and fifty thousand pounds. They were kept in my safe,' said Frampton leading Cross into his house. Ottey stayed in the car on a call with one of her children. She made no qualms about her daughters always coming first. It was something that made complete sense to Cross, so he never had an issue with it. The only problem was that he always forgot to ask what the problem had been and whether it had been resolved. She was okay with that, as it made her feel that she had no need to justify herself to him. So, it was a perfect situation, really.

As Cross followed Luke down to his study something about the house told Cross it was occupied rather than lived in. The air had a still staleness to it, as if it had been settled in there for some time. That no domestic activity had disturbed it for a while. He felt it could do with the doors and windows being left open for an afternoon for some ventilation. The top of Frampton's head was bald, with a ledge of bushy, but suspiciously black, hair encircling it. People tended to crop their hair when they went bald these days, Cross was thinking, but not Frampton. The bald patch was so shiny you could probably see your reflection in it. It was as if Frampton buffed it in the same way he shone his shoes. The remaining hair that surrounded this gleaming circle of visible scalp was like the meticulously tended tonsure of a monk who cared too much about his appearance, with the sharp geometric edges of a perfectly strimmed lawn. He reminded Cross of Professor Calculus from Hergé's Tintin books.

The study had a wooden parquet floor. The walls were covered with wooden panelling and bookshelves. On one side of the room the shelves were bulging under the weight of dozens of volumes of law reports and other legal tomes. On the other side, a smaller bookshelf contained Frampton's other reading: biographies, upmarket hardback fiction, history, together with a section of what looked like antiquarian books. The study wouldn't have been out of place in a set of law chambers. It had the dry air of dehydrated manuscripts and settled dust. There was also something of a gentleman's club about it. Slightly gloomy, fusty almost, with original Edwardian legal cartoons framed on the spare wall space. A large glass-topped humidor with a number of expensive, fat Cuban cigars resting side by side, at a perfect temperature and level of humidity. There were a couple of empty bottles of Mouton Rothschild claret on the mantelpiece with their bespoke artist-painted labels. One was from 1961, which Cross knew was considered to be one of the greatest vintages of the last century. Obviously souvenirs of decadent occasions. The unassuming man bending down to open the safe behind his desk was clearly a man of expensive tastes and commensurately obliging income.

Frampton opened the safe and pulled out an old wooden box. He unlocked it with the small key that was already in the lock, revealing a lining of crushed purple velvet inside. He lifted up a small tray sitting at the top of the box to reveal that the box was empty.

'They've gone,' Frampton said. He looked genuinely shocked, as if he still didn't believe this could have happened. Maybe it added insult to injury that, as well as her death, her precious family heirlooms should also have been taken from her family.

'Will you be able to itemise the missing pieces?' Cross asked.

'Yes, I can look at the insurance documents,' he said, locking the box and putting it back in the safe. Cross noticed a small number of stacks of fifty-pound notes bound together with paper slips, the way they are normally kept together in a bank.

'How much money is that?' he asked.

'Ten thousand. Rainy-day fund. In case of emergency.'

'What kind of emergency were you thinking of?'

'I don't know. I'm a little old-fashioned, I suppose. I like to have it on hand and it's not as if it's earning anything in the bank the way interest rates are.' Cross thought he had a point, but was still trying to think what kind of emergency would need that amount of money in cash. Didn't everyone use credit cards and bank transfers these days? As they turned to leave, Cross indicated the leather-bound antiquarian books on the bookshelf opposite them.

'Are those first editions?' he asked.

'Most of them, yes. A hobby of mine.'

'You're a collector.'

'I wouldn't go that far.'

'Do you read the books or just admire them?'

'Just admire. I wouldn't dare read them. I even use gloves when handling them. Are you interested in old books?'

'I am not.'

'I sold one recently. A first edition *Great Gatsby*. An American collector was desperate. It seemed the decent thing to do. English authors are really more my kind of thing. Dickens, Hardy, Lawrence.'

Carson called a meeting first thing Sunday morning. Never a popular move. Matthews was there but took a back seat, literally and figuratively. Carson behaved as if the jewellery being stolen was a major breakthrough in the case, all thanks to him. He pointed out that their known list of burglars had all, so far, denied any knowledge of the crime, but the stakes had changed now with the theft of the family jewels. Several had corroborated alibis. Carson's feeling was that it was unlikely to be any of them because, bar a couple of instances in the past, violence had never been used in the commission of their crimes. Murder hadn't happened in connection with a burglary for several decades on their patch. It seemed highly unlikely that any of these seasoned pros would react so violently to being disturbed. Their general modus operandi was to flee quickly, avoiding any confrontation – violence just wasn't in their tool box. But Carson now wanted the team to persist with the canvassing of these professional burglars because of the theft of the jewels. It had taken skill and knowledge to open the safe and someone had to have known of the contents.

'It's possible it was a burglary to order,' he announced grandly, looking over at Matthews to see if she was impressed with his deductive prowess.

'But the point of entry was so unsophisticated,' Ottey commented.

'Possibly because there was no need for any sophistication,' said Matthews. 'They knew what they were going for and it was the quickest way in and out. No need to cover their tracks.'

'The cracking of the safe implies a level of sophistication, though,' said Ottey.

'So, we are talking about a burglary gone wrong. Interrupted,' said Carson who couldn't help smiling as this had been the first thing his copper's nose, his detective's gut had told him.

'I think that's a fair assumption,' said his superior officer.

'I disagree,' came a familiar voice from the back.

Ottey, like everyone else, turned round to see Cross standing by the door. He still had his cycling gear on as he'd just come in. Cross was startled as fifty heads all turned round in unison and stared at him. So, he marched across the room, head down, towards the safety of his office.

'Any particular reason?' asked Matthews.

'Too many inconsistencies,' Cross replied over his shoulder, before entering his office and closing the door behind him. Ottey noticed he leant back against the glass door, either out of relief or to confirm it was properly shut.

'I have to say I'm not used to being contradicted so publicly, DS Cross,' Matthews began as she sat in the chair across from his desk. Carson entered the room, out of curiosity. Ottey followed out of a protective instinct for her partner.

'If you make such presumptive and precipitate statements in public I'm not sure how any contradiction as such could be anything other than public also. Force of circumstance,' Cross stated.

'Force of habit would be closer to the truth,' said Carson.

'How could I be in the habit of contradicting Detective Superintendent Matthews when I only met her a couple of days ago?' Cross asked.

'Is that your way of apologising?' Matthews asked. George looked at Ottey for guidance. She nodded discreetly, to suggest he agree. But he couldn't.

'It is not.'

'Inconsistencies. Explain.'

'Upstairs. If it's a burglary to order, why go upstairs and root around for things far less valuable, when you've got what you came for?' Cross asked, not unreasonably, thought Ottey.

'What are you suggesting?' asked Matthews.

'I'm not suggesting anything.'

'Then what are you thinking?'

'As I said, it's inconsistent. That, together with the fact that I'm fairly sure the pathologist is going to come back with evidence that Mrs Frampton was murdered.'

'In the commission of a burglary,' said Carson.

'On the contrary. This murder was quite separate from the burglary. The indications are there, we just await confirmation.'

'Can you elaborate?' asked Matthews.

'The intruder empties the safe of the family jewels but leaves two stacks of brand new fifty-pound notes in plain sight. Then goes up to the bedroom and rifles through a bedroom drawer containing nothing of any real value and kills Peggy when interrupted. Why bother, when he could've simply removed the money from the safe, and not stayed any longer than he had to? He also left a diamond bracelet on her wrist. It doesn't make sense.'

'Maybe he panicked,' suggested Carson. 'That's why he left it there?'

'He panicked and then went upstairs?'

'Who's to say he didn't go upstairs first?'

'Fair point, although one that does fly in the face of your saying it was a burglary to order which surely implies he knew where to look.'

'What point are you trying to make, George?' Carson asked tersely.

'I'm not trying to make a point. I'm merely pointing out the inconsistencies in the evidence we have, that seem to have eluded you.'

'What if there were two burglaries?' Carson proposed.

Cross thought about this. 'That would make sense of the facts as they present themselves. But I think it's highly unlikely. I wonder what the actual statistical odds of that would be, though.' He immediately started doing calculations on his notepad.

Carson nevertheless took this as a crumb of encouragement. It hadn't been discounted out of hand. 'I'll get the Shard to have a look for a second point of entry.' Cross looked up at Ottey, mystified.

'Tallest building in the UK,' she explained.

'I know what it is.'

'It's the unit's nickname for Michael Swift,' Matthews elaborated as she and Carson left.

Cross finally looked up from his mathematical scrawlings and said to a completely disinterested Ottey, 'Can't be done. Too many variables.'

The logic of Cross's objections to the burglary theory were further endorsed later that day, with the appearance of the vertiginous Michael Swift. Alice noticed this unfamiliar figure crossing the incident room, as did Ottey. If it weren't for his height, she wasn't sure she'd've known who he was. He looked very different when not cocooned in a head-to-toe hooded white forensics suit. Long thick hair drawn back into a tight ponytail, his eyelashes so thick you could be forgiven for thinking he was wearing mascara. But he wasn't. He wore a long mohair overcoat that reached down to just above a pair of fourteen-eyelet Doc Marten boots, over a black Joy Division *Unknown Pleasures* T-shirt. He knocked on Cross's office door and waited politely for an answer. He didn't know this was a prerequisite when visiting Cross, he just had good manners and could see that Cross was busy at his desk. This small gesture was one of the simple things in life that Cross held great store by. He motioned Swift in who entered, lowering his head instinctively as he did.

'Mr Swift.'

'It's actually Doctor. Not important to me, but I have a feeling you like to get things like that right.'

'Dr Swift. Do you always lower your head when coming into a room?'

'I wasn't aware that I did. I think it must be instinctive.'

'The result of several scalp-on-low-architrave encounters, perhaps?'

'Absolutely. If I ever go bald I'm sure my pate will be a criss-cross map of scars.'

Cross didn't reply but just looked up at the forensic scientist who just looked back. Ottey joined them and filled in the ever-increasing silence.

'Dr Swift.'

'DS Ottey.'

'What brings you here?' she asked.

'I've been back to the house.'

'And what did you find?' Cross asked.

'No sign of a second entry. To my mind there's only one burglary here, contrary to DCI Carson's hypothesis. But I had a couple of observations I thought might be useful.'

'You could've phoned,' Cross pointed out.

'I would have normally, but it was pointed out to me that you prefer to talk in person rather than use the phone. So here I am. Ten thousand pounds was left in the safe.'

'It was.'

'Does that not strike you as odd?'

'It does.'

'The safe was professionally cracked which seems inconsistent with the crude break-in through the back door.'

'Agreed,' said Cross, offering no more.

'I checked the French windows and the front door. Neither had been picked, in my opinion.'

'Has anyone checked with the alarm company about the alarm's status?' asked Cross.

'I'll check with Carson,' replied Ottey.

'The fingerprints on the bath tap. Were they just the victim's?' asked Cross.

'Mostly. There was one partial that wasn't hers. But there's not enough of it to provide a positive ID,' Swift replied.

'The killer's presumably?' Ottey asked.

'I would've thought so.'

'Odd that. Just the one print. What happened there?' mused Ottey. Cross was thinking exactly the same thing.

'Right. Well, that was it,' Swift said and waited for a second before leaving. He was annoyed not that Cross had already spotted what were, he had to admit, fairly obvious observations, but that he had no excuse to hang around. He definitely had a sense of missing out. Alice watched him leave as Ottey turned to Cross.

'Impressive. I like him,' she said.

9

At exactly seven twenty-nine the next morning George Cross emerged from his flat, as usual, to have his breakfast in Tony's café, which was conveniently situated below. As he closed his front door, he heard a woman's voice call out. He turned, and was puzzled as he saw a woman in her mid-seventies, who he didn't know, looking in his direction.

'George?'

'Yes,' he replied.

She didn't say anything further, so as he was sure her enquiry was merely as to his identity, which he had answered, he moved over to the café door.

'George.' This time the woman was more insistent. He turned back to her.

'Do I know you?' he asked.

'Not really,' came the answer.

'I thought as much,' he replied, again turning towards the door.

'I'm your mother,' she said, matter-of-factly.

This understandably stopped Cross in his tracks. He had neither seen, nor heard, from his mother since she left him and his father when he was five years old.

'Do you have any identification?' he asked.

'What?'

'A form of ID.'

She thought for a moment, then reached into her handbag, a little flustered. She was well dressed with close-cropped hair. Cross wondered whether this was a sartorial choice or one necessitated by illness. But it was her eyes which confirmed the truth of her identity for him before she'd even produced her driving licence. They were green with, he was fairly sure, flecks of brown in them. He remembered them instantly and reflected how surprising this was. He examined the proffered licence and handed it back to her.

'Satisfied?' she asked.

'About what?' he asked.

'My identity.'

'I am.'

'Good. Shall we have a cup of tea?'

'No.'

'May I ask why?'

'You may.'

'Oh, okay,' she said after a moment's processing. 'Why?'

'I'm on my way to work.'

'You were about to have your breakfast in this café, as you do every morning—'

'Except Saturdays and Sundays,' Cross pointed out for the sake of accuracy.

'Every weekday morning at seven thirty,' she continued. At this point Cross saw Tony wave at his mother from inside the café.

'You've met Tony,' he observed.

'He makes an excellent cup of tea. He actually used leaves.'

'Did you tell him who you were?' Cross asked.

'I did.'

'Well, that will be why you weren't subjected to the usual industrial tea bag.'

They stood there in silence.

'You came to find me, George. So I don't know why my being here should be such a surprise.'

'I did.'

'Well, here I am.'

There was another long pause during which Cross realised he should explain and then this exchange would be over.

'I came simply to inform you that everything had worked out well in my life, since you left me and my father. As you can see. Also, that I'm quite successful in my career as a detective sergeant in the Avon and Somerset police.'

'I see.'

'Now that I've had the opportunity to tell you that, my reason for seeing you has been addressed and so you are free to leave.'

He abruptly turned back to his flat door and disappeared inside. His mother waited outside. Five minutes later he appeared, kitted out in his fluorescent cycling gear and helmet, wheeling his bike outside. He double-locked his flat door, then cycled off without another word.

10

Michael Swift enjoyed his job. No, it was more than that. He loved it and this love was enhanced by the fact that he knew he was really good at it. But he quickly came to realise that his choice of forensic specialism had its limitations when it came to solving crime. But then again, all forensics did. He had to keep his instincts in check, on a daily basis, on a job and stick strictly to whatever his particular remit was at any crime scene. Such was his knowledge about forensic archaeology and anthropology he also had to be careful not to tread on any toes. But all those specialisms had the same drawback for him. They provided vital evidence in their different ways to solve a case, but it wasn't up to him what happened to that evidence. He simply handed it over to the officers assigned, then walked away. He didn't get to see it through, and this had become a source of constant frustration for him. In the case of Peggy Frampton, he was done. Finished. The investigation was far from over, but his role in it most definitely was, as far as he could see. Which was annoying. He wasn't intrigued by the case as such. From his point of view it had been fairly straightforward. He'd worked on cases that were much more forensically challenging than this one had been. It seemed to him that there weren't that many clues as to who the perpetrator was, and this was where his interest lay. He wanted to see how Cross's mind worked in such a situation. From what he'd seen and heard of him he had, at the same time, a completely orthodox but unorthodox way of working. Swift found this fascinating and wanted to know more. As he said to his flatmate, it was a classic case of a man-crush at work. 'Blue on blue,' had come the reply which was almost funny but not quite. But it also made him laugh out loud when he imagined what Cross's reaction to such a comment would have been.

Frustratingly, his second visit to the crime scene hadn't led to any further access for him to Cross. Swift decided the office staffer, Mackenzie, might be the key to open the door. He didn't know much about her, but there was something different about her. It was as if she didn't belong there somehow. So, he started stopping by her desk ever so casually – at least he thought so – claiming to be working on other cases which explained his presence in the MCU. It had to be said this was occasionally true. He would, again casually he thought, ask her how the case was going and in particular what Cross was up to. As she seemed to be a willing conversant on the case, he began to bring guilty culinary pleasures, of a sugar-laden carbohydrate nature, for them to enjoy together.

Every time this happened, Mackenzie was secretly relieved to be getting a break from Peggy Frampton's hard drive. She justified it by saying that, as he was the official forensic scientist on the case, these chats qualified as official business. It was also quite playfully flirtatious which, if she was completely honest with herself, she didn't in the least bit mind.

When she arrived at work that morning, Mackenzie

discovered Swift already sitting with his feet up on her desk – an indication, she thought, that their relationship had moved on from colleagues to mates – drinking a coffee and eating a muffin. They were discussing the 'weirdo in Portsmouth' and whether he might really be capable of murder. This was after she'd jokingly asked him if he wasn't sure the guy was a friend of his, which he pretended to take seriously before answering 'no'.

'Cross and Ottey are driving down to see him this morning,' Mackenzie told him.

'Do they need a chauffeur?' he asked.

'You really are pathetic, do you know that?'

'I didn't before I met you, but I think it's safe to say you've told me so often that I've been coming to terms with it. Is this guy a credible suspect though? Seems an awful long way to go if he isn't. He's probably just all mouse and no trousers,' said Swift, which made her laugh.

Cross then walked in. He stopped at her desk and looked at Swift's elevated legs and boots on her desk. Swift quickly sat up, almost falling off his chair in the process, clearly thinking this was a visual rebuke from the DS. It was in fact no such thing. Cross had stared because he was marvelling at how far away from Mackenzie's desk Swift was sitting, thanks to the length of his legs.

'DS Ottey not in yet?' Cross asked.

'No,' replied Mackenzie.

'George!' came a familiar shout from the other side of the room. He always ignored Carson's cross-departmental yells, in the hope that the more often he did so, the sooner the DCI would get the message and desist. He disappeared into his office. Carson appeared moments later.

'Josie called in. Her daughter was rushed to hospital last night. Appendicitis. They had to operate,' he said.

'So, what time does she think she'll be in?' asked Cross.

'Is that a serious question? She's not coming in at all, George. Of course she isn't.'

Cross thought for a moment and then looked up at Mackenzie who was now standing at the door.

'Do you have your car with you today, Alice?' he asked.

'I do, but I wouldn't trust it to get me to Portsmouth and back,' she replied.

'I have my car,' volunteered Swift, whose head had appeared in the doorway a good two feet above Mackenzie's. 'Four-wheel drive, privacy glass in the back, recently serviced and MOT'd. Could probably do with a valet, though, if I'm being completely honest.'

'Alright, let me just email the Hampshire Constabulary again and let them know we're definitely coming this time.'

Half an hour later the three of them, Cross, Mackenzie and Swift, were walking across the car park towards Swift's Land Rover Discovery. Swift had managed to persuade Cross that he might need to do some forensic investigation at the suspect's house. While Cross thought this highly unlikely, it was enough of a slim possibility for him to justify his commandeering of Swift's vehicle, and his services as a driver. Mackenzie had watched as they left the open area, bereft to be missing out, only to hear her name called.

'Mackenzie, you should go with them. I know it's babysitting but...' said Matthews who had no need to finish her sentence, as Mackenzie had already grabbed her coat and bag and was running out of the door.

Michael Ribble was a thirty-four-year-old man who, according to his online presence, was some sort of freelance computer consultant. What this meant was anyone's guess. He lived in his late mother's house in Portsmouth. The house was in a cul-de-sac of an anonymous-looking 1970s housing estate. The type that seemed to have swallowed up a lot of the English countryside in that decade and the one preceding it. Cross disliked them. His father and he had lived on one for a few years before they'd moved into a flat nearer the centre of Bristol. These places were so unimaginative, homogenous in their lack of distinction. Dull with no aesthetic value whatsoever. It was as if developers were in such a rush to keep up with an onrush of demand that they didn't have time for such things as design. Or had they just inflicted a countrywide scar of cost-effectiveness on the landscape?

Swift parked in the road opposite Ribble's house. After a brief exchange in which Cross couldn't hide his surprise that his two companions were under the impression they were going to join him inside, they all walked up the drive to the house. There was a window box filled with alpines. The front garden was paved with a circle of soil in the middle in which was planted a forsythia providing an early bit of spring colour to the scene. They rang an electronic camera doorbell next to the front door. A disembodied male voice answered.

'Yes?'

'Michael Ribble?' asked Cross.

'Yes.'

'Avon and Somerset police.'

'Do you have any ID?'

Cross held up his warrant card.

'What do you want?'

'We'd like to ask you some questions.'

There was a slight pause. 'I'm in my workshop at the end of the garden. The side gate is open.'

They walked down the side of the house into a surprisingly long garden, about a hundred and fifty feet, Cross thought. The garden was immaculately tended. Green shoots in the beds revealed spring bulbs making their way into the world. Cross noticed that the flower beds had all been mulched recently. The edges of the lawn were sharply cut with military precision. They walked down a path which wound its way through the variously shaped beds and between a pair of eight-foot-tall hedges. These partitioned off the bottom of the garden. It was straight out of the 'creating rooms in your garden' school of landscape design. They approached a long shed, alongside a well-kept vegetable patch. The further down the garden they got, the more distant the urban noise of traffic became, replaced with high birdsong. Cross noticed a beehive at the end of the garden. If Ribble lived on his own, and the indications thus far were that he did, he was a very busy man.

The shed door opened, and Michael Ribble appeared. He was wearing a rust-coloured boiler suit spattered with various dried stains. He had work boots on and had the hands of someone whose work was manual. He looked more like a gardener or caretaker than a computer geek. He wore small round wire-rimmed glasses and was quite bald on top. But he hadn't cut the remaining hair which was shoulder-length, giving him the appearance of an Open University lecturer from the seventies. A security camera over the shed door was pointing back to the house.

'Will the workshop do?' asked Ribble. 'Or would you prefer to go into the house?'

'This will be fine,' replied Cross, interested in getting a look inside. It was a surprise. Stuffed creatures covered the walls and most of the surfaces. Others peered out of the shadows. Birds 'in flight' hung from the ceiling. Foxes and the odd occasional domestic pet sat on the floor, their glass eyes reflecting the light from his desk. It was a ring light which surrounded a magnifying lens. This hovered over Ribble's current project, a pair of ferrets fighting. The whole thing was like a set from a Hitchcock movie. Some of the specimens, works in progress probably, were covered in large clear ziplock plastic bags. There was a pile of them near the workbench. All along one wall, hundreds of tools were hung in order of size and type. It struck Cross as the product of someone very organised.

'Oh, man. This is so cool. This stuff is amazing,' said Swift moving further into the workshop, beaming from ear to ear. He looked through the magnifying glass, rendering his face huge and distorted from Mackenzie's point of view. She couldn't help but laugh.

'Are you serious?' Ribble asked.

'Oh, come on, take a look at him. Of course, he's serious,' Mackenzie replied, still laughing. Cross shot her a look. 'Sorry,' she muttered under her breath.

'Absolutely,' said Swift, ignoring them both. 'You have skills, my friend.' Then something occurred to him. 'You don't happen to have like a black crow, or a raven for sale, do you?'

'I don't, but I could look out for one for you if you want.'

'Only if you've stuffed it, mate. This guy's an artist,' he explained to Cross.

'Is this your main occupation?' asked Cross.

'What does it look like to you?' replied Ribble.

'It looks to me like you're a taxidermist.'

Ribble looked at Mackenzie and Swift to try and get a clue as to whether Cross was taking the piss.

'You don't mention it on any of your social media,' said Mackenzie. 'You make out you're some kind of computer expert.'

'People are judgemental. I don't want to look weird, even though I don't think doing this is weird. It's a skill and I make good money.'

Suddenly an eagle owl on a perch behind him swivelled its head a hundred and eighty degrees and stared at Mackenzie with a pair of extraordinarily large yellow eyes.

'Jesus!' she yelled. 'It's alive.'

'Please don't shout. You'll disturb him.'

'How tall is he?' Mackenzie asked, trying to get control of her breathing back.

'Forty and a half inches, or just over a metre, if you prefer.'

'That is the coolest thing I've seen this year,' said Swift leaning his face really close to that of the owl. 'What's his name?'

'Victor.'

'Victor! Classic! I think I'm in love,' Swift continued. This made Mackenzie smile. Cross needed to get back control of this situation quickly, he thought. Then Ribble opened a tupperware box, took out a dead mouse, and held it up by its tail.

'Would you like to give him his lunch?'

'What? Yes!' replied the ecstatic Swift. This was too much for Cross.

'Dr Swift! Remember why we're here. We're conducting a murder enquiry, not visiting a petting zoo,' he said.

'Doctor?' asked Ribble. 'Are you a shrink?'

'No, forensics,' Swift answered as he gleefully fed the owl. This seemed to disappoint Ribble.

'You haven't asked us why we're here, Mr Ribble, which makes me think you already know. You don't seem in the least surprised,' Cross went on.

'Peggy Frampton,' came the reply.

'Correct. Where were you on the night of the seventh of February?'

'I was here,' Ribble replied, looking Cross directly in the eye.

'How can you be so sure, so quickly?'

'Because it was the night of Peggy Frampton's murder.'

'So, you've been expecting a visit from the police?'

'I have,' Ribble replied.

'Was anyone with you that night?'

'I had a customer, but he left around five thirty, which would've given me plenty of time to get to Bristol.'

'And did you?'

'What?'

'Travel to Bristol?'

'No, I was working, like I said.'

'You disliked Peggy Frampton.'

'I hated the bitch. She ruined my life. She made a mockery of me in front of all her followers. She cost me my marriage.'

'You weren't married.'

'All right, the chance of marrying the woman I loved. She

humiliated me. Carol read some of the stuff people wrote about me and she believed it. So, in the end she didn't want to marry me. Who could blame her? Did you read some of the stuff people said? Some of the stuff Frampton said?'

'I did,' said Mackenzie.

'Then you understand.'

'Then she understands what? Why you'd want to kill her?' asked Cross.

'I may have wanted to,' Ribble started.

'There's no "may" about it. You threatened her on more than five occasions. You wrote in graphic detail about what you wanted to do to her, before you killed her.'

'That's all bullshit. It's the internet. People say all kinds of crap to all kinds of people.'

'But not all of them end up dead,' volunteered Mackenzie, which caused Cross to look at her, surprised. She took it as a reprimand. He was, in fact, taken aback because it was what he was about to say next.

'I didn't kill her. I was angry.'

'But you continued to post about her after she was dead.'

'Now that I do regret. I was drunk. Not the classiest of moves. But I haven't done it since.'

'Do you use that kind of language in any disputes you may have in real life?' Cross asked.

'What do you mean?'

'Face to face. The threats you made to her. The insults.'

'No, of course not,' Ribble laughed and looked at Swift, to share the absurdity of the question. Swift maintained the poker face he'd employed since Cross had put him in his place.

'I'm curious as to why such virulent, violent, abusive language is acceptable on the internet,' Cross went on.

'It's what people do.'

'Is that right? I wouldn't know. I use the internet as a source of information. Verified, of course. But to communicate with people I don't know in a public forum? It seems very unwise, can get you into all sorts of trouble.'

'Like what?' asked Ribble.

'Like the police coming to question you as a person of interest in a murder case,' replied Cross in a flash.

Ribble said nothing but did look a little discomforted. The seriousness of the situation was dawning on him.

'Do I need a lawyer?' he asked, directing this question at Mackenzie, having concluded he would get more out of her than out of Cross.

'I don't know. Do you need a lawyer?' said Cross.

'Don't people usually need a lawyer in these situations?' Ribble asked.

'What situations?' Cross asked neutrally. Ribble didn't answer. 'You obviously understand the problem here, Mr Ribble. How this looks. Otherwise, you wouldn't be enquiring about lawyers. You've made violent threats over the internet, in graphic detail, to a woman you, yourself, say ruined your life. You've threatened to kill her, and she has been murdered. On a night for which you have no alibi.'

'I know how it looks,' said Ribble, quietly.

'Are you sure you weren't in Bristol that night?' Cross asked again.

'I am,' he replied.

Cross couldn't tell whether he was telling the truth or not. What he did know was that he had no proof. If he were to arrest Ribble now, the likelihood was that he would be back in Portsmouth within twenty-four hours.

'Very well,' he said.

A couple of minutes later, he and Mackenzie walked towards the car.

'Shouldn't we arrest him?' she asked.

'By that I assume you mean, shouldn't I arrest him as you have no such powers? Do you have any proof that he did it?'

'No,' she replied.

'Neither do I.'

Swift, meanwhile, turned to Ribble in the small glass entrance hall these houses had and offered him his card.

'In case you come across a crow or raven. I'm really impressed by your work, mate. Why are you so miserable? You shouldn't be embarrassed. You should be out there telling everyone what a world-class stuffer you are, man.'

'That's easy for you to say.'

'Yeah, well, look at me. I work crime scenes, for God's sake. I'm constantly surrounded by dead people and bodily fluids, blood and guts. But I don't hide it. I tell everyone.'

'And what does your girlfriend think about that?' Ribble asked.

'I don't have a girlfriend,' Swift replied. Ribble simply raised his eyebrows in a 'point proven' kind of way.

As Swift walked away, Ribble looked towards Cross, nervously. He knew instinctively that this was not a man easily trifled with and hoped it was the last time he saw him.

11

Cross was more than happy to go along with Mackenzie's suggestion that he sat in the back of Swift's car on the journey from Portsmouth back to Bristol. She had explained that there were a couple of requirements to be a front seat passenger, neither of which he seemed to fulfil. The first was to provide navigation where it was needed, and the second to provide conversation with the driver. His immediate reaction was to point out the flaws in her proposition, namely that navigation was provided more than adequately by the vehicle's satellite navigation system, and that conversing with the driver was potentially dangerous, as it could distract them. She countered this by saying that engaging the driver in conversation ensured that they didn't fall asleep. He conceded that this was a valid point but had already decided travelling in the back would be beneficial. On the journey down he'd found Mackenzie's head constantly appearing between the front two seats, with increasing frequency, to talk with Swift immensely annoying. It was doubly concerning as she released her seat belt to do it. When he pointed this out, the situation only got worse, as their conversation was then shouted at volume between the front and rear seats of the car. The privacy glass was also inexplicably alluring.

Being in the back of the vehicle also gave Cross a chance to learn more about his two young travelling companions. Their being in the front of the car together had made their conversation very different from earlier. More informal, Cross noticed. As if they'd forgotten about him being in the back. Mackenzie talked about her upbringing with her socialist-leaning, politically minded activist parents. How they'd initially been appalled at her career choice – 'if indeed that is what this is,' she'd qualified hastily, as if she were keeping her options open. She was 'working for the state', though, according to them, which made Swift laugh. The last couple of cases she'd worked with the team had given them second thoughts. They had begun to see she was doing something useful. Providing a service to society. Her father had even suggested that she could change the police force from within.

'So, you, Cross and Ottey are a team?' Swift asked.

'Not officially, no. But I like to think so,' she replied.

'Where do you see yourself in five years?' Swift asked.

'What is this, a job interview?'

'No, I'm just interested.'

'I don't know. Maybe actually join the force,' she said hesitantly. This interested Cross. He hadn't considered it a possibility, or even an ambition of hers, up until this point.

'Become police?' Swift asked a little incredulously.

'Why not? What's wrong with that? You're police. You just hide it behind a white lab coat.'

She then turned the questioning round on him. Dr Michael Swift was thirty-one, it turned out, and had three main interests in life: crime, comic books and all things gothic – whether, music, literature, architecture, plays, clothes.

'You're a goth, plain and simple,' Mackenzie had said. It

seemed to irritate him, so he just ignored it and carried on talking. He had a huge collection of comic books.

'A pannapictagraphist!' Cross proclaimed from the back seat.

'What?' asked Mackenzie.

'A collector of comic books,' explained Swift.

He went on to say that he thought, maybe, he subconsciously identified with the superheroes, in their attempts to defeat supervillains and this had led to his interest in crime, as well as a substantial comic book collection – properly catalogued, with the rarer numbers safe within the confines of specialist plastic display envelopes. Cross was delighted to hear the young man also had a large collection of crime books. The most cherished of these were the volumes of crime scene photography books he'd acquired over the years. He had a book of crime scenes from 1920s New York, a volume of Weegee's *Murder Is My Business*. Also crime scene photographs from Paris at the turn of the last century. France had in fact been at the forefront of developing the idea of photographing crime scenes. Everywhere else in the world people were still relying on the contemporaneous notes of the investigators, which couldn't always be relied upon. He had several, less graphic, photographs framed on his walls at home. Images by Bertillon who, Swift was then thrilled to learn, was the inventor of the modern criminal mug shot. Bertillon also developed the tall tripod for taking bird's eye photographs of corpses in situ. Swift's favourite photographer, though, was undoubtedly Rodolphe Archibald Reiss whose crime scene photographs seemed to have a cinematic quality to them. He had a great eye, a wonderful sense of composition and drama. It was these photographs, and their inherent sense of narrative, that really fascinated Swift. Every time he looked at them, he felt they had more to tell. Cross made a mental note to ask him about these books when it was appropriate.

Swift had always literally stood out from the crowd ever since an extraordinary growth spurt in his teenage years. The fact that he temporarily became a goth made him even more noticeable. He stood head and leather-clad shoulders above everyone else. One kid had joked that he looked like an inflatable giant Noel Fielding, which he took to mean, with classic adolescent insecurity, that he was overweight. Which he wasn't. He wasn't bullied at school but something about his height made it difficult to make many friendships. In the end this suited him perfectly well. These days he was pretty at ease with his height. But he did complain occasionally that people were staring at him.

'Well let's face it, if you go round dressed like the world's tallest funeral director with the occasional dab of make-up, what do you expect?' Mackenzie pointed out. Cross thought she had a point. One that he would never have dared make, intentionally at least; unintentionally was another matter entirely. But Swift laughed good-humouredly and told her about a long black coat he often wore to work during the winter. Apparently when he hung it up on the coat rack it would fold up on itself on the floor as the rack wasn't high enough. When other coats were then placed over it people would often stop to pick his up thinking it had fallen off the peg.

It was at school that he started sketching. He had real talent and was soon drawing comics, which he would photocopy and leave around the school. This started to make him a cult figure as he never admitted to it. He was the Banksy of the playground, he liked to think. His cover was blown when he dropped a file of sketches on the floor in an art class and his teacher saw them. She was blown away and insisted they had a little exhibition in the school. He was mortified until he realised it actually made other kids think he was pretty cool. (Cross related to his initial mortification. He'd felt much the same way when Stephen had pressured him into giving an organ recital at the church.) Even the basketball team, who had tried unsuccessfully to recruit him, forgave him. After that he actually earned some money doing digital caricatures of pupils for their social media at a fiver a pop. With A levels in maths, physics, chemistry and art he decided not to go to university but art school. He was determined to become either a comic book artist or go into animation. But during that year he realised that drawing for a living was not for him. There wasn't enough purpose in it. He realised he was inextricably drawn to the world of crime.

In a neat reversal of the normal way of things, he dropped out of art school and went to the University of Dundee to study forensic anthropology. He went there for several reasons. The first was that he'd done his research and saw that the course was run by one of the leading anthropologists in the UK at the time, Professor Sue Black. They had also started using the Thiel method of embalming instead of formaldehyde. This preserved a more natural colour in the cadaver but more importantly rendered them more flexible. Joints could be moved around, rotated; tendons could be made to work. It was enormously useful to trainee doctors learning about the anatomy of the human body. But almost as important to Swift was the fact that Dundee was the home of DC Thompson's classic comics *The Dandy* and *The Beano*. There was even a statue in the city centre of Desperate Dan with his dog and Minnie the Minx. He enjoyed his four years there. He left with a much greater knowledge of human anatomy and the process of death than when he'd arrived. But it had also confirmed to him that a career in forensic anthropology alone was not for him. He wanted to concentrate on forensic science, as this seemed to be a constantly evolving field. So, an MSC in crime and forensic science followed at University College in London. His academic journey then ended back in Dundee, where he completed a PhD in forensic science, concentrating on the transfer and persistence of evidence. He'd been working for various police forces throughout his academic career, and was thus a very experienced, well qualified crime scene investigator/forensic scientist, when he got the job with the south-west forensic team, a few months earlier.

Cross thought he came across as an extremely bright young man who wore his cleverness with discreet ease. He also thought that Mackenzie and Swift made a good pair. But what did he know?

12

On Wednesday night Cross arrived at his father's flat with their regular Chinese takeaway. He was glad of it as he wanted to talk to him about his mother. He opened the door to Raymond's flat and wheeled his bike into the hall. This was something he hadn't been able to do with any ease the year before, as Raymond was something of a prolific hoarder and the flat was crammed from floor to ceiling with all manner of 'invaluable' junk. Cross had taken advantage of his father's spell in a care home (having 'snitched' to social services, as Raymond had put it) to clear it out. The fact that the junk was itself the cause of his fall, and resultant broken hip, seemed to have completely passed Raymond by. The clear-out had been the 'grossest invasion of my privacy I have ever experienced'. But the flat was now clear and clean, with anything Cross had adjudged worth keeping safely in a nearby storage unit. Raymond had had a cleaner since then, well, several in point of fact, but none of them stayed very long. Another thing he'd taken great exception to, particularly as his son refused to have one at his own flat, which was, for Raymond, an act of unfathomable hypocrisy. Tonight, the flat smelled of recently sawed and sanded wood.

'Hello?' Cross called out.

'Back here! In the spare room,' came the reply.

Cross walked round the corner at the end of the small corridor to find several lengths of two by four wood and large pieces of chipboard leaning against the wall. The sound of an electric jigsaw came from the room at the end. Cross walked up to the open doorway and was surprised by what he saw. The spare room looked like a workshop with cast-off bits of wood and sawdust all over the carpet. A waist-high platform had been built around the walls with a long hole in the middle in which appeared a beaming Raymond.

'What's all this?' Cross asked.

'I've made a start,' Raymond replied.

'On what?'

'The model railway.'

'Ah. I see. Perhaps a little planning and thought should've been invested before you actually started construction.'

'I did. I've got a plan. Look.' He held out a crumpled piece of paper which had a rough smudged sketch of the platform he was building together with its dimensions. It looked like it had been drawn by an eight-year-old who had dreams of being an engineer, but as yet only showed more enthusiasm than talent. Cross looked fantastically unimpressed.

Fifteen minutes later the two men sat on chairs, in the middle of the platform, eating their takeaway and surveying the project. They said nothing for a while, then Cross noticed some pencil marks on the back wall.

'What's happening up there?' he asked.

'Mountains. Going to have a ski lift or a funicular. Haven't decided yet.'

'Very ambitious.'

'You know me, "no mountain high enough",' he chuckled, the reference going clean over Cross's head. 'I'd like to build the buildings, but it might be easier just to buy model kits. Feels like a bit of a cheat though.'

Cross said nothing.

'How is Josie?' Raymond asked.

'Fine.'

'Good.'

'Oh,' said Cross as something suddenly occurred to him. 'Her daughter's had her appendix removed.'

'Really? Which one?'

'You only have one appendix.'

'No, which daughter?'

'Carla.'

'When did this happen?'

'Sunday night. Josie's off work.'

'Poor thing.'

'Oh, I imagine she's fine. Carla, on the other hand, probably not.'

'You haven't called her?' Raymond asked.

'No.'

'All right, we'll go and see them when we've eaten.'

'Dad, her daughter's just had an operation. Now is not a good time for a visit.'

'Now is actually the time you're supposed to visit. We'll need to stop and get something for her on the way over.'

'Like what?'

'Not sure. It's at times like this I really miss Woolworth's. You couldn't go wrong with a bag of pick 'n' mix. Life was so much simpler then.'

Cross had to agree with him on this. As a child the fortnightly visit to Woolies' pick 'n' mix section would be the highlight of any particular weekend. They had tried weekly visits, but Raymond had come to the conclusion that this was excessive and also took away some of the magic. Pick 'n' mix could easily be located in any Woolworth's store, either by the number of children crowded in front of it, or the sickly-sweet smell of sugary confectionery that wafted from it. The display was contained in a series of clear plastic boxes which took up a length of wall. Each had a lid, which you lifted up, and a small scoop to help yourself to the sweets, which some children used like a shovel. You filled your bag and then paid by weight. There was a huge choice, from cola bottles to fried eggs, coconut mushrooms, liquorice allsorts, rainbow chocolate buttons and dozens more. Once the young Cross had got over his initial concerns about hygiene, he was enthralled. Raymond remembered their first visit together. His son carefully took a single sweet out of each container, placed them in his bag and later, at home, performed a taste test. He then wrote the results in his notebook, giving each sweet a mark out of ten. Having done this, he asked his father what weight he would be allowed on each visit. He then correlated the scores to the permissible weight and worked out an equation which told him exactly the number of each of the chosen sweets – some hadn't made the cut at all – he should put in his bag. It was quite a process, but one he enjoyed. He also liked it when new varieties appeared and, following a taste test, adjustments had to be made to his order. It was a father–son ritual which lasted into Cross's late twenties, when the store closed.

They set out in an Uber to Ottey's house, stopping at a

service station so that Raymond could buy some things for Josie's children. He came back laden with sweets and turned to Cross.

'Whenever visiting an ill child or a newborn and you take presents, always remember to take something for the other siblings, if they have them. Important to remember that,' he said. Cross made a mental note of this as he always did, despite the fact that he had no idea when it would come in handy. He wasn't in the habit of visiting children, neither sick nor those who'd just been presented with a little brother or sister. They drove on in silence for a while then Cross turned to his father.

'I've been thinking about my mother recently,' he began.

'Oh yes.'

'I'd like to know more about why she left,' Cross went on.

'You and me both,' replied Raymond, laughing in the deflective way he always did whenever she was mentioned.

'You've been doing that a lot recently, when I bring the subject up.'

'What?'

'Laughing.'

'Well, I don't know what to say. I'm as much in the dark as you.'

'I don't actually think that's true. People always laugh when asked questions they're disinclined to answer.'

'I would if I could. Tell you more.'

'Sometimes it's just nervousness. Other times it's a confidence that repetitive use of the ploy will prevent any further enquiries on the matter.'

'Well in my case it's neither, Sergeant,' Raymond replied ironically.

'She's been to see me,' he said, studying his father's face closely. Raymond looked away out of the window.

'She has?' he said.

'Yes, she was at the recital.'

This seemed to disconcert Raymond.

'I didn't see her then, but she reappeared a couple of days ago,' Cross went on.

'I see,' Raymond replied, quietly.

'She was waiting outside my flat when I went to work.'

'Why, I wonder? After all this time?' Raymond said in such a way that told Cross he already knew the reason.

'Oh, that's entirely my fault. I went back to the house in Gloucester trying to find her.'

Raymond didn't say anything to this. There was a lot swimming around in his mind. He felt a little sick, he realised.

'Once she found out I was looking for her she decided to come and find me,' said Cross.

'Why did you go looking for her in the first place? What were you trying to achieve?'

'I wanted her to know that, despite her obvious misgivings about me at the time she left us, things had worked out just fine. As one glance at me would prove. That she might like to consider that she had made a mistake, that had caused a lot of unnecessary pain, and might want to reflect on it,' Cross said, satisfied that not only was it an accurate description of their meeting, but also, hearing it out loud, how much sense it made.

'And what was her response to this?'

'She said there was more to it than I knew.'

'How did she find you?'

'Stephen.'

'The priest?'

'I know! It's infuriating,' Cross said, misinterpreting his father's tone as agreeing with the social outrage that had been inflicted on him. 'But apparently there's no such thing as clerical confidentiality when it comes to non-believers.' Then something tangential occurred to him. 'Do you think that also applies to sanctuary?'

'What on earth are you talking about?' asked Raymond.

'Can you seek sanctuary in a church if you're a non-believer? It seems to go against the whole point of Christianity if you can't. I'll do some research,' he said, fishing out his notebook and writing it down.

At that point they arrived at Ottey's house, and the conversation was over. If Raymond had been at all troubled by it, you wouldn't have known. The moment he walked through the door, he was like a loving grandfather coming to comfort one of his favourite grandchildren; weighed down with sympathy expressed in the form of confectionery, something their mother would normally never let them have. But removed appendices called for different rules. Cross and Ottey walked into the kitchen, as Raymond pretended to be thrilled at Carla's appendix which she was now waving in a jar in front of his face.

'How is Carla, post-op?'

'Good. Absolutely fine, now the drama of the op is over, and the pain can be managed with paracetamol. She's just enjoying being the centre of attention, while it lasts.'

'Was it definitely appendicitis?' Cross asked.

'It was. It's in pretty poor shape, if you'd like to have a look.'

'I read that thousands of operations are carried out on perfectly healthy appendixes every year.'

'I read that article too. We've obviously been googling the same thing.' Cross was about to protest when she stopped him. 'I'm touched that you went to the trouble. It was very thoughtful.'

'It was,' he confirmed. She wanted to say that he'd also done it so he could be the expert on the subject in the room. But she felt that was unnecessarily unfriendly.

'So how was Ribble?' she asked.

'How did you know we went to Portsmouth?'

'Alice told me, which was just as well as I didn't look like a complete dick with Matthews.'

'Matthews called you?'

'No, she came round. Brought flowers.'

'You'd think she'd have the sense to leave you alone at a time like this. What was she after?'

'Same as Raymond. She just wanted to check everything was okay and see if there was anything she could do.'

Cross thought for a moment. 'That is refreshingly different. I can't imagine Carson doing that in similar circumstances. Well, he hasn't, has he? Have you heard from him?'

'He's not a mother,' Ottey replied.

'Matthews has children?'

'Why does that surprise you?'

'I don't think it does. I just didn't know.'

'Well, she knows how difficult it is being a mother and trying to juggle that with a career in the force. So how was Ribble?' she asked again.

'Still on the whiteboard,' said Cross.

What this meant was, he was still a person of interest. But Cross looked concerned.

'What is it?' Ottey asked, now familiar with his thoughtful expression.

'The alarm. According to the alarm company, it was switched off half an hour before she was killed. How would he know the code?'

13

Carson busied himself holding endless, interminable meetings about the progress, or lack of, in the case. Ottey, now back at work, was relieved that she and Cross had been excused from these meetings by Matthews. She felt the team was best left alone to do the time-consuming tedious jobs that were required this early on in an investigation. Door-to-door enquiries continued, as did tracking down any CCTV footage in the relevant time window. Neighbours with video doorbells were also being approached, to see if they had recorded anything that might be material to the investigation. There was a whiteboard in the open area of the MCU on which photographs of the crime scene, in all its bloody detail, and the missing jewellery were displayed. The team tended to congregate around this, as if it focused their attention. The incident room was a busy place. People flitted in and out. There was the constant buzz of low volume conversations as detectives bashed their phones, chasing leads and eliminating others.

The board in Cross's office was much more ordered and organised. The photographs were so accurately aligned and spaced that you could be forgiven for thinking that Cross had used a spirit level and ruler. But the content of the photographs was also different. They were photographs of all the people involved, or who might be involved, in the case. It was as if he liked to be faced with all the major players as he worked at his desk. He was standing up close to the board, looking at Michael Ribble, when there was a knock at the door.

'Yes?'

A DC from the main team came in. His name was Wilkins. 'I was reading the paper at breakfast this morning. Frampton's recent case was being discussed. It was quite interesting actually...'

'Relevance?'

'The date the case ended. It was three days before his wife's murder. But he stopped in London.'

Cross said nothing.

'His chambers and home are in Bristol. Just thought it seemed odd. Do you want me to look into it?'

'No.'

'Oh, okay.' Wilkins turned to leave.

'I will,' said Cross. Wilkins had been around for long enough to know that this was practically a compliment from Cross. He'd determined that the DC's thinking was worth pursuing. So Wilkins walked across the open area smiling as if he'd just received a pat on the back. What he didn't know was that it was exactly the kind of small detail, something that didn't make obvious sense, a break in routine or what someone might reasonably have been expected to do, that often opened up an important line of enquiry for Cross. Luke Frampton now interested him a little more than he had a few minutes ago.

* * *

Justin Frampton had been back in the country for almost a week, but Cross had delayed meeting him until Ottey had returned to work. This had pleased her secretly. Cross asked if they could meet all three of the family together. He wanted to see them as a unit. Get a sense of the family dynamic. They arranged to meet at Justin's flat in Abbots Leigh.

Ottey and Cross drove across the Clifton Suspension Bridge. A bridge George knew almost intimately. He could tell you the dates of its construction, number of fatalities, original cost, competing tenders, even the number of rivets, and where the wrought-iron chains on each side had been forged. This information had been relayed to him, over the years, every time he and his father Raymond had either driven or walked across it. Raymond was a devoted Brunel fan (George's middle name, not known to many, was Brunel thanks to his father's obsession), and it was an enormous, indescribable highlight for him when it was discovered, quite recently, that the abutment of the bridge on the Leigh Woods side actually contained arched vaults. After many years of campaigning, hard-hat tours had now been initiated and it was Cross's intention to treat his father to one in the near future. He told Ottey this as they drove across it.

'Oh my god, that's so cool. He'll love that. I should take the kids.'

'Preferably on a different day.'

'George, that's rude. Even you must be able to see that.'

He thought about this for a moment. 'No. It would definitely be preferable for all of us, children included.'

'You may have a point,' she then conceded.

Cross looked like he was about to say something but

changed his mind. This was unlike him. Generally, as soon as he thought of something he wanted to say, it just hurtled out of his mouth, even if others were speaking.

'Is everything all right?'

'You'll have to be specific. I have no idea what that question alludes to.'

'With you? You don't seem yourself.'

Cross was conflicted by this question. He was, as it happened, preoccupied with something personal, but it went against the grain for him to talk about personal matters on police time. When he'd originally told Ottey this point of principle she claimed he was just using it as an excuse to get out of talking about such things. But he said they weren't paid out of the public purse to discuss their private lives. They could do it at the end of a day in the pub or when they went out for dinner. But as she pointed out, he didn't go to the pub or out for dinner with colleagues. So, his principled attitude was just a convenient way of avoiding ever talking about anything personal. Privately, he admitted to himself that he'd been 'found out', as Ottey would put it. But he had no intention of telling her that.

This morning, however, he was caught in two minds. The fact was he did have something he wanted to tell her.

'I saw my mother a few of days ago,' he said, as if it were the most normal thing that happened on a daily basis, instead of for the first time in over four decades.

'What?'

Ottey was so thrown by this that she pulled over to the side of the road.

'What are you doing?' he asked.

'Your *mother*?'

'We'll be late. Please continue driving.'

'What happened? Where did you see her?' Ottey continued, ignoring him. Cross now related the events in detail.

'You're kidding.'

'On the contrary. I find nothing about this amusing.'

So, what did you do then?' she asked, still a little shocked.

'I went straight over to see Stephen, of course.'

'The priest? Why am I thinking it wasn't to get some spiritual advice at this life-changing moment?'

'Because that would be ridiculous. I knew that Stephen was the only way she could've found out where I lived.'

'And how did you figure that one out?' asked Ottey.

'Because only you, human resources at work, my father, Tony the café owner and Stephen know my address. It had to be him. So, I told him that he had no right to divulge my personal details to a stranger.'

'She's not a stranger, she's your mother.'

'He didn't know that for certain. Anyway, he wasn't in the least bit apologetic, not even when I pointed out that the relationship between a priest and one of his parishioners is supposed to be like that of a doctor with a patient – confidential.'

'I think calling yourself a parishioner is a bit of a stretch.'

'That's what he said. But then he went on to say he would've done the same thing with any parishioner or congregant, the only difference being he would've informed them first.'

'And he didn't with you because he knew you would've said no.'

'Have you spoken to him?' he asked, a little surprised by her reaction.

'I have not.'

'Well, he went on to say that he was only doing his job, offering pastoral care whether or not I'd asked for it, or indeed thought I was in need of it.'

'I love that man.'

'He's celibate,' said Cross.

'Oh, George. So, are you seeing your mother again?'

'Of course not. I've made my point and there's an end to it.'

'Oh, I don't think so. Not for a minute.'

He had no idea what she meant by this, but the fact that she'd pulled out and was driving again meant that the conversation could be deemed to be over. Thankfully. Although, to his surprise, it hadn't exactly gone the way he thought it would. But he'd told her about it, and so ticked it off on his mental to-do list. It would never have to be mentioned again.

The Frampton family were waiting in the front room. Parminder the family liaison officer was there with them. She volunteered to make them all tea when the detectives arrived. The front room wasn't overly large, and the sense of them all being in perhaps uncomfortable proximity to each other was enhanced by the fact that it was crammed full of antique furniture, cluttered but assembled in an orderly and tasteful fashion. It was a bit like a curated room in a museum, only homely and comfortable.

'You've been abroad, Mr Frampton,' Cross began.

'Justin. Please. Yes, I had a short break in Portugal. I came back as soon as I heard.' The young man seemed nervous, Cross observed. Perhaps it was just the shock of it all.

'What line of business are you in?'

'Antiques. I have a small antiques shop in Bath. But I mostly do online orders now.'

'That makes sense,' said Ottey, as she looked around the room.

'Don't look at anything for too long, or he'll try and flog it to you,' said Sasha.

'That's probably true,' Justin laughed nervously.

'Have you always been interested in antiques?' asked Cross.

'He has from a young age. Gets it from his mother,' said Luke. 'He, well they both, spent their childhoods trawling round the south-west at weekends, going to various antiques fairs, or shops that Peg had read about in a magazine article. Happy days.'

'Maybe for you two, but not for me. I was bored out of my mind,' said Sasha, doing her best to deflate the nostalgic bubble which was in danger of encasing them.

'Oh, it wasn't that bad,' Justin protested quietly.

'Her picnics were the worst of it,' Sasha continued.

'Now that's true!' Justin laughed loudly.

Luke, basking in the warmth of their wistful memories, then said, 'She bought the most gorgeous picnic hamper when they were young, nineteen thirties, I think it was. Boy, did she put it to good use.'

'If only her food had been as attractive as that hamper. I've been scarred for life. If my kids begged me to take them on a picnic I'd say no. Even now I get a sickly feeling in the bottom of my stomach whenever we pass a sign for a picnic lay-by on an A road.'

'Oh, stop it,' said Justin smiling. 'You have to admit things improved when she discovered you could put things in sandwiches other than just sandwich spread.'

'Oh my god, do you remember sandwich spread?' Sasha asked the two police officers.

'I don't,' replied Ottey.

'Well you've been spared, trust me.'

'I was rather partial to it,' said Cross.

'You'll be saying you liked condensed milk next,' said Sasha.

'As long as it was Carnation, then yes.'

'Blimey, I'm not coming round to your house for supper any time soon,' Sasha laughed.

'No, you're not,' Cross replied.

There was an awkward pause.

'Have you noticed anything else missing from your study?' asked Ottey.

'No, just the jewellery,' Luke replied.

'The jewellery? What jewellery?' Justin seemed shocked by this.

'Mum's sapphires and diamonds,' Sasha answered.

'No! Why didn't you tell me?'

'Well obviously we were going to tell you, but we haven't had a chance,' said Sasha.

Justin's phone rang. He looked at the number and seemed startled.

'I have to take this,' he said getting up and leaving the room.

'He's still in shock,' Luke explained, somewhat unnecessarily, Cross thought. 'I think being out of the country made it a lot more difficult for him. If you know what I mean.'

'I don't.' Luke was taken aback by the bluntness of Cross's reply.

'It's just a feeling. His being here wouldn't have made any

material difference, of course, but he feels irrationally guilty about it happening when he was away.'

'It's certainly irrational,' commented Cross.

'George,' cautioned Ottey.

Luke travelled quite a lot as a judge or recorder and as a barrister on higher profile criminal cases at the Old Bailey, apparently. It was on one of these cases that he'd been in London at the time of his wife's death.

'*R. v. Swinton*,' Cross proclaimed out of nowhere.

'Yes?' Luke replied.

'Your recent case at the Old Bailey.'

'Correct.'

'You won.'

'Thankfully.'

'Why thankfully? Was there any doubt?'

'Trials are complex organisms, as I'm sure you're well aware, Sergeant. My client was innocent. But it was a difficult case to prove, or more accurately convince the jury of. The lawyer for the prosecution is an excellent barrister but he's rather like a Battle of Britain ace.'

'He likes a dogfight,' Ottey volunteered.

'He does indeed and is far more interested in marking up his tally on the fuselage of his aircraft than in anything else.'

'The case actually finished a few days before your wife's murder. Three, to be precise,' Cross went on.

'What?' Sasha asked.

'That's correct,' said Frampton. Justin came back into the room. He looked like someone who had received bad news.

'Everything all right?' his father asked.

'Yes, just a friend calling about a piece he's seen up in Gloucester he thinks I might like,' Justin replied.

'Why did you stay in London? Why didn't you come straight home?' Cross continued.

'I had other business to attend to.'

'*Three* days?' Sasha asked, looking directly at her father.

'That's right,' he replied. Sasha looked away as if she'd decided not to press this any further.

'What's this?' asked Justin.

'I'm asking your father why he stayed in London for three days after his recent trial had finished,' said Cross.

'I had meetings with solicitors, that kind of thing,' Frampton continued.

'On other cases?'

'No, actually, I was meeting with them trying to drum up some work.'

'Really? I had no idea barristers did that, did you, DS Ottey?'

'I did not,' she replied.

'I thought your clerk would do that,' Cross continued.

'He does.'

'Surely a barrister of your standing doesn't need to "drum up" business, as you put it. There's always plenty of crime about, isn't there?'

'And plenty of other barristers to take them all on. It's a competitive business, Sergeant.'

Cross now turned to Ottey, which she knew was her cue to continue with the interview.

'People often find this a ridiculous question in these circumstances, Justin, but in case your mother's death wasn't caused in the commission of a burglary, do you know of anyone who might want to cause her harm?' she asked.

'Me? Why me?' he asked defensively.

'Well, we've already asked your father and sister.'

'Do I know someone who would want to kill my mother? No, of course not.' He laughed nervously at the very idea.

'Justin, calm down. You never know, you might think of something. Something might come to mind,' his father said gently. Justin looked at him for a moment then sighed.

'I'm sorry. Of course, it's a perfectly reasonable question. No, I don't, off hand, but I will think about it. If anything occurs to me, I will let you know.'

Cross got up to leave. Ottey followed. 'Thank you for your time,' she said. 'If you need anything just ask Parminder. That's what she's here for. If any of you think of anything which might be relevant, she'll let us know.'

As they got to the door Cross stopped so abruptly that Ottey walked straight into the back of him. It was a little comical. Justin looked at his sister as if to say their lack of coordination didn't bode well for the investigation. Cross then asked the next question with the air of an absent-minded professor giving a badly attended university lecture.

'Who knew about your wife's family jewellery?'

'Um, I'm not sure. She used to wear it quite often. Particularly when she was mayor,' said Luke.

'There was that article,' Sasha suddenly piped up. 'Justin, you organised it.'

For a moment Justin looked like he was being accused of doing something wrong. But the defensive expression disappeared as quickly as it had appeared.

'Oh yes. That's right. It was in an antiques industry mag. They were lovely pieces. Very attractive,' he said.

'Very collectible,' said Ottey.

'Were?' asked Cross.

'No, you're right. Are. Hopefully we'll get them back,' Justin added quickly.

'But the article was picked up by the *Telegraph*, remember,' Sasha went on. 'Mum was thrilled. They sent a photographer and did a piece on our family history.'

'Yes, but it was years ago,' Justin replied.

'No, it wasn't. We were all relieved that, being a Bristol family, we had no links to slavery.'

'That's right,' laughed Luke quietly.

'So it's possible someone saw that piece in a national newspaper and decided to steal them,' said Ottey.

'I suppose so. But kill her? That seems unlikely,' Luke said.

'There's something up with that young man,' Ottey said as they walked to the car.

'He certainly seemed on edge. But then again, his mother has just been murdered,' Cross replied.

'It was more than that. He was nervy. Jumpy. Defensive.'

'His taking a call in the middle of a meeting with the police struck me as strange. If it was just an antique dealer friend, that is,' added Cross.

14

Since their fruitless trip to Portsmouth, Michael Swift had spent a good deal of time studying the crime scene pictures of Peggy's bedroom. He really wanted to be able to offer more to the case. But it was one of those rare occasions where the photographs didn't really seem to tell a story. The lack of logic in the events intrigued him, though, and kept swimming around in his head. He was already working on other crime scenes as they presented themselves, but he couldn't forget about Peggy. He had to find a way to stay involved and observe more of Cross at work. There was one thing they didn't have yet. A cause of death. If the answer wasn't in the victim's body, it was possible it was in the pictures. Then, in the early hours of the morning, that was exactly where he found it, with Robert Smith of The Cure serenading him through his stereo. It was an old Quad system with a turntable. He was a vinyl man, was Michael Swift. Something he was sure George Cross would approve of.

Matthews looked up from her desk. All she could see was a Gorillaz T-shirt, and Michael Swift's chin through the glass pane of her door.

'Come in.'

'Dr Michael Swift, ma'am, forensic investigator.'

'I thought so,' she said, looking up at him. He sighed instinctively; his habitual disappointment that his height was the main thing people remembered about him rose to the surface. 'Nice to meet you.'

'Likewise,' he replied.

'How can I help?'

'I think I have a cause of death in the Frampton case.'

'Well, that's pretty impressive, when you consider the fact that the pathologist, who has performed the autopsy, still doesn't have one.'

'Well, sometimes you have to look outside the box – beyond the corpse to find the answer.'

'Why are you telling me this and not DS Cross?'

'He's not in his office. He told me if I came over and couldn't find him, to report directly to you. If I thought it was important.'

Matthews was surprised by this. Most detectives were proprietorial about the lines of communication with their teams. Possessive about information, deciding when or indeed whether they shared it with their senior officers. Apparently George Cross wasn't like that, which she liked.

Ottey saw Swift with Matthews as she and Cross came back into the MCU from their visit to the Frampton family. Matthews got up as soon as she saw the returning officers and followed them into Cross's office with Swift in tow. Mackenzie, as eagle-eyed as ever, knew there had to have been

TIM SULLIVAN

some development in the case. But they closed the bloody
door which meant she couldn't hear.

'Ma'am,' Cross and Ottey said, practically in unison.

'Michael came to me with something, as you told him to if
you were out,' Matthews began, explaining the looming FE's
presence. Ottey thought this was interesting for two reasons.
Firstly, that Cross had told Swift to do this – it was something
he'd never told anyone to do with Carson – and secondly there
was something slightly apologetic in Matthews' explanation.
As if she, the senior officer, needed to explain anything to
anyone anyway.

'Michael, could you elaborate?'

'I don't think Peggy Frampton was killed by the blow to
the head.'

'Neither do I,' said Cross.

'Why?' asked Matthews.

'No aspiration from either the mouth or nasal passages. Dr
Swift has now confirmed this with a microscopic examination
of the carpet fibres, I assume,' Cross went on.

'I have. There is no aspirated blood on the carpet,' Swift
confirmed.

'Which is puzzling,' replied Cross.

Swift smiled and reached for something in his pocket but
Cross had already left the room.

'Where's he going?' asked Matthews.

'My money's on Clare. The pathologist. You should
probably tag along too,' Ottey said to Swift.

'Are you sure?'

'Oh yes. This is his way of asking. Come.'

'Let me know what happens? Please?' said Matthews,
mock-pleadingly as they disappeared.

'I will,' said Ottey over her shoulder, thinking again how refreshingly different this was to working with Carson, who then walked into the office.

'What did I miss?' he said to Matthews.

'I think they may have found a cause of death. But I'm not entirely sure,' she replied, causing him almost to spin theatrically on the spot, to ask Ottey what was going on. But she'd gone. He looked at Mackenzie as if he was going to ask her something, only for the absurdity of such an idea to hit him. He then walked off, shaking his head.

'Wanker,' she said, under her breath.

'Could you bring Mrs Frampton in?' Clare asked the mortuary assistant. 'I'm assuming you think I've missed something?' she asked Cross who had arrived with Swift.

'Why would you assume that?'

'Why else would you be here? And come on, you have to admit you get a kick out of showing me up.'

'I get no pleasure when you make mistakes. On the contrary, it's time-consuming.'

'Aren't you going to introduce me?' she said, looking at Swift.

'Dr Clare Hawkins, Dr Michael Swift,' Cross replied. She waited for further explanation, but none came from him.

'Forensic scientist, crime scene investigator,' Swift explained.

Ottey now entered the room. Cross looked at her pointedly, implying she'd forgotten something vital, which he wasn't going to show her up by saying aloud. She thought for a moment, then sighed and reached for her warrant card.

'DS Ottey,' she said holding it aloft.

'Morning, Josie. How are you?'

'Thrilled that George has seen fit to include me on one of his regular visits to see you. So, what are we looking at?'

'Peggy Frampton's body,' Cross replied as a trolley clattered noisily into the room. 'I wanted to have a closer look at something. Dr Hawkins mentioned something in her autopsy report which together with Dr Swift's observation I thought might benefit from our combined re-examination.'

Ottey didn't like these visits to the mortuary, unlike her partner who seemed to have an enthusiastic fascination with them. Not that he was in any way a thanatophile. His experience simply told him that the answer to whatever murder he was investigating often lay within its walls. That, as the final witness to any murder, the victim's body would more often than not have the answer, or at least a very strong indication as to what befell them. But Ottey couldn't stand the smell. It wasn't of death, far from it. It was of layers of disinfectant and cleaning fluids that covered any residual smell of the mortuary's late residents. One of the few benefits of the pandemic was that she could wear a mask which she liberally doused in perfume when visiting the mortuary.

As the assistant was about to uncover Peggy Frampton Cross stopped him. 'Just her face and neck.' As if to preserve some modicum of modesty for the poor woman. Something this place and its process had taken away from her some time ago.

'Dr Hawkins,' Cross began.

'Clare,' she said for the umpteenth time.

'Dr Clare Hawkins,' Cross said, correcting himself and making a mental note for the umpteenth time to remember this. 'You found no evidence of blood in the victim's lungs or respiratory tract, according to your report.'

'Correct.'

'With that in mind, and the fact that you also believe that the blow to the head wasn't forceful enough to cause death, would you not have expected the presence of blood from the victim's inhalation of it?'

'I would.'

'So…?'

'So, it's a puzzle. As you know we haven't been able to conclusively give a cause of death. There's no previously undetected aneurysm released by the blow. Nor a cardiac event brought on by the assault.'

'What other factors, then, could account for a lack of aspiration on the carpet beside the victim's mouth?' Cross asked.

'The lack of blood ingested by the victim, as I just said.'

'Let's look beyond that.'

Ottey had no idea what Cross was after, but she recognised the look in his face as he led them all through his thought process. It was a look of confidence.

'What other reasons can there be for the absence of such blood? Could it have been caused by an external factor?'

'Something that prevented her from inhaling the blood from the head wound in the first place,' offered Ottey.

'Yes,' said Cross. 'The absence of petechiae – that's bloodshot eyes—' he explained to Ottey.

'George…' Ottey growled.

'—threw me initially. But I did some research. Crime scene photographs!' he instructed.

'What?' replied Clare. Then realising what he meant,

turned to the lab assistant who typed into a computer at the side of the room. Dozens of thumbnails appeared on a monitor mounted on the back wall.

'Face close-up. In situ,' Cross instructed. The photograph came up of Peggy. Her hair was matted with blood. The one visible eye now lifeless as the cornea had clouded over post-mortem. Her head was arched back, and the mouth was wide open.

'What struck me as unusual as I studied this picture and several others from differing angles, was not only the unnatural angle of the head, as if it had been pulled back,' he arched his head back, looking up at the ceiling to demonstrate what he meant, 'but also the way the mouth is so wide open.'

'It looks like she's struggling to breathe,' said Ottey.

'Yes.'

'After your last visit the only conclusion that I could come to was that she was suffocated immediately after being struck on the head,' said Clare.

'She wasn't strangled?' Ottey asked.

'No, the hyoid's intact, there's no bruising to the neck, and no evidence of petechiae in the eyes,' Clare confirmed.

'Dr Swift has the answer,' said Cross, looking directly at the forensic examiner, who seemed to be momentarily lost in his own thoughts.

'I do?' he said.

'It's in your pocket. You reached for it when I interrupted you back in the office, did you not?'

'I did.' He looked at Cross for a moment then put his hand into his packet and produced a small evidence bag with an earring in it. 'Was there an earring missing from one of the victim's ears?' he asked Clare.

'There was.'

'But it's not just the earring, is it, Dr Swift? You've found a trace of plastic material either in the clasp or on the carpet near where you found the earring,' Cross went on.

'How the fuck do you know that?' asked the nonplussed, but at the same time bemused, FE.

'Because it makes sense of the facts as they are presenting themselves to us. She was asphyxiated with a plastic bag, immediately after she was struck. From the research papers I've studied it appears to be a difficult, if not impossible, conclusion to come to through a post-mortem, without adjunctive evidence. But the presence of the plastic—'

'In the clasp,' Swift filled in.

'—together with the lack of blood in the victim's lungs and respiratory passages, and therefore the lack of aspirated blood on the carpet, adjacent to the victim's mouth, makes it more likely than not that the victim's face was covered with a plastic bag after she'd been knocked down. This prevented both the inhalation and exhalation of blood from the head trauma.'

There was silence in the room. Swift wanted to clap but knew that would be totally inappropriate. Cross was singularly impressive, and he determined to ensure he worked with this detective as often as he could, from then on. Ottey smiled, not just at Swift's slightly stunned expression, or indeed Cross's impressive deductive skills, but the fact that he liked a bit of theatre, did dear old George. He could just as easily have let Swift produce the earring back at the office, but that wouldn't have had the desired effect, the *coup de théâtre* of the big reveal in the autopsy room.

117

'So, this changes everything,' said Ottey, as she drove Cross back to the office.

'It doesn't change anything. It merely confirms what was looking likely last week,' Cross replied.

'I thought you didn't deal in "likely".'

'When it comes to theories and hypotheses, no. The evidence was likely pointing in this direction, however.'

'You went to see the body without me. Clare referred to your "last visit".'

'I did,' he replied in a way that he hoped conveyed that this was inconsequential.

'Again.'

So, she was going to make an issue of it. 'There was no need for both of us to go. I saved you an unnecessary excursion.'

'"Team", George.'

'We should go back and see the family with this new information.'

'We should talk to Matthews first.'

'We don't have to do that,' replied Cross.

'We don't *have* to, but it won't do us any harm. Remember what I told you about managing the higher-ups.'

'You said it was important, and that I should leave it up to you.'

'That's right.'

'So, you do that, and I'll go and see the family.'

'That may be literally what I said, but it is not what I meant, and I know you know that, by the way.'

Ottey had become something of an expert in spotting when Cross used his condition conveniently to get out of something he didn't want to do. He, of course, knew he did this from time to time, but was equally aware that it was working less and less frequently with his partner. Which was annoying.

'She was deliberately murdered?' Carson asked in disbelief. They were all in a hastily convened meeting of the entire team.

'It was premeditated. It wasn't accidental. It wasn't an interrupted burglary,' said Ottey, speaking for Cross, as usual, in a large meeting.

'Are you sure?' he persisted.

'She was suffocated with a plastic bag held over her head. It seems highly unlikely that a burglar saw a bag full of her hair curlers and decided to use it on the spur of the moment.'

'Most supermarket carrier bags have small holes to provide ventilation, together with which, if such a bag had been used to store hair curlers, they would doubtless have perforated it, rendering it ineffective for the purposes of suffocation.' It was the first thing Cross had said in the meeting. There was a snigger from a couple of young detectives in the room.

'What's so funny?' Matthews asked.

'Nothing, ma'am,' one of them replied.

'Then, why are you laughing?'

'Sorry, ma'am.'

'Don't apologise to me for behaving like a couple of immature twats. Maybe you should apologise to the DS who has come up with a cause of death. Which I'm sure neither of you would've done, even if it had been written on a piece of paper and held up in front of your face. A cause of death which will have a significant impact on the direction of our investigation.'

There was no reply.

'So, this was a premeditated murder and for my money it was either professional with the perpetrator knowing it would be difficult to detect – a plastic bag is more often than not used in cases of suicide in my experience – or it's personal.' She paused as she thought this through for a moment.

'Uniform should do another sweep of the immediate area, and see if we can find this bag. The rest of you find the jewellery. It's our only lead.'

'The jewellery is irrelevant,' said Cross dismissively. 'We have a burglary to order, as DCI Carson has described it, and a murder with a staged burglary designed to throw us off the scent.'

'I take your point, however indelicately put, Sergeant.' Cross immediately looked to Ottey for clarification, but she was looking the other way. He was simply making a valid point. 'The burglaries, whether a single burglary or two, are both lines of enquiry we should pursue. They may or may not turn out to be linked. So, as I said. Find the jewellery.'

'The jewellery, if it was indeed stolen to order, probably had a buyer lined up and we'll find no trace of it,' said Carson.

As the meeting broke up Carson walked over to Matthews. 'Sorry about George,' he said.

'Why?'

'The way he contradicted you in front of the entire team. Twice.'

'He did?' she said, sounding surprised. 'I didn't notice. I was just thinking he made a good point. Put more bodies on the fingertip search. We need to find that plastic bag.'

'And the paperweight,' Carson added.

'Not forgetting the paperweight.'

15

Cross was eating his breakfast in Tony's café when a voice caused him to look up.

'Good morning, George.'

It was Stephen the priest. He'd got into the habit of dropping in on Cross, at breakfast, to badger him about something. The last thing had been an organ recital he'd coerced Cross into doing at the church to raise funds for a new heating system. If he persisted in ambushing him like this, Cross might have to find somewhere else to enjoy his early morning repast. Not an easy prospect with the number of demands he had for the way his perfect cooked breakfast was prepared and served, though. It would be difficult to find another Tony. Twelve months previously Cross had decided to change to porridge for a while. A huge change for him and one that needed to be taken with appropriate considered research. Tony put together a blind tasting not only of various brands but also cooking methods. In the end Cross had, of course managed to plump for the traditional oats in a pan with milk. More time-consuming, but there wasn't much Tony wouldn't do for his most regular customer.

'Stephen,' George replied, laying down his cutlery. He chose not to address the priest as 'Father' as he wasn't a believer and so not a part of his flock. He also had a perfectly acceptable father in Raymond.

'I've brought someone to see you,' continued the priest. Cross knew that the smile plastered across the man of cloth's face meant trouble.

'Good morning, George,' said his mother, Christine, who appeared from behind Stephen. Cross was quite startled by this. It took him by surprise and not in a pleasant way. He immediately started to wipe down his cutlery with a paper napkin and put it back in his pocket. He was prepared to forgo his breakfast, in its entirety, to avoid whatever this meddling young priest and woman had in mind.

'Don't do that, George. Tony went to such a lot of effort,' said Stephen.

'For which he will be adequately compensated.'

Stephen was unaware that this situation constituted a real social crisis for Cross. He didn't experience many occasions where he was put on the spot out of his work environment, and at work it was different. There, he had equipped himself with various strategies to cope. Ottey told him once that she thought he coped at work because he was shielded by his persona as a police officer. She then went on to say they all did it, which made him feel better, as it wasn't one of those moments where she was singling him out. This morning in the café just confirmed to him what he'd suspected for a while. That these ever-increasing awkward moments in his life had one factor in common. The priest.

'George, you can carry on with your breakfast. This won't take long,' Stephen said.

'He can't,' Cross's mother interjected. 'He doesn't like to be watched eating. It upsets him.'

Cross was taken aback by this observation. Not just because she was right, but the fact that she had remembered after all these years.

'Very well. We'll go and sit over there,' said Stephen, pointing to a table in the far corner. 'When you've finished eating, why don't you come and join us for five minutes?'

Cross looked at his mother. Other than her eyes she was someone he didn't actually recognise. There had been no photographs of her, nor of them all together, in the flat when he'd grown up. What was odd to him in that moment, though, was that her expression exactly mirrored how he often felt when he was determined to see something through. Was it possible this was how he looked when he felt the same way? He didn't know. He'd never been facing a mirror or reflective surface when 'determined', as far as he knew. One thing he was sure of, though, was that this woman wasn't going to leave until she'd got what she'd come for, and that if she left without it, it would only be a matter of time before she returned.

'Very well,' he said reluctantly. They retreated to the other table and ordered a couple of cups of tea. Cross ate his breakfast. He tried not to think about what his mother wanted from him, so as not to cloud his responses when he did talk to her. He finished eating and walked over towards them. Stephen was about to stand when Cross went straight past him to the till, to pay Tony. Only then did he turn, join them at the table, and take a seat opposite his mother. He looked at his watch.

'I will leave in ten minutes,' he announced.

'I've come back to see you because Stephen told me to,' his mother began. Cross looked at the priest and then back at his mother. 'The reason being that I wanted to correct some of the impressions you gave me in our last brief meeting.'

'I wasn't aware I gave you any.'

'I'm so pleased you've done well with your life, but I'm not surprised. I see you in the local paper occasionally. You seem to be doing very well in your work.'

'Best conviction rate in the force,' Stephen added, as if telling Cross something he wasn't already aware of.

'You seemed angry,' his mother went on.

'Is that in the least bit surprising?'

'No, of course not. I left you and your father when you were very young. Have you ever discussed it with him?'

'Not really.'

'I see.'

'But I saw the letter.'

'What letter?' she asked.

'Presumably the last letter you wrote to him, telling him why you left.'

'I don't remember it exactly.'

'Really? A letter ending your marriage? Abandoning your son. Something you don't remember?' he said, sounding as if he were in the MCU interview room.

'I said I don't remember it exactly. But of course I remember writing it.'

'Do you remember saying you couldn't accept me the way he wanted you to?'

She looked confused for a moment. 'That's not true. I wouldn't have said that.'

'As I said. I've read the letter, and that's what it says.'

'That is not what I meant. You've misread it.'

'I can assure you, I paid a lot of attention to it. Certainly more than you, it would seem. I don't blame you. I've never blamed you, if that's what you need to hear.'

'It isn't. It really isn't.'

'I've accepted it. It's a fact of my life. I'm sure I wasn't an easy child. In fact I know from my father I wasn't. But you made your choice. The easier choice, it has to be said, and you have to accept that. You left me with Raymond and it's worked out fine.'

'I felt, rightly or wrongly, that he was best equipped to bring you up. That you, being the way you were, wouldn't be able to cope with being shared between the two of us. You liked order and routine, even at that age. Ray seemed to communicate with you better than I could. So, as the marriage was over by then, I thought leaving you was the best option. For everyone. I think, looking at you now, I was right.'

'The marriage was over, George. That's why she left,' said Stephen.

'And we all know why that was,' said Cross.

'Do we?' asked Stephen.

'Because of me,' Cross stated neutrally.

'That's not true,' said Christine.

'I don't blame you,' Cross repeated.

'You keep saying that, which makes me think, if you don't mind me saying so, that you do blame her. Very much so.'

'I do mind,' Cross answered. 'I have Asperger's syndrome, or autism spectrum condition, however you prefer to refer to it.'

'Which your mother didn't know at the time.'

'No one knew, but that is precisely my point. Had you known then, maybe, things would have worked out differently.'

'They absolutely would not,' she asserted firmly.

'At least you're honest,' said Cross, getting up.

'George, don't leave,' Stephen urged.

'It's fine,' said Christine. 'Let me say just one last thing. You think you know what happened, but as your work as a detective should tell you – nothing is ever that straightforward. In this situation it's not even as if there are two sides to the story. Stephen says you have two passions in life. The organ – and I have to say you're a wonderful organist, all the more remarkable given that you're self-taught—'

'She came to the recital, George. That's how she and I met,' added Stephen. Cross was surprised by this.

'—the other is the truth. Stephen says you can't let go of a case until you're absolutely sure you've got to the truth. You can't settle until you know justice has been served. Well, your view of me and my actions is unjust. Because yes, I left you and your father, but you don't know the truth behind that decision. You have your version of the facts. But that's your version. The version that Raymond has let you believe. You need to find the truth, George. You need to speak to your father, and if he won't tell you, then do what you're obviously good at. Get to the truth yourself.'

He was fairly sure she was upset and possibly angry, which he found surprising in the circumstances. But, before he could say anything, she had grabbed her handbag and scarf and left the café.

'Do you know what she means by that?' Cross asked Stephen.

'I do not,' he said, then added mischievously, 'And even if I did, I couldn't tell you.'

'You told me there was no such thing as—'

'But,' Stephen interrupted him before he could finish, 'the difference is she's a believer, George. A churchgoer. You are not, and what she tells me, she tells me in confidence.'

16

The fingertip search still hadn't turned anything up which was immensely frustrating. So a text from Catherine in CCTV was a welcome development. Cross liked the CCTV room at the MCU. Although to call it that was something of an exaggeration. It was, in fact, Catherine's drab little office where she and an assistant (she used to have two, but one was reassigned and never replaced; a subtle way of making departmental cuts) viewed hours of footage on their desktop computers. But he liked its singularity of purpose. The tasks at hand were simple and, while tedious, crucial. Catherine had covered some of the dull walls with printed frame grabs from past cases. These were like trophies. Images that had led to breakthroughs in cases and arrests. She had explained to Cross that they were a visual source of encouragement for her. Particularly at times when the hours of fruitless eye-straining pixel-gazing got her down.

Her text announced that Catherine had found something of interest. She could easily have just sent the image over electronically but she liked the human interaction (and interruption) of people coming to the office. Most of the detectives in the MCU were aware of this and indulged her, however busy they were, often with coffee and muffins. This wasn't just to demonstrate their appreciation of her work, it was because Catherine was a police officer, now deskbound, thanks to an injury she suffered on duty some years before. She didn't want to leave the force and they had been very good in finding her work that she could manage. Everyone was conscious of how easily, and at any moment, they could be in her shoes and so made time for her.

'Catherine, good morning,' began Ottey, handing her a soy latte, as Cross greeted her with his customary awkward nod of the head. 'What have you got?'

'I've been looking at footage from the council planning meeting. Peggy's final meeting,' Catherine replied.

'Why?' asked Cross, as it wasn't something they'd actioned.

'Matthews asked me to do it,' Catherine replied.

'So shouldn't you be showing it to her?' Cross asked.

'I'm sure she already has, George, and Matthews has asked her to show it to us,' Ottey said patiently.

'Correct,' said Catherine. 'And look who I found in the public gallery.'

It was Michael Ribble. They looked at it for a moment.

'Let's bring him in. Thanks, Catherine. George?' said Ottey, indicating that this was one of those times where an expression of gratitude was normally expressed. But he was already halfway out of the door.

'Don't worry. Him leaving like that's his way of saying what I've shown him is important,' said Catherine smiling.

'I've never managed to see it like that before, but I'm definitely going to try to in future.' They laughed and she left.

17

Michael Ribble had that particular look of fear people often had when, having already been visited by the police at home, they thought the matter had gone away, only to be arrested a few days, or even weeks later. With Ribble, Cross couldn't read whether it was the fear of the guilty, or that of an innocent man who has just realised he could get into trouble for something he hadn't done. People were well aware, these days, that the police often got it wrong. Cross thought the public had a right to be sceptical of their ability to always get it right. As he sat opposite Ribble and organised his files, he noticed his suspect continually taking off his glasses and rubbing his eyes. He also noticed that he had a surprising amount of dandruff on his shoulder, considering only about an eighth of his scalp was producing hair and the rest of it seemed clear of any obvious dermatological issue.

'Do you know why you're here?' Cross began after a long pause, during which he simply studied his interviewee.

'Because you've made a mistake,' came the reply.

'In what way?'

'I didn't kill Peggy Frampton,' Ribble answered, calmly.

Cross consulted his notebook carefully, then, having found what he was looking for, looked back up.

'Do you remember my asking you how you imagined your behaviour to Peggy Frampton, both online and in person, her subsequent death at the hands of a third party, and your lack of any alibi, might appear to us?' Cross asked.

'I do.'

'Where were you the night of February the seventh?' Cross asked.

'I've already answered that question,' Ribble replied.

'You have, but not under caution,' answered Cross.

'I was in my workshop at my house.'

'You're quite sure of that?'

'I am.'

'How can you be so sure?'

'Because, like I told you, Peggy Frampton was killed that night.'

'So, you made a note of it?'

'Yes.'

'Why?'

'You know why.'

'Perhaps you could answer the question again for the tape?'

'Because I was having a row with her online.'

'A row during which you threatened to kill her.'

'Yes, but I didn't mean it.'

'More than once. Five times, to the best of my knowledge.'

Ribble sighed, as if there was never any chance of his convincing this detective of the conventions of internet trolling.

'But you didn't, kill her that is, because you were miles away in Portsmouth?'

'Yes.'

Cross looked at Ribble as if he were giving him the chance

to think again about his answer. Then he opened his file and passed an A4 printout across the table.

'For the tape, DS Cross is showing the suspect a frame grab from the Bristol City Council meeting of February the seventh,' said Ottey.

Ribble looked at it and said nothing.

'Do you have a particular interest in Bristol planning matters?' Cross asked.

'Oh, very funny,' said Ribble, rattled.

'I can assure you I'm not joking. I'm trying to understand your presence at the meeting. So do you?'

'What?'

'Have an interest in local planning matters in Bristol?' asked Cross.

'No, of course not.'

'So, why were you there?'

'I wanted to see her in the flesh. That's all.'

'Which was something you'd done several times before. So many, in fact, that Mrs Frampton had a restraining order taken out against you.' He looked at Ribble who took off his glasses and rubbed his eyes. He put them back on and looked at Cross. 'Why the need to see her in person that night? The night she was murdered?' Cross continued.

'I wanted to be there when she failed. When that bloke got his application through. I wanted to see the look on her face when she lost something that was important to *her*.'

'But you had no idea whether that would happen or not.'

'From everything I'd read, I thought the application would get through.'

'And that was it?'

'She was obsessed with that development. Totally obsessed.

And with him. Chapel. You should maybe take a look at him, instead of wasting your time with me.'

Chapel was the property developer whose harbourside scheme Peggy Frampton had opposed.

'You knew it meant a lot to her,' Ottey said.

'Yeah. I'd even signed one of his petitions for the development. Written to the local MP.'

'Why?'

'Why not?'

'But she didn't lose,' said Ottey.

'No,' he mumbled.

'That must've pissed you off.'

'It was disappointing, yes.'

'Driven all that way, maybe for a bit of closure. To see her suffer. But instead of that you saw her in another moment of victory,' Ottey went on, trying to push his buttons.

'She was so pleased with herself,' he answered, scowling at the memory.

'It was a big moment for her,' Ottey added.

'Oh yeah, and how she loved it.'

'That must've really pissed you off,' she said.

'I'm not going to lie,' Ribble agreed.

'About what?' asked Cross.

'I'm not going to lie – I was pissed off. Is there something wrong with you?'

'No.'

'I wouldn't be so sure, mate. I thought it when you came down to my place. Now I'm sure of it. You should get yourself checked out.'

'So pissed off you went round to her house and killed her,' said Ottey, ignoring him.

'No! I did no such thing.'

'So, what happened then?' asked Cross.

'I went home,' Ribble replied.

'Having killed Peggy Frampton.'

'No!'

The four of them sat there in silence. The duty solicitor hadn't said a word. Presumably he was just listening in order to get up to speed.

'I thought you said you weren't going to lie,' Cross said finally.

'About being pissed off. It's an expression.'

'Oh, I think I understand. You're not going to lie about that, but you feel free to lie about anything else. Is that correct?'

'I'm not lying. I'm telling the truth because I don't want to be here. I want to go home.'

'To play with your dead animals?' asked Ottey.

'You won't get a rise out of me, Sergeant. I've heard them all,' replied Ribble, wearily.

'Heard all what?' asked Cross.

'Taxidermy jokes.'

'Really? All of them?' asked Cross.

'Is he serious?' asked Ribble.

'How about this one? A taxidermist walks into a pub, orders a drink and the barmaid asks him what he does for a living.'

'Oh, you know, *stuff*, he replies,' said Ribble finishing it for him.

Cross said nothing. It was possible, Ottey thought, that he was trying to come up with another joke to see if Ribble knew that one as well. Instead, he just said:

'You are lying, Mr Ribble, and not for the first time. You

should know that juries take a very dim view of people who lie constantly in their interview. It quite often leads to them forming the opinion that nothing that comes out of the accused's mouth can be trusted. So, with that piece of advice in mind, I'm going to ask you once more. Where did you go after the planning meeting finished?'

'I told you. I went home.'

'Mr Ribble, I'm going to ask you one final time. Where did you go after the planning meeting?'

'Blimey, you ever give up?' Ribble asked.

'I can promise you, he most definitely does not. You might want to bear that in mind over the next few hours. Well,' Ottey said, looking at her watch, 'the next twenty-three if you're lucky. If you're not, he can go on like this for days.'

'Mr Ribble, could you answer the question truthfully.'

'I went home,' he said very slowly, leaning over the table as if speaking to a very small child. Then he leant back in his chair. Cross looked at him for a while. Then he opened his folder, leafed through a few pages, and produced another A4 screen grab.

'This is a frame grab from the video doorbell three doors down from the Framptons' house. It shows a delivery being made to the house, quite late at night. Ten fourteen, to be precise. You can see it from the time stamp as well as the date, February the seventh, 2022.'

Ribble looked at the photo. 'What am I looking at?'

'As I'm sure I said, it's a frame from the doorbell...' Cross began.

'Is he for real? Are you trying to irritate me?' Ribble asked.

'Not deliberately, no. But as you seem to be getting a

little heated, let me show you another frame. As you can see it's taken a couple of minutes later, at ten sixteen. The delivery man is turning away from the door. But what's really interesting is what's appeared in the background on the other side of the road. A car has pulled up, pointing in the direction of the Frampton house.'

Ribble had a look.

'That's your car, isn't it, Mr Ribble?' Cross asked innocently, as if he was trying to be helpful. Ribble said nothing, but the blood had drained from his face. So much so, Ottey thought he might be about to pass out. The solicitor suddenly sprang into action.

'I'd like to speak with my client, please.'

'He has the look of a very worried man. Don't you think?' asked Ottey as they walked back to the open area.

'He does,' Cross agreed. They heard a loud row coming out of Matthews' office. They looked in as they passed and saw her yelling at Carson.

'What was the very first thing everyone was told at the meeting with the Chief?' she asked at volume.

'I was caught off guard,' came the defensive reply.

'Don't talk to the media. All media goes through the Chief's office on this one.'

'Like I said. It was unexpected.'

'If you're caught off guard, you say nothing.'

'But the media's all over us!'

'Which is not your problem. You refer them to the Chief. Why can't you accept that?'

'I can. I get it.'

'Bullshit. You have a reputation for this kind of crap, Carson.'

'I do not.'

'If I've heard about it, you can be sure you do. Now get out. Do this again and you'll be having this conversation with—' she looked at her phone, 'the Chief, who is now calling me. Great. Out.'

Everyone in the open area had stopped what they were doing to listen in. Carson appeared, looked down the corridor into the open area, decided he couldn't face the silent ridicule and walked off in the opposite direction. Ottey went over to Mackenzie's desk as Cross, who had no interest in what had just happened, went into his office.

'What was that about?' Ottey asked Mackenzie.

'Motormouth,' she said, pulling up a news video on her computer. It was Carson talking to a reporter.

'We've made significant progress in the Peggy Frampton case. Michael Ribble of Portsmouth, who had made several death threats to her, has been arrested,' he said.

'He just can't help himself, can he?' Ottey commented.

18

Mackenzie had put together a background report on Ribble. Mostly stuff she'd gleaned from his social media. Ottey read it and summarised it to Cross, whose mind seemed to be elsewhere.

'Well, that's unsurprising,' she began. 'He wanted to be a doctor but didn't get the grades. Worked in a tannery for a while straight out of school. Didn't go to university. Lived with his mother after his father's death. Lists his interests as gardening and animal anatomy. Member of various taxidermy guilds and societies.'

But Cross wasn't listening. He was thinking about Adam Chapel and that, depending on how it went with Ribble, they might need to pay the developer a visit. He was also thinking about Luke Frampton. Statistically, the majority of murders like this turned out to be domestic having been committed by someone in the family, predominantly the spouse. Cross liked numbers and concrete statistics. So, Luke Frampton was still someone of interest to him. His attitude to not taking silk intrigued Cross. Something about it just didn't ring true. He had protested a little too much when he finally spoke about it years later. It sounded more like a justification for not attaining something that might have been expected of him, rather than a cogent explanation of a firmly held belief. Cross had looked into it. As with so many businesses or trades, the legal profession had several professional trade magazines. These not only discussed cases and points of law, changing legislature, the legal aid crisis, but also the movements of lawyers between firms and chambers. Cross looked for any references to Frampton. There were several in recent years to do with some of the bigger criminal cases he'd been involved with, but when he went even further back, to around the time Frampton would have been of the right age to apply for silk, generally early forties, he came across an article which interested him. When he was forty-one Frampton had left what was generally considered to be one of the best sets of chambers in Bristol for another lesser known one. The circumstances of the move seemed rather vague. Often barristers split off from chambers in groups to set up their own outfit, but this didn't seem to be the case with Frampton. He'd just left and gone to what seemed to Cross to be a less prestigious chambers. In one interview (there were only three, one of which was just a brief generic statement about his looking forward to a new and fresh challenge), he was asked whether the move had anything to do with his not applying for silk, as many people had expected him to do. His reply was that silk wasn't everything. He was more interested in the actual work than a couple of initials following his name. For Cross it begged the question – was it a voluntary move or had he been pushed?

An hour later Ribble's solicitor read out a statement to Cross and Ottey. Ribble had indeed driven to Peggy's house the night of her murder. She had gone for drinks with her supporters after the meeting, presumably to celebrate. So, he drove to her house to confront her. But when she got back, he relented and just drove home. He was conscious of the fact that he'd lied at the beginning of the interview, but this was the honest truth. Cross got up immediately and left. He hadn't given Ottey a signal, so she remained and continued the interview without him.

'I'd like to extend holding Ribble for another twelve hours,' Cross told Matthews in her office.

'Okay. Is that because you think you'll get a confession out of him in that time?' she asked.

'Whether he confesses or not is dependent on whether he committed the crime.'

'You're not convinced?'

'We have no proof,' Cross pointed out.

'But he lied about being in Portsmouth on the night of the murder. Lied about going home straight after the planning meeting ended, when he in fact drove to her house to wait for her. Has made numerous threats against her in person and online. I'd say things aren't looking great for Mr Ribble,' Matthews summed up.

At this point Carson appeared in the door. His body language said he was there just to listen.

'So, we can have the twelve hours?' Cross asked.

'Oh, absolutely. I'll do the paperwork,' said Matthews.

'We might need to extend that for a further thirty-six,' Cross went on.

'On what grounds?'

'To enable us to gather evidence. Once we have the bag and the paperweight, things will be more conclusive, one way or the other,' Cross explained.

'I think we should just charge him,' Carson volunteered. He'd looked initially still chastened but just couldn't resist coming out with his usual refrain in such situations. The only difference, here, being that he wasn't in charge.

'Oh, I'm sure you do, Ben,' said Matthews.

'I disagree,' said Cross.

'DS Cross—' Carson began, before Cross continued.

'It's a pointless course of action and completely unnecessary. All it does is fulfil DCI Carson's need to be seen to be making progress on a case, particularly when we are not actually doing so. It just makes us look foolish when we later have to release the suspect.'

'Well, as I don't give a hoot whether we're seen to be making progress or not, I'm going to go with George on this one,' finished Matthews.

Cross now stayed away from the interview room. Some members of the team took this as a sign he thought Ribble was innocent. But not Ottey. She knew that this just meant he thought his time was best spent elsewhere. She no longer minded this, so long as Cross kept her informed of what he was doing. Which, of course, he never did. On this case he just hadn't turned up for the interview that morning. So, she ended up annoyed anyway. But then she told herself his absence might actually be helpful to her. Even though Ribble had adopted the 'no comment' mantra to every question, such lengthy interviews often produced a confession in the end.

The relentless questioning often wore the interviewee down. Cross was an expert in this, but only when they had the evidence to back it up. Which they didn't here. Secretly, she hoped she could produce a confession from Ribble before any further evidence was found and, more importantly, without Cross's help. A little point-scoring in a working relationship never did anyone any harm. The problem she had was that Cross probably wouldn't notice. He'd be happy just so long as the right result had been achieved. Ottey also enjoyed the freedom she had without Cross at her side across the table from a suspect. She sometimes liked to hypothesise about the events of a murder; suggest to the suspect what she thought might have happened. She felt it could reap rewards, but Cross had no truck with this. He was sufficiently self-aware, though, to know that, while it didn't sit well with his process, it did occasionally bear fruit.

19

'Morning, Tony! A cappuccino, please,' said a familiar and currently, to Cross's mind, unwelcome, voice which went on to say, 'Good morning, George.'

Cross looked up at Stephen, then beyond him to the café entrance and finally, at the outside street, through the window.

'Christine isn't here. I'm on my own,' Stephen said cheerfully, pulling out a seat and sitting opposite Cross, which of course meant he immediately had to stop eating. 'Your breakfast will get cold,' the earnest young man of the cloth said, looking at all the plates with Cross's separate breakfast items.

'As Christine told you, I prefer not to eat in front of other people,' Cross said.

'That must make dinner parties interesting.'

Cross was about to answer, when Stephen saved him the bother. 'I know you don't go to dinner parties. Tony, could I have that coffee to go?'

Tony lifted up a takeaway cup he was already preparing. He knew as soon as Stephen sat down opposite his most regular customer that the priest would be taking his coffee away.

'I'll make this quick,' Stephen continued. 'You didn't come in to practise the organ last night.'

'Work prevented me from doing so,' Cross replied.

'Not the fact that you're angry with me for bringing in your mother the day before?'

Cross didn't answer. He didn't like being ambushed in this way, and being put on the back foot despite the fact, or maybe because of it, that he did it to other people all the time, in the course of his work.

'I want you to feel you can come and play the organ whenever you want. I know how important it is to you, and selfishly I enjoy it when I have a chance to listen. I promise that I won't spring Christine on you unannounced again if that's what's worrying you.'

Cross thought about this for a moment. 'Very well then.'

'But I want to ask you something before I leave.'

At this point Tony came over with his coffee. Stephen went to his pocket to pay.

'No, Father,' said Tony. 'It's on the house.'

'Why, thank you,' said Stephen. He turned back to Cross, who obviously disapproved of what had just happened. 'Oh, don't look at me like that. You're making me feel like a bent copper taking kickbacks. I'll say a prayer for Tony later, as a quid pro quo. Fair enough? Anyway, Christine – here are the facts as I see them, Sergeant.' He'd decided to inject a little jocularity into the conversation. It must have slipped his mind back at the parsonage, when he came up with this strategy, who he was actually dealing with. He promptly dropped this approach. '*You* reached out to her, George. She didn't instigate any of this. She didn't try and get in touch with you, despite having wanted to for years.'

'I just wanted her to know that she was wrong. That was all. I didn't want to have anything further to do with her after that.'

'Well, life isn't like that. People aren't like that. It's just not so simple. Everyone has feelings, needs and regrets.'

'She *should* have regrets.'

'And she does. She's your mother. She just wants you to do one thing. Ask your father what really happened all those years ago. It sounds to me like there's a lot more to it than you think.'

'I have asked. He doesn't want to talk about it.'

'Which should maybe tell you something. So, do what you're good at, George. Do some detective work. You may owe your mother nothing, but you owe it to yourself to find out the truth.' He grabbed his coffee, waved to Tony and left. George thought about what had just been said, then looked at his barely touched breakfast and realised he'd lost his appetite. He pushed the plates away and grabbed his coat. Tony appeared and looked at the uneaten breakfast.

'Everything all right?' he asked.

'Not particularly,' Cross asked.

'Do you want me to heat them up?'

'Not necessary,' Cross answered then took the exact amount he owed for the breakfast out of his pocket and put it on the table. Tony pushed it back.

'Not necessary,' he said and walked away. But Cross left it there when he walked out a couple of seconds later.

20

'Do you know where George is?' Matthews asked Ottey. She had just got a further extension from a magistrate, at Cross's request, to detain Ribble for another thirty-six hours.

'I do not,' Ottey replied, probably more emphatically than she meant to.

'Does he often do this?' Matthews asked Ottey into her office.

'Not as much as he used to. But yes, he does.'

'And are you happy with that?'

'Sure,' she answered in a way that didn't even convince herself.

'I see. You asked for a new partner a couple of times last year, apparently. I'm sorry I didn't know that. You were presented as a package by the Chief.'

'It's fine. Things have changed. I'm happy working with George, and you might have had a hard time finding anyone else to partner him.' This was, she realised, the first time she had said this either to herself or anyone else. 'As for this morning, I've come to realise there are times when it's best he's left alone. I think he needs it occasionally, and he always comes up with the goods.'

'I can see why Carson is reluctant to split you two up.'

'The thing about George is, it's never personal. It may be thoughtless, rude, annoying. But it's never deliberate. He doesn't have it in him. Once you've grasped that, it's all fine.'

'I'm not sure Carson has grasped it. I get the feeling he tolerates Cross more than understands him.'

'Well, to be fair, you have to start somewhere and besides…' But she thought better of finishing the sentence.

'Besides what?'

'I suppose I shouldn't say this, but it is quite funny sometimes seeing him try to cope with George.'

'I can see that,' Matthews said, smiling. 'I imagine working with George you need to find the fun wherever you can.' She looked at Ottey for a moment before going on. 'He's lucky to have you. *We're* lucky to have you. But it does beg the question – what happens when the inevitable occurs? Promotion.'

'Oh, George doesn't want promotion. He's very happy where he is.'

'I wasn't talking about George.'

'Oh, I see,' said Ottey, flattered. 'Well, I'm sure we have a long way to go before we have to cross that bridge.'

Cross was at that precise moment crossing Queen Square, a beautiful Georgian square which housed Frampton's original chambers. For many years this square had been an area Cross avoided. Not because it was unsafe but because it had been the victim of a gross planning decision many years before, which he found intolerable aesthetically. So he simply avoided it. The square had had a long, troubled history. In the mid-nineteenth century it had been the scene of a riot in support of the Reform Bill in Parliament. Several people were killed in these riots. Four were later hanged. Thirty years later it was proposed to build Bristol's main railway station there. But the city burghers felt it would divert trade from the nearby docks, and rumour had it that local washerwomen had protested against it. They claimed the smuts from the engines would ruin their laundry. The station was eventually built at Temple Meads, not too far away. But the biggest travesty to befall the square, in Cross's mind, happened in the 1930s, when the Bristol Corporation sanctioned the building of a dual carriageway diagonally, right across the square. Destroying it in one aesthetically crude and vulgar swathe of concrete and cement. It was recognised by later generations of the council that their forebears had made a dreadful mistake, and the square was fully restored in the early 2000s. Cross and his father made a day of it when it first reopened, coming down with sandwiches and a flask of tea to admire the refurbishment.

The chambers were in one of the Georgian buildings that had survived the initial destruction caused by the dual carriageway. Cross had made an appointment with a senior barrister, who was head of chambers at the time Frampton had left.

'Dreadful business about Peggy. I was very fond of her. A true Bristolian,' Alex Simmonds began. 'You know she had a huge hand in applying for the lottery fund to restore this square, back in nineteen ninety-eight?'

'I didn't know that,' replied Cross.

'Indefatigable she was. How can I help? I have to confess I haven't had much contact with Luke since he left. I'm an employment specialist, so our paths don't ever cross in court.'

'Why did he leave the chambers?' Cross asked.

'I think he just wanted to move on.'

Cross looked at the man closely. There was definitely more to it than this, so he pressed. 'But he went to a much smaller, less successful chambers than these.'

'Perhaps he wanted to be a bigger fish in a smaller pond.'

'Surely, if he wanted to be a bigger fish, he would've applied for silk. Are you a QC?' he asked, although he already knew the answer.

'I am.'

'And when did you take silk?'

'Nineteen ninety-five.'

'A couple of years before Mr Frampton left.'

'Is it? I can't remember the exact dates.'

'Are you surprised he didn't take silk? Did he apply, do you know?' At this, Simmonds looked a little uneasy.

'Not as far as I know.'

'Were there conversations about it when he was here?'

'Sergeant, I'm a little busy this morning. Perhaps you could do me a favour and just come out with whatever it is you want to know. What brings you here?'

'I don't really understand these things. I don't understand a lot about the Bar, other than what I see in court. But many people think it's an antiquated business, out of touch with the modern world. Wearing wigs and gowns, for example. I myself think that's a good thing, by the way. It adds a certain formality to the proceedings, while giving the barrister a certain amount of anonymity. But the title of QC strikes me as a little old-fashioned.' Simmonds made no response. 'It seems to me an arbitrary honour, enabling two things – the right to wear a silk gown in court, and to charge your clients a higher fee.'

'What is your point?'

'Now that I think about it, I can see that Mr Frampton might have a point. He seems to think it's an unfair system that he wants no part of. Seems quite an honourable stand.' Simmonds couldn't help but scoff at this notion. Cross realised the man had let his guard down.

'You don't agree?'

'The word honourable and the name Luke Frampton don't sit together easily, in my opinion.'

'But he's on record about the fallibility of the system.'

'Well he would be. He's not a QC. The Bar is filled with bitter men and women who didn't get silk because they realised it was pointless to apply, or applied and didn't get it.'

'And which was he?' Simmonds looked at Cross for a moment. It was an expression Cross had seen many times in various people he'd interviewed, and one he now recognised immediately. The resignation that this irritant in the form of a policeman wasn't going to stop until he'd got what he came for.

'Frampton left these chambers because we refused to support his application for silk.'

'A refusal which presumably would have guaranteed his failure to attain it?'

'Well, if your own chambers isn't going to support you, it's highly unlikely you're going to get it. Particularly when the circumstances for that refusal become known. The Bar is actually quite a small place.'

'So he left because of that.'

'Yes,' came the qualified response.

'Would his new chambers have supported him, do you think?'

'I doubt it and even if they had, I don't think it would have been successful.'

'Why not?'

'Because the reasons for our lack of support were known.'

'Which were?'

'His predilection for the opposite sex.'

'I see,' said Cross making a note of this.

'It became a problem. Affairs with relatives of clients, young impressionable lawyers, and then he crossed the line.'

'None of that was crossing the line?' asked Cross, surprised.

'Wrong choice of words. His position basically became untenable when his behaviour involved someone in the practice.'

'Did he have an affair with a colleague?'

'A colleague's wife.' He paused, whether for dramatic effect or weighing up whether to go into further detail, Cross wasn't sure. 'My wife.'

21

Ottey was taking a break from interviewing Ribble and was making herself a coffee when Mackenzie appeared brandishing an A4 printout.

'From Mark Coombes. He heard about Ribble's arrest and talked to his wife about it. She had plenty to say, so put it all down in an email for him to give us.' Ottey looked at her blankly, her head still across the table from Ribble in the interview room. 'Mark, Janette's husband. Janette, Peggy's assistant.'

'Of course,' replied Ottey and took a look. Janette was initially circumspect in her email. She didn't want to get anyone into trouble, but Peggy definitely thought of Ribble as a threat. It had been one thing when it was online, but quite another when he'd first shown up in Bristol. He'd found out where she lived and kept turning up. He became progressively more aggressive on each occasion. That's when she called the police. Peggy Frampton clearly felt threatened by the man.

'We now have a witness to some of your altercations with Peggy Frampton,' Ottey began, when she went back into the interview room. Ribble said nothing. 'Janette Coombes,' she explained.

'Never heard of her,' Ribble replied.

'She was Peggy's assistant.'

'Oh, her.'

'She says you were physically intimidating to Mrs Frampton,' Ottey went on.

'Really? Tell me, do I look intimidating to you?'

'People of all shapes and sizes can be terrifying to others.'

'I'll have to take your word for it,' he replied.

This was interesting to Ottey. It was the first time Ribble had engaged with her in over eighteen hours beyond the repeated 'no comments'.

'Here's what I think happened. You were disappointed at the outcome of the council meeting. You hadn't had the chance to gloat. So, you went to her house and things got out of hand. I don't think you meant to kill her, but that's what happened. You became frustrated when you couldn't get her to understand how you felt. When she wouldn't acknowledge the damage she'd done to you.'

'According to her, she hadn't done anything,' he said.

'Exactly. That must have been so frustrating,' Ottey commented.

'It was just arrogant. People should be held to account for what they say online,' he said, without the slightest trace of irony.

'Which you told her,' Ottey said, encouraging him to expand.

'I'd told her loads of times.'

'Michael,' she said quietly, almost confidentially, as if it were just between the two of them, 'is that what you told her in the house that night?'

He was about to answer when the door suddenly opened and Carson walked in. Ribble clammed up. Ottey gave Carson a look of reproach. She was furious. The usual protocol when people, even senior officers, wanted to go into an ongoing interview was to check the monitor first. Then, when a suitable lull or natural break in the interview occurred, go in.

'DCI Ben Carson has just entered the room,' she announced, for the tape, through gritted teeth.

'Do you recognise this?' Carson asked, as he produced an evidence bag in which there was a plastic ziplock bag.

'No.'

'It's a plastic bag which we found discarded near the Clifton Suspension Bridge, together with the paperweight used to strike Peggy Frampton, before she was asphyxiated using the bag. If you look closely,' he said, helpfully holding the bag up to Ribble, who recoiled, 'you can see traces of her blood and hair inside.'

Ribble said nothing but was obviously shocked.

'What's more interesting is nearer the bag's aperture. There's another stain there. Dried now, of course. But the chances are, it's either the sweat or saliva of Peggy Frampton's killer.'

Ribble just stared at Carson, who said nothing. He then produced another evidence bag which contained several unused ziplock bags, identical to the bloodstained one.

'Perhaps you recognise these?' Carson asked.

'No comment.'

'These were taken from your taxidermy studio. They're the ones you use to protect your specimens.' Ribble began to look frightened. 'They are exactly the same make and size as the one used to kill Peggy Frampton.'

Ribble looked at his lawyer, which prompted him into action.

'Pure coincidence. The use of these bags must be quite widespread. You have no proof.'

'Not quite, but we can easily clear the whole matter up, if your client is willing to provide us with a DNA sample,' Carson said. Ribble's expression changed dramatically as he leapt at this.

'Yes. Absolutely. Take a swab and let's end this,' he said.

'That wasn't the reaction we were expecting, I take it?' Matthews said to Ottey. 'Do you think it means he's not our man?'

'I'm not so sure. People often want DNA proof just to get the whole thing over and done with. To be caught without actually admitting it,' Ottey replied. 'I think he was about to tell me something before DCI Carson burst into the bloody room.'

'Yes, I saw that. Where is he? I'll talk to him,' replied Matthews.

'Thanks,' she said, happy that someone else would have the row for her.

'It's completely unprofessional, but unsurprising, when you consider who it was,' said Cross when Ottey told him about Carson's behaviour. He'd looked at the tape and agreed with Ottey that Ribble might have been about to say something of interest. But he'd also noted the initial panic on Ribble's face when he learned how the bag had been used. It was news to him. He hadn't been told the mechanics of Peggy Frampton's killing, deliberately. But he was clearly horrified by the grotesque manner of her death and couldn't hide it. It was an involuntary reaction. Bearing in mind there were no mental health issues at play, it wasn't a case of horror, at realising what he'd done. It was simply truly shocking to him. But moments later there was a slow-dawning relief after the DNA had been mentioned.

'Look at that.' Cross pointed to the screen as they watched the playback of the interview. Ribble sat back as he was told about the DNA. There was a hint of a smile.

'Only an innocent man would react in that way. Because he knows the DNA can't be his. Up until this point he must have realised that things were stacking up against him, circumstantially. But if there was DNA and it wasn't his, it could work in his favour.'

'Possibly,' Ottey pointed out. 'It won't necessarily be conclusive,' she added tersely. She was still irritated by his latest disappearing act.

Cross, though, was now fairly convinced they had the wrong man. His reaction to the presence of DNA was pretty much all Cross needed. His thoughts had moved onto the plastic bag. The fact that no similar bag was found in a search of the Frampton household meant that it had been taken there for the sole purpose of killing Frampton. It was a premeditated act. Cross couldn't be sure that Ribble had gone to Bristol with a plastic bag in his possession to kill Peggy Frampton. The more he thought about it, the bag was shaping up as their biggest clue. Not just for the potential DNA traces it held, but the reason for it being used. Why a plastic bag?

22

Ottey's anger with Carson seemed to ramp up her frustration with Cross for going missing and not keeping her in the loop. That was supposed to be the deal. It had annoyed her all weekend, which in itself annoyed her. She hated taking her work home in any form. This was exacerbated not only by the possibility that Ribble could be innocent, but also that somehow George knew this before she did. Which was why he'd left her to waste her time in the interview room and gone out doing whatever it was he was doing. She didn't want to give him the pleasure of speaking to him again about working as a team, though. This was something she'd done again and again, and it obviously wasn't working. So, a new week, a new plan. She was going to demonstrate to him how frustrating his behaviour was by behaving just like him, right back at him. Maybe this would be more effective. It would certainly be more enjoyable.

Mackenzie was busy still trawling through Peggy's laptop. But she had also owned a Filofax, which Ottey had concentrated on. She reflected how strange it was that the Filofax had now become an indicator of someone's age or vintage. She'd yearned for one when she was younger, but never had one. She had to settle for being inexplicably jealous of her friends who did. They were the must-have accessory; so grown-up and sophisticated. She found a lot of appointments in Peggy's Filofax with 'JLK'. They weren't regular, but they were there right up until her death. Five in all. Not a lot but interesting all the same. The purpose of the meeting became a little clearer to her when she found some written notes on those dates. They concerned money and assets. She had her suspicions about what was going on and this was finally confirmed when she found a business card for a Melissa Morse, a family lawyer at a firm in Bath called James, Lantern and King. Bath rather than Bristol. Was that because of a need for privacy? Ottey wondered. A quick call to Morse's office confirmed what she already thought. Peggy Frampton was divorcing her husband. Did he know? Did the children know?

Mackenzie had also come across a number of interesting photographs on Peggy's laptop in an innocuous-looking file in her downloads. The file was untitled but contained several photographs of Luke Frampton and a much younger woman, out and about in London. At first glance you could be forgiven for thinking they were pictures of Frampton with a client, or maybe a goddaughter. They were having lunch at Scott's of Mayfair, sitting outside so the young woman could smoke. Laughing, eating and drinking a bottle of white wine. But the last couple of images as they said goodbye, kissing in an intimate embrace, painted an enitrely different picture.

'Who do you think took these? Private investigator for her lawyers?' asked Mackenzie.

'More than likely,' Ottey replied.

Later that afternoon she grabbed her things together and announced, 'Right, I'm off,' loudly enough to alert Cross, sitting in his office. By the time she'd retrieved her coat, he was at her desk.

'Where are you going?' he asked. Anyone else might have done this casually, to disguise their interest. But Cross couldn't play these kinds of games. He just came straight out with it.

'To do a little police work,' Ottey replied.

'I see.' He pondered this for a moment. 'Would you like to inform me what it is you're doing?'

'I would not,' came the reply. He gave this due consideration, weighing up the possible implications of this refusal. She almost laughed at his deadly serious expression.

'I don't think that's going to work,' he said finally.

'Why ever not?' she asked.

'Because, as you keep telling me, we're a team.'

'Right…' she said, inviting him to go on.

'Which, by its very definition, means we should work together.'

'Oh, I see, so when you want to wander off and do something on your own on a case, that's okay. But when I want to do it, you have a problem with it.'

'Yes,' he replied, as it seemed a perfectly accurate summation of the situation. She laughed, as did Mackenzie who quickly looked away when he turned to her.

'Fine. Then I'll see you later.'

'But where are you going?' he protested.

'No need for you to know. Just like there was no need for me to know where you were on Friday when you buggered off solo and I couldn't tell Matthews where you were.'

'I was at Luke Frampton's first chambers,' he stated defiantly.

'And when were you going to tell me that, exactly?'

'When appropriate.'

'You know what? I'm going to go now. I'll let you know where, when I deem it appropriate,' she said.

'I see,' he replied, still confused.

'Do you get my point now?'

'Not exactly, no.'

'Are you being deliberately obtuse?'

'Not deliberately, no.'

She looked at him for a moment, realised she just couldn't keep this up and surrendered. Even she wasn't that cruel.

'Oh, come on. Grab your coat. I'll tell you where we're going in the car.'

They were sitting on a bench in front of City Hall, with the shallow moat behind them, facing the large area of grass in front of the building. Cross had always thought it was shaped like a baseball ground. He had looked at the photographs of Frampton with the young woman and listened as Ottey explained how she'd tracked down the investigator they were meeting, through Peggy's divorce lawyer, who wanted to do anything she could to help find out what had happened to her client.

'I think we should take a look at Adam Chapel, the developer,' was Cross's immediate reaction. Ottey knew this wasn't a lack of interest in what she'd found, merely him saying what he was thinking at that moment.

'I used to come down here with my father and feed the pigeons. I'm fairly sure I remember being in a pram, so I must've been really young,' Ottey said as she watched a couple with their young child doing exactly that.

'Me too,' Cross replied.

'Really? I wonder if we were ever here together as small children at the same time on the same day. Imagine that, two small kids with no idea that their lives would intersect at a much later date.'

'Possible, but highly unlikely. I am a little older than you.'

'You're so unromantic.'

He looked at her with that expression which she found completely endearing and infuriating at the same time – total confusion and a little alarm.

'I don't mean it like that, you idiot. I mean it like the romance of the universe and the role of serendipity in it. The romance of uncertainty. Don't you find it a weird thing to think about?'

'I do.'

'You mean that in the wrong, weird way, don't you?'

'There's a right "weird way"?' he asked, even more confused.

'Oh, I give up.'

'You seem to do that a lot.'

'With you probably not as often as I should.' She looked around them. 'I've always wondered why they call this College Green. It's nowhere near the university or a school. Think I'll look it up,' she said, taking her phone out of her pocket.

'The cathedral used to be St Augustine's Abbey back in the twelfth century, which owned the land. It formed part of the abbey. With the dissolution of the monasteries, it became a collegiate church and the land was renamed College Green.'

'I don't know why I bother when I have my own walking Wikipedia at my side most times of the day.'

'Oh, I wouldn't go that far.'

'Well I would. Don't put yourself down all the time.'

'I think you'll find my information and knowledge far more accurate than Wikipedia,' he said confidently.

She laughed. Nothing was said between them for a few moments.

'I saw my mother again,' Cross said.

'Really? How come?' Ottey asked, intrigued.

'She came back to Tony's with Stephen.'

'I bet that went down well.'

'On the contrary, I was most put out.'

'Did you talk to her this time?'

'Yes. But not through choice.'

'Good.'

'Why is that good?'

'That you spoke to her is good, George.'

'It seemed the most efficient way of getting rid of her,' he said. But he made the decision that he would elaborate no further. He was fairly sure her tone wasn't sympathetic. It was something about the way she was looking at him.

'Are you really not going to tell me what happened?' she said.

'It was the usual story we hear all too regularly at work. That there are always two sides. That she thought she was doing the best for me. That I didn't understand the complete picture of what happened.'

'Okay,' Ottey replied.

'She told me I should speak with my father and ascertain the truth.'

'And have you?'

'Of course not. I don't see the point. On the one hand it would upset him—'

'Look at you, George! Thinking about someone else's feelings. You see, you can when you put your mind to it. Way to go,' she said, genuinely pleased.

'It has nothing to do with being considerate. His being upset would simply mean the chances of getting the truth out of him would be considerably diminished. But I suspect it isn't something he would relish discussing on any basis,' he continued.

'So, what are you going to do?'

'What she suggested. Do what I'm good at. Find out the truth for myself.'

'You don't think maybe you should just leave it alone?' she asked, playing a little devil's advocate.

'I know it's a weakness of mine. I seem incapable of leaving things alone. I can't settle until I know the truth,' he said quietly.

'I can certainly vouch for that,' she said ironically.

'As she and Stephen correctly point out, it was me who went looking for her, not vice versa. Having reflected on it, I'm not entirely sure I was being honest with myself when I said I just wanted to demonstrate to her that things had worked out well for me. I think I wanted to know why she left.'

'That's all fair. There's another factor though. Which is why she doesn't just come out and tell you what happened. She doesn't think you'd believe her,' Ottey said.

'Which has an element of truth to it. Anyway, I have my father's belongings and papers all catalogued and filed in storage.'

'I know.'

'I'm sure the answer lies in there somewhere.'

'Sergeants Cross and Ottey?' enquired a man approaching them.

Ottey didn't really want to like Peter Miller. As a rule of thumb she didn't like private investigators. She put them in the same category as the persistent local journalists who had been calling the unit continuously for the past few days. Their self-importance and obvious belief that they were working on an exclusive on the scale of Bernstein and Woodward really irritated her. That and the fact that they wouldn't take 'no' for an answer. But Miller proved to be charming, intelligent and helpful, without wanting anything in return. Maybe that was his play, she thought – to be straight and useful. Create a good impression knowing that you could then return at a later date and ask for something you needed.

'He's got quite the reputation,' Miller said as he confirmed that he'd been taken on by JLK but also that he had done further work for Peggy. 'It surprised me how widely known this was at the Bar. I mean, it was common knowledge.'

'He doesn't look the type,' said Ottey.

'What exactly do you mean by that?' asked Cross.

'Well, he's very unprepossessing, hardly good-looking. I can't see the attraction,' she said.

'Or the success rate,' added Miller. 'I completely agree he seems an unlikely Casanova, but apparently women just love him. Can't get enough of him. No angry exes in the wings either. He gets on with all of them and is still in touch with some.'

'Who's the woman in the photographs?' Cross asked.

'Agnesha Dragusha. She's the daughter of one of Frampton's previous clients.'

'That sounds a little worrying,' said Ottey.

'It is. Her father's a really nasty piece of work. He's inside serving life with no chance of parole for a string of murders. Head of an Albanian organised-crime family based in the UK, but with strong ties to the mother country. He didn't always just order the killings. That wasn't enough for him. He wanted to carry out some of them for himself, which is why he got caught. He's an out-and-out psychopath.'

'Where's he in prison?'

'Belmarsh. But he still exercises power both outside and inside the nick. His son Mikki runs things now. Even worse than his father, by all accounts.'

'Why would Frampton get involved with that family?' asked Cross.

'I got the feeling maybe she came fishing for him. Why, I don't know. Maybe Dad wants something.'

'Did Peggy know?' asked Ottey.

'About this one, yes.'

'But not all the others?'

'Not initially, but she did before she died.'

'No wonder she wanted a divorce,' Ottey commented.

'Did Frampton know that?' asked Cross.

'He did.'

'And was he happy?'

'Surprisingly not. He promised to end the affair, which of course he didn't, which just made Peggy all the more determined. But he still pushed back. She then threatened to go public with all the affairs.'

'Which could have ruined his career at the Bar.'

'I wouldn't have thought it would be exactly helpful,' commented Miller. 'She wanted a quick, uncontested divorce and the more he pushed back the more aggressive she became with her demands. She was very angry.'

'Possibly not the best tactic, as things worked out,' said Ottey.

'Do you think he might've killed her?' Miller asked Cross.

'I don't know. At the moment we can't rule anything out.'

'To be honest, it is something that occurred to me. Particularly with the Dragusha connection,' said Miller.

'Did you like her?' Ottey asked.

'I did, actually. Very much. I had a lot of respect for her. She could be quite full-on but that was part of why I liked her. You knew where you were with her. She didn't suffer fools gladly. It's funny, I'm normally quite detached in my work, but with this one, even now, well particularly now, after what's happened, I look at those pictures and I'm just really sad. I obviously liked her more than I thought. I've found her murder really shocking. Upsetting.'

'You sound like you became quite close,' Ottey observed.

'In a way. She was one of those people that made you feel close to her. She made you feel she cared. It was a skill. I was actually having some trouble of my own at home, and she took my wife and me out for dinner. "Counselling à la carte", she called it. She was very funny.'

'Thanks for meeting with us,' said Ottey.

'Have you looked at her social media? I did at the beginning to get to know my client. Some of the stuff on there is vicious. I know most of it is just abuse for the sake of it. But there might be something there.'

'We are looking, of course,' replied Cross.

'Sure. Well, if there's anything you need doing on this which, well, you know, your job prevents you from doing, just let me know. On the house. It's the least I can do for her.'

'The things we can't do because of our job are generally the things that lead to other things being inadmissible in court,' Cross replied before walking off towards Ottey's car.

'You have my number,' Miller said to Ottey. 'Seriously, if there's anything.'

'I'll call. Thanks.'

23

Cross looked out over the gorge as he stood on Sion Hill across from the Framptons' house. Ottey was opposite him, waiting for the front door to be opened. It was a cold March afternoon. The sort that made your nostrils flare and resemble half-eaten redcurrants. Rather magically the gorge was filled with a low layer of fog, which Cross, from his elevated position, was looking down on. The late afternoon sun gave the fog a sulphurous yellow hue. It looked almost artificial, like a shot from a movie where the director had gone a little overboard with the CGI, to create an atmosphere. Movies, or films as Cross preferred to refer to them, were far too reliant on CGI these days, he felt. It was like watching a video game. The fact that most films were actually made digitally now, rather than on celluloid, just compounded the problem. There was something about absurdly stunning landscapes, impossible stunts being manufactured in a computer, that completely disengaged him from a movie. The fact that anything was possible, could be achieved with such ease and had nothing to do with reality, took much of the magic out of going to the cinema these days, he thought.

'George!' Ottey called him, as Marina had opened the door.

They followed her into the kitchen where Luke was sitting with a coffee, going through a stack of bills.

'Peggy always did these,' he said, without looking up or greeting the two police officers. 'I didn't realise how many bills we had. She hated direct debits. Said people were making millions, flying in private jets, buying superyachts from all the uncancelled direct debits and subscriptions in the world.'

'Colman's mustard,' said Cross.

'Yes, exactly,' Frampton replied. Cross turned to explain this to Ottey.

'I know! He made his fortune from the mustard left on the side of plates, not from the mustard actually eaten. No mustard mansplaining required,' she said, before he had a chance to open his mouth.

'Can I make you tea? Coffee?' asked Marina.

'Coffee please,' replied Ottey.

'No thank you,' said Cross.

'She really does make an excellent cup of tea. Loose leaf, in a pot,' Frampton assured him.

'Bone china?' asked Cross.

'A man who appreciates his tea,' Frampton observed, approvingly.

'That's one way of putting it,' Ottey commented.

'I will have tea,' Cross acceded. Marina left the room with the slightest suspicion of a look in Cross's direction.

'So how are you, Mr Frampton?' Ottey began.

'I'm finding the fact that it's murder, and the way it happened, increasingly hard to deal with.'

'You mean the plastic bag?' asked Cross.

'Exactly. But otherwise, fine in the circumstances. We've

been busy clearing up after your forensics team. What a mess. All that fingerprint dust.'

'Sorry about that,' replied Ottey.

'Can't be helped and they were very polite. The tall one – how tall is he?'

'Six foot eight,' replied Cross. He looked at Ottey as if to say he knew this information would come in useful at some point.

'He offered to clear up, but frankly Marina couldn't get him out of the house quickly enough, so she could clean. Shall we go through to the drawing room? She can bring your tea through.'

Once sat opposite them, Cross detected a defensiveness in Frampton's posture. It was as if he was preparing himself for whatever they might be about to either ask him or inform him of. Cross was fairly sure he wasn't expecting a progress report so much as an interview. But why was Frampton thinking this way? Was it because his experience of dealing with the police over the years at the Bar had made him skilled at reading them? Or was it because he hadn't told them everything he might have?

'So, Sergeants, how can I help?' was not a question people normally asked when waiting to be given an update.

'Why haven't you taken silk, Mr Frampton?' Cross asked.

'I beg your pardon?' Frampton looked at Ottey, who was as surprised as him at this opening line of questioning.

'You are not a QC,' Cross continued.

'Correct. But what does that have to do with anything?'

'You're on record saying the QC system is outdated and should be done away with.'

'That's right.'

'Too political. Too clubby.'

'Correct. Which is why I didn't apply.'

'Really?' Cross looked confused and reached into his pocket for his notebook. 'That's odd because I was told... where is it now? Yes, here it is. You were going to apply but then discovered your chambers wouldn't support you.'

'Who on earth told you that?'

'Alex Simmonds.'

Frampton looked uncomfortable at this. It seemed to take him off guard. 'I'd actually decided not to apply when they told me that. The horse had already bolted.'

'That's not how Mr Simmonds remembers it.'

'That's hardly surprising,' Frampton said, looking like he immediately regretted it.

'Really, why do you say that?' Frampton didn't answer. Cross looked through his notebook, as if he'd forgotten why, but knew the answer lay in the pages somewhere. Ottey loved him when he was like this, playing the slightly bewildered policeman who didn't seem to get out much. He finally stopped at a page.

'Ah, that's why,' he said, looking back at Frampton. 'Because you slept with his wife.' He let this remark hang in the air, then noticed Marina standing in the door to the room, with his tea. She'd heard everything. She came forward and placed the tea on a small table next to Cross and gave Ottey her coffee. Ottey thanked her, as Cross was too busy staring at Frampton.

'What has any of this got to do with my wife's murder?' Frampton asked tersely. Cross continued to look at him for a moment, then turned to Ottey.

'Where do you stay when you're in London?' she asked Frampton.

'I have an apartment.'

'Interesting you should say "I" instead of "we".'

Frampton thought about this for a moment.

'My wife is dead, Sergeant.'

'I'm well aware of that. But you very much see it as *your* apartment, do you not?' There was no answer to this. Ottey then produced a file and took out the photographs of Frampton with the young woman at lunch. She set them out on the table between them, one by one.

'Who's this young woman?' she asked.

'A client. Well, more accurately, the daughter of a client.'

'Do you always take the daughters of your clients out for lunch?'

'She was taking me, as a matter of fact. It was to thank me for all my work on behalf of her father.'

Ottey waited as if she were giving him a chance to tell the truth. When he said nothing, she produced the photographs of him and the young woman kissing in the alleyway. He looked at them and said nothing.

'Before you say anything, Mr Frampton, you should bear in mind the fact that your building has a concierge. Who happens to be an ex-policeman. Never misses a thing. This young woman is quite a regular guest of yours apparently. An overnight guest.'

'Your marriage was in trouble. Your wife was seeking a divorce. Were you aware of this?' Cross asked.

'Of course I bloody was.'

'You didn't mention it before,' commented Ottey. 'We know about all the other affairs, Mr Frampton. It would seem that marital fidelity wasn't exactly your strong point.'

'All right, I was a shitty husband. In a way. But a good

husband and father in many others, which I would never expect you to understand,' he said, looking directly at Cross. 'Yes, she wanted a divorce and who could blame her? Why she had the need to have these photographs taken, I have no idea. We had agreed to get divorced.'

'But you hadn't agreed terms,' Cross pointed out.

'Well, she became impossible. Her demands were outrageous,' Frampton protested.

'Because she was angry,' said Ottey. 'Was she using these photographs to pressure you?'

'I've never seen them before.'

'Because she never had the chance to show them to you,' Cross pointed out.

'Now, wait a minute,' he said, laughing nervously. 'Are you honestly suggesting I decided to kill her because she wouldn't be reasonable?'

'We haven't suggested anything,' Cross pointed out.

'Had she decided to expose you?'

'What? For being unfaithful?' he asked incredulously. 'This is the Bar we're talking about. What exactly do you think would happen?'

'Extra-marital affairs are one thing,' Cross said. 'But with the daughter of an Albanian warlord, convicted of murder?'

'Wouldn't be that great for business, I would imagine,' Ottey chimed in.

For the first time in the interview Frampton seemed unsure of himself and went slightly pale.

'I did not kill my wife, however unpleasant the divorce was becoming. It's up to you whether you believe me or not. But you would be better spending your time finding out who actually did, rather than waste your time in an absurd pursuit of me.'

'Mr Frampton, your integrity – both personal and professional – is questionable at best. You are in a relationship with a woman whose father has no compunction when it comes to ending the lives of others for whatever reason. So your advice is difficult to take seriously,' said Cross.

Marina appeared at the door in her coat and scarf with her handbag over her arm.

'I'm leaving now, sir.'

'No, Marina. Wait. Could we just talk about this?'

'Okay. I'll wait in the kitchen.'

'Everything all right?' Ottey asked.

'Marina's handed in her notice. She doesn't want to work here any more.'

'Oh.'

'Because of what happened to Peggy, no other reason. She finds it too upsetting coming here. I'm doing my best to persuade her to stay but it's proving to be an uphill battle. She's devastated. Like we all are.'

The two detective sergeants waited in Ottey's car a hundred yards away from the Framptons' house, up the hill towards the bridge. It took just ten minutes for Marina to appear at the front door. Something about her gait told Cross that she hadn't been persuaded to continue working for Frampton. She walked with purpose and quickly, as if she couldn't get away from there fast enough. When she drew level with the car Ottey wound down the passenger window and, to Cross's irritation, shouted across him.

'Marina? Could we have a word?'

Marina hesitated and looked back at the house. She then opened the door and got into the back seat.

'Can we drive you home?' Ottey asked.

'I'm going to the supermarket,' Marina replied.

'Then the supermarket it is. Which one?'

Fifteen minutes later they were in the car park of a large Sainsbury's in Bedminster.

'Is this your local?' Ottey asked.

'Yes, but they also have a large message board with jobs. I want to have a look.'

'Good idea,' Ottey replied with a smile. This quiet friendly approach was immediately undercut by Cross.

'You had a job. Why did you leave it?'

'I didn't want to work there any more,' Marina replied.

'Because Mrs Frampton was killed in the house?' Ottey asked sympathetically.

'A bit, yes. But I really worked for her, not him. She was a good woman.'

'You don't like him,' Cross stated baldly.

'He was a bad husband,' came the answer.

'What makes you say that?' asked Ottey.

'Because I know. Because she told me. Mrs F and I talked a lot. If she was there, she always made me sit down for a coffee. She said we both deserved a break and a chat.'

'Like friends,' Ottey suggested.

'She was my friend. A good friend.' She began crying.

'It must be very hard for you, such a shock.'

'Yes. For lots of people. She was important to so many people. Helped them. People relied on her.'

'So, you knew her marriage was in trouble?' asked Cross.

'No, not trouble. Over. She found out about his affairs. So many of them. She wouldn't forgive him, and she's dead.'

'Do you think the two are connected?' Cross went on.

'What? I don't know. But do you know who this woman he's with now, is?'

'Yes,' answered Ottey.

'And her father?'

'Yes.'

'Yes. Mrs F was very unhappy. She said it was a bad family.'

There was a pause as this woman thought about the awful situation she suddenly found herself in the middle of.

'Poor you. You've lost a friend and a job,' said Ottey.

'Two jobs. I'm not working for Joanna any more.'

'Why not?'

'Because it's next door.'

'Did Mrs Frampton say anything else about Mr Frampton's mistress?' asked Cross, sounding characteristically old-fashioned.

'I think it was just another thing that made her want to punish him,' she said.

'What do you mean, punish him?' asked Cross.

'She wanted to make him pay. I think she was right. Even Sasha agreed.'

'What about Justin?' asked Cross. He noticed an immediate hesitation in her at the mention of the son.

'He tried to persuade her not to. He thought things were fine as they were. They got along and were getting older. Why divorce now? It was pointless, he said.'

'That sounds a little detached from reality. A little spoiled, maybe,' suggested Ottey.

'Which is exactly what he is.'

'Go on,' Ottey prompted her gently.

'He's a hopeless boy. They were always arguing about him. She said her husband was always making excuses for him, whatever he did. She said he'd never grow up if he kept... what's the word? Indulging him. Sasha was with her mother when it came to Justin. She puts up with him because he's her brother and she has to. I think if they weren't brother and sister she'd have nothing to do with him.'

'Were there any major problems with Justin? Bigger than usual in the last few years?' Cross asked.

'Any particular crisis?' Ottey elaborated. Marina took a deep breath as if she was summoning up the courage to speak and concentrate on getting it just right.

'Four years ago, the Framptons redecorated their house. As you saw they have quite a lot of pictures. It was one thing they still had in common, art. They were always going to sales and art shows, sometimes final shows at art colleges. Always looking, always buying. So, they packed up all the paintings, wrapped them in bubble wrap and put them in the attic. When they came to put them back up a month later, one of them was missing. They couldn't find it anywhere. Then a friend of Peggy's saw it for sale in a gallery in Cheltenham. The same painting,' she said with incredulity.

'Okay. So how did it get there?' asked Ottey.

'Justin. He sold it to them.'

'He stole from his parents?'

'What else would you call it?'

Cross hadn't asked a question for a while, so Ottey continued. 'What did his parents say about it?'

'Mrs F was very upset. She couldn't believe he would do such a thing, whatever the reason. Mr Frampton just made excuses for him. He even tried to persuade her how well Justin had done. Said he got such a good price. Can you believe it? Mrs F told me she couldn't believe her family was in such a mess, and that she couldn't do anything about it.'

'Time for a change,' Ottey commented.

'Exactly.' Marina checked her watch. 'I have to go.'

'Of course, and thank you. You've been really helpful. Here's my card. Could you give me your number?' asked Ottey.

'I'll text it to you,' she said, getting out of the car and walking away.

'You went awfully quiet,' Ottey said to Cross. 'What was going on in that head of yours?'

'I was trying to decide whether it would be inappropriate for me to offer her employment,' he replied.

'You? Have a cleaner?' she asked in disbelief.

'No, obviously not me. My father.'

'I thought you'd fixed him up?'

'I have. Three times in the last nine months. The most recent one has just walked out.'

'Why would you want to put her through that? Hasn't she had a hard enough time recently without having to deal with Raymond?'

'I happen to believe with Marina he might have met his match. What's more, he's always talked about wanting to learn Spanish.'

'No.'

'Really?'

'It wouldn't be inappropriate. Go for it.'

He immediately got out of the car and walked towards the supermarket.

'I didn't mean right this minute!' she shouted after him.

24

Ribble had been interviewed by Carson and other members of the team in Cross and Ottey's absence. But no further progress had been made. Then the DNA results from the bag came back. The trace proved to be saliva, not sweat. But it also proved, conclusively, that it did not belong to Ribble. He was released on police bail, as Matthews wasn't convinced it completely exonerated him. The fact that it wasn't his didn't prove his innocence. The trace could have been left there after the event, or even been on the bag before the murder. Nor did the lack of his DNA in the bedroom exonerate him. He remained a person of interest in the case. Frustratingly, there was also no match on the criminal database for the DNA either. Cross was impressed by her diligence and following the evidence. He liked people who adhered to working by the book.

Mackenzie had continued with her victimology of Peggy and had discovered that she had quite a few enemies in the south-west property development world. She really didn't seem to like them, on the whole. A sentiment which was vociferously reciprocated. She seemed to take them on at every opportunity. There was even a winter where she had insisted that developers let the council house the homeless in their buildings before work on the sites began. As some of these involved properties that were scheduled for demolition, she was able to argue successfully against the developers who tried to claim their property would be damaged. A group of developers, former sparring partners, normally at each other's throats, competing for contracts or the purchase of tracts of land, suddenly had an enemy in common. An unlikely alliance was formed which became rancorously personal about Peggy. Three of them, in particular, spearheaded this with their combined influence and money, working against her at every opportunity. Even on local social issues that had nothing to do with development. Any issue she backed, they opposed. Vocally. A smear campaign was launched against her person. None of it was true but it was relentless.

The three developers were called Adam Chapel, Pat Morris and Simon Trethorne. The leader of this unholy trinity was Chapel. This was the man Ribble had mentioned in his original interview. He'd made his initial fortune doing developments in the south-west countryside. He built large housing estates with his USP being that the designs of the houses were varied and not identical. People seemed to like the fact that their house was slightly different to their neighbours'. The style was homogenous, but they came in all sorts of different shapes, sizes and configurations. The purchasers obviously felt it gave them some individuality and that in a snobbish way it was one step above the jerry-built, box-like housing estates of the 1970s. As people started to flock back to the city, Bristol in particular, and the price per square foot of property rose inexorably, Chapel stepped in to satisfy demand. Peggy's beef with him was mainly to do with the renovation of historic properties in Bristol. He seemed to have scant regard or concern for historic conservation.

One development had been particularly contentious and occupied a lot of Peggy's time in her last years of office. It was a large harbourside development, the planning application for which had originally been submitted to the council six years before. He'd originally received permission to make an old paper mill into a block of luxury flats. But at the eleventh hour he'd decided to knock the entire thing down and replace it with a modern building whose controversial design had divided opinion. Peggy had vetoed the initial change to the harbourside development while still on the council. A long, protracted and unpleasant war erupted between the two of them with Chapel aided by his two new best friends. Peggy knew it was pure greed that was driving him. He could get more units onto the land's footprint if he started again. It was all to do with profit. He tried to make several compromises but was knocked back again and again by Peggy and the council. In the end they agreed to keep the entire original façade. This was duly refused.

Chapel then took the decision to try and settle the dispute in the court of public opinion. He waged a media campaign to demonstrate the enormous value of the development to Bristol, both economically and aesthetically. This seemed to backfire. The more attention he drew to it, the more opposition he seemed to attract. As is often the case in these situations, it wasn't long before this PR campaign morphed into a war. The longer it went on, perhaps inevitably, the more personal it became on both sides. Chapel caricatured her as someone who was stuck in the past, entrenched in architectural values that had no relevance to modern life. She made him out to be a classic, capitalist egotist prepared to trample on anything that got in his way, including sites of historic importance. He was a veritable child of Thatcher. There were TV debates on local news, radio phone-ins, even advertising campaigns. It seemed to Cross and Ottey that it had grown completely out of proportion and become absurdly personal. The local press had turned it into a David and Goliath battle. The retired politician against the billionaire property developer and his gang of powerful friends. They made comments about how much easier life would be if Peggy Frampton had taken her retirement seriously. Chapel was caught on camera saying that she was 'a huge pain in my arse' whose main aim in life was to stand in the way of progress, whatever that might be. There was certainly no love lost between Peggy Frampton and Adam Chapel.

In the weeks before the meeting on the night of Peggy's murder, it seemed that things might be swaying in the developer's favour as he'd made so many compromises to the project. But Peggy had been victorious again, just hours before her death.

25

Chapel's HQ was on the outskirts of Bristol. It was a tastefully designed complex of two-storey buildings set in beautifully landscaped grounds with a circular artificial lake immediately in front of it. This reflected an upside-down image of the main building back at itself. Chapel would later tell them that his 'campus' (he referred to the place in the same way big tech companies in Silicon Valley referred to their premises), had won several architectural prizes. He was hugely proud of it. One thing Cross noticed as they parked in the car park, shielded from view by strategic arboreal planting, was that Chapel's name was nowhere to be seen on the building itself. It was etched on a large piece of glass behind the receptionists' curved desk, but that was it. Was this a lack of ego? wondered Cross, only to be told, when he enquired, that Chapel felt it ruined the integrity of the building. The only sign of ostentatious wealth was a helipad with a hangar beside it, and a helicopter being washed down.

As Adam Chapel came into reception to welcome them, Ottey thought he wasn't someone you'd want to pick a fight with in a hurry. He was muscular and strong-looking. There wasn't an inch of fat on him. He was well turned out in a

Richard James Savile Row suit and an open white shirt. He greeted them politely.

'Can I get you a tea or coffee?' he asked.

'Coffee would be great,' said Ottey.

'No,' said Cross.

Chapel then turned to the girls behind the reception desk. 'Nancy, Debs, can I get you anything?' he asked.

'No thanks.'

'No thank you, Adam. I'm good,' said the other.

'Follow me,' he instructed the police officers.

He walked at pace, with the purpose of a man who felt there weren't enough hours in the day to get everything he'd set out to do, done. They followed him up a free-floating industrial metal staircase, which seemed to hover in mid-air, until they came to a very smart kitchen. Its walls were covered with white tiles and it had black slate work surfaces. There was an array of fresh home-made biscuits and flapjacks, a bowl of fruit and a vase of artistically arranged fresh flowers on an island in the middle of the room. It smelt of freshly baked bread and coffee. There was an internal window behind which was a stainless-steel kitchen. In it a team of chefs were busy preparing food. Through a matching window on the far side of the kitchen, a large staff canteen could be seen. It was beautifully appointed and comfortably laid out with variously designed tables and chairs. It was bohemian-homely on a grand scale. This place was going out of its way to be a great place to work.

Chapel grabbed a large coffee cup and saucer and walked up to an enormous black and chrome coffee machine sitting on the counter.

'Cappuccino, latte, flat white. Whatever you like. I think we've even got some syrups in the cupboard.'

'Flat white, skimmed milk if possible.'

'Of course.'

Cross noticed the whole coffee beans in a clear box which formed the top part of the machine. 'Bean to cup,' he noted with approval.

'Best you can get. My partner practically had an aneurysm when he saw the invoice for it. Ten grand. By far the best investment we've made in years. Do you know the single most morale-busting thing a business can do to its workforce?'

'I do not,' said Cross, who was genuinely interested in this kind of thing.

'Charge the staff for coffee and tea. You'd be amazed how many businesses do it. Provide an industrial-sized tin of instant coffee and milk, then charge fifty pence a cup. It causes an absurdly disproportionate amount of resentment in the staff. And what's the upside? It's not as if you're going to make a profit anyway. So what's the point?'

Cross and Ottey were thinking the same thing. Finally a piece of empirical evidence to put in front of Carson who had pissed everyone off last year by charging them all for coffee and tea.

'You should talk to our boss,' Ottey said. 'Mind you, I don't think he'd go this far. This is like from one extreme to the other.'

'Yes, but it wasn't entirely unselfish. I get to benefit from it as well.'

Cross then noticed another machine. 'Is that an ice cream machine?'

'Mr Whippy? Yes. They love it. And that's the kitchen,' he said, waving at a couple of the chefs through the window. 'The refectory is on the other side.' Cross noticed he didn't use the word canteen. Too vulgar perhaps? 'We provide lunch every day.'

'Free?' asked Ottey.

'We started free but frankly it just cost us too much. So we asked the staff what we should do, and they came up with a subsidy system. So basically, we pay half each. We also do individual orders now, so as not to create waste. Everyone orders from the menus by text when they arrive in the morning, then has a choice of picking it up in the refectory, or if they're really busy, we deliver to their desk. We were throwing out so much food before and I can't bear waste. This way is much more efficient, and people feel they have more choice because, well, they do. We try to be sustainable in everything we do, from the buildings we create to the food we provide for our staff.'

The coffee machine had been grinding and puffing away in the background quietly. This machine even *sounded* like it made coffee perfectly. Chapel heated the milk then poured it expertly into Ottey's cup, complete with a leaf pattern in the foam, which she received gratefully. She couldn't help but inhale the aroma appreciatively.

'Wow, that smells good.'

'Doesn't it? Fairtrade Ethiopian this week. Think I'll have tea though.' He opened a cupboard and took out a teapot. Another cupboard was opened and revealed an array of loose-leaf tea caddies, many of them from Fortnum & Mason. Ottey almost laughed out loud when she saw Cross's face.

'I've changed my mind,' he said suddenly.

'Of course, any preference? I was going to have Darjeeling.' Cross checked his watch. 'Yes, Darjeeling would be fine.'

'You're such a tart,' said Ottey quietly to Cross as they

followed Chapel, who was now carrying a tray with the teapot and cups and saucers to his office. His approval rating on the tea front had soared as soon as Cross saw him getting out bone china without even asking.

'What?'

'He had you at Darjeeling. I bet you now think he's as clean as an Egyptian laundered sheet.'

'I resent that implication.'

'Sorry, I forgot. Sense of humour. Lack of.'

Ottey quickly realised they were being given a surreptitious grand tour of the building as no one with this amount of interest in design would have located their office so far away from the kitchen. It was completely impractical. They walked through vast open areas, with creative-looking people hunched over computer screens staring at 3D architects' plans. Each open area had a designated rest 'space' with sofas and bean bags, where employees lounged around with cups of tea and coffee, brainstorming. Chapel gave the detectives an ongoing commentary as they walked through. Then Cross stopped abruptly. They were outside a design studio where people were making incredibly sophisticated and intricate models of buildings.

'You have a model workshop,' Cross observed, thinking in part about his father.

'We do.'

'I thought most architects used 3D modelling on computers these days.'

'Well, firstly, I like to think our architects aren't like most architects. Architects do still use models. It gives the clients a more easily read representation of their building. They can, as it were, walk around it. For the architects it can be part of their process. They actually come across problems with the design. One of them told me she wasn't happy unless she got her hands on the building this early, which I rather liked.'

Cross had noticed a young woman pouring what looked like cement into a model.

'Is that concrete?' he asked.

'Yes, we don't do it often, but that particular building will be finished in concrete. The architect wants to give the client a more realistic impression of the finished building. A more tangible impression, if you'll forgive the pun.' Cross looked at him blankly.

'She's making an impression of the walls with the moulds,' Ottey quickly explained.

'Would you like to go in and have a closer look?'

'No.'

'Are you sure?' asked Ottey, who thought she detected a slight hesitation in her colleague. This could either mean he was really interested, or he was weighing it up as a possibility of gleaning more information about Chapel and his set-up at a later time. It was in fact the former. Cross, though, responded like a child who, having succeeded in behaving like a grown-up in front of a stranger with his mother, was then treated like a child by her; completely ruining the effect and wasting his effort.

'It's irrelevant to our purpose in being here,' came the terse reply. They moved on.

'You know who would love that,' Ottey continued. 'Raymond, his father,' she explained to Chapel. 'He's building a railway set in his spare room.'

'How do you know about that?' asked Cross.

'Look, here's the plan.' She got out her phone and scrolled

through her messages till she came to Raymond's childlike sketch of a landscape with buildings, mountains, lakes and a railway snaking through it. Chapel looked at it politely while Cross stood there silently fulminating about how, firstly, Ottey knew, and secondly, what on earth was she doing with it on her phone?

'Gosh, that is ambitious. You should definitely bring him in, Sergeant. I think he'd find it interesting and I'm sure he'd learn a thing or two. Our team is one of the best in the country and they love nothing more than talking about the intricacies of what they do to anyone who's willing to listen.'

Cross didn't answer as he was still trying to process what he saw as the total inappropriateness of this suggestion. This was a murder enquiry, after all. For Ottey it was one of the rare moments in their working relationship where she could smile to herself as she fondly wound him up. 'I'll let him know,' she couldn't help saying, eliciting the inevitable...

'You will do no such thing,' from Cross.

'Murder? I read it was a burglary gone wrong,' said a surprised Chapel.

'Either way a woman is dead,' replied Cross.

'Yes, of course.' Chapel thought about this for a moment then looked up. 'Oh, I see! You surely don't think...' He paused briefly. 'Well, I suppose I can see how you might have come to that conclusion.'

'What conclusion?' Cross asked.

'That I might have had something to do with it.'

'Why?'

'We had history, Peggy and I, as I'm sure you're well aware.

She's been a thorn in my side over the harbourside development for years. I've bent over backwards to accommodate her views. We're building affordable housing nearby on another of our sites. The building's completely sustainable, and on the conservation front we've pretty much agreed to everything she asked for.'

'So why hasn't it been given approval?'

'The truth is she kept moving the goalposts. For some reason she just didn't want to see it built.'

'She's cost you a small fortune,' Ottey pointed out.

'The delays have actually cost us millions. But then again that's my fault. As soon as I figured out that it was irrational on her part and she wasn't going to let it get built, whatever concessions we made, I should've walked away. But I'm one of those people who don't like being told something isn't possible. Gets my back up. I have to prove everyone wrong, and she was wrong. It's such a beautiful development. Would you like to have a look?'

'No,' came the quick answer from Cross.

'She just wouldn't back down. We even met privately, to see if there was any way we could thrash the problem out between us. But there was just no persuading her. I was the devil incarnate and she wouldn't budge. You can't win an argument if the other person won't listen to reason. I'm a hundred per cent in favour of heritage preservation and conservation. I mean, I'd like to think people will be as protective of our buildings in a hundred or so years to come. But there has to be a line. If there isn't, there'll be no progress. There has to be room for vision, but every vision has its detractors. History tells us that, more often than not, they're in the wrong. What if they'd got their way with Brunel over the suspension bridge? It doesn't bear thinking about. Brunel was years ahead of his time and thank goodness for him.'

'That sounds like a speech you've made a few times,' said Ottey.

'Are you a visionary?' asked Cross.

'Not really. I'm an enabler. I enable others' vision. I'm not creative. But I make sure I'm surrounded by people who are. I give them licence to exercise their creativity to the fullest. The kind of licence Peggy wouldn't afford me.'

'All of which explains why your name cropped up as a person of interest,' said Ottey. Cross was watching the man closely, but as yet didn't have a read.

'Oh, of course. But you're wasting your time. No development is worth the cost of a human life whether in construction or, well I don't know how to put it, whatever scenario you're imagining.'

'We're not imagining anything,' replied Cross. 'Simply trying to ascertain the facts. Where were you on the night of February the seventh?'

'That was the night of the latest appeal before the council,' Chapel replied, looking at the calendar on his computer.

'It was the night Peggy Frampton was murdered,' said Cross.

'Yes, quite.'

'You lost that appeal.'

'We did.'

'So were you there for the meeting?'

'I was not. There are only a certain number of planning meetings at Bristol Council that a grown man should have to endure. Here we are. I was at a dinner. A fundraiser for a friend's new foundation.'

'Can you prove it?'

'Of course, there were hundreds of people there.' He typed something into his computer, then swivelled it round for Ottey and Cross to see. There were several photographs of the event including a few of him.

'There was a sit-down dinner. I could get my secretary to let you have all the contact details of the people at my table.'

'Why would you have those?' asked Cross.

'Because I paid for the table. They were all my guests; therefore I have their details. Otherwise, how would I have invited them?'

Cross detected a slight tetchiness to this answer but said nothing.

'That would be helpful, thank you,' said Ottey.

'You said at one point that your life would be much easier without Peggy Frampton in it,' Cross continued.

'You never have people asking you sensitive questions, at exactly the wrong time, all the time, do you, Sergeant?'

'No.'

'But it's precisely *what* you do. It's your job to catch people out. For people in the public eye, even in as small a fishbowl as Bristol, or the south-west, we're on the other end of it. It's something we have to deal with on a daily basis, and sometimes we're not as good as we should be managing it. Then the quotes, or often misquotes, do the rounds and before you know it, have become facts written in stone. Would my life, my professional life, have been easier without Peggy Frampton snapping at my heels? Undoubtedly, as far as the harbourside development was concerned. But that's as far as it goes. As I've said, I acknowledge the whole mess is my fault. I should have backed down when I realised my opponent wasn't just formidable, but closed to all reason.'

'We'd like those names at the function,' said Cross getting up.

'Of course. It's the least I can do.'

'It is,' observed Cross.

'I actually liked her,' Chapel said, as he walked them to his office door. 'She fought hard and always above board. A rare thing in a politician. Especially a local one.'

'Thank you for your time,' said Ottey.

They saw themselves out. Ottey always preferred not to have an 'escort' she'd told Mackenzie once. She liked to get an 'unsupervised' look at any place before she left.

'It's quite the operation he has here,' she said. But Cross didn't reply. He was looking through the glass pane of a conference room, where a group of about ten young people were sitting at a long table. A man in a smart suit was standing at the head of the table berating them, at volume. Cross couldn't hear anything, but the man was red-faced, shouting so forcefully that the veins on his neck were sticking out. At one point he swept a pile of architectural plans off the table onto the floor. He then obviously dismissed them all, as the door opened and they trooped out, pale and shaken. Except for one, Cross noticed. A young man, with something of a swagger, who walked away in the opposite direction from the group, shaking his head and smiling.

'He wasn't exactly what I expected,' Ottey said, as they walked towards the car.

'What "exactly" did you expect?' Cross asked.

'Someone more combative, maybe. More confrontational and defensive about our being there,' she replied.

'Why?'

'He's a property developer, for a start. Not the most sociable species, in my experience. Like many of them he has a reputation for getting what he wants.'

'Except in Peggy Frampton's case.'

'Exactly. I'm not sure he's the flowers and chocolates type.'

Cross looked at her. 'You really are a puzzle to me at times,' he said.

'Well, at least that places me in about three-quarters of the population.'

Cross was thinking Chapel may well not be the hard-edged face of the business. That didn't mean that someone else wasn't.

26

Bristol Cathedral befitted the funeral of a local dignitary such as Peggy Frampton. The building seemed much grander now that it was no longer bordered by a main road. The south part of College Green had become traffic-free in 1991. It had added hugely to the amenity of the building, Cross thought, a little like the improvements to Queen Square. The front of the cathedral and its approach had a little in common with Westminster Cathedral, perhaps. It wasn't an enormously imposing building outside. Indeed, many people over the years had made the mistake of thinking that St Mary Redcliffe was the city's cathedral because of its strikingly decorative exterior and tall spire. But the cathedral more than made up for that with its glorious interior, the vaulted nave being lit in a way that accentuated its beauty.

It was a dull March morning, more cold than fresh. Mourners dressed formally in black greeted each other outside briefly before agreeing it might be warmer inside. They could always catch up after the service. As Cross and Ottey walked into the cathedral she estimated there must have been at least four hundred in the congregation. She chose a row of seats at the back of the church as they normally did, to keep their presence as discreet as possible, but Cross continued to march down the aisle until he found a row, just before the quire screen, which was to his liking and stepped into it. She followed him and sat next to him but before she could ask what she was doing this close to the family, he looked up at the organ above the choir stalls beyond the screen and said, 'Much better acoustics here.'

Cross loved the cathedral, even though not a person of faith. His only objection was that at some point in the past the pews had been removed. This seemed to be happening all over the country, which he thought was a shame. The need for versatility seemed to override the need for conservation. He would've liked to have had a conversation with Peggy about that, had he ever known her. He often came to lunchtime organ recitals at the cathedral, if he was free and in the vicinity. He knew the complete history of both the building and the organ itself. He could recite the technical specifications of the instrument down to the last stop. It had been renovated in 1907 then not overhauled again until the late eighties. Before that, a retired organist he'd spoken to had told him, it was drastically outdated. 'Playing it was a bit like driving a 1907 car on the M4 motorway,' he'd said.

Like many murder detectives, Cross and Ottey routinely made a point of attending a victim's funeral. For Ottey it was part of her process in dealing with the crime. The memory of it at a later date when the investigation might have hit a low or fallow patch, often gave her the added motivation she needed to find out who had ended a life so prematurely. For Cross it was mainly an exercise in observation of who was there and how they conducted themselves. Particularly the family and anyone else linked to the victim who was already in their purview. The congregation that day was made up of local politicians, members of local media organisations and people whose lives Peggy Frampton had touched in some way.

Adam Chapel was there and far from melting into the background he seemed to be making a point of drawing attention to himself. This seemed odd to Cross. Why would someone who had such a public falling-out with the deceased, calling her all manner of things, even at one point impugning her integrity, behave in this way? As if nothing had happened? Chapel spoke to and greeted many people. He seemed quite popular. Far from trying to avoid him or ignore him, people actually seemed to welcome his approaches, and not from fear. It was respect. After the service Cross watched as Chapel sought Luke Frampton out. They shook hands with noticeable warmth, Chapel holding onto the widower's hand comfortingly. There seemed to be absolutely no animosity.

'Isn't that Mark Coombes?' Ottey asked Cross at one point.

'It is,' Cross replied as he watched him shaking Frampton's hand and then hugging a startled Sasha. 'I thought he said he didn't know the children.'

'He did, but people do odd things at funerals,' Ottey replied.

Mackenzie was also at the service, much to Cross's surprise.

'She's doing the victimology, of course she's here, and if she wasn't you'd be complaining,' Ottey commented. But then Michael Swift appeared and moved into the seat next to Mackenzie.

'And Dr Swift?' Cross asked.

'I would've thought that was obvious,' she replied, which puzzled Cross even more than when he'd asked. But the service began, and he couldn't pursue it.

The service was well orchestrated. Politicians and friends spoke warmly about Peggy. The choir sang beautifully. There was something completely unpompous about it, Ottey thought. This was also reflected in its length. It wasn't too long. There was welcome humour in some of the speeches, none of which overstayed their welcome. Bob Dylan and David Bowie songs were played. Ottey thought that Cross might disapprove, but he didn't, surprisingly. He explained that he viewed the whole thing from a secular point of view, so it was neither here nor there. He was also very complimentary about the organ playing.

People milled about afterwards as the family held back to receive condolences, before leaving for a private burial. Chapel seemed to know a lot of people and was doing the rounds. Mackenzie was never too far away from him. Because none of the principals involved in the case actually knew who she was, she could get close to them and, on occasion, eavesdrop in a way that the two detectives were unable to.

'It seems that while the recent spat took all the headlines they had actually got along on several other earlier property developments,' she told them later. 'Basically, he was saying he had a lot of respect for her. That she fought as hard as he did and he had a lot of time for that. The interesting thing was how receptive Frampton was to this guy. I didn't expect that. Then Chapel started talking about the need to memorialise her in the city in some way. He thought the council should name a street or square after her and that he was going to get on their case if Frampton was in agreement.'

'Which of course he was?' asked Ottey.

'For sure.'

'Could be the ultimate mislead,' Ottey suggested.

'Chapel seemed quite sincere to me. But what do I know?' said Mackenzie.

'Not enough to make that judgement, certainly,' said Cross.

'It was an opinion, and a qualified one at that. In no way could that be construed as a judgement,' Mackenzie replied emphatically.

'Good point,' Cross agreed. Ottey smiled at this, Mackenzie was getting used to her boss and was having less and less truck with his nonsense.

A couple of things that happened after the service interested Cross in particular. As people offered their condolences to the family, a couple of suited men made their way over to Justin. They made no effort to speak to or greet his sister or father. They smiled at Justin and shook his hand, but he looked discomforted. As if he'd been taken by complete surprise and that they were the last people he was expecting to see. Cross watched as the two men walked away, simultaneously adjusting their jacket buttons unnecessarily, to a waiting black Range Rover. One of them had a tattoo which covered the entirety of his neck up to his jawline and chin. Cross didn't understand tattoos at all, but these seemed even more peculiar to him. From a distance it looked like the man had been in an accident and was wearing a neck brace. The two men got into the back of the car and Cross wondered whether they had in fact even attended the service. He also noticed that Justin didn't take his eyes off them as they left.

'Friends of yours?' he asked as he approached him.

'No! I mean, no. They knew my mother, apparently.'

He was lying, Cross realised, though he had no idea why.

'New suit?' he went on. Justin was dressed in an immaculate black pinstriped three-piece suit.

'No.'

'Looks it. Great cloth,' Cross said.

'It is. Anderson & Sheppard.'

'Savile Row indeed. Prince Charles's tailor.'

'His and mine,' said Justin a little pompously. Expensive tastes like his father, Cross was thinking.

The other thing was the unexpected presence of Alex Simmonds, Luke Frampton's former chambers' partner. He had hugged Sasha warmly and it was reciprocated affectionately. They spoke as he held both of her hands and looked very directly at her. This was followed by another hug. He turned and gave Luke a reluctant, formal handshake, then he left. Cross was surprised to see him there and wondered why he'd come.

Ottey didn't normally offer her condolences to the bereaved relatives of the victims at funerals. She'd already done it at the beginning of the investigation. But she wanted Frampton to know they were there and were watching him.

'Lovely service,' she said.

'It was,' he agreed. 'She would've been amazed at the turnout.'

'Oh, I don't think so. She was well liked, by all accounts. Which, needless to say, isn't making my job any easier.'

'These things take time, Sergeant. I know that only too well.'

'Of course you do. Forgive me if I'm wrong, but am I recognising a lot of these people for, what you might call, all the wrong reasons?'

Frampton gave a small nervous laugh. 'You mean my clients, or more accurately my former clients?'

'Yes. I have to say I'm a little surprised.'

'Well, they're very grateful, I suppose.'

'Did any of them know Peggy?'

'No, of course not. What are you trying to suggest?'

'I'm not trying to suggest anything. They must be here for you, then, rather than your late wife.'

'Yes.'

She said nothing further but smiled and walked away, leaving him wondering exactly what she was thinking. Which was of course what she'd intended.

As they reached Ottey's car a voice called out to them, 'Detectives!' They turned to see Mark Coombes approaching them.

'Mr Coombes,' said Ottey.

'Mark, please. Lovely service,' he commented.

'I thought you didn't know the family,' Cross commented.

'Not well, no.'

'Then why were you here?' Cross went on.

'Janette asked me to come. I was her representative, if you like. She asked me to pass on her condolences. The more she thinks about it, the more upset she gets. She wanted to come back for it, but you know, Peggy's gone. What would be the point?'

Nothing was said in response to this.

'The reason I came over was I had a chat with her last night. She wanted to know how things were going. I told her about that Ribble weirdo. She was a bit surprised he'd been released, actually. She thought he was a good bet. But then she said…' He got his phone out of his pocket.

'You made notes?' Cross asked, impressed.

'No, we talked by text. She'd run out of credits on her phone card. So this was much cheaper. Here, you can read it.' He was about to hand the phone over when something caught his eye. 'Actually, maybe not,' he said, laughing nervously. 'It gets a little… personal.' He laughed again. 'Sexting, they call it, don't they? Anyway, the gist of it was that if Ribble's out of the picture she thought you might want to look at the argy-bargy with Chapel. It'd gone on for years and got quite personal.'

'Does she think Chapel would kill Peggy because of the dispute?' Ottey asked.

'Not in so many words. But she talked about a bloke called…' He looked back at his phone. 'Bland. His right-hand man. Nasty piece of work, apparently. Anyway, I just thought you would like to know.'

'Thanks. That's very helpful,' said Ottey.

'Oh good,' Coombes replied, pleased he'd been of some use.

'We'd like to speak to your wife,' said Cross.

'Really? Okay. I mean I'm not sure she'd have much to add,' he replied.

'You'd be surprised what can be useful,' said Ottey.

'Sure. She's going to be a little hard to get hold of in the next week or so. She's trekking and white-water rafting. Can you imagine?' he said, looking directly at Cross.

'No. I can't,' Cross replied.

'Well, let me set something up.'

'We can always call her if it's a question of cost,' added Ottey.

'Really? Oh, that would be great,' Coombes replied, as if this was a relief.

'Meanwhile perhaps you could send over the relevant parts of that text conversation to us?' said Cross.

'Of course.'

★★★

'Got time for a coffee?' Swift had asked Mackenzie a little earlier, as she was discreetly approaching Adam Chapel. She'd said yes quickly just to get him to go away. She was sure his height would draw attention to them both and ruin her clandestine operation 'Overhear', and acquiescing seemed to be the easiest way to achieve this.

Half an hour later they sat down in a coffee shop at the bottom of Park Street.

'So, spill,' he began. 'What's happening?'

'Not much. I have a relatively quiet life,' she teased, as she knew full well, he was asking about the case.

'Ha-ha. With the case.'

'Well Matthews doesn't feel Ribble can be ruled out completely, even though it wasn't his DNA on the bag and there's no trace of it in the bedroom.'

'Absence of evidence is not evidence of absence in the eyes of the law,' replied Swift.

'Her point, exactly. I agree with her. I don't think he can be ruled out completely.'

'I'm in agreement there.'

'But I get the feeling George disagrees.'

'Wow.'

'What? It's not that surprising.'

'You call him George.'

'Not to his face. Of course I don't.

'How on earth does anyone get a feeling off DS Cross?' Swift asked.

'It comes with practice. He has various tells,' she said.

'Like what?'

'Like walking out of a room, with complete disinterest, whenever Ribble's name is mentioned.'

'Yep, that would do it,' he said, smiling at the thought of it.

'You're just a little besotted with him, aren't you?' she said.

'I am not,' he answered defensively.

'Yes you are. Be a man and admit it.'

'I am *completely* besotted with him and am mature enough to admit it. There is, without question, a level of hero-worship in my relationship with him,' he pronounced.

'I had no idea there was a relationship of any kind between the two of you,' she replied.

'I stand corrected. You are of course right. It was presumptuous of me in the extreme to think that.'

She laughed. He was very charming when he wanted to be.

'That's very sweet,' she said.

'And that is very patronising,' he replied. 'But I'm willing to take it on the chin and…' He trailed off. He seemed to have been a little on edge from the moment he sat opposite her. As if he wanted to ask her something and was trying to summon up the courage.

'And what?' she probed.

But whatever it was, he seemed to have lost confidence and didn't elaborate any further. She found herself feeling strangely disappointed.

27

Cross was reading Coombes's text exchange with his wife.

JAN: They must have looked at Chapel dispute.

MARK: I'm not sure.

JAN: CTTOI they should. Was her main thing recently. Got quite unpleasant. His second in command Bland's a nasty piece of work.

MARK: But murder? Really?

JAN: I know. Can't believe even he would resort to this. But. Wouldn't put anything past him.

MARK: Okay I'll tell police.

JAN: Anything else LMK.

> MARK: Will do.

> JAN: BFN!

Cross hated text acronyms and initialisms with a vengeance. He'd welcomed the idea of emails at the outset, thinking it would encourage people to correspond more; reinvent the idea of letter writing. But even they had their own form of shorthand now. One which infuriated him as he often had to study them closely to interpret them. Which was clearly counter to the purpose of electronic communication – to be speedy and efficient. There was nothing of particular interest in this text communication between Coombes and his wife. But they definitely needed to talk to Janette. He was sure she might know something that could be key to the investigation.

He did a deeper dive into the property developer Chapel and his business. Married twice, with two children, there didn't seem to be any ostensible problems with his domestic life. He still got on with his ex-wife, to the extent that she and her new partner often spent Christmas with Chapel, his new wife and all the children. He had a degree in architecture from King's College London, which meant five years of undergraduate study followed by two years' professional experience before final exams. That was a lot of time to invest in something, just to walk away from it. Apparently, during his final two years of study he made up his mind not to pursue it, per se. He said in an interview at the outset of his business that he'd come to realise he would only ever be a middle-ranking architect. There were so many better people around, with more talent and vision than he could ever hope to have. But he also realised that he understood other people's visions and ideas and maybe had an ability to facilitate them and, more importantly, sell them. So he wasn't walking away from it completely.

He set up the company with a friend from university. An economics graduate called Mike Rowbottom who, in the four years since his graduation, while Chapel qualified as an architect, had decided working for other people wasn't for him. Together with Chapel's ambition and taste, and Rowbottom's not inconsiderable business acumen, they built up a hugely successful company. This wasn't just limited to the south-west. Their building projects were now to be seen worldwide. From the Far East through the Middle East, across the Atlantic to the States; the Middle East had been a particularly lucrative market for them. But five years ago they had parted company. This split had attracted a lot of attention in business and architectural trades. The falling-out was apparently over Chapel's determination to take the company public. He saw it as becoming a new Balfour Beatty or Arup. Rowbottom not only had doubts about this, but was also on record as saying that it was too soon, and if they weren't careful they could open themselves up to a hostile takeover. It was fraught with danger, in his opinion. The only thing it seemed they could agree on was that he should leave the company. Which he did. The cost of buying him out put paid to the idea of going public, in the short term at least, which was a little ironic. A new COO was appointed from within. His name was Clive Bland, he'd been in the company for just under a decade and had been promoted to the board a couple of years before Rowbottom's departure. When it came to Bland's public and digital profile, his name appeared to be somewhat aptronymic. Bland to the point of non-existence.

Something about that struck Cross as a little strange. His rise, if not exactly meteoric, coincided with the company becoming more bullish and aggressive in public. Cross decided to go and meet Clive Bland. He didn't want to go back there as part of the investigation, though. He wanted their guard to be down and he had the perfect excuse to do it.

The next day Marina opened the door to his father's flat as Cross was looking for his keys.

'Good morning, sir,' she said.

'Yes,' he replied, as he often did to this salutation. Ottey had been confused at first and asked him about it. He'd replied that she had made a statement and he had agreed with her. 'What statement?' she'd asked. 'Your observation or statement that it's a good morning,' he replied, surprised at having to explain it.

He picked up his bike and walked inside. He was about to put it down when Marina stopped him.

'Wait!' she instructed, before disappearing into the front room. She returned moments later with a newspaper, which she opened and placed on the floor under each wheel of the bike.

'Okay, now put it down.'

He did so, obediently, then followed her into the kitchen. He noticed the wooden floor was gleaming and the hall smelt of floor polish.

'Have you used different polish on the floor?' he asked.

'Different? What do you mean different? There was no polish, just varnish. I use beeswax polish. Old-fashioned, but much better,' she explained.

'It smells nice.'

'Everything smells nice when it's clean,' she said pointedly. What was this about cleaners, Cross wondered. All the ones who had come to clean for his father spoke as if the flat hadn't been cleaned in years. The obvious implication being that the previous cleaner had been completely inept, but they were there to rescue the situation and put it right.

In the kitchen there was a teapot with three teacups and saucers. One of Raymond's bone china sets. She began to pour. Cross was about to speak when she read his thoughts.

'It's a fresh pot. Raymond said you were coming at nine thirty and that you were always on time.'

'I see,' he replied, taking the cup when it was proffered.

'Is the job to your liking?' he asked.

'Yes, thank you. I'm very grateful.'

'I wasn't seeking an expression of gratitude. You have no need to be. It makes a lot of sense. How are you getting on with Raymond?'

'We'll be fine,' she said cautiously.

'That sounds like you have doubts. He does take a little getting used to.'

'Wrong way round, sir. He needs to get used to me and we'll be fine.'

Cross had no answer to this, but thought he may have done the wrong thing here, and might be looking for a replacement sooner than he thought. He'd made the mistake of underestimating her, probably because of the circumstances in which they met. She was in shock and stressed then. As he sipped his tea he hoped this wouldn't be the case as she made such a fine cup. Raymond walked in.

'*Buenos dias*, Marina! *Como estás*?' he proclaimed loudly as he came into the kitchen.

'*Bien, Señor* Raymond. *Te he hecho un té y tostadas*,' Marina replied.

'*Eso es amable. Gracias*,' said a beaming Raymond, looking to his son for approval, which was not forthcoming.

The Chief had convened a meeting at the MCU that morning and on the face of it didn't seem at all surprised or put out by the fact that Cross wasn't there. The team ran through the case for his benefit. There hadn't been a 'whiff' of the jewellery, Carson said. He was of the view that if it turned up at all it could take months. Their theory of it being a burglary to order, which the evidence still supported, in his opinion, particularly the leaving of the ten thousand pounds, meant that a private sale had probably followed. In terms of the murder, they had no solid evidence that the burglary and murder had happened on the same night. In fact, there was little evidence to go on with the jewellery theft in terms of date or time, other than that Peggy Frampton had been wearing it eight days before. So the burglary had taken place sometime between then and the discovery that it was missing. But he was no longer sure how profitable the burglary was as a line of enquiry regarding the murder, and thought that he and his team would be better off concentrating on other leads in the murder case.

'Which are?' asked the chief. This flummoxed Carson, who was desperately thinking of something to say when Matthews stepped in.

'None. We have no leads as such,' she said with a candid

confidence that conveyed normality and no need for concern. 'Lines of enquiry. But no leads.'

Before the Chief left, he took Matthews to one side.

'If Cross isn't going to be present at these meetings, a heads-up would be appreciated,' he said.

'I entirely agree,' she said and smiled.

'Ah, I see.'

'But your presence is a great gee-up for the team. So not a wasted visit, sir.'

'No, of course not. I didn't mean to imply the opposite. If there's anything I can do, just yell.'

Matthews had come to the conclusion, over the last few weeks, that the Chief's interest in the case was more personal. It wasn't simply in response to external pressure from the media or political forces – either within or outside the police. He'd been personally affected by this death. She'd also realised how much faith he seemed to have in Cross, which in turn gave her the courage to stand back and let the detective dance to his own tune.

'I think we should look into the political side of all this,' Carson suggested to Matthews in her/his office. 'She may have been popular on one side of the council chamber, but she had a lot of enemies on the other.'

'Okay, fine. Murder in local politics is almost unheard of in this country. It feels like a stretch,' she replied.

'Sure, but what if it was personal, not political?'

'What are you suggesting?'

'The husband was having affairs, left, right and centre. What if she found romantic solace at work and it all went pear-shaped?'

'Sure,' said Matthews again, who couldn't have sounded

less convinced if she'd tried, Carson thought. 'Send someone over to City Hall and see what they can dig up. But it was a while back.'

'Well, bearing in mind how little we have, ma'am, isn't it worth a shot?' he said.

'No, you're right. Of course you are. Can you also find a couple of bodies to give Mackenzie some help with Peggy's social media? It's too much data for one person to get through.'

'Of course.'

'Cross still thinks we can't rule out someone from her social media world. The internet is a universe of resentment, pain and misread messages.'

'Sure.'

28

'This is very thoughtful of you,' said Raymond, as he and Cross took a taxi to Chapel's HQ. Cross had called and asked if he could take Chapel up on his offer to show his father their modelling room. Chapel was delighted to say yes and so it had been arranged.

'Not really. I want to go back there without them thinking it's part of the investigation,' Cross replied.

Raymond was neither surprised nor disappointed by his son's frank response. He'd become used to his son's directness and on the whole he liked it. But he flattered himself that Cross, even though the primary reason was work-related, also knew that such a visit would be welcomed by him. So there was a vestige of subconscious thoughtfulness in this, and that was enough for him. Situations like this often demonstrated consideration in his son. Difficult to see or discern at times, but when he did, Raymond made the most of them.

Cross was also eager to talk to Raymond about his mother again, but decided to wait until their visit to Chapel's was over. This was in case it upset him and in some way led to their visit being cut short. So he'd ask him on the trip back.

'Did Josie not want to come today?' Raymond asked.

'No,' Cross replied quickly, as the truth was he'd neither asked her nor informed her of where he was going.

'Stupid question. If she'd been with us these people would've seen straight through our little ruse. Do you need me to try and find anything out?'

Cross looked at his father, puzzled. 'Certainly not.'

'Understood. I will keep my eyes open though,' he said, fancying himself to have just been deputised by his son as an undercover operative.

'What for?' asked Cross.

'I don't know. Anything that strikes me as fishy. How is Josie?'

'Fine.'

'Good.'

'And Carla?'

'Recovering at home.'

Raymond was visibly impressed from the moment they drove past a large concrete slab engraved with CHAPEL at the entrance gates to Chapel's campus. Cross had missed it on his first visit. The letters were up lit from lights buried in the ground. As they approached the main building, a helicopter at the side of the building started its rotors. They got out of the taxi.

'Do you mind if we wait and watch it take off?' Raymond asked Cross.

'No.'

The passenger door of the helicopter then opened and Chapel appeared, trotting towards them. He was fashionably and informally dressed from head to toe in black, offset by a white T-shirt visible in the V of his cashmere sweater, and a pair of black and white Vans skateboarding shoes.

'DS Cross!' he called.

'Mr Chapel.'

'Hello, I'm Raymond Cross, George's father.'

'Of course you are,' said Chapel as they shook hands.

'This is most kind of you,' Raymond said.

'Not at all. I love showing off the modelling shop. I hope you'll find it interesting.'

'Oh, I'm sure I will.'

'I have to go on a site visit in London otherwise I'd show you round.'

'Well, it's very nice to meet you. We mustn't hold you up,' said Raymond.

'How's the investigation going, Sergeant?'

'Slow at the moment, but we'll get there in the end,' Cross replied.

'Oh, he always gets his man. Or woman, of course,' said Raymond. 'He doesn't discriminate when it comes to arresting folk,' he added, laughing at his own joke.

'I'm sure he doesn't,' said Chapel, looking straight at Cross. 'Call me if you need anything else, Raymond. You too, Sergeant.' He ran back to the helicopter. Raymond and Cross waited as the rotors got up to speed. The downforce made the water on the ground rise up like a circular skirt around the chopper. Chapel waved as it took off. Raymond waved enthusiastically back. Then the helicopter turned and disappeared into the distance, quickly becoming a speck on the horizon.

'What a fabulous thing,' said Raymond, shaking his head in admiration.

They were greeted in reception by Chapel's PA who gave them visitors' lanyards and showed them to the model room. Raymond was immediately awestruck.

'What a wonderful smell,' he said, referring to the scent of aerosol glue which hung in the air.

A young woman showed them round. She was charming and illuminating about all the different processes. Like Cross the previous week, Raymond was amazed that one particular model building was being made out of concrete. Eventually, without much prompting, Raymond produced the rough sketch of his plans for his railway landscape.

'Dad, I'm sure they don't want to see that,' said Cross.

'Of course we do. Adam said that was the whole point of the visit,' the young woman said before calling over another colleague. As a couple of others joined, Cross decided this was probably a good moment to slip away, unnoticed. He knew what he was looking for, just not where it was. So he wandered around the open areas of the building until he came to some offices in the vicinity of Adam Chapel's. He scanned the names etched on the door glass until he finally found what he was looking for. An office bearing the name *Clive Bland*. In it sat a muscular-looking man with cropped hair. Unlike Chapel he was wearing a suit, shirt and tie. The ensemble was very well put together. This man either had taste or knew someone who did. Cross recognised him as the man who had been tearing a strip off a number of employees, at volume, on his previous visit. There was an architectural model on a table by the door. It was the controversial harbourside development. Cross knocked on the door and went in. He immediately stopped and looked at the door where he'd knocked.

'Well that's annoying,' he said as he pointed to the smudge his knuckles had made. He got out a handkerchief and started to wipe away the offending mark.

'Don't you find that's often the way of beautifully designed things? Completely impractical. I mean, if I'd pushed the door, look, it's even worse,' he said and demonstrated to prove his point. He then sighed as he realised he'd now have to wipe away the large palm print.

Bland saw the visitor's lanyard hanging round Cross's neck. Cross was dressed informally today, which meant he looked like a trainspotter on his way to nearby Parkway station who had got lost.

'Can I help you?' he asked, managing to sound completely unhelpful. Behind him were several photographs of him taking part in different athletic events – marathons, bike races, triathlons, iron-men competitions, in what looked like north Africa. The man was obviously fit, and wanted people to know it, thought Cross.

'You wouldn't want to be a cleaner in this place, would you? Unless you couldn't get another job, I suppose, in which case, nice building, could be worse. But the amount of glass. I should imagine your cleaners have nightmares about smears, don't you think? Having been staring at glass from all angles all day, trying to spot a smear, and by virtue of its reflective quality staring at themselves, I wouldn't be surprised. Mind you, I'd be very interested in knowing what liquids they use to clean them, and if they have any tips.'

'Are you lost?'

'No, not at all, I meant to come in here. I wanted to have a look at this,' he said, pointing at the model. 'Do you mind?'

'I actually have a meeting.'

'It's the harbourside development in Bristol, isn't it?' Cross, ignoring him, asked.

'Yes,' came the curt reply.

'Gosh, looking at it close up like this, seeing all the detail, I really can't see what all the fuss is about,' Cross went on.

'How do you mean?'

'Well, what's the problem? Is what I mean,' said Cross, as if stating the obvious.

'You tell me,' replied Bland.

'It looks very sympathetic to the original building. You've kept the entire façade intact,' Cross went on, bending down to check.

'Well, it wasn't enough for some people, I'm afraid. So there we are.'

'Oh no. Does that mean it won't be built? Such a shame. It looks like a lot of work and money went into it.'

Bland laughed. 'I daren't even think how much money we've wasted on planning. But we'll get it done, by hook or by crook.'

'By crook? What does that mean?' asked Cross.

'It just means we'll do whatever it takes to get it done. I think we have a better chance now.'

'Why's that?'

'Certain obstacles have been removed from the process,' Bland said, checking his watch.

'What sort of obstacles?' Cross asked, giving the impression of being the kind of bore who won't let a conversation go until he's in possession of every detail.

'One of our major opponents is no longer around to oppose, as it were.'

'How did you manage that?' Cross asked.

'We didn't manage anything. She died, unfortunately,' Bland replied.

'That is sad. But good for you, I suppose.'

'If you were hard-hearted, you could look at it that way.'

'What happened to her?' Cross asked.

'She was murdered.'

'No! Wait a minute. I read about that. The former mayor,' Cross said, thinking out loud.

'That's right. Look, as I said, I have a meeting arriving any minute.'

Cross turned back to the model then back at Bland, as if he were seeing him in a different light.

'What?' asked the COO, falling for it.

'Very convenient for you,' Cross replied.

'I beg your pardon?'

'Her dying. Being killed like that. What was it you said? "Certain obstacles have been removed."'

'That was just an unfortunate choice of phrase.'

'Was it? Or just a slip of the tongue?' Cross asked, holding Bland's look. Chapel's PA appeared, walking past.

'DS Cross, are you lost?' she asked. Cross noticed the tiniest of reactions in Bland's otherwise immovable face at the mention of his police rank.

'No, I was just admiring this model and talking to your COO. He seems very hopeful it will now proceed in light of Peggy Frampton being murdered. I was actually on my way to make some tea,' Cross replied indelicately.

'Let me show you the way,' the PA replied politely. Cross followed her. Bland seemed a little unsettled as he watched them disappear down the corridor. He then walked over to his desk, picked up his phone and dialled a number.

'The police have just been in,' he said. 'Any rumblings your end?'

★ ★ ★

Cross declined the young woman's offer to make his tea, preferring to do it himself. It was a ritual he not only enjoyed, but was fairly confident he was more skilled at than everyone else. As he was waiting for the teapot to warm before adding the leaves – he'd told Ottey he was able to tell whether a pot had been preheated or not, when drinking a cup someone else had made – a young man arrived to make himself a coffee. He was fantastically slim, wearing tight-fitting black jeans, a pair of Grenson's light brown boots with a triple welt sole, and a white T-shirt. Cross noticed that he had no tattoos which, to this policeman's mind, was a real sign of independence. His hair was cropped round the sides but long on top where it had been drawn back into a tight bun which sat on top of his head towards the back. Cross recognised him as the man who'd walked out of Bland's dressing-down meeting the week before, looking completely unfazed by it.

'Hey, you all right there?' he asked Cross.

'Yes.'

The young man made his selection on the meister coffee machine. The beans were ground, filling the room with a rich coffee aroma.

'Are you an architect?' Cross asked.

'I am. You?' came the reply.

'I am not.'

'Okay, so what do you do?'

'I'm a policeman,' Cross replied.

'Yeah? Cool. You don't actually look like one.'

'Really? And what do policemen generally look like?' Cross asked.

'Right response. I have no idea. As a rule, I just like to subjugate myself to society's accepted prejudices when convenient, or when they are basically anti-establishment,' replied the young man, laughing again.

'How long have you worked here?'

'Seven years. Can you believe that? I can't. But I'm leaving next month.'

'Why's that?' Cross asked. The young man had paused as he realised this was a lot of questions. From anyone else, fine. But this man was a policeman and his 'accepted prejudices' kicked in.

'Why are you here, Inspector?'

'It's sergeant. My father is building a model railway in his spare bedroom and Mr Chapel invited him to come in and visit the model shop.'

'Classic Adam,' the young man laughed affectionately.

'So have you got a better job?' Cross asked.

'I'd like to think so.'

'Must be quite a wrench leaving this place. It's so beautifully designed. Must be a nice place to work, for the coffee alone.'

The architect laughed. 'That's funny. The coffee did actually come into the equation when I was deciding what to do. But then I thought that was a bit shallow, and the fact is, where I'm going is surrounded by good coffee shops.'

'In Bristol?' Cross asked, genuinely interested.

'No, I'm going north. Manchester. But you're right, I will miss this place and loads of the people.' Cross said nothing. The young man felt the need to fill the gap in the conversation, as people often did with Cross. 'But it was the right time to move.'

'Why?'

'Well, this place hasn't really been the same since Mike left.'

'Mike Rowbottom?' Cross asked.

'Yeah, it was a really cool place back then. Look around you. The two of them conceived this, then built it. Recruited really talented people from all over. Mike was a numbers guy. They fitted together so well. He was empathetic to what Adam wanted. Interested in it all. Now it's all about the bottom line, profitability and money.'

'Why's that?' asked Cross, who was pretty sure he already knew the answer.

'Oh, various reasons.'

'Like what?'

'Management.'

'But Chapel is still the man in charge. It's his company,' Cross pointed out.

'Yeah, but he's very susceptible to whoever has his ear, if you know what I mean.'

'The COO? Clive...?'

'Bland. He drives the financial side of things, he's brutal, man. Adam is the kindly artistic, green face of the company. Bland is the hatchet man.'

'That's unfortunate,' said Cross.

'It is for anyone who crosses him.'

'That doesn't sound good.'

'Here's the thing. Cutting budgets and managing costs on a project has always been difficult. But it's part of the job and there's always a way. We box and cox and get there. You disagree on the numbers with Bland and you're out the door. Just like that. If you happen to come across Adam on the way out, with your cardboard box in your arms, he asks, all innocent: "Oh no. What happened? You're leaving? Surely we can sort this out." But he's known all along. He doesn't like confrontation, so just looks the other way.'

'Why doesn't anyone just tell Adam the truth?' asked Cross, not unreasonably.

'Why do you think I'm leaving?' the young architect said, picking up his coffee.

'You did?'

'Had to. But he doesn't listen. I told him I didn't want to work in a place where profit is the only thing that matters, and I thought he'd always thought the same thing. Everyone is unhappy. They feel they're being constantly judged and about to be fired. You cross Bland at your peril.'

'What's his background? Do you know?' Cross asked.

'He's an accountant, came from a huge building supply company originally. Very political. Manoeuvred his way into Adam's ear. His mother's Albanian, apparently. Rumour has it she's part of some huge Albanian crime family. But I'm sure that's bullshit. Anyway, nice to meet you. Sorry for venting.' He picked up his coffee. 'Venting, nice one.' He laughed, and left.

Cross sat there for a moment, thinking. Then he saw the ice cream machine in the corner of the room. He'd forgotten about that, and however early in the day it was, it was too good an opportunity to miss.

Raymond was thrilled with his morning. He came away with a couple of large bags of glues, materials and drawings.

'One of the lads in there took a copy of my rough plan and is going to put it in his computer like a proper architect's drawing. How kind is that?' Raymond told his son.

'Very,' Cross replied.

'That was such a fun morning. Thank you so much. Did you get what you were looking for?'

'I'm not sure.'

'Why ever not?' asked Raymond.

'It's always more difficult when you don't know what it is you're actually looking for.'

29

'I didn't get to see much of him. He had to go to London. But I did have a wander and encountered Mr Bland.'

'The COO?'

'Correct. Not the most popular man in the firm. Something of a voracious cost-cutter. Several people have lost or left their jobs since he rose to his present position in the firm. They call him the rottweiler.'

'So, good cop–bad cop,' Ottey suggested. Cross didn't understand. 'Chapel and Bland,' she explained.

'Very much so. It seems that Bland will go to any lengths to get what he, or what he thinks the company, needs. He described Peggy Frampton as an obstacle that needed to be removed.'

Ottey smiled. 'He didn't know you were a cop when he said that, did he?'

'He didn't ask,' Cross pointed out.

'He would never have said it if he'd known. So he warrants a closer look,' Matthews commented.

'He does. I think we should also look at the company finances over the last few years.'

'I can get a forensic accountant on it,' Matthews offered.

'No,' Cross said abruptly.

'George likes to do that stuff himself. I know,' Ottey said in response to Matthews' look of surprise. 'We all run a mile, but it's one of his things.'

'What do you mean, one of my "things"?' Cross asked.

'One of your things that you particularly like to do,' Ottey explained.

'I see. It might be helpful in future if you actually completed your sentences,' Cross replied.

'George,' Matthews said, chidingly.

'It's fine,' Ottey interceded. 'He's right. When it comes to him I should.' Cross gave her a look and she laughed, 'Finish my sentences completely for his benefit.'

'Not just mine,' Cross protested.

'Point taken. Move on, George,' Ottey replied.

'I discovered something else. It could be nothing but if it is it's quite a coincidence. Bland's mother is Albanian and, rumour has it, is related to a big Albanian crime family.'

'Really? Name?' asked Matthews.

'I don't have it.'

'Why is that a coincidence?' asked Carson. There was a moment's silence as the three other people in the room wondered whether they'd heard right.

'Frampton's girlfriend is Albanian. The father is the head of an Albanian crime family and a convicted murderer,' Matthews said with as little side as she could, which was quite difficult in the circumstances.

'Oh, right. Sorry, that was so obvious I thought there must be something more to it,' Carson spluttered.

'I'll look into it,' said Cross.

'Anything else?' asked Matthews.

'If you're looking into Chapel a little more, I've come

across a group of activists helping Peggy with her campaign. They might be worth talking to. I could probably track them down,' Mackenzie offered.

'Good idea. They might be able to cast more light on Chapel,' said Matthews who then went on, 'You know what. I think we should step back and go over what we have right now. Also the night of the murder.' She knew from Ottey that this was a process that Cross found useful, and they often did together. Matthews thought it might be profitable to do it with the whole team. She also knew that Cross's contribution would be negligible in such a forum, but Ottey had told her he secretly liked to hear other people discuss the case. It often set trains of thought running in his head. A meeting was convened in the open area an hour later.

'So, we have Peggy Frampton, an eminent Bristolian, ex-mayor, brutally murdered in her bedroom. An attempt was subsequently made to make it look like a burglary in the bedroom and we now know jewellery was also stolen from the study safe,' Ottey began.

'There is nothing to tell us that the jewellery was taken on the night of the murder,' Matthews pointed out.

'That is true. It could've been at any time during the previous eight days, according to her husband.

'That was the last time he opened the safe,' Ottey qualified. 'On the night in question Peggy is at the council chamber to attend what is thought to be Adam Chapel's last chance to get his development through planning. Peggy speaks as a member of the public and reiterates what she's been saying over the years against the application, which is then turned down for what is possibly the final time.

'A group of them go out for a drink to celebrate the result. Then Peggy is driven home by a friend, an ex-colleague, arriving at approximately ten thirty. Some time after that she goes to her bedroom and turns on the bath. We assume she didn't go into the rear of the property or she would've noticed the back door window had been smashed. If only...' she said, for the first time thinking that had she done so the chances were she would've called the police and still been alive.

'It's so clumsy. Such a giveaway. Didn't the killer realise that?' asked Matthews.

'What?' asked Ottey.

'What you're saying. That the back door could have alerted her to their presence,' Matthews explained.

'It's a good point,' said another detective. 'It just doesn't fit with a professional burglar who can crack a safe.'

'It doesn't,' Carson concurred.

'Who did his job so well in the study that the theft of the jewellery wasn't discovered for days,' the detective continued. At this, Cross scribbled something down in his notebook.

'Also true,' said Matthews, thinking out loud.

'It lends credence to the idea of there being two separate events. George's objections to that were that the chances of two burglaries happening on the same night were ridiculously small. But as you point out, ma'am, we have no proof that the jewel theft and the murder occurred on the same night,' said Carson.

'Forensics are confident the killer in all probability is male, from the size of the covered shoe imprints on the bedroom carpet. He was waiting behind the bedroom door. He killed her before disrupting the bedside drawers and turning off the bath, leaving a partial fingerprint,' Ottey continued.

'Which has proved to be useless,' Carson commented.

'He doesn't know that. The fact is he still left it which could be useful,' said Ottey, who wasn't entirely sure why, but was repeating something Cross had said to her.

'What about motive?' said Matthews, changing tack.

'Revenge for all the trouble she was causing Chapel? Or maybe a solution to the problem?' suggested Carson.

'It's possible.'

'If that's the case it would seem that Chapel's contacts don't extend to professional experienced killers,' said Matthews, casting some doubt on it. 'Clumsy break-in, partial fingerprint on the taps, DNA left on the bag which is then discarded carelessly.'

'Yeah, right. Don't think this guy would get a load of five star reviews on Trustpilot as a killer for hire,' said Mackenzie, immediately regretting it in the silence that followed.

'Let's talk about the family,' said Matthews, a little like a chairwoman at a local parish meeting that had veered irritatingly off topic. 'Frampton's in London, alibi confirmed. But his case was over three days earlier and he chose to remain there with his girlfriend.'

'A girlfriend with a very dodgy family background,' said Carson.

'Her father is a killer. He's also in prison,' Matthews pointed out.

'But he still has influence on the outside,' said Ottey.

'Frampton could have stayed in London as part of a plan to be out of Bristol for the murder,' Carson suggested.

'Why would he want to kill his wife?' asked Ottey.

'Because he wanted to move on.'

'So, divorce her. Don't have her suffocated in a plastic bag,' Matthews protested.

'He may not have known how they were going to do it,' Carson replied, realising how absurd he sounded as he did so, but his instinct to be at the middle of any meeting he attended got the better of him momentarily.

'He's been regularly unfaithful to her. Why bother killing her when he'd always got away with it? Doesn't sound like she'd've been much of an obstacle if he'd said he wanted the marriage to end,' said Matthews.

'Maybe it was the girlfriend's idea. She'd grown up with that kind of thing going on around her and it was the first time it was a real possibility for him. Having her killed,' said Carson.

'Okay,' Ottey said to Carson. 'Why don't you check communication with Dragusha at Belmarsh and any recent visits? Who they were with and when.'

Carson's mouth dropped open in an expression of exaggerated disbelief for the benefit of the others in the room. 'Are you actually giving me, your senior officer, last time I looked, an order?' he spluttered.

'You know full well she can't do that,' said Matthews.

'The question is does *she*, ma'am?' Carson pointed out indignantly.

'I, on the other hand, can. So please either do it or delegate it to one of your team which is, I'm sure, what DS Ottey meant, DCI Carson.'

Ottey decided to ignore all of this and carry on. 'The daughter is a GP who lives in Cheltenham. Not a huge fan of the brother, it would seem. She has that resigned attitude, when it comes to him, from years of being constantly disappointed and the beneficiary of dozens of broken promises. The cleaner told us he's stolen from the family before. Alice is still trawling through the victim's social media presence but it's a huge task.'

'Didn't you get some help?' asked Matthews, looking at Carson

'It was offered, ma'am,' Carson replied defensively.

'I'm good thanks. It's easier if one person is across it,' said Alice, justifying her refusal a little too quickly.

'So, three areas – family, father and son – seem unlikely. Property developer, a possibility, or maybe someone from her social media career?' Matthews summed up.

'I'd put money on Chapel and his mates,' said Carson.

'You haven't even met the man,' said Cross, speaking for the first time. 'And yet you have him down as a killer.'

'Like you, George, I'm not making any judgements, I'm simply following the facts and evidence.'

Matthews checked herself as she was about to ask Cross what he was thinking and said instead, 'Is something about all of this bothering you, George?'

'The plastic bag. Why a plastic bag? Why not strangle her or drown her in the bath?' he replied. He didn't want to elaborate any further, or be pushed on it, so he simply left the room.

30

When it came to examining company accounts detectives often made use of the accountants in the force, either in the fraud squad or, if they weren't available, the accountants who ran the force's finances. Cross, though, liked nothing more than a juicy, complex spreadsheet to get to grips with and so always did such investigations himself. Looking at Chapel's business wasn't especially difficult, as he was looking at what Ottey often referred to as the 'headlines', and not doing a complete forensic overhaul at this juncture.

While still largely profitable, things had definitely changed at Chapel over the last few years. More specifically: since the time that Mike Rowbottom had left and Clive Bland's ascent to the top table. His cost-cutting could easily be seen in the numbers. The outgoings of the company had been significantly reduced, but then again so had the annual turnover. This was down by at least five hundred million pounds a year. It was still showing a profit but the firm seemed to have taken a major backward step. From quotes in various business journals, always given by Adam Chapel, they were reshaping the company to make it more 'lean and mean', before they thought seriously about going public. A decision hadn't been made on that as yet, but it was still in the mix. This was exactly why Rowbottom had left in the first place. Cross wondered what Bland's plan was. Surely a company with a larger turnover, admittedly one with larger costs, was a better prospect for potential shareholders? That expansion would surely lead to further profit and therefore higher dividends. He decided to get in touch with Rowbottom, who had relocated to Australia.

'I bought a ranch,' Rowbottom explained, when he got hold of him on a Zoom call the next morning. 'My wife is originally from Australia and with the children all grown up, it finally seemed possible. It's something we've always wanted to do.' He looked tanned and relaxed. 'Best thing I ever did, leaving Chapel and all that stress behind. Life is wonderful.'

'It was stressful?' Cross asked.

'It became more so after Adam decided to go public. I thought the idea was insane. It was something we'd said we had no interest in doing, no matter how well we did. We just loved what we were doing. Making a shedload of money but still keeping our original ethos and objectives we set out with. We still had integrity. We embraced sustainability years before everyone else. When they all thought it was hippy-dippy shit and fought tooth and nail against it, we were evangelical. We were years ahead of the curve, because we were financially independent and had a good sense of how things should be done properly, from an artistic and ecological standpoint. Adam was more passionate about it than I was, for God's sake. Until he wasn't.'

'So what happened?'

'Clive Bland happened.'

'Go on.'

'Right from the moment he joined the company...'

'What was his job when he started?'

'Chief finance officer. He worked Adam from day one. Looking back, it was like he had a plan. In retrospect, I can see part of that plan, long term, was to get rid of me. I tried to tell Adam, but he wasn't having any of it. Decades of friendship and partnership, family holidays together, dealing with each other's bereavements, all counted for nothing in the end. That's the saddest part of it for me.'

'Are you still in touch with Mr Chapel?' Cross asked.

'No. We're way beyond that.'

Cross detected an element of sadness and regret in his voice.

'In the end I was just glad to get out. Whatever you say about Bland, he's a master at manipulation and getting what he wants. If he wasn't so unpleasant it'd be quite impressive. I warned Adam about him. I wouldn't put it past him to be the last man standing at the company,' Rowbottom said.

'Really?'

'You don't know him.'

'Can I ask you about Peggy Frampton?' Cross asked. Rowbottom laughed.

'Oh God. I don't know why I'm laughing. I liked the old bat. I was so shocked to hear what happened. I wrote to her husband. But she was a royal pain in our arse. After we were knocked back by planning the first time, I told Adam to walk away. I just had a sense about her. She was one of those people who, when they have a cause, cannot see beyond it; cannot see a compromise. It just has to be their way completely. They have a kind of madness in their eyes when they talk about whatever their passion is.'

'Why didn't he listen to you?'

'He was convinced it was his legacy project. That he was going to make his mark on Bristol. Something that would be there for hundreds of years.'

'Did you see it that way?'

'To an extent, yes. But it became obvious that Peggy was going to do her best to stop it, no matter what we did, or however many changes we made. At one point I asked Adam if he had history with her, because it seemed so irrational, so disproportionate to what we were proposing. He assured me he didn't.'

'She was that determined?'

'Yes, but in an increasingly maniacal, obsessed, totally unhealthy way. I told Adam early on that we should swallow our losses, before they became unmanageable, which I could see happening, and admit defeat.'

'He seems to regret not having done so,' said Cross.

'Oh sure, he'll say that, but he doesn't mean it for a minute. The whole situation has made the entire company stagnate. They can't plan, not knowing if this huge project is going to happen or not. Dozens of other great projects have gone by the wayside. Really great projects artistically, really terrific for the reputation of the company, have just been ignored.'

'What was Bland's position on the development?'

'Oh, he was all up for it. Called it a landmark project. Told Adam, would you believe, it would make him his generation's Brunel.'

'But Brunel was an engineer, a genius,' protested Cross.

'Exactly, and Adam knows that. But he let himself believe it. Then Bland said Harbourside would put fifty pence on a potential share price. Absolute bollocks, of course. There was no evidence to back up that claim but Adam was completely sold. He's always had a latent ego problem. It just took a while to come out with the right encouragement.'

'From Bland,' said Cross.

'Exactly. He has a reputation for getting what he wants at all costs. He's a liability, that man. He's going to drag the company down and Adam with it, if you ask me. Particularly now that Peggy's out of the way. The current indications are that the development will go through.' Cross said nothing to this. Rowbottom quickly realised how this sounded. 'Listen, I'm not saying Bland had anything to do with Peggy's murder. I think that's a step way too far. Even for him.'

'But why would you think they'll be going under now the development might actually go through?' asked Cross, not following the logic of it.

'Because since I left, Bland has not only cut costs, he's quadrupled the company's credit line to the banks. If the development goes ahead and Bland convinces Adam to take the company public on the back of it, which has always been his long-term plan, they'll have to mortgage the company to the hilt, leaving them vulnerable,' Rowbottom explained.

'Vulnerable to what?' asked Cross.

'A hostile takeover by one of the behemoths like Balfour Beatty. Look we have, sorry, *they* have a beautiful campus, as Adam insists on calling it, but they're a minnow in comparison to some of those beasts out there. Peggy cost us serious money, Sergeant. A bloody fortune, and that could finally come home to roost if someone launches a bid for the company.'

31

Sasha Connor appeared in the MCU a few days later. She was in Bristol visiting her father. Ottey and Cross met her in the VA suite.

'How are you?' Ottey began.

'Um, well, you know how it is. Losing your mother strikes me as difficult enough. But when you add murder into the mix it makes it all the harder to process,' Sasha replied.

'I completely understand,' said Ottey.

'Oh, was one of your parents murdered?' Sasha countered aggressively. She regretted it immediately. 'I'm sorry, I didn't mean that. I'm a little all over the place at the moment.' Cross was a little thrown by this apology. He thought she had a point. Neither of Ottey's parents had been murdered, so how she could understand, and 'completely', for that matter, was beyond him.

'No need to apologise,' Ottey continued. 'It was a thoughtless, automatic reflex on my part. Are you back at work?'

'I am. I thought it would distract me, and it has to an extent. The main problem is dealing with the patients endlessly expressing their sympathies. It's exhausting. It was bad enough at the beginning, but now it's been in the papers that the police are treating it as a murder, the patients can't seem to get enough of it. Does that sound terrible?'

'Alex Simmonds was at the funeral. You were pleased to see him. Why was he there?' asked Cross.

'He's my godfather,' Sasha replied.

'That must've been awkward,' Ottey commented.

'Nope. He's actually one of the best of my godparents. It's weird how parents manage to mostly screw that up. Choosing godparents for their children,' Sasha went on.

'Oh, don't,' agreed Ottey.

'You said you had something to tell us, that you didn't want to speak about over the phone?' Cross said.

'Yes. It's a bit awkward really but I thought you ought to know. It's about my brother Justin,' she said.

'Is it about the painting he stole?' Cross asked. Ottey gave him a look which he ignored. He just wanted to get on with it.

'How did you know? No one knew about that.' Cross and Ottey said nothing. 'Marina,' she said, thinking it through. 'My mother must've told her. But yes, that's why I'm here. I just thought you ought to know.'

'Why?' asked Cross.

'Well, because my brother has stolen from my parents before. You might not have been aware of it, and I thought it might be of interest to you. He has form. Isn't that what you say?'

'No,' replied Cross.

'Whatever. It was the first thing I thought when I heard her jewellery had gone missing – I couldn't believe it. Didn't want to believe it. I know this sounds awful, but I was so relieved when you said you were treating it as murder and not a burglary gone wrong. Because what if he *was* involved and it ended up in my mother's death? I can't imagine what would've happened.'

'So, you do think it's possible he's involved?' asked Cross.

'Of course it's possible. He's an antiques dealer who was stupid enough to steal an Augustus John from his parents and think he'd get away with it.'

'Why would he need to? Why did he steal the painting?' asked Ottey.

'Money, obviously,' she said with no edge. 'My brother has a problem, a weakness, an addiction, call it what you will. He gambles. Can't stop himself and I'm not just talking about horse racing. It's any sport, cricket, darts or anything – he'll bet on the sock colour of the next man who enters a room. It's awful. He's banned from every licensed betting shop in the south-west, did you know that?'

'We did not,' answered Cross who was taking careful notes.

'He's even been banned from internet websites and can't get on others because all his credit cards are maxed out. So now he goes to private bookies, who are the only ones willing to take his bets, and you know what that means.'

'No,' again from Cross who didn't look up from his notebook.

'Well, they're criminal. He must be up to his eyes in debt and God knows who he owes it to or what they'll do if he doesn't repay it.' Cross said nothing but was thinking, as was Ottey, that this shed an interesting light on the case.

When Ottey was showing Sasha out she turned to her and said, 'That must've been really hard for you.'

'What, dobbing my brother in? Not really. I mean, I don't even know whether he did it.'

'Did you ask him?'

'I didn't have to. He accused me of thinking it before I'd said a word. Possibly a case of offence being the best defence. But I think maybe it's like an alcoholic with him. He's got to hit rock bottom before he can begin to recover.'

'Well, we'll see. But thank you.'

'My mum wouldn't have expected anything less. Tell me one thing, though. Are you absolutely sure the burglary and her murder aren't related?'

'I think so. We don't even know if the theft of your mother's jewellery happened the night of your mother's murder or some time before.'

Justin Frampton used to have an antiques' shop in the Cotham area of Bristol but had recently moved to an antiques' mall in Bath. When Cross and Ottey arrived the following day, it turned out that Justin's shop was more of a stall than an actual shop. It was in a large, classic Bath sandstone building, which housed some small shops and stalls. There were also display cabinets with phone numbers inside them for sellers who weren't there physically, so that if anyone had any interest in buying anything they could contact them. Cross thought this hardly constituted an efficient way of doing business. They had decided not to give Justin any advance warning of their visit, and as a result he wasn't actually behind his stall. A nearby stallholder was looking after it for him while he had his lunch. Probably in her eighties, she walked with an air of faded glamour and a stoop. Whether this was an osteoporotic symptom, or the result of the enormous amount of gold jewellery round her neck, pulling her head towards the ground, was difficult to say. Her lipstick and eyeliners were more smudged than applied.

'Is Justin around?' asked Ottey.

'You police?' she asked.

'What gave you that idea?' Ottey laughed.

'Gorgeous young Black woman with *him*?' she said, eyeing Cross disparagingly. 'What else are you going to be? He's at lunch. Should be back in ten minutes. Mind you, his word is worth about as much as an inner tube, with a hole, on a bike.'

'Okay, thanks. We'll come back,' said Ottey, still smiling. Cross had noticed that Justin's stall was only open four days a week, so either he was just lazy, or business wasn't so good.

'We might as well have a look around while we're here,' Ottey said, as she wandered off. Cross walked in the opposite direction. He wasn't particularly interested in the place until he saw a small shop whose window was filled with toys. Something in the centre of the window attracted his attention.

Ottey returned to Justin's stall about fifteen minutes later, empty-handed. She hadn't bought anything as she was still feeling the vacuum in her bank account that her annual extravagance at Christmas, as a single mother of two daughters, inflicted. Despite promising herself, and negotiating with the girls, that it would be a restrained Christmas, with them only having a couple of presents each, partly so as not to spoil them, but also as another lesson in her 'value of money' curriculum, she'd gone overboard. Again. The truth was she enjoyed spoiling the girls and why shouldn't they have fun at

Christmas? Was it an attempt to compensate for all the times over the past year where her job meant that she'd missed birthday teas, school plays and dance displays? Yes. Probably.

Cross reappeared a couple of minutes later with a large rectangular box, in a bin liner, under his arm.

'George, what have you bought?'

'Nothing,' he replied.

'That's a bloody great big bin liner of nothing under your arm. So, unless you're taking out someone's rubbish, which I very much doubt, you've bought something.'

'Is he not back yet?' George asked, deliberately ignoring her.

'No. Show,' she instructed him, pointing at the bin liner.

He reluctantly pushed back part of the bin bag to reveal a worn Hornby cardboard box with a picture of a train on it, specifically, the Flying Scotsman.

'It's a Hornby train for my father. He's constructing a train set in his spare room.'

'That's great. He'll be so pleased. I love spontaneous presents. They're so much more exciting than ones at Christmas or on birthdays.'

'Oh, it's not a gift,' he said, producing the receipt. 'But I'm sure he'll think it's worth the money. If not, I can bring it back.' Ottey was about to suggest that Cross experimented, gave the train to Raymond as a gift and took note of his dad's gratified, gratifying expression of gratitude, when Justin appeared at the other end of the room clutching a cup of coffee. He saw them, smiled, and waved. Dressed in a herringbone three-piece suit, complete with fob watch on a chain in his waistcoat pocket, a bright yellow silk pocket square and matching tie, decorated with horses, adorning a checked Viyella shirt, he was the image of what he obviously thought an antiques dealer, albeit with only a small stall to sell from, should look like.

'Officers, how are you?' he began brightly. 'Any news?'

'No. We'd just like a word, if that's all right,' Ottey answered.

'Yes, of course. Let me get a couple of chairs.'

'I think somewhere more private would be better,' she replied.

'Oh, okay. That sounds a little ominous,' he laughed jokingly, pulling a faux expression of apprehension, then turning to the neighbouring stallholder. 'Dorothy, would you be able to keep an eye on the stall for a few more minutes?'

She looked at her watch irritably and scowled. 'I should be on my lunch.'

'And you will be soon enough. I promise.'

She nodded her assent, secretly curious as to what the two police officers wanted from him.

As they walked out Justin noticed the package under Cross's arm.

'Taken the opportunity to do some shopping while you were here?' he asked. Cross didn't answer straight away, suddenly fearful that it had been unprofessional of him to shop while they were on police business.

'Train set. For his dad,' Ottey answered for him.

'Did you get it from Stanley?' As they walked past the shop Cross had bought it from, Justin shouted at the shop owner.

'I hope you gave my friend here a good price, Stan!'

'If I'd known he was a friend of yours I'd've charged him double!' came the reply. Cross wasn't sure whether this was said in jest or whether the man actually meant it.

They continued into the entrance hall of the building.

'Will this do? It's probably a little chilly to talk outside, don't you think?'

'Yes, this'll be fine,' said Ottey.

'Augustus John,' stated Cross.

'What about him?' replied Justin, still smiling.

'Interesting character. Would you say his colourful life accounts for his continuing fame, rather than artistic talent?' asked Cross.

'Partly. But he was a great draughtsman and a talented painter.'

'Not in the forefront of twentieth century artists though. Would you agree?'

'Not at all, he was a hugely important artist in his time. Why this interest in him?'

'Oh, I think you know the answer to that, Justin,' replied Ottey.

'I'm afraid you've lost me.'

'The burglary on the night of your mother's murder wasn't the first theft from the house, was it?' asked Cross.

'It's the first successful burglary I'm aware of, Sergeant.'

'I didn't say burglary, Mr Frampton. I said theft,' said Cross, correcting him. 'Burglary generally involves breaking and entering. But you didn't have to break in to steal your parents' Augustus John. So, it's just theft in our book.'

Justin Frampton laughed at this.

'I didn't steal it. I'm afraid you've got your information all wrong. I merely took it to have it valued. I've been constantly badgering my parents to have their collection properly valued. This was one of their most expensive pieces and I wanted it correct for their insurance. It was way out of date, and you know what those companies are like.'

'If you took it just to have it valued, how did you end up selling it?' asked Cross.

'I would've thought that was obvious. The guy had a buyer, a collector who was willing to pay well over the odds. It would've been ridiculous to turn it down.'

'Even though you were selling something that wasn't actually yours,' Cross pointed out.

'I wouldn't put it that way. It belonged to the family.'

'Really? That's a fairly liberal interpretation, isn't it?' he said, turning to Ottey.

He looked back at Justin. 'Does the family home also belong to all of you?'

'Obviously not,' replied Justin, tersely.

'Why didn't you tell your parents about the sale? More to the point, why didn't you give them the proceeds of the sale?'

'They were abroad, in South Africa at the time. The house was being renovated.'

'And yet you didn't tell them when they got back.'

'It slipped my mind. Then, when they discovered it was missing, well, that's when I made my mistake. The truth is, it coincided with a slight cash flow problem I was having. I used the funds to solve the situation, intending to pay it back when things had sorted themselves out. It then became too late to explain, and too awkward to tell them what had happened.'

'Did your parents claim on their insurance for the picture?' asked Ottey.

'Well obviously.'

'Which of course made you guilty not just of theft, but also fraud,' she pointed out.

'No. I put a stop to it as soon as I heard they were making a claim.'

'This cash flow problem. Was it a personal one or business-related?' Cross asked.

'I don't remember.'

'I find that hard to believe,' said Ottey.

'Well, bearing in mind you know nothing about me, that's neither here nor there.'

'Your father was very forgiving,' Cross said.

'Understanding rather than forgiving. He took the view there wasn't anything to forgive.'

'And your mother?'

'Less so.'

Cross turned to Ottey who took it as her cue to take over.

'Why the move from Bristol? With your business?' she began.

'Partly as a result of the pandemic, but also I never really got the footfall I needed in Cotham. The footfall I did get wasn't ideal. I think Bath probably attracts a better sort of clientele for the antiques business.'

'Better off, you mean?' said Ottey.

'If you like, yes.'

'Why not get a shop? I mean, what you have here's more like a stall. Bit of a comedown, isn't it?'

'It's a start. Needs must. Once I've built up my clientele here, which I will, I'll move into new premises. This is a stopgap while I look at what's around. I also have an online business which is where I sell most of my stock now. The things at my house, for example. I sell a lot of that online.'

'Were your mother's jewels insured?' Cross asked.

'What kind of a question is that? Of course they were.

Look, I ought to be getting back. Was there anything else?' he asked irritably.

'You haven't asked why we're here, Mr Frampton?' said Cross.

'I don't need to. I'm not stupid. You've found out about the Augustus John incident, and my parents have just been burgled. Of course it makes sense to talk to me. I can see that. The fact that I was out of the country when she was killed is neither here nor there, apparently. And I'll answer the burning question you seem reluctant to ask. Did I burgle my parents' house? No. Did I murder my mother? No.'

'You must understand why we'd ask,' said Ottey.

'I just said I did, Sergeant.'

'But you've left out one thing. One major factor that might have led us to have an interest in you.'

'Which is?' Justin asked irritably.

'Your gambling.'

There was a moment's hesitation in the antiques dealer.

'That is all in the past, thankfully. I've stopped. I go to gamblers anonymous meetings. I haven't placed a bet in months.'

'And you've paid off all of your past debts?' Cross asked.

'That is part of the recovery process, yes. Now, if that's all, I really must get back. You can see what an old harridan Dorothy is. Don't be fooled by the over-friendly demeanour,' he joked.

'I thought she was far from friendly,' replied Cross. Justin looked at him then handed Ottey a card, turned and left.

As they walked out to the car Ottey was looking at the card. 'He has all the markers of a Walter Mitty confidence man, don't you think?' she asked.

'It's quite a skill. To be that plausible in the face of the facts. To have an outrageously rational reason to counter all arguments. People like that have to come to believe their lies after a while, don't you think?' Cross asked.

'I suppose so.'

Cross looked out at the front of the building as they drove off and saw Dorothy walk out, wrapped up head to toe in fur, lighting a cigarette on the end of a long black and gold cigarette holder. She returned his look and followed it as Ottey pulled away.

'If he took the jewellery it would explain how the alarm was switched off,' she said.

'If he took the jewellery, it wasn't on the night of the murder. He was out of the country,' Cross replied.

'That's true.'

Another dead end.

'George…?'

'Yes.'

'The train set. Give it to your father. He'd be so surprised. It would mean a lot to him,' she said imploringly.

'Really?' he asked, interested that that would be the case.

'Genuinely.'

'Well, I shall give it some thought,' he replied.

32

That weekend Cross stopped by the storage unit where he'd deposited all of his father's excess belongings and memorabilia. Cross was there because Raymond was convinced he had various components for a train set in his stuff, which he'd been meaning to sell before the accident. (He'd tripped over something in the flat and broken his hip.) Raymond had been meaning to do many things with his stuff over the years. But of course they'd never happened. Now, though, with his new-found enthusiasm for building a train set in his spare room, it would come in handy.

'Told you they'd be of some use some day,' he'd said to his son, as if proving a point. Cross remembered seeing railway paraphernalia, including a complete, boxed train set, when he was clearing out the flat. Hornby, he was fairly sure. There were odd signal boxes, models of waiting rooms, ticket machines and platforms. All of Raymond's belongings were sorted in a logical order. There was also an intricate logging system which Edwin 'The Evidence' at work had come up with. So Cross, armed with the log book, found the relevant three boxes in under five minutes. Having found them he didn't leave immediately, because the truth was he wanted to look for something else. He wanted to go through the stuff he'd come across about his parents' early married life. He was sure Raymond didn't know it was there. He would surely have thrown it away if he did.

Cross had discovered a letter from his mother when they were clearing out the flat. It was this letter which had led him to reaching out to her. He felt there was an innate injustice in the way he and his father had been treated by her. This was based on the assumption he'd held all his life, that she had left because of him and his condition. She hadn't been able to cope. This struck him as deeply unfair, particularly since he had grown into the sort of man she could've been proud of. But it wasn't approbation he wanted from her. He wanted nothing from her but to witness how wrong she'd been. This letter had confirmed to him what he'd thought all along. In it she said she couldn't *accept him the way you want me to. He's driven a wedge between us and we now live a life I no longer recognise... If when little George has grown up he wants to find me, let him know I would welcome that.*

Cross had read the letter a few times the day he discovered it and had memorised it. So when he came across it in one of the storage boxes, he didn't need to look at it again. He was mature enough now and sufficiently self-aware to know it couldn't have been easy for her. While in his mind he didn't excuse his mother, he understood the situation. But over the years, in his work, as he'd often witnessed the strong, inextricable bond that existed between a mother and her children, he began to wonder why that hadn't emboldened his own mother to persevere and see it through. Was that what she meant by telling him to find out the truth? He decided to investigate his parents' marriage as he would a case at work. He would need to be clinically detached and open to everything. He'd already put what little he'd found about his mother into a storage box, together with anything else relevant to their marriage. But he needed to go through everything around that time, to get a complete picture.

He'd found their marriage certificate along with his birth certificate – which he'd taken away with him. He saw some photographs of the wedding, but they didn't seem to have had an official wedding photographer. The pictures were quite informal and a little chaotic, which he thought built up a good picture of the day. They'd got married in a small church in Bristol and had their reception in the adjoining church hall. It was a modest affair, but the pictures seemed imbued with fun and jollity. They even had a dance band. There was a group photograph of the happy couple with their parents, bridesmaids and Raymond's best friend, Ron. He was Raymond's colleague at work and had been his friend until his death in the nineties.

He found wage slips, tax forms, bus tickets. Raymond seemed to have kept everything. He knew already that Christine and Raymond had met at the Concorde factory in Filton. She continued to work after they were married, then, a year later, George arrived. He was interested to see that his mother went back to work, when he was three years old. A couple of things occurred to him when he discovered this. Had his mother gone back to work to get away from her troublesome child? Also, did they never discuss having another child? He put together the boxes with his father's train set, and called a taxi.

He delivered the boxes to Raymond but didn't go into the flat as he'd kept the taxi waiting. He did ask him on the doorstep, though, about his mother returning to work. Why had she done that when she had such a small child?

'Well, you were at nursery, and I think she got bored. She liked it at work. She had friends there. At least, that's what she said.'

'What does that mean?' asked Cross, who immediately castigated himself for having preconceptions about the answer. He needed to be clear-headed and objective.

'Nothing,' his father replied. 'We had a childminder who looked after you till she got back from work. It cost her just about all she earned.'

'You didn't contribute?'

'I was paying for everything else.'

'It seems an odd arrangement. I mean, you were married. Didn't you share all the money you earned?'

'Yes. Like I said, I paid for everything else,' Raymond said, deftly avoiding the question, Cross thought.

'What about other children? Did you ever think of having more?' Cross asked. He detected a slight hesitation in his father.

'Not that I recall, no.'

'What is it?' Cross asked directly.

'Nothing. I was just trying to remember. It was so long ago.'

'Did she not want any more?'

'No, it wasn't that.'

Cross decided not to lean any harder on Raymond's obvious discomfort. He thought his father was probably trying to protect him. He spent the rest of the evening in his flat, picking through the evidence of his parents' lives together. Theatre programmes, cinema tickets, restaurant receipts, football tickets, old cheque books with the stubs filled in meticulously, matchbooks from bars. He built up a picture of his parents' relationship. It seemed fun and full. But then, suddenly, it all stopped. The year before she left them, their social life, going out, the fun, all seemed to suddenly end. What had happened? If this were a case at work Cross would have deemed this detail important. The pattern of their lives had been broken. Why?

33

Faye Settle arrived at the MCU a few days later. She was a member of Peggy's conservation group and had been very active against the Chapel development. Mackenzie discovered the group was meeting in a pub that week. She'd gone along as Cross didn't like pubs, mostly because they were too noisy, but also, as someone who rarely drank, the whole exercise seemed pretty pointless. Mackenzie listened in as instructed, worked out who was in charge and had given her a business card. She also formed the view that Faye was probably a close friend of Peggy's. Faye was accompanied to the MCU by a young man called Tom Snape. He was partly dressed in surplus army camouflage and a beanie, from which protruded long dreadlocks. He had earrings that stretched a large hole in his ear lobe. Years ago, Cross remembered, people had gasped in amazement at photographs in *National Geographic* magazines of tribes in Africa or South America, who had large discs inserted in their ear lobes which were several inches in diameter. Now you could see them on any First World high street, urban or rural.

'What do they call those earrings?' Cross started by asking.

'The earrings are called plugs. The process is called gauging,' the young man replied helpfully, with a thick Bristol accent.

'You ever get into trouble because of it?' Cross went on.

'All the time. But that's other people's problem, if they don't like what they see.'

'He's not as frightening as he looks,' interjected Faye good-heartedly.

'Am I not? That's disappointing,' he replied, smiling warmly.

'I was thinking more along the lines of cultural appropriation. Tribal earrings and Rastafarian dreadlocks on a young, middle class, white man, might well fall into that category,' Cross explained.

'Ah, I see what you mean,' Tom answered reasonably. 'Yes, I do, as it happens. But it is what it is.'

'That seems a very un-woke attitude for someone of your generation.'

'Truth of the matter is, we live in a multicultural society. I think we'd all be better off if we just got on with it and borrowed off other cultures when we want. As long as it's respectful, I just don't have a problem with it.'

'You make a sound point,' Cross replied.

'Perhaps we could get on with whatever it is you've asked us in for. I have to say I don't feel this is the friendliest of environments,' said Faye.

'Adam Chapel,' Ottey began. 'Have you ever had any problems with him?'

'Where do you want me to begin?' Faye said, laughing nervously.

'What I mean is, did he ever cross the line?' Ottey went on.

'Of course he did. He's a property developer. These people are practised in the dark arts. There is no line they won't cross when it comes to getting what they want. It's what makes them so successful, if you can call it success,' Faye answered.

'Could you be more specific?'

'He tried bribery at first. Subtly, contributions to various charities Peggy supported. Nothing direct. Then, when it was clear that was never going to work, he moved onto smearing Peggy. Discrediting the group. His initial charm offensives gradually became media campaigns against us. He even took out full-page adverts in the local press,' Faye explained.

'He basically tried to make us out to be a load of local busybodies and nut jobs. Which, to be fair, is about halfway right. Yours truly representing the nut job section of our membership,' said Tom, laughing.

'You have membership?' asked Cross picking up on this.

'No, what I mean by that is our regular members. We're not an organisation as such. We're just a group of committed concerned citizens, holding those in positions of power to account,' said Tom.

'Did Peggy ever feel threatened by anyone during this dispute?' asked Ottey.

Faye thought for a moment then looked up, a little startled. 'Oh my god. Do you think...? I thought it was a burglary gone wrong.' Tom also looked a little shocked.

'I told you, Faye. I told you these people were capable of anything,' he said.

'Do you really believe that?' asked Cross. 'We are talking about murder here.'

'I do,' Tom replied quietly.

'But might that be because you're the type of person who sees a conspiracy in every corner?' asked Cross.

'You'll be asking me if I'm vaccinated next,' said Tom.

'Are you?' said Cross immediately.

'I am. Okay, no bullshit here,' said the young man, as if

doing them a favour. 'A good woman has died. Yes, people call me a conspiracy theorist at times, because they don't like the awkward questions asked. Because they want a quieter life. But sometimes the truth is uncomfortable, and the fact is that while Chapel might be the gleaming white-toothed front of the company, his consigliere is something else.'

'Clive Bland,' said Ottey.

'That's the one. He made threats to all of us, didn't he, Faye? And they weren't particularly subtle.'

'Yes, but we didn't take them very seriously, did we?' said Faye.

'And yet here we are, answering questions about Peggy's death, in a police station,' Tom pointed out. Faye was silenced by this. She looked at the floor and frowned, as if trying to make sense of something.

'I know. I feel dreadful about that now. We all do. But do you really think he would go that far?' she asked.

'We have no idea at present. But it's not something we feel able to rule out just yet,' said Ottey. She turned to Tom. 'We'd appreciate it if you didn't tell anyone outside of this room what's been discussed here. As soon as rumours start swirling round it makes our lives just that bit more difficult and impedes the investigation.'

'I'm sorry, but I feel a little queasy. Could I use your ladies' room?' Faye asked. The colour had indeed drained from her face and she was looking very pale.

'Yes, of course. Why don't I take you?' Ottey said sym–pathetically. 'George, could you get Mrs Settle some water and maybe a couple of biscuits?'

* * *

When Cross returned a couple of minutes later, Tom was sitting forward on the edge of the sofa, as if prepared to say something.

'You need to talk to Faye without me. Maybe the lady officer should do it. Faye and Peggy were tight. I think she may know more than she's letting on. Stuff she doesn't want to say in front of me.' Cross hadn't as yet formed an opinion of the scruffy young activist sitting in front of him, but this made him think the young man was perhaps sensible and considerate. Both pluses in Cross's book. Most people of his type were virulently, irrationally in his opinion, anti-police. But if Tom Snape was, he was hiding it well. Presumably because he wanted them to get to the truth of his friend's murder.

Faye and Tom left the building together, about an hour later. Tom had waited for her while she spoke to Ottey on her own. Ottey came into Cross's office.

'So, things changed between the opposition group and Chapel pretty radically, almost to the day that Mike Rowbottom left,' she began. 'The tone of the dealings between the two of them became unpleasant. Faye said constant threat hung in the air. Chapel seemed to retreat into the background as Bland rose to the fore. Bulky-looking ex-military types started appearing wherever they held their meetings. The group would regularly change the venues for their meetings but these guys would still appear, sitting in the shadows watching them.'

'How did they know where to be?' Cross asked.

'They thought Bland must've got someone to infiltrate the

group. It wouldn't be that difficult, after all. But, before they became paranoid and started looking into everyone who'd joined the group recently, Peggy told them to just ignore it. What did it matter if they knew where they were meeting? It was irrelevant if they knew what their next move was. Then Peggy and Faye started meeting separately from the group, to discuss things they actually didn't want to leak to Bland, and therefore Chapel. They became pretty close, according to Faye. They even went on holiday a couple of times together, just the two of them. Things gradually escalated. Peggy became convinced she was being followed. Kept seeing the same car again and again when she was out. The same men hanging around near her house. Peggy was a strong woman but, according to Faye, this started to wear her down. Faye became concerned about Peggy's mental health. Peggy's car was vandalised. A condolence wreath was delivered by a firm of undertakers. That kind of nonsense.'

'How unimaginative,' said Cross.

'I know, but it seems to have been the final straw for Peggy. You have to remember this was happening at the same time as the breakdown of her marriage. Her worries about Justin. The poor woman had a lot on her plate. She went with Faye to see Chapel about the intimidation. He was appalled by what she said and tried to assure her that none of this had anything to do with his people. Bland was summoned to the meeting and a shocked Chapel relayed everything Peggy and Faye had just told him. Bland was charm itself and promised them that none of this had anything to do with them. They simply weren't that kind of people. He turned to Chapel, apparently, and said that maybe they should take a closer look at those, other than themselves, who stood to gain from the project.'

'Like whom?' asked Cross.

'Contractors, suppliers, et cetera. It was obviously bullshit, but Bland said he'd get right onto it. Then Chapel asked to speak with Peggy privately. Later she told Faye he'd wanted to assure her, face to face, that they would look into it, and if it transpired to be someone within the company, which he very much doubted, they would be instantly dismissed. If it was any of the contractors, he would sever all links with them.'

'Did she believe him?' asked Cross.

'I don't think so. She told him to look closer to home. She basically came straight out with it and said that it was Bland. Of course she didn't have any proof. He told her it just wasn't possible. Meanwhile, Faye's waiting in reception and Bland comes over to her. It's like he's a different person, standing too close to her, almost choking her with his excessive aftershave. He shoved his card at her and said he was sure that he and she could sort the situation out. He knew about her delicate financial situation, just getting by, apparently, and thought they could come to a mutually beneficial arrangement. She refused to take the card. He then stepped even closer to her, she thought maybe so no one could hear, and told her they needed to stop being a pain in the arse and move aside before anyone got hurt.'

Cross thought this through. 'But we have nothing to connect him to Peggy's death.'

'Exactly. Faye did say something else, though. She was a little coy at first, thinking it was personal, and maybe she shouldn't say anything.'

'There's nothing too personal when it comes to murder.'

'Which is what I said. I'm obviously learning from you, George. Faye asked if we knew about Justin's gambling. It caused Peggy an enormous amount of pain. He was playing both parents off against each other and getting money from them, but it became such a problem, even they couldn't bail him out after a while. Bland knew about this. It's an open secret in certain circles in Bristol, thanks to Peggy's profile. Apparently, he still owes a small fortune to various parties.'

'Which is exactly the opposite of what he told us.'

'He's still gambling,' Ottey went on. 'But, as he's barred from most legit outlets, has no credit left for the internet, he's gone over to the dark side. Illegal betting, and we know what they're like if you don't pay up.'

'But how could Bland use that against her?' Cross asked.

'He told Peggy she should be worried in case his debts should get into the wrong hands. But she lost me there.'

'Debts get sold on. Bookies are owed, say, a hundred thousand and they can't get the money whatever they do. Mr Big comes along and offers them thirty pence on the pound for the debt and flashes a briefcase with thirty thousand in it,' said Cross.

'That's a hell of a loss,' said Ottey.

'Needs must and it's not as if it's money the bookie has lent to someone. It's a gambling debt. Thirty thousand is better than nothing,' Cross concluded.

'So, presumably Mr Big manages to enforce payment, and walks away with seventy k at a cost of a few well-aimed threats and maybe a spot of torture,' said Ottey glibly.

Then, as if to seal the deal of a good day's work at the office for the two of them, Mackenzie knocked and came into the office.

'So I did a bit of digging into Clive Bland,' she began. Cross immediately sat up and looked at his actions book, a little worried. 'No, you didn't ask me to. But his name kept coming up and I'm afraid curiosity got the better of me.' Cross couldn't help but sigh and give Ottey a look which said, *Why do I bother?* 'The rumour that he is half Albanian is absolutely true. His father, Dick Bland, is English but married an Albanian lady he met on holiday. She already had family settled in the UK, so moved over and had two children. Both boys. One died in his twenties. I'm not sure how.'

'His mother's maiden name. Do you have it?' asked Cross.

'I do. Somewhere. Here we are. Dragusha,' she said. Cross and Ottey looked at each other. 'That rings a bell,' Mackenzie said.

'Doesn't it just,' replied Ottey. 'George?' she said expectantly.

'What?' came the answer.

'Hasn't Alice done well? Again? Using her initiative?' Ottey explained. Cross looked at her blankly, as if she'd lost her mind. She wrote something on her pad and thrust it across the desk at him.

He read it, sighed, then looked up and said, 'Well done, Alice. Good work.' He turned back to Ottey, only to be faced with the same expectant expression, eyebrows raised expectantly. He looked back at Mackenzie. 'Thank you,' he said.

'Oh, you're welcome. You saying that makes it all the more worthwhile,' she said and left the room. Cross looked back at Ottey.

'Sarcasm?' he asked.

'I think irony, possibly,' Ottey replied.

34

One of Carson's team had already ordered the visitor log sheet for Andi Dragusha from Belmarsh's High Security Unit, but only for the previous six months. Cross now asked them to go back five years and also provide a log of the calls he made out of the prison. Prisoners in the HSU weren't allowed to receive calls, only to make them. Prison officers would monitor these calls to make sure nothing criminal was being planned. Andi Dragusha had several calls a week, mostly to the same number, which turned out to belong to his son Mikki. Andi still managed to have some control over his criminal empire through his son, and Cross surmised they must have formulated quite a sophisticated oral code for communicating with each other over the phone by now.

The visits made more interesting reading. Frampton had been an occasional visitor a few years before. When cross-referenced they corresponded with the last of Dragusha's unsuccessful appeals. But the visits had started again the previous year, amounting to three in all. But as far as Cross could ascertain, he had no new appeal pending. So why was Frampton visiting? The other person of note was Clive Bland. He had been twice in the last six months. When Cross asked Belmarsh to go back the further five years, he discovered that

Bland hadn't visited his uncle once in that period. To Cross this was a clear indication that something had changed. These visits were more interesting than Frampton's, but he couldn't rule out the possibility that they were connected.

Cross and Ottey paid Luke Frampton a visit. This time at his chambers. They were quite different to the ones in Queen Square, modern and functional. Dressed in a well-cut three-piece pinstripe suit, he looked very much like the criminal defence barrister he was. But he seemed unhappy at their presence there.

'I could have come to see you. All you had to do was call,' he began.

'We did. Which is why we're here. As suggested by your clerk,' replied Ottey.

'Does it make you uncomfortable? Us being here?' asked Cross.

'It's never a good look for someone to have the police visit them at their place of work,' replied the lawyer.

'Slightly odd on two counts. First, that you're a criminal barrister, and secondly that we are the detectives looking into your wife's murder. How could that reflect badly on you?' Cross asked.

'Yes, well, what can I do for you?' Frampton replied dismissively. Again, Cross noted, no enquiry as to whether there had been any developments in the case. Not normal, in his experience.

'Andi Dragusha,' Cross stated.

'Yes,' came the blank reply.

'Have you seen him recently? Had any contact with him?' Cross asked.

'That would depend on what your definition of recent is.'

'In the last six months,' said Ottey.

'I can't recall.'

'A few years ago you were quite a regular visitor at Belmarsh,' said Cross.

'That would have been around the time of his last appeal. So yes, I was.'

'An unsuccessful appeal,' Cross pointed out.

'Correct.'

'What's it like working with someone like that?' Cross asked, as if going off topic and asking out of personal curiosity. 'Is he frightening? Intimidating perhaps?'

'Not to me. I'm his barrister.'

'But you must get a sense,' Cross pushed.

'He doesn't frighten me, if that's what you're asking.'

'He's killed seven people.'

'Correct.'

'Even as a detective, I think I'd find that quite intimidating.'

'Perhaps because, as a policeman, your relationship to someone like my client is invariably antagonistic.'

'I try not to be antagonistic with persons of interest in investigations. I find it counterproductive,' Cross replied. Frampton laughed at this.

'I find that hard to believe. But let's compromise and call it combative then,' he said. Cross thought for a moment.

'No, I don't think that does it either,' he said. 'Does he look like a killer? I mean, do you think people who are proved to be killers, look like killers? Is there a killer type?'

'No, I don't. Do you?'

'Cesare Lombroso was convinced of it in the nineteenth century. He had a huge following in the US. They liked what he had to say, especially the eugenicists. They thought that criminality could be managed out of the population. Seems inconceivable now. Does Andi Dragusha look like a killer, Mr Frampton? I mean, if you didn't know who he was, and you were shown a photograph of him, would you say, "killer"?' Cross asked with great interest.

'I would not. Look, I'm actually quite busy this morning.'

'Too busy to talk to the murder detectives investigating your late wife's tragic death?' asked Cross.

'No, of course not, but perhaps you could just ask me what it is you want to know.'

'Why the assumption that we're here to ask questions of you, the victim's husband?' Frampton didn't answer. Cross turned to Ottey. 'What could Mr Frampton here possibly think we needed from him?'

'Beyond me,' said Ottey, quietly enjoying Cross's performance. She often did, she was coming to realise. He was very deft at the curious, slightly unworldly and possibly stupid detective.

'Do you have any links with Dragusha, other than as his client?' asked Cross.

'You know very well I'm in a relationship with his daughter.'

'Has that changed at all since your wife's death?'

'I suppose I have seen a little less of her lately.'

'Because you haven't been in London?'

'That, and out of respect for my wife.'

'The respectful thing might've been not to have an extra-marital affair with her when your wife was alive,' Ottey said. She couldn't help herself, even though she knew it would irritate her partner. Frampton shifted uncomfortably.

'Have you met his son? Her brother?' Cross went on.

'I have.'

'And what's he like?'

'I couldn't tell you. I've only met him once.'

'Are they close? Agnesha and her sibling?'

'No.'

'They don't get on?' asked Ottey.

'Agnesha wants nothing to do with the family business,' said Frampton, as if this was some kind of positive reflection on her.

'Business? That's an interesting way of describing a criminal enterprise,' observed Cross.

'The truth is more likely to be that, as a woman, there wasn't any room for her. Not exactly the most feminist of environments, the Eastern European crime family,' Ottey pointed out.

Cross winced and couldn't help correcting her. 'It's inaccurate to call an Albanian an Eastern European in the modern sense of the word, wouldn't you agree, Mr Frampton?'

'I have no opinion on the matter.'

'Here's what's puzzling me in all of this. Is it not in the least bit awkward, or professionally compromising, for you to be in an intimate relationship with the daughter of a convicted killer? He's your client. Isn't there some sort of professional conflict?'

'He *was* my client,' Frampton corrected him. Cross looked puzzled.

'Really? He's no longer a client?'

'No.'

Cross nodded, as if acknowledging this information was new and might change things. 'So you can't recall visiting him at any time in the last six months, and yet you have. Three times in all. Once, only last month. Just after your wife's death. Perhaps you visit so many prisons, with so many clients, that they all merge into one after a while.' Frampton didn't respond.

'Now that I've pointed that out perhaps you could try and remember what the purpose of those visits was?' Frampton made no answer. 'They weren't professional visits, presumably. As you've just told us, he's no longer your client.'

'What I meant was that I'm no longer retained by him as his barrister.'

'I'm sorry, I'm confused. Is he, or is he not, your client?' Cross asked.

'To an extent, yes,' came the reply.

'To an extent?' Cross repeated, and shook his head as if trying to grasp a very complex concept. 'You'll have to explain that to me,' he went on. 'I'm not well versed in lawyer–client relationships. How is it possible for someone to be someone's client "to an extent"?'

Frampton didn't answer.

'What were those three meetings about?' Cross asked, changing tack a little.

'You know I can't tell you that. Lawyer–client confidentiality,' Frampton replied.

Cross looked at Frampton directly. 'Doesn't that confidentiality apply only to an extent, Mr Frampton?' Ottey smiled. Cross really was funny at times, even though she wasn't sure he always meant to be.

'Maybe it would be better if we asked Mr Dragusha himself,' she said.

'Good luck with that,' said Frampton, before quickly checking himself.

'You know something, Mr Frampton, you're absolutely

right. We do need a little luck in our jobs sometimes, and right now we need all the luck we can get in finding the killer of your wife. Especially if everyone is as unhelpful as you,' said Cross getting up. Frampton was quite taken aback.

'Thank you for your time,' said Ottey.

'You should know Dragusha's not particularly fond of the police,' Frampton said helpfully.

'I've yet to meet a convicted criminal who is,' Ottey replied.

'Why would he worry about us, Mr Frampton? We're simply looking for the killer of his barrister's wife. He can't possibly object to that, and even in the unlikely situation we thought he might've been involved in that murder, his presence in the HSU at Belmarsh rather puts paid to that theory,' said Cross.

'You just don't want to get on that man's radar, Sergeant,' said Frampton.

'Is that a threat?' asked Ottey.

'No. Merely a word of advice.' There was an air of smugness about Frampton as he made this reply. As if he'd regained the upper hand. As if a natural order had been restored. He didn't bother to stand as they went to leave the room. Then Cross stopped and turned.

'Clive Bland,' he stated.

'What about him?' asked Frampton.

'Do you know him?' asked Cross.

'I've never met him,' Frampton replied.

'But do you know him?' Cross repeated.

'I'm aware of who he is.'

'Through your wife's campaign?'

'Yes. I didn't have much to do with Peggy's activities on that front. It was very much her own thing.'

'You didn't ever offer legal advice?'

'I'm a criminal barrister, so planning matters are not my expertise. I did get a colleague more versed in that field to give them legal opinion on a couple of occasions.'

'Peggy thought she was being harassed recently. Did you know that?'

'No.'

'She never shared that with you?'

'No,' came the reply, which Cross didn't believe for a minute.

'Did you know that Andi Dragusha is Clive Bland's uncle?' Cross asked. Frampton seemed unsettled by this. His face tensed as the blood drained from it.

'Bland?' was all he could mutter.

'Powerful man to have as an uncle, wouldn't you say?' asked Cross before he left. Frampton sat in his chair, looking slightly stunned.

35

Ottey picked Cross up at six thirty the next day. To her surprise, as she parked outside his front door and waited, he appeared from Tony's café.

'Gosh, he opens early,' she said as Cross got into the car.

'Oh, he isn't open. He doesn't open till seven. But when I told him yesterday that I wouldn't be in this morning, because you were picking me up at six thirty, he told me to knock on his door at six, and he'd make me breakfast. Here, this is for you,' he said, handing her a greaseproof bag. 'It's a fried egg and bacon sandwich on brown toast.'

'George, that's so thoughtful of you,' she said, quite touched.

'Nothing to do with me. Tony just gave it to me for you when I was leaving,' Cross said. She smiled. Classic Cross. Tell it as it is, even if it means not taking credit for something you hadn't done, but could have got away with and scored points. How kind of Tony not only to open for Cross, but to think of her as well. It was amazing how people so often put themselves out for Cross, without being asked. Maybe it was because he would never think of asking that encouraged people to do it. He was one of those people in life you knew wouldn't take advantage of anyone.

She'd picked Cross up early because she wanted to do the return journey in as much daylight as possible. Belmarsh was in south-east London, in an area called Thamesmead. It was a schlep from central London, let alone Bristol, from which it was a three-hour drive at least, depending on traffic. Initially when Ottey went on long trips with Cross, she'd been offended by the silence of her front-seat passenger. How could someone in such close proximity to her be silent for so long without feeling in the least bit awkward? She'd be infuriated with herself for her constant, unsuccessful attempts at instigating a conversation. But over time she'd realised that the silence actually had its benefits. She knew Cross was using his time in the car to go over the case microscopically and repeatedly, in a way no one else did, or could do. He would ask occasional questions when he needed to. She came to appreciate the silence. It almost became an oasis of calm, a rare moment of peace for a working mother of two. She was able to sort things out in her head; either problems at work, or teenage crises at home. It also had to be said that, when compared to what some of her previous colleagues considered 'banter', Cross's reticence was positively luxurious. The fact was that Cross was good at many things, but small talk and non-work-related conversation were not two of them. The other benefit, which couldn't be dismissed in a rush, was that Cross, unlike every single one of her male colleagues, was not a back-seat driver. This was an enormous plus in her book. What was it with men and their firmly held belief that their driving talents were so god-given that a mere woman couldn't even begin to comprehend them? That is when they actually deigned to let her drive, which wasn't often. This normally occurred on 'morning after' occasions, when they attempted to articulate through a sickly haze of stale alcohol. This was always accompanied by the steady soundtrack of crunching Polo mints. They were worried they might be over the limit and the prospect of being driven by a woman was better than losing their licence and possibly their job.

Cross never had any driving tips or alternative navigational advice to offer.

She stayed south of the river that morning and obviously avoided central London. Their journey was made a little longer by a diversion that Cross had insisted they make to the northside of Clapham Common in south London. He felt that they needed as much up their sleeve as possible when visiting Dragusha. Not so much leverage, as insider knowledge. The Belmarsh inmate had nothing to lose by not giving them anything. He could just sit there and bask in the knowledge that he had made two detectives waste the best part of seven hours in a car, for nothing. So they were going to pay Agnesha Dragusha a visit. She lived in a grand building on the north side of Clapham Common. Built in 1860, the imposing terrace originally consisted of five six-storeyed houses that were famed for having fifty-foot-long drawing rooms. They were built originally to rival Kensington and Chelsea. Book-ended by two French-style turrets, it still looked grand even though it was now divided into flats. Agnesha's apartment took up the entirety of one of the turrets. It was a two-floor duplex and had to have been worth over a couple of million pounds, in Cross's estimation.

Agnesha answered the video door entry herself, but was unwilling to let them up into the flat. She obviously got the sense, though, which Cross always managed to impart with silent efficiency, that he wasn't going to leave until she'd talked to them. They then had to wait a full fifteen minutes before she finally made her appearance. She had obviously been on the phone, as a short time into their wait Ottey received a call from Luke Frampton, which she declined. From the look of her when she finally made it out of the door, she'd also spent a fair amount of time doing her make-up. She was wearing designer tracksuit bottoms and top, with a leather jacket thrown over. Black Ugg boots on her feet. She was undoubtedly a beauty, with dark hair and almost black eyes. But she was also one of those young girls who thought they could be even more beautiful with a little help. Collagen in her lips, Botox in her lineless forehead. The kind of things that made her face look like it had a permanent Instagram filter on it. But the fact that she had come out at all told Cross she had things to say. He had fully expected it to be a wasted diversion and thought Frampton must have told her he would make them go away. But Ottey hadn't taken his call. Agnesha didn't have to come down from her ivory tower. They had no warrant. They couldn't make her speak to them, yet here she was.

There was a communal garden across the private road outside the building, which she took them over to. She indicated they should sit on some ornate cast-iron chairs near a rhododendron bush. It wouldn't be too long till it was in flower, Cross thought. As it was still winter the seat cushions had been stored somewhere, which meant the seats were fantastically uncomfortable, whichever way the detectives tried to organise their buttocks.

'What do you want?' the young woman began irritably.

'We're investigating Peggy Frampton's murder. But you know that already,' answered Ottey.

'So what's that got to do with me?' she said in perfect

English, with the accent of a privately educated young London woman.

'Is that a genuine question?' asked Cross.

'It's nothing to do with me. I know nothing about it.'

'We know that,' said Ottey, causing Cross to give her a reflex look, as they knew nothing of the sort.

'I'll come straight to the point. What does your father think of your relationship with Luke?' Ottey went on. The young woman wasn't expecting this.

'He only just found out,' she replied.

'Really?'

'Yes. We've been very discreet.'

'His being incarcerated can only have helped,' added Cross unhelpfully.

'When did he find out?' asked Ottey.

'About three months ago.'

Which was around the time of Frampton's first visit to Belmarsh.

'How did he take it?' Ottey went on. Agnesha didn't answer. 'Was he unhappy? Is that why he summoned Luke to the prison?'

'Yes.'

'What happened?'

'He told him to end it. Luke refused.'

'Are you frightened, Ms Dragusha?' Cross asked.

She laughed nervously. 'I shouldn't even be talking to you.'

'How do you and your father get on?' asked Ottey.

'How does anyone get on with someone like that?'

'But you're his daughter,' said Cross, doing his best to understand.

Then she just opened up. It sounded like it was a relief for her to be able to talk. 'I didn't even know what he did for a living, if you can call it that, until my teens. Can you believe that?'

'Yes, I can.'

'I just thought I had a normal dad, who worked really hard at his normal job. Until I found out the truth, I grew up thinking the problem was with me. Other kids didn't like me, no matter what I did. No one wanted to be my friend. Do you know how hard that is?'

'Actually, I do,' said Cross.

'Other kids knew the truth about my father, and when one of them told me I didn't believe him. We had a terrible fight. Our parents were called in. My dad said it was all untrue. That he worked hard in the city. In financials with some Albanian bank. It all sounded perfectly plausible to me. But there was one thing that puzzled me. The boy's father, the one I'd had a fight with, looked terrified throughout the meeting. Absolutely shit-scared, couldn't look at my dad, and kept apologising, telling him it wouldn't happen again.'

They said nothing for a while.

'Would you want to be friends with a girl who's driven to school in an armoured car by a couple of bodyguards? All the kids were scared.'

'As were the parents, by the sound of it,' suggested Ottey.

'Exactly. But I didn't know that. It messed with my head completely. I have so many issues from all that, to this day.'

'Was he a good father to you, though, despite all that?' asked Cross.

'He was never there. He was often away all night, which meant huge rows with my mum the next day. He'd not be around for months then mysteriously reappear around my birthday. He gave me a big party for my tenth. Kept calling it the "big one zero". No one came. Not one child. So what did he do? He sent a couple of his goons to go round the neighbours, persuading them to let their kids come to the party. They bribed them with Gameboys. Can you believe that?'

'He knew it was going to happen,' said Cross.

'How d'you know that?' she asked.

'Because he'd bought the Gameboys for such an eventuality,' he replied. She thought about this for a moment.

'Oh my god, you're so right. It never even occurred to me. Thank you for adding another layer of pain to the memory, mate,' she laughed. 'I'm like everything else he has. A possession. He owns me, or at least he thinks he does.'

'What about your mother?' Ottey asked, annoying Cross as he already knew the answer, and thought Ottey's ignorance of it showed them in a bad light.

'Dead. Cancer,' she replied.

'I'm sorry.'

'Oh, it was a long time ago. But it made my dad even more protective of me, as he called it. The truth was he just became even more possessive. I can't do anything, see anyone, go anywhere, without him knowing.'

'But he's in Belmarsh,' Ottey replied.

'And I might as well be too,' she said. Then she looked over the road where a black Range Rover, with tinted windows, had just pulled up. Two men wearing suits, with open white shirts, got out. They then stood, clasping their hands together before them, staring at the group at the garden.

'And here they are,' she sighed, looking up at her building.

'My brother has to have someone in there on the payroll. Mikki's muscle, I call them.'

'Has your father told Mikki to keep his eyes on you?' asked Cross.

'What do you think? Every time Luke comes round, they appear and frighten him off. When I got on a train to Bristol once, to go and see him, one of them actually got on the train. So there was no point in me going. God, I hate my life right now.'

'Maybe it would be better just to call it off?' suggested Ottey, whose gut told her this relationship didn't have the makings of a long runner anyway.

'Now you sound just like my aunt,' came the reply.

'Would that be Clive Bland's mother?'

'Yes. But what would be the point of that? Nothing would change. It would all be the same. No one will ever be good enough for me, that my father hasn't chosen. My marriage has to be of use to the family.'

'How?' asked Ottey.

'In the shape of some kind of alliance.'

'An arranged marriage?' said Cross.

Another car now pulled up; a black limousine with tinted windows. One of the guys standing beside the Range Rover walked over and opened the rear door. A man in his thirties stepped out. He had thick blond wavy hair, and a suntan. He was wearing crisp jeans, starched white shirt and a classic blue blazer, with a pair of aviator sunglasses, which the overcast day certainly didn't warrant. He waved cheerfully at the three of them then flashed a very expensive white smile.

'Agnesha! Hi,' he shouted.

'I do not, I repeat, I do not want to go with him,' she said quietly.

Mikki came close and kissed her on both cheeks.

'I'm a little busy at the moment, Mikki. As you can see, I have friends here,' said Agnesha.

'Oh, I'm sure they'll understand, won't you, DS Ottey and Cross?' he said, with a threatening emphasis on their names. He took his sister by the wrist and placed his other hand firmly in the small of her back, guiding her forcefully away.

'Actually, we were in the middle of a conversation which we'd like to finish,' said Ottey, who began to walk after them, before Mikki's muscle stepped in her way. She decided not to press the point as their interview with Dragusha later could suddenly find itself cancelled. Cross noticed the neck tattoo on one of them. They were the same men who had paid Justin a visit at the funeral.

'Give my love to Dad!' he called over his shoulder.

36

HMP Belmarsh stood in sixty-four acres on part of the old Woolwich Arsenal site. It was next door to Woolwich Crown Court but felt like it was in the middle of nowhere, despite nearby housing and a dual carriageway. Opened only twenty years earlier, it already had the reputation of being one of Britain's toughest prisons. It housed just under a thousand prisoners, some of whom were Britain's most notorious criminals: from terrorists and murderers to paedophiles, rapists, burglars and fraudsters. It was surrounded by a one point three mile, twenty-foot-high perimeter wall, topped with razor wire. No one had escaped from the prison since it had been in operation, and certainly not from the section Cross and Ottey were headed to. The high security unit was effectively a prison within a prison, with its own perimeter wall. It was a two-storey structure with four spurs, each containing twelve single-occupancy cells.

Security at the prison was predictably tight. At the main prison reception Cross and Ottey had to go through airport-type security, with body scanners, their belongings going through another. They were then patted down and sniffed by a pair of dogs. By the time they got to the golf buggy that was going to take them to the HSU, they had been through at least a dozen locked gates. The clanking of keys really was a constant soundtrack in prison, Cross reflected. They were driven through the prison grounds and Cross was quite glad for the burst of fresh air it provided. When they reached the HSU they were taken into another reception area. The first thing Cross noticed was how hot and stuffy it was in there. They were then subjected to another airport security-style check, another sniffer dog and, for good measure, another pat down. Their belongings were put into a locker and they were then made to wait at a final gate for at least five minutes, while staff in the control room checked their credentials.

'Blimey, he'd better be worth it,' said Ottey who, despite her best efforts, found herself inexplicably nervous. Her pulse was racing. How could such a nondescript utilitarian building like this be quite so intimidating? Cross didn't reply. He was finding the whole experience alarming. He wasn't generally a claustrophobe, but as a rule he liked to be in control of every aspect of his life, which included the ability to open any exit door. This many locked gates behind him were definitely imbuing a sense of unease in him. Added to this, the fact that the HSU was like a two-thirds scaled-down model of a normal-sized prison gave it an unrelenting sense of restriction and lack of space. It was also unbearably hot. The prison officers were all dressed appropriately in shirtsleeves, unlike Cross and Ottey in their winter clothing.

They were escorted into a room with two chairs facing a glass panel, on the other side of which was another empty plain room. After a few minutes a couple of prison guards entered followed by the prisoner himself, dressed in grey prison jogging bottoms and just a T-shirt, thanks to the oppressive heat. He didn't look at all threatening. He had a thick head of white hair. So thick it looked as if it was just sitting on top of his skull, like an ill-fitting wig. Cross was staring at it, trying to figure the hair out. But the overall impression was of someone quite ordinary. Someone who could have been a baker, or butcher, a builder or plumber, who worked with his hands, which Cross had also observed were huge. But nothing about him shouted head of a crime family, killer of seven men – seven, that is, known to the authorities. There was something about his eyes, though. They were light grey, so light as to be almost colourless. As lifeless as the clouded eyes of a recently deceased person. Chillingly so. It was as if he had cataracts, which they knew he didn't. He looked at the two police officers in a completely disinterested way.

'Thank you for seeing us, Mr Dragusha,' Ottey began. He made no reply, just fixed her with an expressionless gaze.

'I expect you're curious as to why we're here,' she went on. He took his time to answer.

'I don't care. It makes for a break in the day, even if it's to see two country bumpkin plods. You look hot.' He glanced at Cross who was in fact thinking about Dragusha's accented familiarity with the English vernacular. 'So have at it. I'm all ears.'

'We're investigating the murder of Peggy Frampton,' Ottey continued. He shrugged his lack of interest.

'She was a well-known figure in Bristol, so you could be forgiven for not knowing of her. But as she was your barrister's wife, I'm sure you know exactly who I'm talking about.'

At this he raised his eyebrows in a flicker of surprise.

'You knew she'd been murdered, surely?'

'I did not,' came the reply.

'He didn't mention it on his last visit?'

'He did not.'

'That seems strange,' Ottey said, as if thinking aloud.

'He's very professional, Mr Frampton. Doesn't bring his personal business to the table.'

'Then what was the purpose of his visit?' Ottey asked. He didn't answer but looked at Cross who hadn't spoken yet.

'You've run out of appeals,' Ottey pointed out. Again, no response. 'So why was your barrister here?'

'You'd have to ask him,' said Dragusha. He obviously knew they already had, but Ottey wasn't about to give him the pleasure of telling him so. Dragusha exuded an innate calm, as if he had all the time in the world. Which in a sense he did. He wasn't going anywhere. Didn't have things to do. He turned to Cross.

'How is your father?' he asked. Cross decided not to play Dragusha's game and didn't answer. 'Has he recovered from his fall?' Again, Cross didn't answer. Dragusha turned back to Ottey. 'And your daughters?'

'Mr Dragusha, you're not the first person in your situation to have had people research us and our families. But you're wasting your time. We're neither surprised, nor particularly bothered. But one thing it makes me wonder is, why you went to the trouble?'

'It was no trouble,' he answered.

'Why would you feel the need to threaten us?' she asked.

'What is it with the English? How can you think a polite enquiry is a threat? I simply like to know about the people who come and visit me. After all, you know a lot about me, so why shouldn't I know a little something about you? I thought it might give us something to talk about, as there's really nothing else for us to discuss. I have no idea why you're here.'

'I've already told you why.'

'Then you've wasted a trip. I know nothing of this poor woman's murder and if I did I'd tell you. After all, I might get something out of it.'

'As you seem to like discussing family, why don't we discuss yours? Clive Bland,' Ottey went on. Dragusha's face seemed to light up, genuinely, at the mention of his nephew's name.

'Clivey-boy, we're very proud of him. Every family has a black sheep but he's our white sheep. He's done so well, doing so well.'

'Why didn't he join the family business?' Ottey asked. But Dragusha was looking at Cross.

'Does this one not speak?' he asked. Neither Ottey nor Cross replied. She knew Cross had made a choice. Why, she wasn't sure. But it was always interesting to see how these things played out.

'Clive,' she said, bringing him back on track. He continued to look at Cross for a moment, before looking back at Ottey.

'It's not compulsory. To join the family,' he replied.

'Was it something to do with his brother's death?'

He thought about this for a moment, then looked at her as if this hadn't occurred to him before. 'Yes, that might be why.'

'He visited you recently.'

'He did.'

'Why?'

'He wanted to see me. How else is that going to happen unless he comes here? Or did you expect me to book a table at the Ritz?'

'What did he want?'

'He didn't want anything.'

'So, what did you want?'

'He's family. Why should either of us want anything?'

'That was his first visit to you in prison. In five years no visits. So why now, all of a sudden?'

'I was sixty recently. He came to pay his respects. It's a tradition. Check the visitors' log and you'll see they've all been in. Cousins, nephews, nieces, children, they've all been in.'

'Except for one.' Cross spoke for the first time. Dragusha turned to him. 'Your daughter. She hasn't been in. Not once since you've been in prison. Why is that?'

'This is no place for a young woman. I don't want her here,' he said defensively.

'Maybe she's just too busy with her new beau,' said Cross suddenly. 'Sixty? So that makes you younger than Luke Frampton. By at least eight years.'

Dragusha gave nothing away.

'What's that like? Your daughter, beautiful young Agnesha, your most perfect creation, your special, precious girl, having an affair with an older man? A man older than her own father. Isn't that a little – I don't know how to describe it, I don't have children – but isn't it a little strange? Uncomfortable perhaps?'

Again, no answer. Just an inscrutable stare from the other side of the glass.

'Maybe that's what you want for her though. What you had planned all long. Your daughter sleeping with a man who's almost seventy.'

Dragusha suddenly slammed his fist on the desk in front of him. One of the guards behind him said something. He settled into the back of his chair again. Cross continued as if nothing had happened.

'Is that why you asked Luke Frampton to come in and see you? To ask him, tell him to stop? It seems completely proper to me. Mr Frampton's behaviour strikes me as, at the very least, unprofessional. How about you, DS Ottey?'

'It crosses a line, definitely,' she replied.

'Have you thought of reporting him to the Bar?' Cross asked.

'He's no longer my barrister,' said Dragusha.

'But you have considered it, or discussed it with him? Was the relationship ongoing during the time he was representing you?' Dragusha didn't reply. But Cross was satisfied that he was getting gradually wound up, so he continued to press. 'Not only is he older but he's also married. Well, was married.'

'So maybe you should be looking at him,' Dragusha said. Cross thought about this for a moment, just long enough to make the Albanian suspect he might be being played by this strange cop.

'You think he might have killed his wife, so he could be with your daughter?' Cross looked at Ottey as if this wasn't something they'd considered. 'It would make a lot more sense than you, I suppose.'

Dragusha laughed a great bellow of a laugh. 'Why would I have his wife killed? That would set him free. How would it benefit me?'

Cross thought about this for a moment then looked at Ottey.

'Have we got this wrong?' He turned back to Dragusha. 'You actually want your daughter to be with Frampton. You can presumably have people killed even though you're in the most secure prison in the UK. You had her killed so your daughter could have what she wanted.' Cross looked at the floor, trying to work out how he could have been so stupid not to have thought of it. 'We've been looking at this the wrong way round.'

Another bellow of a laugh. 'Are you having fun with me, or are you just stupid? Of course I don't want her to be with that old fuck. Like you said, he's older than me!'

'It's no wonder she's terrified of you. Such a shame. Lovely young woman. We saw her on our way here. We thought she'd refuse to see us but no, she was very happy to talk.' Dragusha didn't take the bait. 'Absolutely terrified and resentful. She feels imprisoned by you, which is a trifle ironic, considering where you currently reside.'

'You saw her?' Dragusha asked quietly.

'We did,' replied Cross.

'How was she?'

'Unhappy, Mr Dragusha. Beautiful and unhappy. And I think we both know whose fault that is. But you know all this. You keep your tabs firmly on her, through her brother Mikki.'

Cross stopped for a moment. 'Did you try and persuade Luke Frampton to break things off with your daughter? Is that why he was here?'

'Of course,' Dragusha replied, perhaps seeing no good reason not to answer truthfully. 'What father wouldn't? She'll spend the best years of her life being a carer for him. What father would want that for his daughter?'

'Which brings us back to Clive. Here's the thing. Most detectives will tell you the same thing the world over. They don't believe in coincidence. You must know that from all of your many court appearances. I've read the transcripts. Fascinating stuff. Took me an entire weekend to read, and I do have some questions for you, which I've made a note of. But that will have to wait for another time. Maybe I could arrange another visit and we could have a chat?' Dragusha looked at Ottey with an expression she was now familiar with, from her witnessing many first-time interlocutors with Cross. He was trying to make sense of what was going on in front of him.

'I'd have to come on the train,' Cross continued, oblivious to this as he attempted to work out the logistics of his next visit to Belmarsh. 'So, we'd probably best aim for mid-afternoon, if that suits? The train journey will also give me an opportunity to get my queries in order. Now where was I?' he asked Ottey, who duly played her part.

'Coincidence,' she said.

'Ah yes, coincidence. So, Clive, your nephew, is the COO of a company that has been in dispute with Luke Frampton's late wife at a cost, to them, of millions. Clive pays you a visit, the first in the three years since your incarceration, then shortly after, Peggy is murdered. Could it be that he wanted to use your unique, how shall I put it, skillset to persuade Peggy to back off, and it all went horribly wrong?'

Dragusha said nothing but stared at Cross blankly. Cross returned the glare, unblinkingly. He then stood up, indicating the meeting was over. Ottey went to the back of the room and pressed a button by the door.

'As for Agnesha, I think she's looking for a father figure in her lover,' Cross continued, staring straight at Dragusha. 'A figure not to replace one that she's lost but to fill the void of one she's never had. But more importantly, Luke Frampton gives her something you never could. Still can't. Particularly from in here. Even if you had it in you.'

Cross stopped for a moment and studied Dragusha, who he knew was now sitting with every tendon and ligament in his body tensed to breaking point. Before he finally lit the fuse.

'Love,' Cross said quietly. The convict leapt up, knocking his chair backwards across the other room into the wall, and flew into a psychotic rage, banging his fists against the safety glass, shouting obscenities in Albanian, spittle hitting the window. His eyes suddenly came alive, for the first time, with a fiery anger, bulging and becoming bloodshot. His face was inches from Cross's, who just stood there looking at this blur of wild, manic thrashing around in front of him. Several prison officers ran into the other room and forced Dragusha to the ground. He looked up at Cross as the side of his face was pressed to the floor. His expression was distorted but even so, unmistakably threatening. Cross seemed completely unmoved, unlike Ottey who was leaning against the back wall, stunned by the violence of the outburst they'd just witnessed.

37

Cross had found another stash of Raymond's photos in one of his father's storage boxes and was going through them that Saturday back at his flat. The most interesting bunch were photographs of him with his mother. They seemed to have been taken on various trips around the country. Brighton, with the pier in the background. London, on the river somewhere. What occurred to Cross was that the majority of the photographs had been taken by professional street photographers, who still plied their trade in the 1970s, around famous landmarks or beaches, taking pictures of tourists and holidaymakers. His father had always been a keen amateur photographer, so he was surprised at the number taken by these strangers. Going through the albums Raymond had actually compiled, it was clear where his interests lay; in feats of British engineering, Isambard Kingdom Brunel in particular, not his family. He had taken a number of unsmiling Cross as a child. The fact that he hadn't taken these holiday snaps, and wasn't in them, meant only one thing. He wasn't with them on these trips. Presumably he was busy at work. He freely admitted that his work at Filton, the aircraft factory where his parents had met, had been all-consuming. The other thing that struck Cross, looking at the pictures of him and his mother, was how happy she looked. Him not so much. He had the identical, taciturn frown chiselled into his features in every picture. But Christine didn't look like someone who was annoyed with her child, or at the end of her parental tether, as Raymond had often described her. These were mementoes of happy occasions for her. Cross realised he'd never seen these pictures before. In fact, now that he put his mind to it, he couldn't recall ever seeing one of him and his mother before now. It had never occurred to him to ask his father if any existed. For Cross she had left and simply didn't exist in his life.

He was putting the photographs back into the box when he saw that one of them had another, stuck to its back. The photograph on top was of him and his mother in Brighton, on the beach this time. Christine was helpless with laughter as a disconcerted four-year-old Cross looked in horror at a parrot perched on his outstretched arm, flapping its wings, as if trying to escape. He peeled off the photograph that was stuck to the back of it. It was a photograph of Raymond with his best mate from work, Ron, or Uncle Ron as Cross had always known him, until, that is, the moment he discovered Ron wasn't in fact an uncle at all, and so refused to address him as such. According to the seven-year-old Cross it was an 'inaccurate description of our relationship'. The photograph was of the two men in front of Blackpool tower. Raymond had dated the back *September 9th, 1972*. Cross would've been four, but something seemed familiar about the date. He went back through the photographs and found the one of him and his mother in Trafalgar Square. On the back was the same date, 9th September, 1972. So his father wasn't working that weekend. He and Uncle Ron were in Blackpool. Maybe it was work. A conference? A meeting with a supplier? He would ask his father.

38

It was Sasha Connor who opened the door of her father's home on Sion Hill to Cross and Ottey. She looked disappointed when she saw the two police officers.

'Detectives, I was expecting my husband and children.'

'Is your father at home?' Ottey asked.

'Yes, he's upstairs,' she said, moving aside to let them in.

'Day off for you?' Ottey continued.

'We're sorting through my mum's things. Well, her clothes mostly. So, I've taken some time off as it'll never get done if he's left to do it on his own.' They followed her upstairs to the master bedroom. Luke was sitting in the middle of a Stonehenge circle of black bin liners.

'Ah, hello,' he said as they walked in. He pointed to three different groups of bin bags and announced, unprompted, 'Sasha, charity shops, recycling.'

'Making room for someone else?' Cross asked, with such a lack of tact that even Ottey looked surprised.

'I beg your pardon?' Frampton replied.

'I rather got the impression that your relationship with Agnesha might now progress to one of a more permanent nature, now that it's no longer an extramarital affair, thanks to your wife's death.'

Frampton stood up as if to emphasise his outrage.

'I am packing up my late wife's, my murdered wife's, clothing and you have the nerve to ask me that?'

Ottey stepped in before Cross went any further. But even she couldn't quite help herself from calling it as it was.

'I think in the circumstances your indignation is a little rich, Mr Frampton. You were, after all, in a relationship with another woman at the time of your wife's death and let's be frank, it wasn't the first.'

'They have a point, Dad. Get off your bloody high horse. It has glass legs,' said Sasha.

'Oh, don't start,' her father said irritably. 'What do you want?' he asked Cross.

'Again, your first instinct is to ask what we want. Not whether there have been developments, or any news in the case,' Cross observed. There was no response to this. 'You neglected to tell us that Andi Dragusha didn't approve of your relationship with his daughter.'

'Well, that's one way of putting it,' added Ottey.

'You didn't ask,' came the terse reply.

'She's a very beautiful woman, Agnesha, but deeply unhappy,' said Ottey. 'With that in mind, some people might look on your relationship as being purely exploitative. She's very vulnerable and in her words "imprisoned". You're so much older than her. One could ask the question – what is it she sees in you?' Ottey continued to try and push his buttons.

'Why did you visit her? You need to leave her alone,' said Frampton.

'Because we're investigating your wife's murder,' Cross pointed out.

'Don't be facetious,' snarled Frampton.

'Oh, he's not. He couldn't if he tried. What you see is what you get with DS Cross, Mr Frampton, but what I'm seeing in front of me now, is a worried man,' said Ottey, trying to bring the conversation back on track.

'If her father finds out the police talked to her…' Frampton trailed off.

'He knows,' said Cross.

'How?' asked an increasingly panicked Frampton.

'I told him,' Cross explained helpfully.

'What! Why?'

'It just came up in our conversation.'

Frampton thought about this for a moment. 'How was she?' he then said.

'Difficult to say, as our conversation was cut short by her brother and his muscle, as she called them, taking her away,' said Ottey.

'Mikki…' the lawyer said under his breath. 'You have no idea who you're dealing with.'

'Then perhaps you could enlighten us,' suggested Cross.

'I can't get hold of her. She's not in her flat. She's not taking my calls and now I know why.'

'You've been trying to get in touch with her?' asked Sasha in disbelief.

'Sasha, please,' he pleaded.

'You're unbelievable. I'm sorry, but I don't want to hear any more of this bleating,' she said and left the room. But Cross heard her footsteps stop about two-thirds of the way down the stairs. She might not want to be in the room, but she wanted to hear what was said, nevertheless.

'Have you had any dealings with Mikki?' asked Cross.

'Rather too many.'

'Why?'

'Why do you think?'

'He shares his father's disapproval?' asked Cross.

'I've no idea. It seems to me he just does what he's told. His father still exerts a huge amount of influence in the outside world.'

'Has he made any threats, directly or otherwise, against you and your family?'

'No,' he said after a moment's hesitation.

'What was your meeting with him, in the weeks prior to Peggy's death, about?' asked Ottey.

'As I keep telling you,' he said, exasperated. 'I can't say. I am governed by lawyer–client confidentiality.'

'Let's not go down that path again,' suggested Ottey.

'Mr Frampton, do you think it's possible that Andi Dragusha was involved in your wife's murder?' asked Cross.

'How exactly would that make any sense, Sergeant? If he wanted me to stay away from Aggy, how would killing my wife be to his advantage? Clearing out the main obstacle to my being with her?' Frampton pointed out.

Cross reflected that this was the second time someone had referred to Peggy Frampton as an 'obstacle'.

'Interestingly, that's exactly what Dragusha said,' remarked Cross.

'Well, there you are then. Frankly, if this is as far as you've got, I'm not exactly confident that my wife's murder will ever be solved.'

'What exactly has he said to you in reference to your relationship with his daughter?' Cross went on.

'He's asked me to end it.'

'And your reply?'

'I told him I loved her and had her best interests at heart.'

'His reaction?'

Frampton seemed conflicted as to whether to reply. Was it because he was already worrying about what had happened to Agnesha?

'He said that if I didn't end it, he would.'

'And now you can't find her, nor make contact with her,' Cross summed up out loud.

'Correct.'

'You need to tell us whatever it is you're holding back, Mr Frampton. Before things get worse,' Ottey said.

'My wife's been murdered. How could things get any worse?'

'That's for you to tell us,' said Ottey. 'Like I said, the sooner the better.'

'You don't think he'd hurt his own daughter, do you?' Frampton asked.

By the time they decided to leave, Frampton looked like someone who had the weight of the world on his shoulders. Cross turned back at the door.

'Your wife's jewellery,' he said.

'What about it?'

'You haven't asked about it. Not once since you reported it missing have you asked how the search for it is going.'

'Well, maybe I have a little more on my mind like my wife's recent murder than a piece of family jewellery, Sergeant,' Frampton replied.

Cross thought about the merits of this answer for a second. 'Unless…'

'Unless what?'

'You're not asking because you know it's a pointless question,' he replied.

Sasha showed them to the front door.

'Sasha, I don't want to alarm you, but just be careful,' Ottey said. 'With everything going on, take extra care of yourself.'

'You don't think I'm in any danger, do you?'

'I'm pretty sure you're not. But you can never be too careful, okay?' She gave the young woman her card.

'He has no idea how ridiculous he looks. She's seven years younger than me, for God's sake.'

'Does that make it more difficult for you?' asked Cross with genuine interest.

'It makes it well weirder.'

'Justin not helping you today?' asked Ottey.

'No, thank goodness. He'd be more of a hindrance than a help.'

'Why's that?'

'He just walks round the house spotting potential items to sell. It's a nightmare.'

The two police officers left. But for Cross this was the most interesting thing anyone had said that morning.

'He's frightened,' said Ottey as they got into the car.

'More conflicted than frightened. Worried maybe,' Cross suggested.

'He's keeping something back.'

'As you made abundantly clear.'

'Is that a criticism?'

'No. Merely an observation. MCU,' he instructed.

'Oh. Okay. Let me just put the meter back on.'

He looked at her, not knowing what she was talking about. They didn't have a meter. This was a police car. This often happened. His not understanding her when she spoke. He'd asked her about it once and she'd explained that what she had just said, which he didn't understand, was a joke. So he assumed on this occasion that it must have been one of her 'jokes', albeit one unfathomable to him. Unfathomable and therefore unfunny, he reassured himself.

39

M ark Coombes was sitting in reception, waiting for Cross, when they got back. He was holding a manila envelope file.

'DS Cross,' Coombes said, cheerfully, holding out his hand.

'Mr Coombes,' Cross replied.

Coombes withdrew his unwelcome hand. 'I spoke with Janette a couple of days ago. She remembered she had a file on Chapel's Harbourside development. She brought loads of stuff back during the pandemic, when she was working from home. She thought it might be useful. So, I dug it out.' He held the file out for Cross.

'Did you organise a time for us to call her?' Cross asked, taking it from him.

'You know what, I did ask, but she said she was about to go on a five-day fast at some hippy-type spa in Malaya. They have to give themselves self-administered enemas. Can you believe that? So, she's incommunicado for a little while. No human contact allowed, apparently. First I'd heard about it. Anyway, I'll chase her next time,' Coombes assured him, eagerly.

'If you would,' Cross said and turned to go.

'Did you know Clive Bland has links with an Albanian

crime family, by the way? That is to say, they *are* his family,' Coombes called after him. Cross turned back.

'We did,' he replied.

'From what I've read in that file, he wasn't shy of using them to do his dirty work,' Coombes continued.

'Explain,' said Cross.

'Intimidation, that kind of thing. Peggy became more and more aware of it and was quite upset. J kept everything. There are logs of when things happened and text conversations between her and Peggy. Luke Frampton told her to keep a record of it all, in case it ever went to court.'

'Thank you,' Cross replied.

'You're welcome, and I will fix a time for you and Janette to talk. Promise. Probably a lot more efficient than all this message relaying,' said Coombes, before Cross turned and left.

'So, we're obviously dealing with an organised crime hit here,' began Carson. He often did this – started a meeting with a bold, generally unfounded statement. 'And in my experience, organised crime hits are difficult to prove at the best of times.' There was a small titter among the detectives in response. The closest he'd come to organised crime was when watching an episode of *Breaking Bad* on TV. Matthews stepped in.

'Well, I'm sure we can all learn from that experience at some point, DCI Carson,' she said, causing another unintended ripple of laughter through the rows of seated police. This kind of thing was why Cross hated these large meetings. They so often descended to this level of playground antics. Someone being picked on, someone being the butt of a joke. He had too many unpleasant memories of his own playground at school.

'DS Ottey?' Matthews asked.

Ottey looked at her notes. In reality Cross's notes, which he'd given her prior to the meeting.

'So, the main question George and I have is whether Dragusha is involved in this case at all.'

Carson sighed a little too loudly and shook his head. 'For real?' he asked.

'And the answer seems to be, yes and no,' she continued, ignoring this, but looking directly at him. 'The evidence, such as we have, certainly points in his general direction. But to what purpose? To intimidate Peggy on behalf of Bland? If that were the case, what happened? Did he mean for her to be killed – an obstacle removed – or did he mean to scare the life out of her and it went too far? We think it seems unlikely.'

'I thought DS Cross didn't speculate?' mocked one of the other detectives, looking for approbation from the others, which he didn't get.

'He isn't speculating. He's asking questions based on the little we know. Bland has distanced himself from that side of the family for his entire life. Why would he want to get involved now?' Ottey continued.

'But you said he went to Belmarsh to see the old man,' the vocal DC pointed out.

'Sure. But why?' asked Ottey.

'Well, to set the whole thing up, obviously. Bloody hell.'

'Frampton is having an affair with Dragusha's daughter—' Ottey said before being interrupted.

'Irrelevant. Completely bloody irrelevant,' said the detective. He'd been seconded from another unit, such was the amount of manpower being thrown at this case, and clearly liked the sound of his own voice.

Ottey was about to reply when Cross got up and walked over to his office, saying as he did so, 'That's a ridiculous statement. Nothing is irrelevant at this stage. Because we don't know what is relevant. The fact is that Dragusha has two links to this case, through his daughter to the victim's husband, and his nephew who works for the company the victim was at loggerheads with. To call his daughter's affair with the widower of the victim irrelevant is either ill-considered or incompetent. But in your case it's probably both.'

'What did he just fucking say?' said the detective, getting up to follow Cross.

'Sit down!' said Matthews in a voice that brooked no dissent. 'I think what Cross is saying, DC Goodwin, is that maybe you should think more before you open your mouth. You should know nothing can be ruled out at this point. So it's a little hasty calling anything irrelevant.' She then turned to Carson. 'But for what it's worth, this doesn't have the hallmarks of a professional hit, in my book.'

'The plastic bag,' he said, as if to prove his point. In his office Cross's ears pricked up at this. He was interested to hear what Carson had to say in reference to the bag. Unlike Ottey, who had a habit of dismissing what Carson had to say out of hand before he'd even spoken a word, he was always willing to listen. 'For me it raises the possibility of this being a professional contract. Not necessarily to kill her but to persuade her to back off the Chapel dispute. What if the killer tortured her? Suffocated her just enough till she was about to pass out, then asked her if she'd back off? She said no, so he did it again and again until he went a little too far and killed her?'

Ottey had to admit this theory wasn't without merit. As did Cross.

'What about the DNA on the outside of the bag not being in any database?' asked Matthews.

'He's just good at his job. Never been caught. Isn't in any database,' Carson replied.

'But why throw it away so carelessly?' asked Ottey.

'Good point,' agreed Carson.

'It's a bloody puzzle,' added Matthews.

After the meeting she walked over to Cross's office. He'd left the door open, so she walked straight in. As she turned to close the door she saw Carson following her. She closed it anyway.

'This is a mess,' she said.

'I don't think so,' he replied.

'Go on.'

'Well, there are links here. Bland, Dragusha, Frampton, Chapel. We just need to find out how they work.'

'And how do you suggest we do that?'

'Concentrate on the "why" rather than the "how". I need to do a little research.'

'Do you need any help?'

'No.'

40

Cross went into his usual self-imposed purdah. Ottey was quite accustomed to it by now and never attempted to interrupt. He would normally lock himself, metaphorically, into his office, not appear for days, not eat, not go home, just methodically research whatever it was he decided needed his undivided attention. For him this was really where a lot of satisfaction lay in his work. 'Finding a link, blind' was how he'd described it to a bewildered Ottey once. He had no idea what he was looking for and was never particularly concerned if his efforts didn't turn anything up. He differed in this respect to most of the other detectives on the MCU. He was not only happy to do this kind of 'donkey-work', as they referred to it, but if his efforts did indeed turn out to be fruitless, he just saw it as part of the process they had to go through in order to solve a case. He saw the closing of an avenue of investigation as a mark of progress. Obviously not as useful as one leading somewhere, but progress all the same. It excluded something. Brought that avenue to a close, meaning they didn't have to waste any more time investigating it any further.

He began by looking into Chapel's business in detail. The turnover and profit of the last decade. Directors on the board, loans, investments, outstanding projects, credit lines. He came across a portfolio for potential investors in a restructuring of Chapel's company. It was dated eighteen months earlier, so Cross dug down into the company's financials for the last twelve months and discovered that this restructuring had indeed taken place with several hundreds of millions invested into the company. This made sense in light of his conversation with Mike Rowbottom. They had obviously anticipated the dangers he feared and had done something to protect themselves. All of the investors seemed to be legitimate and transparent. Then he came to one who wasn't identified by name. The investment came from an offshore corporation. Cross felt a flicker of excitement at the discovery of this small, hidden detail. Complex offshore networks were often an indication of some sort of illegal activity. It took him almost another twenty-four hours, oblivious to all the activity in the open area, to weave his way through a myriad of offshore companies and foreign banks until he finally found the answer. Satisfied that his intensive 'blind' search had paid off dividends – a pun he must remember to use with Ottey – he shut down his computer at three in the morning, and cycled home.

The first thing he did when he got there was take a shower. Then he went to bed. No food, no drink. He just needed to switch off. But he couldn't. He got into bed and ran through his findings step by step. If someone had cross-examined him about his marathon search, he would've been able to take them through it, not only in the minutest of detail, but in the exact sequential order he had gone about things when he discovered them. He often reflected what a shame it was that no one ever asked him to do this, because he loved it. It was his party trick. It would have to be a pretty dull party, Ottey had once told him when he described it thus to her. Which he thought just proved his point. A defence barrister had once, famously, made the mistake of asking Cross, in court, how he could be so certain about a conclusion he'd come to concerning the guilt of his client, when all he'd done was go through thousands of emails and dozens of corresponding receipts for fictitious expense claims. Cross was delighted to be asked and set off on a microscopically detailed, forensic description of his investigation, step by step, accompanied by an exact timeline of when, during this search, certain facts became apparent to him. After an hour of this, the judge stopped him and told the jury that he felt they'd heard enough from this 'most conscientious of sergeants', to convince them of his diligence and accuracy.

Cross played the search back in his head moment by moment, piece by piece, revelling in his discovery. It was like a golfer who, having played a great round of golf, well below his handicap, will play the entire round in his or her head, shot by shot and bask in the memory.

He had first become intrigued by the complexity of offshore companies, together with the full extent of their illegal use, with the appearance of the so-called 'Panama Papers' in 2016. Fraud was something that had always interested him, having spent some time in the fraud squad in his late twenties. It was deemed to be the best place for the idiosyncratic young detective by his superiors, who really weren't sure what best to do with him at the time. Chained to a desk and computer, analysing endless financial spreadsheets, seemed an appropriate way of dealing, or not dealing, with him. He was happy enough. Numbers had always fascinated him, and this work required less human interaction than normal, which was a bonus. The Panama Papers comprised over eleven million leaked documents from a law firm in Panama called Mossack Fonseca. They detailed the activities of over two hundred thousand offshore entities, some dating back to the 1970s . Thousands of them had been used for illegal purposes such as money laundering and tax evasion.

Cross then became something of a self-taught expert in offshore corporations and was secretly delighted that he had been able to put this to good use in the last twenty-four hours. The anonymous investor in Chapel's company had made a significant investment, well over a hundred million pounds. It was made by an offshore company based in the Marshall Islands. This was what immediately interested Cross. It was a red flag for him. Shell companies have no employees and no physical presence. They are designed to hide the identity of the owner and make the source of any money hard to trace. The identity of the owner is easily hidden by the corporation being registered as a subsidiary of another corporation, which in turn is a subsidiary of another, and so on. It is like a Russian doll, with more and more companies revealed as each one is uncovered. The major advantage of them is that they aren't subject to any kind of regulation or tax implications. The bank accounts of several of this investor's companies were themselves registered in the name of the banks in which the accounts were held. Large transactions of cash were regularly moved between the various corporations and bank accounts in different countries.

He discovered there were eleven corporations in all, with intricate and complex links in six different jurisdictions:

Cyprus, the British Virgin Islands, Liberia, the Marshall Islands, Malaysia and the Seychelles. He followed each of them doggedly, including all their offshoots. This network had more tributaries than the Amazon. He was impressed with the complexity of the network, which concealed both the movements of cash and the owner's identity with great, adroit, accounting skill. But the trail had to end somewhere. All you needed was patience, which Cross had in abundance when it came to this kind of thing. The architects of this scheme – another pun he had to remember for Ottey – probably thought that, if it came to an investigation, people would inevitably give up at some point, as they became entangled in the thorny branches of this impenetrable maze. But they hadn't accounted for the indefatigably persistent George Cross. His search eventually ended up with an onshore company called Dhermi Holdings, quite possibly named after the owner's hometown. But, more importantly, there was his name in black and white, and it was of significant interest to the case. When Cross had stopped playing it back in his head, he saw it was six thirty and decided the sensible thing to do was get some sleep.

He came into work a little after midday. Ottey knew this was the usual pattern after an intense session like the one Cross had just put himself through. As they left the unit in her car a little later, she said nothing. She knew he'd found something because he said nothing when he arrived. If his discovery led to the shutting down of a line of enquiry, he was quick to say, to prevent the team wasting any further time on it. In turn, her reticence to ask him was because she knew that Cross preferred to deliver whatever he'd unearthed directly to the person of interest. She also, secretly, liked to watch it unfold in front of her in real time. At times, she thought, Cross was like her own, individually curated, true crime TV series.

41

Clive Bland was out of the office that afternoon. He and Chapel were on a site visit in Swindon. Cross was reluctant to delay speaking with him, so he and Ottey set off eastbound, down the M4. The building site was enclosed within tall hoardings in the centre of town with several signs proclaiming them to be 'considerate constructors'. The rain and heavy trucks coming in and out had made it into an enormous mud bath. Ottey went to the trunk of the car and produced not one, but two pairs of wellington boots.

'You still have them,' Cross observed, secretly pleased.

'Why would I have thrown them away?'

'Good point.'

She'd actually bought each of them a pair the year before, for a particularly muddy crime scene. She decided she wasn't going to ruin another pair of perfectly good heels, and be laughed at in the process. Heels were an unimaginable nightmare in deep mud. Ottey often wore heels to work, not always, it had to be said. But the memory of wearing those appalling, unsightly black shoes when in uniform had scarred her. She'd also bought a pair of wellingtons for Cross selfishly, as she didn't want him to get mud all over her car. They reported to the site office which was adjacent to the fifteen-storey-high central concrete pillar of the building. Numbers were painted on its sides to indicate where all the floors would be. They looked at the artist's impressions of the finished building inside the office. Ottey wasn't impressed.

'I would never have said that was a Chapel building,' she commented, as they followed a man in a high-vis suit and hard hat towards the concrete monolith. They were now also sporting high-vis jackets with 'Chapel' emblazoned in large black letters on the back, and hard hats similarly adorned.

'Why not?' asked Cross.

'It's just so functional. Very little architectural merit,' she said grandly.

'I didn't know you were an expert,' Cross confessed.

'I watch *Grand Designs* on the TV,' she protested facetiously, knowing full well he'd never heard of it. But the grin was quickly wiped off her face when she learned that Chapel and Bland were on the twelfth floor of the structure. To reach them they'd have to travel in a wire cage that seemed attached to the side of the concrete edifice in the most perfunctory way. Ottey hated heights. It was one of her worst fears but she wasn't about to tell the two men this. Cross looked positively gleeful.

'I've always wanted to go in one of these,' he told the young man, as he closed the gate behind them. The lift started with a jolt. Ottey stayed at the back of the cage next to the building clutching the metal mesh with a white-knuckled fist. The young man looked at her and beamed. It was this kind of fear on the faces of visitors that made his day. Cross, on the other hand, was standing right at the front of the cage looking directly down at the ground disappearing rapidly below. It was a thrilling sensation, reminding him of his trips to amusement parks all over the country with Raymond. He had briefly become obsessed with amusement park rides, aged ten, learning the names of every major ride in the UK, together with their technical specifications, height and speed. Raymond had indulged his son's interest as, from an engineering point of view, it was of interest to him too. He even went along with Cross's determination to experience every single ride in what he had determined, by a series of compare and contrast lists, to be the main amusement parks in England, Scotland and Wales. Over a couple of years they succeeded in doing this. Then one morning Cross came down to breakfast a little crestfallen. Thorpe Park had just built a brand new, only-one-of-a-kind-in-the-world rollercoaster, where the riders were suspended below the track. He had no longer ridden *all* the rides in the country. Raymond quickly offered a solution. They would now go to all the new rides as they were opened. And so they did. Over the next few years Cross kept notes in an A5 notebook and took photographs, before moving onto filming them on his phone and dictating his notes. They continued to visit Thorpe Park and Alton Towers as new rides were built. Over time Raymond felt he'd become too old to actually go on them any more. But he was just as happy watching his son's expressions of glee as he was hurtled around the sky in some modern instrument of self-inflicted torture for the paying public. They even had an entire album of those pictures that are taken automatically on some rides, at the most hair-raising moments of the experience. Raymond loved these pictures, particularly the ones where they were together. They were rare moments of real connection between the two of them.

They duly found Chapel and Bland on the twelfth floor, having a meeting with various construction workers. Chapel looked up and saw them approach, Ottey looking unwell and Cross very pleased with himself.

'Sergeants. You should've waited till we came down,' said Chapel.

'*You* definitely should've,' Bland said to Ottey.

'I'm good,' was all she could mutter.

'How can we help?' Chapel asked charmingly.

'I have to say, if I'd driven past this building site without knowing it was one of yours, I would never have guessed,' Cross began.

'Really? Why's that?' Chapel laughed nervously.

'What was it you said, DS Ottey?' But she wasn't quite recovered enough to have a conversation as yet. 'No architectural merit, that was it. I was under the impression, having visited your "campus", as you like to call it, though I for one couldn't see any teaching going on there, that you went in for big concepts and "bold landmark designs". I think that is how your website describes your work. But this is very... how can I put this? Functional? Utilitarian?'

'Functionality is one of the most important tenets of good architecture, Sergeant. All good buildings have to function well or else, well, they're not good buildings,' Chapel asserted.

'Besides, every business needs a certain amount of bread-and-butter work to keep on top of operational overheads,' Bland volunteered.

'I wouldn't exactly call this bread and butter, Clive. One of the great things about this particular building, Sergeant, is its sustainability. It's a virtually carbon neutral building.

315

Now that may not sound glamorous, but it's more and more essential for the future of the planet.' Cross had noted Chapel's reaction to Bland's comment. There was a definite tetchiness there. The creative and business parts of the building butting heads, perhaps?

'Mikki Dragusha,' Cross said.

'What about him?'

'Do you know him?'

'I do not. Who is he?'

'Mr Bland's cousin.'

'Ah, I see. Yes of course, Dragusha is Clive's mother's maiden name. I am well aware of Clive's relatives. He was completely open about it from the outset. That and the nature of the family business,' Chapel replied confidently. 'We're very transparent in all of our dealings within the company.'

'What nature would that be?' asked Cross. 'The family business.'

'What are you driving at, Sergeant? We are all well aware of that side of my family's criminal activities. So, what is it you want?' asked Bland.

'We're investigating the murder of Peggy Frampton,' Cross went on.

'You don't say,' sneered Bland.

'Clive, please,' Chapel interjected.

'This company has been in a dispute with her for a number of years, costing you a small fortune,' Cross continued.

'With respect, Sergeant, haven't we covered all of this? What is more, don't personalise it. We are in dispute with a group of objectors headed up by Peggy Frampton. Or it was,' Chapel pointed out.

'You failed to mention that the cost of this dispute had necessitated a financial restructuring of the company.'

'It's not a restructuring. More a re-leveraging, and it had absolutely nothing to do with the planning dispute,' said Bland.

'Well, I'll leave the business terminology to you,' Cross replied.

'There have been other factors. The economic downturn, record inflation, the pandemic,' Chapel pointed out.

'Of course, all of which has necessitated new investment, from new partners,' said Cross. Ottey suddenly had an idea where this was going.

'That's true,' said Chapel.

'I've spent the last couple of days looking at the new investment structure of your company, and your financial health over the last few months. Without this new injection of funds you were seriously exposed and certainly not in a position to go public.'

'I wouldn't go that far,' said Bland tersely.

'Really? Well, I'll have to take your word for that, as you know a lot more about business than I do. But as a layman, I think your backs being against the wall can't have been advantageous, when it came to negotiating the terms of this new investment. You couldn't have had much leverage.'

The two men said nothing, so Cross went on.

'So, I was slightly surprised at the high levels of new investment you did manage to secure – some five hundred and fifty million pounds. I mean, surely, with all the expert advice the investors were getting, they could see the fragile state of the business, financially. Then of course I got it. Your intention to go public. These investors realised they could double or even triple their investment.'

'Is there a question in there somewhere?' asked Bland.

'No. Merely an observation. Here is my question though. If you weren't actually able to go public, what would that mean for their investment?'

'We're confident we won't find ourselves, or be putting our investors, in that position,' replied Chapel.

'And if you do?' Cross pressed. There was no response. 'Well, as I've already said I'm no expert. But looking at other situations historically, I would imagine the investors would want to withdraw their investment and your company would collapse. But would all of them be able to get out in time?'

'It's a risk, and one they and their advisors will have taken into account. There's no such thing as a sure-fire investment, otherwise we'd all be billionaires. Speculation carries an inherent risk, which is why when it pays off the profits are so high,' said Bland as if addressing a five-year-old child.

'I am well aware of what to speculate means. It comes directly from the Latin *speculationem*, meaning contemplation or observation, the noun being *speculatus*. *Spek*- is also a Proto-Indo-European root, meaning to observe. But thank you for your explanation. So to sum up. It's very much in your interests and the interests of your investors to go public.'

'Of course,' said Bland.

'And the harbourside development is a cornerstone of that strategy, yes?' They didn't answer. 'Let me answer that for you, as I've read the prospectus you put together, Mr Bland. It's vital. You need that development to go through and Peggy Frampton was in your way.'

'Are you honestly suggesting we had anything to do with that poor woman's murder?' asked a startled Chapel.

'Not you, but perhaps one of your new investors. A less legitimate one,' Cross suggested. Bland looked uncomfortable.

'What is he talking about, Clive?' Chapel asked.

'I have no idea. I think he's making it up as he goes along.' Cross often got this reaction from people, Ottey was thinking, and it was when he was at his most dangerous.

'One investor caught my attention, simply because it was so difficult to find out who it was. Their identity was hidden behind so many complex, what you might call, company firewalls. A spider's web of interlinked shell corporations, which was curious, I thought, for a legitimate business. It took me hours to track him down through various shell companies and offshore financial entities located all over the world. Most of your other investors were easily identifiable and transparent, as you would call it. But not this one. When something is this complicated, I'm reliably informed by our fraud team that it's generally indicative of something illegal going on somewhere down the line – like money-laundering.'

'Clive?' Chapel repeated. He was starting to become concerned. But Bland said nothing.

'Does a company called Dhermi Holdings mean anything to you, Mr Chapel?' Cross asked.

'It does not,' he replied.

'But I thought you knew all of your investors personally. Mike Rowbottom said it was a core philosophy of your company. To know who you were in business with.'

'He's no longer with us,' said Bland.

'I am well aware of that. Your very presence in this

conversation, Mr Bland, is proof enough of Mr Rowbottom's departure. But he left specifically because of his opposition to the public offer, he told me. Again, I know nothing of the inner workings of a business like yours but, from what I can glean, there was a certain amount of what politicians would call "briefing" against Mr Rowbottom. How exactly did Mr Bland manage to turn you against your oldest and best friend, Mr Chapel? The co-founder of your company, godfather of your eldest child, best man at your wedding?'

Chapel didn't answer.

'I can understand your hesitation in answering because, when put like that, it does sound a little implausible, doesn't it? But as we all know, it did happen. However, let's go back to Dhermi Holdings. It meant nothing to me, of course, but the clue is in the name. It's a beautiful village on the Ionian coast, with a lovely beach and beautiful architecture. It's famous for its remoteness. I imagine that might have played a part in the investor's naming of it; wanting their identity to be remote, as it were – hard to get to.'

'The clue? What on earth do you mean?' asked Chapel impatiently. He was getting fed up with Cross's act, unlike Ottey, the blood having fully returned to her head, who was now a willing and intrigued audience.

'The clue?' Cross asked, as if trying to remember when he'd said this. 'Oh yes, the clue is where Dhermi, the village, is located. It's in Albania.' He said no more, but just looked at the two suited men. After a suitable pause he went on. 'Mr Bland here is, as we all know, half Albanian.' He looked from Bland to Chapel who said nothing. 'The mysterious owner of Dhermi Holdings and now a major investor in your company, Mr Chapel, is none other than Mikki Dragusha.'

'Small world,' Ottey interjected.

'Is this true?' Chapel asked Bland.

'Your company now has direct links to one of Albania's largest and most dangerous crime families, the head of whom is currently serving seven life sentences for murder – those the authorities know about, or can prove, that is. Your company has money in its coffers that almost undoubtedly has criminal provenance.'

'Clive?' Chapel said quietly, inviting an explanation.

'Mikki is not like his father. He wants to make the family legit.'

'And you didn't think to mention the source of this investment because?' asked Chapel.

'I knew you'd say no.'

'And you were quite right. You seem to be forgetting whose company this is.'

'Mr Chapel, did you really not know about this investment?' asked Cross.

'I did not. Was there anything else, or do you have any further surprises for me? I have quite a busy afternoon.'

'No, that will do for today. But who knows what this new information might lead to.' Cross looked directly at Bland. 'I will leave you with one thought. Nothing happens in the Dragusha – I hesitate to call it a business, but for want of a better word I will – business that Andi Dragusha doesn't know about. We all know how far he will go to get his way. After all, he's in prison for it. The question is, how far are Mikki and his father willing to go to make sure their substantial investment, just over one hundred million, as it happens, Mr Chapel, pays off? For a family that's no stranger to murder?'

* * *

Ottey clutched the mesh at the back of the construction lift cage again, as Cross looked down. They started to descend.

'It's a pity this isn't quicker, like Detonator at Thorpe Park,' Cross exclaimed with childlike enthusiasm. 'That ride has a one hundred and fifteen foot drop. I think we're a little higher here, but what makes Detonator much more of a thrill is that it doesn't just work on gravity alone. It has a pneumatic system which actually pushes the ride towards the ground as well.'

Ottey wanted to make some caustic response to this useless, and in the circumstances, not terribly helpful piece of information, but found she couldn't speak. The lift then gave a little jolt and she screamed. Even in her terror, she noticed this made Cross smile.

They sat in her car waiting for her to recover so that she could drive.

'Bloody good work, George.'

'I know,' he replied. She shook her head at this and laughed. 'What?' he asked innocently.

'Oh, nothing. Are you thinking that this might fit in with Carson's theory that the murder might have been intimidation gone a step too far?'

'I'm not.'

'Are you thinking anything?'

'I'm thinking that Dragusha senior had absolutely nothing to do with Peggy's murder. As both he and Luke Frampton pointed out – it doesn't make any sense for him to have had her killed.'

'Which leaves us with Mikki.'

'Possibly.'

'I didn't know you were acrophobic,' he said.

'I'm not. I have vertigo,' she replied.

'You do not have vertigo, I assure you. What you have is acrophobia, an extreme or irrational fear of heights. Vertigo is just a symptom of acrophobia. People often confuse the two,' he said as if this should make her feel better. She actually wanted to pull over and strangle him.

42

Cross decided to widen the investigation. He'd by no means excluded Mikki Dragusha, but had planted enough uncertainty with Chapel and Bland that he thought something might happen. The idea of fully investigating a crime family at this point wasn't an option. It would waste hundreds of police man-hours, which they didn't have. A couple of detectives were put on Bland. Faye Settle had confirmed that the car Peggy was sure was following her was a black Range Rover with tinted windows. She didn't recall seeing a man with an extensive neck tattoo among the thugs who sat in on their meetings. Cross also asked the team to find out if there were any sightings of a black Range Rover around City Hall and Peggy's house on the night of the murder. He himself sat down with a mound of reports compiled by other detectives working on the team. The ones he was interested in initially were the canvassing reports. Not so much the ones of the neighbours and people in the immediate vicinity of Sion Hill where the Framptons lived, but of the people Peggy actually knew well. He read dozens of interview transcripts from people she'd worked with at City Hall. Yes, there were those with political differences, but she seemed to be respected, on the whole, if not universally liked. After an extended day of going through these reports nothing, nor anyone, flagged themselves up as a serious potential threat to their victim's life. One thing he did come away with though, was the feeling that life in local politics was somewhat dull, with everyone attaching themselves to various local causes, then fighting for them to the exclusion and possibly detriment of everything else. Peggy Frampton had been guilty of this to an extent, as an espoused evangelist of conservation and defender of Bristol's heritage.

He and Mackenzie had also compiled several spreadsheets of contentious or 'of interest' interactions with people on Peggy's website, organised by date. They had photographs pulled from the internet of various correspondents on a whiteboard in his office. Mackenzie had built up profiles of some of them from their social media which were placed alongside the photographs. Their marital status, their friends, websites they liked, tastes in music and film, books. She had also downloaded photographs that she thought were of interest – at parties, sporting events, on holiday. As ever, Cross was amazed at how much information people were willing to give away about themselves, made public for anyone to see, on the internet. Surely it wasn't safe. He was also impressed by the amount of work she'd done.

'She had quite a lot of help from her new friend,' said Ottey mischievously.

He assumed from her tone that this was some sort of office gossip. The kind of thing he didn't approve of. His view was that such rumour-mongering was an unwelcome distraction from the very serious work of solving murder. Although closer to the actual truth was that he found it exhausting, trying to navigate all the different implications and innuendoes that flew around the ether of the open area when a new source of tittle-tattle appeared. As Cross looked at her blankly, she explained, 'Swift. Ever since your little road trip to Portsmouth, he's found all sorts of excuses to come over to the MCU.'

Cross thought about this for a moment. 'That would make sense,' he said.

'What? You got the vibe too? Or do you just think they make a good couple?'

'Certainly not,' he said, horrified at the very thought of it. 'I was merely thinking that her approach to the work had been much more organised and scientific of late. So, it would make sense that Dr Swift had helped her.'

'George, do yourself a favour. Don't say that to her.'

'Why ever not? It's a compliment. It says a lot about her. That she's able to recognise her weaknesses and do something about it, by enlisting someone brighter and more capable than her to help.'

'Oh right,' she replied. 'I hadn't thought of that.'

'Of course you hadn't,' he replied. She looked at him and was about to retaliate, when he tapped his nose and winked in a most ungainly way.

'Irony,' he then said, looking immensely pleased with himself.

He was methodically working away in his office when Mackenzie burst in, in exactly the way he hated. He looked at her, shocked.

'I'm so, so sorry, but you have to hear this,' she ex–claimed.

'A knock on the door would have been just as quick as

your apology for not knocking and would have had the added benefit of not startling me. As well as being just plain good manners,' Cross commented.

'Okay, but listen to this. It's a comment from Peggy to a man in the public forum of her website discussing problems in his marriage. "You are smothering the life out of your wife and your relationship with her. She feels she can't do anything without your agreement or consent. She obviously can't think for herself any more. She's lost her identity outside of you and your marriage. She's lost her independence. You have to give her room to breathe and be herself." He then disagrees saying that despite everything he's told Peggy, she obviously doesn't understand him. But she ends it by saying, "You are suffocating your wife emotionally and crushing the life out of your marriage. If you carry on like this, you may as well just put a plastic bag over her head. It'll have the same effect."'

She looked at Cross. He thought for a moment.

'Who is this?' he asked.

'I don't know. His username is glassman86,' she replied.

'Put together a profile of him. Whatever you can find online and let me have it as soon as possible.'

'Okay,' she said, leaving a printout of the exchange on his desk. He picked it up and studied it for a few minutes. He had a friend at Cambridge University, Oliver Black, who was a linguistics expert. They had been at school together. Cross had always been slightly in awe of him as he had worked out early on in their relationship that Oliver was much, much, cleverer than him. He decided to send Oliver some documents for him to cast his critically analytical eye over.

He'd pressed 'send' when there was a knock at his door. Ottey appeared.

'Justin Frampton's gone missing.'

43

'So, this is good news,' announced Carson, silencing the room of thirty detectives in an instant. Something he never managed to do when he actually wanted to. Sensing the tumbleweed moment, together with the increased temperature of his cheeks, he went on, 'I mean, obviously not for the Frampton family. What I meant was, that in a case where little headway is being made, this is a positive link. The murder and the kidnapping have to be connected.'

A further silence.

'Someone help me out here,' Carson jokingly pleaded.

'I think you have a point, boss,' said a detective sitting to one side. 'It's too much of a coincidence. I mean, what are the chances of the two of them happening to the same family, within a couple of months? They have to be related.'

'Yeah. Find Justin, get hold of the kidnappers and we get closer to Peggy Frampton's killer,' added another detective.

Justin Frampton hadn't been snatched in an off-the-pavement grab and stuffed into the back of a mysterious black transit van, idling nearby. Two men had simply turned up at his antiques stall and appeared to persuade him, with very little effort apparently, to accompany them out of the building.

'How did he seem?' Cross asked the next-door stallholder, Dorothy. She was more preoccupied with how long she was expected to be in charge of Justin's stall than his well-being.

'He looked like he'd shit himself,' came the caustic reply. Ottey made a note of the date and time it had happened. It had been a full eighteen hours before Luke Frampton reported it, and about a week after they'd visited Andi Dragusha in Belmarsh. When Dorothy had been asked to describe the two men, she had used the expression 'muscle men', much like Agnesha's nickname for her brother's colleagues. But she'd also noticed that one of them had a tattoo which completely covered his neck.

'George?' Matthews said, turning in Cross's direction.

'What?'

'What do you think of DCI Carson's theory?'

'I think he's quite right in one respect,' replied Cross.

'Which is?' she asked.

'That it's progress.'

'Gosh, well, that's a first. So, we're agreed for once.'

'Absolutely not. Quite the opposite, in fact,' Cross protested.

'What?' Carson spluttered in disbelief.

'The abduction and holding of Justin Frampton go to prove that the Dragusha family had nothing to do with Peggy Frampton's murder,' Cross went on.

'And how do you figure that one out?' asked Carson.

'I thought it was possible that Mikki Dragusha had Peggy Frampton murdered, either deliberately, or accidentally in an attempt to frighten her. Even though the cack-handedness of the entire event might suggest otherwise. Her death meant that their main obstacle against the proposed development had been removed. Fairly extreme, but when you consider the company going public was dependent on that deal going through, not implausible. But then I asked myself, why abduct Justin when all you risk doing is drawing attention to yourself?'

'Wait a minute. You're saying the Dragushas have Justin?' Carson said.

'And the answer is that it is exactly what they're trying to do. Draw attention to themselves,' Cross went on, ignoring him.

'Do you have evidence for this?' asked Matthews.

Cross and Ottey answered at the same time.

'Yes,' said Ottey.

'No,' said Cross.

'We have an eyewitness who's identified them,' Ottey continued.

'You might have led with that,' said Carson.

'There were two men at the funeral who talked to Justin and seemed to disconcert him,' said Cross.

'One of them had a distinctive tattoo which covered the entirety of his neck. Some sort of serpent. The same guy was with Mikki when he took Agnesha. One of the guys who came for Justin also had a full neck tattoo,' said Ottey.

'That seems fairly conclusive to me, George,' said Matthews.

'It's certainly a solid lead. I wouldn't go as far as conclusive, unless he is the only person in the country with such a tattoo, which I think highly unlikely,' Cross insisted.

'Okay, so if it is them, why would they want to draw attention to themselves?' Matthews asked, indulging him.

'For that answer I suggest we ask Luke Frampton,' Cross said.

'But we want to hold back telling him about the Dragusha involvement for the moment,' added Ottey.

'Possible involvement,' Cross corrected her.

'Ever the contrarian, George,' Carson observed.

'Only when the contrary opinion is the only valid one, DCI Carson. This development means that we should now be looking elsewhere for Peggy Frampton's killer. However disappointing that might be to those in this room looking for a quick and convenient result.'

At this point the chief constable walked in, hat under his arm. Everyone stood.

'As you were,' he said. 'Could I see you in your office, Heather? You too, DS Ottey, Cross.' He then strode through the open area. Matthews followed with Cross and Ottey in her wake. Carson had made an instinctive movement to get up, initially assuming he would be required as well, but then decided he'd suffered enough humiliation for one day without a public rebuff, so just stayed put.

'The Justin Frampton situation is bound to hit the press soon. It'll inevitably highlight the fact that we're making little or no progress on the Peggy Frampton murder,' the Chief began.

'No chance of keeping a lid on it?' Matthews asked hopefully.

'I'm getting a lot of pressure from the council, which I can deflect fairly easily, but it's actually reached ears at Number Ten.'

'Hardly surprising as she's one of a number of public figures who've been murdered. Jo Cox and David Amess both killed in their constituencies. It's becoming a major political problem,' said Ottey.

'So, we think it's politically motivated?' the Chief asked.

'No,' replied Cross.

'But the optics would probably play into the political narrative, in the short term at least. Which will only bring additional unwelcome pressure,' said Matthews.

'Quite so. The main priority right now though is to find Justin Frampton. Not only for his sake, but so we can get ahead of all of this,' said the Chief.

'Are we to investigate this as well as the murder?' Cross asked.

'Aren't they part and parcel of the same thing?' asked the Chief.

'George thinks not,' Matthews replied.

'Okay, I'm not going to ask you why. Heather, how would you like to work this?'

'Well, George's theory might be correct,' Matthews began.

'It's not a theory. It comes from a logical appraisal of the facts as known,' Cross interrupted.

'Link or no link, I think it would be negligent on our part not to investigate these in tandem. Not the least because of how it would look from the outside if this team handed it over to a new one,' Matthews went on.

'Not a great look politically,' said the Chief. This kind of big picture consideration never occurred to Ottey. It confirmed to her that Matthews would go far. She found herself wondering if they were in the presence of a future chief constable.

'Exactly so. I suggest George continues his investigation into the murder and Ottey joins Carson's team and tracks Justin Frampton down.'

Perceiving this as an instruction, Cross got up immediately and left the room. Matthews shook her head and smiled. 'He really doesn't give a toss who anyone is, does he?' she said, looking at the Chief.

'Not so much,' said Ottey.

'Which is why he's so good at what he does, and why we all let him get away with it,' replied the Chief.

For her part Ottey was less than happy to be seconded onto Carson's team, but she wasn't going to argue in front of the Chief, nor a potential chief-in-waiting. She definitely gave a toss who they were.

She and Carson went to see Luke Frampton. The story of Justin's abduction had made its way not only into the local press, but also the nationals and various TV news networks. Photographers, journalists and TV reporters with their crews now occupied the grass verge opposite the Frampton house, waiting for any sign of life. They descended en masse as the two police officers made their way from their car, asking for comment. Ottey was surprised by Carson's restraint in the situation. Then she remembered his recent bollocking at the hands of Matthews. The Chief had also seen Carson's comments on the local news and was not best pleased. No wonder he was so quiet.

Frampton was as distraught as you would expect. He didn't know who had his son and no contact had been made. But there was something about him, Ottey told Cross when she reported back to him at the MCU, that was off.

'It wasn't so much that he was holding something back,' she said. 'More like he felt guilty about it, responsible in some kind of way.'

'Interesting observation,' replied Cross.

44

That night, Cross went to Stephen's parish church to practise the organ. It was a night for Bach, he'd decided. Pieces he'd played for years, that were as familiar to him as the bicycle route home from work. He wanted to free up his mind to think about the case. But that night he found himself thinking about something else. His mother and his father's friend Ron. He was sure the answer to his mother's enigmatic assertion that he didn't know everything about her decision to leave still lay somewhere in the boxes of Raymond's storage unit. But he would have to wait till the weekend to go back and look. Cross looked up at the car rear-view mirror he'd attached a few years before, so the parish organist could see both the celebrant and the congregation during mass, and noticed that Stephen had secreted himself into the pews to listen. He often did this. This particular night Cross just hoped that it wasn't another opportunity to harangue him about his mother.

It wasn't. The priest had discovered, much like Cross, that the music cleared his mind. He found the weekly sessions an ideal opportunity to think about his weekend sermon. He would sit in the empty church as the organ pipes filled the air, listen and jot down the occasional thought. Once or twice he'd actually written the entire sermon by the time Cross had finished. He'd really missed Cross's session the previous week, when he'd declined to come. He hadn't realised that it had become as important a part of his weekly routine as it was to Cross. The prospect of him not coming back was a miserable thought, which had prompted his pleading visit to the café. He was glad Cross was back. It was like the return of a wayward, errant cat who'd briefly gone missing, presumably fed by well-meaning neighbours. So determined was he not to deter Cross from returning, that he slipped out through the sacristy back to the parsonage before the detective had finished playing. This was in the hope Cross would think the danger of him pressing him about his mother, every time he saw him, was past. It was easy to achieve as Cross practised for exactly an hour – to the minute. Stephen left with two minutes to spare. Cross felt refreshed and energised after playing and went home in as good spirits as he ever managed to muster.

45

There was a polite knock on Cross's office door. He looked up. Mackenzie was standing there. He couldn't be sure, but he thought she was bouncing up and down on her toes like an overexcited child. He motioned her in.

'Plantar flexion,' he announced.

'What?' she asked.

'What you were doing. Standing up and down on your toes like that,' he replied.

'Oh, okay. Good to know. Glassman86. I couldn't find a photo, but this is what I've managed to dig up.'

Cross read it carefully then looked up at her.

'Remind you of anyone?' she asked.

Mark Coombes actually seemed quite pleased to see them later that day and welcomed them into the house without hesitation. Cross had observed this in people on the fringes of an investigation. After a while they often came to think of themselves as an integral part of it. They sometimes fancied themselves as amateur sleuths, or maybe they were just lonely. Coombes was presumably unused to being on his own, after twenty years of marriage, so it was possible he was filling the void left by his absent wife. Mark and Janette Coombes lived on a modern housing estate in Knowle West, in the south part of Bristol. There was a caravan parked outside the house. It was dark by the time the detectives arrived, although the clocks had recently gone forward, something Ottey always welcomed. She found doing the school run in the dark particularly grim. It seemed so much more difficult to get up, even more difficult to get her children up. She then wouldn't see them till it was dark again. Carla had once joked that they were a family of vampires, only seeing each other at night.

Dressed in his work clothes, Coombes probably hadn't been in for long. 'So how can I help?' he asked eagerly. 'I see the Frampton boy's missing. It's got Bland written all over it. At least that's what Janette said.'

'You've spoken to her?' Cross asked.

'Yes. Last night. Oh bugger,' he said. 'I keep forgetting. I'm so sorry. I will organise a time for you to speak. I promise. Particularly in the light of this latest development. Maybe she could help.'

'She might, but we won't actually know that until we've spoken to her,' said Cross.

'Of course.'

'We've got a number of names we've taken from Peggy's website. We'd like to talk to Janette and see if she feels, in retrospect, they might have posed a threat of any kind,' said Cross. Coombes's face lit up at this like someone watching a complex thriller on TV and suddenly understanding where an obscure plot point was leading.

'Bloody hell, do you think the killer might be someone from the website?'

'We're investigating all possibilities,' replied Ottey.

'Problem is, some of the stuff people wrote to Peggy was right out there. They do that, don't they, these nut jobs? Think it's okay to say anything they like. They're cowards basically, hiding behind the internet. J says some of the stuff was awful, sick. You know Peggy went to the police?'

'We do.'

'Blimey, it just goes to show, doesn't it?' Coombes said.

'Just goes to show what?' asked Cross.

'I'm not sure, now you ask,' he laughed. 'Just one of those things you say, isn't it?'

'I'd like to speak with Janette herself,' said Cross.

'Of course. Like I said, it's a bit tricky, but I'll ask her the next time she calls and set something up. I'm assuming normal office hours?' he asked helpfully.

'No, we'll speak with her whenever it's convenient for her.'

'Okay, I actually think she'd like that. She still feels guilty being away while this is all going on. Which is daft,' Coombes said.

'Is this one of your conservatories?' Ottey asked, looking at a glass structure attached to the back of the house.

'It is. It's called the Versailles,' he replied.

'It's great,' she said, walking into it. Coombes followed. 'Such a good space.'

As the two of them walked into the conservatory Cross noticed the number of books in the house. They seemed to be everywhere. Someone had a good reading habit.

'Are you aware of the etymological roots of the word conservatory?' asked Cross.

'I'm not,' Coombes replied cheerfully. 'But I get the feeling you might be about to tell me.' He laughed again, then looked at Ottey as if they were sharing a private joke.

'It comes from the Italian *conservato*, meaning stored or preserved, together with the Latin *-ory*, meaning a place for.'

'Fascinating,' Coombes replied genuinely.

'They were originally the preserve of the upper classes—'

'Excuse the pun,' joked Coombes.

'What? Oh, I see. Of course, they no longer fulfilled their original purpose when introduced in the nineteenth century.'

'So, you know your stuff about conservatories then?'

'He's one of those people who knows his stuff about practically everything. It's very irritating,' said Ottey.

'You've never complained before. I thought you liked learning things,' replied Cross, surprised.

'What? You're unbelievable. I've complained about it loads. It's just that when I do you don't hear, because you're still talking.'

Cross then continued, as if to prove her point.

'Originally introduced by botanists and explorers, returning from their travels with samples they wanted to propagate. The English climate being too cold and harsh, they built glass structures to keep them warm and encourage them to grow. The rich then built them primarily to grow citrus fruits for their dining tables.'

'That's right. All the stately homes started to add orangeries for that purpose, like Chatsworth,' added Coombes.

'Correct, a fine example constructed by the gardener Joseph Paxton. The problem was, glass was expensive and subject to a tax at the time. When that was finally abolished, so the popularity of conservatories grew. Of course, they are now more of an extra room rather than anything else, with the added advantage of not requiring planning permission.'

'It comes under permitted development rights, unless

you're in a listed building or conservation area,' Coombes explained to Ottey unnecessarily.

'Well. This has all been fascinating, but we should go,' said Ottey.

'Is this conservatory new? I can smell fresh paint,' asked Cross.

'No, we've had it a few years now. I've been doing some odd jobs around the house while Janette is away. I'll email you with a time and date as soon as she's got back to me.'

'Thank you,' said Ottey as he showed them to the door. He picked up a conservatory brochure from a pile on the dining table and gave it to Ottey.

'In case you're thinking seriously about getting one,' he said.

'Thanks.'

He then stood and waited at the door as they walked to the car. Like someone waving off relatives who'd dropped in, and he wouldn't be seeing for a while. Cross turned at the car.

'I hear you're frightened of flying,' he said to Coombes out of the blue.

'Who told you that?' Coombes laughed.

'Sasha Connor.'

'Well, she's not wrong. It's true. Flying and lifts. They're my weak spots. Probably why I ended up working in conservatories – they're always on the ground floor.'

'Actually,' said Cross, 'it was a fashion with some Victorian London builders to place them as first-floor annexes.'

'I stand corrected,' he said amicably.

'But I thought you said you were planning a trip to see your wife in Australia at the end of her adventure,' Cross observed.

'The wife says it's never going to happen. But I'm trying

hypnotherapy, and if that fails get some knockout drugs from my GP,' Coombes replied.

'A twenty-two-hour flight sounds like an ordeal for an aviophobic.'

'All in the name of love, Sergeant,' he replied cheerfully, then waved as they drove off.

'All in the name of love indeed,' commented Ottey.

46

With Justin Frampton still missing, detectives had been unable to track down either Mikki or his tattooed muscle. This was hardly surprising, particularly as Cross had made it known that he didn't consider it a priority. The kidnap was something of a sideshow for him which he knew would eventually be resolved. He was more interested in working the murder. He asked Mackenzie to check Mark Coombes's phone records. He wanted to see how often he was making and receiving calls to Asia.

Luke Frampton arrived at the MCU with his daughter Sasha. Ottey got the distinct impression that she had forced her unwilling father to come in. He had the look of a child being dragged to the dentist. As she showed them into the VA and was about to get Carson, Luke Frampton specifically asked for Cross.

'He's working your wife's murder, not your son's dis-appearance,' Ottey informed him.

'But they're related, surely?' Sasha suggested.

'DS Cross takes the view they're not.'

'I'd very much like him to join us if that's possible,' he said.

Cross was very happy to do this, but insisted on clearing it with both Matthews and Carson. This wasn't in any way to ensure that he wasn't treading on anyone's toes. It was simply a matter of protocol. The former never concerned him in the least.

Luke Frampton's hand was shaking as he handed over his mobile phone to Cross. On it was a photograph of Justin Frampton slouched against an internal brick wall, probably in a warehouse or factory. His shirt and suit were covered in blood. His left eye was so swollen it was completely closed. There was a cut in the eyebrow above the right eye and another on his top lip, which was also grotesquely swollen. He was a red and purple picture of pain. Cross handed the phone over to Ottey for her to have a closer look.

'Did you receive any message with this?' Cross asked.

'No.'

'Do you know who's responsible for it?'

'Obviously not.'

'Do you have any idea why this might have happened to your son?'

'I do not.'

Cross thought about this for a moment. 'You have no ideas at all? No theories? No possibilities?'

'No.'

'Then why have you asked to see me?'

'Look at him. He's been beaten to a pulp,' Frampton said desperately.

'He has. But if you have nothing to add I have nothing to offer. You should've forwarded this to us and saved yourself the trouble of coming in,' said Cross who then turned and left.

'Where's he going?' Sasha asked in disbelief.

'Back to his office, I'd imagine,' Ottey replied.

Sasha walked out and called down the corridor, 'DS Cross?'

'Yes,' he replied, turning round.

'What are you doing?' she said.

'Going back to the case I'm investigating. Your mother's murder.'

'But what about my brother? My father asked to see you.'

'To what purpose?' Cross asked.

'To show you the photograph. He looks barely alive.'

'Well, I've seen the photograph,' he replied, and continued walking away.

'George?' Ottey had appeared from the VA suite. 'Mr Frampton says he would like to talk.'

'Justin is a troubled soul,' Frampton began.

At this Sasha sighed. 'Dad, enough of the excuses.'

'His gambling has always been a worry to us. We've paid for rehab—'

'Paid his debts, you mean,' Sasha interrupted.

'Yes, that as well, when we could. We thought it had stopped, that he'd got past it. What with therapy—'

'And the fact that he's been banned from all betting shops in the south-west, all tracks, racecourses, anywhere he could possibly place a bet,' Sasha interrupted again.

'Correct, but like all addicts he always found a way. He found illegitimate outlets who would take his bets and, as you know, once you stray down that path it's only going to end one way.'

'So, he owes money,' said Ottey.

'He does. A great deal and you really don't want to owe these kinds of people anything.'

'How much?' asked Ottey.

'It started out at just over two hundred thousand pounds,

but now with what they laughingly call interest it's increased obscenely and remains unpaid.'

'What? Did Mum know about this?'

'She was the first to know.'

'Because Clive Bland brought it to her attention,' said Cross.

Frampton looked up at him enquiringly.

'Faye Settle told us,' said Ottey.

'Well, you know what happened then. He tried to use it against her in this wretched property saga. Told her how embarrassing it would be for her if it got out that Justin had been gambling illegally and owed a small fortune. She reminded him that she was no longer a public figure, so the embarrassment would be completely personal and something she could easily deal with. She taunted him that it might even do her online branding some good. He was welcome to do with it whatever he wanted to.'

'The obvious question here, Mr Frampton, is how he came to be in possession of that information,' said Cross.

'I've thought about that, of course. But I have no idea.'

'Do you really expect us to believe that?'

'I'm telling you the truth.'

'If we're dealing with the truth perhaps you could tell us the truth about whether the people who have done this to Justin had been in touch prior to sending the photograph?'

Frampton thought about this for a moment, then decided to say what he'd obviously been withholding.

'They texted me almost immediately he went missing, but told me not to involve the police.'

'That's not uncommon in these situations,' replied Cross. 'What did they want?'

'Three hundred and fifty thousand pounds.'

'The amount he owes his bookies, presumably?' Cross asked.

'Yes. They have him. His bookies. But I have no idea who they are.'

'It's irrelevant,' said Cross.

'What are you talking about?' asked Frampton.

'The debt is no longer theirs. It's been sold on.'

'What? To whom?' Frampton asked, confused.

'At this point it might be helpful to remind you who Clive Bland's mother is.'

'Oh, Jesus.' The colour drained from Frampton's face as the full horror of who they were dealing with now sank in. Cross let him dwell on it for a few minutes.

'Was there any further contact between Bland and your wife?' Cross went on.

'Yes. He came back and offered to pay off the debt and get Justin out of trouble.'

'As long as Peggy backed down from her opposition to the development,' said Cross.

'Precisely.'

'Which presumably she refused to do, or we might not be in this situation.'

'We had a terrible row about it. I asked her what was more important to her, his life or a small piece of Bristol's heritage being preserved. She'd lost all perspective when it came to that wretched dispute.'

'Maybe she'd have retained her sense of perspective if you'd been around more often and not off shagging everything in sight all the time,' Sasha protested.

But it was as if she hadn't spoken. Her father was lost in his own world where this latest crisis was threatening to engulf him.

'She could be quite hard-headed and cold-hearted at times. She said Bland paying off Justin's debt wasn't the solution. He'd just carry on because this was proof that however desperate things became, someone would always step in and save his skin. That there would always be a way out for him no matter how bad things got.'

'But why would they kill her?' asked Sasha.

'They didn't,' replied Cross. 'Peggy Frampton's murder had nothing to do with her son's inability to pay off his gambling debts. Because this isn't where this narrative ends, is it, Mr Frampton?'

'I have no idea what you mean.'

'I mean you have more to tell us,' said Cross.

'I've told you all I know,' Frampton protested.

'Let me ask you another question, then, Mr Frampton. Did you manage to secure another means of paying off your son's ever-increasing debt after your wife turned down Clive Bland's offer?'

'I did not,' he said quietly.

'Seriously, come on, Dad, you've always been such a shit liar. What have you done?' Sasha asked. There followed a long silence which Cross decided to end.

'Shall we discuss your wife's jewellery?'

Frampton looked up at Cross desperately.

'You only discovered the theft of the jewellery a few days after the murder,' Cross continued.

'Correct.'

'But at that point it looked like the murder might have

been an interrupted burglary. Why didn't you check the safe immediately?'

'I wasn't allowed back into my house, if you remember.'

'But once you were, it still took a couple of days.'

'My wife had just been killed, Detective. I wasn't thinking straight.'

'Possibly not. But what happened when you were? Thinking straight?'

'I checked the safe and…' he began.

Cross waited for a good minute before saying, 'And the jewellery was there.'

Frampton paused before he answered. He looked up at Cross. He knew.

'Yes.'

'What?' exclaimed Sasha, desperately trying to keep up with what was going on.

'How much did Justin manage to sell them for?' Cross asked.

'Two hundred and fifty thousand pounds.'

'So a hundred thousand below their actual value and not quite the full amount of the debt. But the insurance claim would cover the shortfall. In fact you'd actually be in profit,' Cross elaborated.

'Mum wanted me to have that necklace, it's a family heirloom,' said Sasha.

'I was going to give you the remaining insurance money,' Frampton said pathetically.

'I'm not interested in the money. Money you would've obtained fraudulently, by the way.' She turned to Cross. 'Have you known this all along?'

TIM SULLIVAN

'I wasn't entirely certain, as I had no proof. But your father's persistent lack of interest in the recovery of the jewellery was instructive. It was as if he knew there was no point in asking because he knew they weren't going to resurface any time soon.'

Luke Frampton suddenly looked a good decade older than his age. The weight of his jowls, now grey in colour, seemed to be dragging his head inexorably towards the ground, in granite-like folds. He looked like an ancient Shar Pei dog on what he knows is his final visit to the vet.

'Perhaps a cup of tea?' Ottey suggested.

'You thought, even though burdened by the white-collar criminality of what you'd done, the matter had been put to rest. But it hadn't. The real horror didn't hit you until your son went missing. That could only mean one thing. Your son hadn't used the money to pay the debt. He'd used it for one last final hurrah. Placed one final bet.'

'You're kidding,' said Sasha.

'And now Andi Dragusha has decided to use it to his advantage.'

But Frampton was no longer looking at her. He was weeping, staring at the floor.

'I'm done with this. I'm done with you, and I'm done with my brother. I couldn't give a shit what happens to him, or you,' she said on her way out of the room. After a moment Cross decided to follow her.

'Tea?' he called after her.

'What do you want?' she asked wearily.

'Very perceptive of you, Mrs Connor. I need to talk to you about your mother.'

* * *

Cross made them tea in the MCU's small kitchen. Sasha watched the process and when he poured it into a couple of bone china cups said, without any malice, 'You're not exactly a normal detective, are you?'

'You'd have to define what you mean by "normal" before I can furnish you with an accurate answer. But you're certainly not the first to make that observation. Not quite as politely as you, usually, it has to be said.'

'How can I help?' she asked, smiling despite the situation. She had calmed down quite quickly, to her surprise. Perhaps it was because they were going to talk about her mother.

'Do you know Janette Coombes?'

'Of course, she's practically part of the family.'

'You like her.'

'Very much, I'm tremendously fond of her. But now you've brought her up, I'm feeling like a complete cow for not getting in touch with her about Mum. I've been so wrapped up in my own grief. She must be bereft. Are you in touch?'

'Yes.'

'Could you forward an email for me?'

Cross paused a moment. 'Of course. I'll give you her contact details and you can email her yourself. Was she close to your mother?'

'Very much so. They were like peas in a pod. They really enjoyed each other's company, which made working together so easy.'

'What exactly was her role with your mother?'

'Well, it started as a general PA. Mum was completely hopeless when she left politics and didn't have the support system of a big office behind her. So, the first thing Janette did was organise my mother's life. She was uber-organised,

Janette. She used to be a librarian years back but then, as all the libraries started to be closed down, she found work harder to come by.'

'And that was it?'

'She became my mum's right-hand woman. Particularly when all the internet stuff took off. They started discussing people's problems with each other, and Mum discovered they had so much in common emotionally. Their approach to life was so similar.'

'Peggy had an enormous amount of correspondence,' Cross observed.

'She did, and that's where Janette became so indispensable. After a while Mum even let her answer letters on her behalf. But the online forum really became Janette's domain. It grew exponentially. So much so that Mum had decided to announce Janette to her followers and make her officially another agony aunt, alongside her. It's just occurred to me actually that she could take over Mum's website. Sad. But it shouldn't go to waste. We thought we'd close it down, but there seems to be no reason why Janette shouldn't have a shot at it when she's back. Don't you think?'

'It certainly makes sense. So why did she leave, with things going so well?' asked Cross.

'Oh, that was all Mum's idea. It wasn't permanent. Polly's been great, but as Mum said, it wasn't the same. She's very professional, but too young. They didn't have the same rapport and Polly isn't really up to dishing out advice.'

'Whose idea was the sabbatical?'

'That was Mum. She'd never really travelled, Janette. Mark doesn't like to fly. Well, he's terrified of it, apparently. Peggy told her she needed to spread her wings. There was more to the world than Bristol. More to see than the south-west of England out of the rear window of a caravan. If Mark wouldn't fly, that was really his problem. There was no reason why she shouldn't travel the world. They called it her silver gap year.'

'Do you think there was more to it than that, maybe?'

'In what way?'

'How was Janette's marriage?' Cross asked.

'I honestly have no idea. Why are you asking?' she said, surprised.

'I'm thinking that maybe the state of their marriages was also something they had in common.'

'Possibly,' she said as she thought it through.

'Do you know Mark, her husband?'

'Never met him.'

'Until the funeral,' Cross reminded her.

'Oh yes,' she replied, remembering him hugging her. 'That was odd. He seemed so upset.' She drank another sip of tea. 'Great cup of tea, by the way.'

'I know,' he replied.

She laughed. Being a GP, it hadn't taken her long to work out that this detective was somewhere on the spectrum.

'Don't forget to send me Janette's contact details,' she said as she left.

47

'Plan of action, George?' asked Matthews in the doorway of his office.

'For what?'

'As a result of your meeting with Frampton,' she went on.

'He had nothing relevant to the murder case to say. He was here about his son's kidnapping,' Cross explained.

'That's what I meant.'

'But I'm not working the kidnapping,' he pointed out.

'I'd like you to work both,' she said. This pleased Cross. Approbation of his skill at his job was always welcome. He thought for a moment.

'In that case, I think we should pay Chapel and Bland another visit,' he replied.

'Why?'

'Because at present we have no lines of communication with the kidnappers. Bland could be a conduit for us. It's more than possible he's set in motion a sequence of events that have got out of hand and he now has no control of and might want to rectify. It's also possible that he's unaware of this latest development, and so will be at pains to help.'

'I still don't understand why they would buy the debt,' she said.

'You would if you'd met the father,' said Cross. 'The photograph of the beating. It's not about the money, Dragusha senior is using it as leverage over Frampton senior.'

'None of this is getting us any closer to Peggy Frampton's killer.'

'It isn't,' he agreed.

'But we need to sort it before it gets worse.'

'I suspect that will be down to Luke Frampton in the end,' said Cross.

'So, you'll go to Chapel's?' she asked, wanting to make sure they were both on the same page.

'I will.'

'Good. Now you're working both cases, are you sure you don't need any help?'

'No, DS Ottey can drive me.'

Matthews looked surprised, which he noted.

'I don't drive. I can. I just choose not to,' he explained.

'So, what, Ottey's just your chauffeur?' she said.

'Interesting you should say that. She asks me the exact same thing on a daily basis,' he replied, completely straight-faced.

'Let me know how you get on,' she said and left. She walked past Ottey's desk. 'You deserve a medal. You really do.'

'Oh no, what's he done now?' Ottey asked.

'Nothing. He was just being... Cross.'

'Yeah. I get that a lot.'

Cross and Ottey waited in the glass-walled boardroom of Chapel's HQ which sat majestically above the entrance to the building. The front entrance had a swirling roof of slate sticks arranged like a three-dimensional cross-hatch sketch.

It gave the impression of being constantly on the move as you walked towards the building. It reminded Cross of a murmuration of starlings swooping through the sky. A black swirling mass at one point, then seeming to disappear in an instant, before immediately reappearing. The structure announced to the visitor not only the success of the company, but also that any building project they had in mind, would be in the best of hands. Cross looked out over the landscaped grounds and man-made lake, drinking his perfectly brewed cup of tea. He turned as he heard Chapel and Bland enter the room. Chapel was in his default setting of unctuous charm. But Cross noted Bland's previous shell of machismo bravura seemed somewhat in check.

'There's been a development in the case which we hoped you might be able to shed some light on,' Ottey began.

'Specifically you, Mr Bland,' Cross added.

Ottey then handed over her phone, showing the photograph of Justin's beaten face, to the two men. Chapel looked suitably shocked. Bland attempted a neutral reaction, designed to imply that he had no idea why they were showing it to him. But a quick look shot in Cross's direction gave away the fact that this was news to him, both unwelcome and frightening.

'Who is this?' asked Chapel.

'Peggy Frampton's son,' Ottey informed him.

'What the hell's happened to him?' Chapel went on.

'He's been badly beaten. This photograph was sent to his father,' Ottey explained.

'And you're showing this to us, why?'

'Were you aware of Justin Frampton's gambling problem and his enormous debts?' asked Cross.

'I wasn't aware of Justin Frampton at all up until this point,' Chapel replied.

'Unlike your colleague here, who was aware of both, and tried to use it to your mutual advantage,' said Cross.

'Clive, what on earth have you been up to?' asked Chapel.

'Do I need a lawyer?' asked Bland, ignoring his boss's question.

'Mr Bland attempted to pressurise Peggy Frampton into backing off from her opposition to Harbourside by threatening to go public with her son's problems. But she was having none of it,' said Cross.

'Is this true?' Chapel asked Bland.

'I think that as we, the police, are informing you of this, you can take it as fact. When Peggy was unmoved by Mr Bland's threats, he very generously offered to pay off her son's debt, in return for her ending her opposition to the development,' Cross explained.

'I would never have sanctioned such a payment, no matter how large or small,' Chapel insisted.

'Three hundred and fifty thousand pounds, in point of fact.'

'Jesus!'

'But you wouldn't have had to. Would he, Mr Bland?' There was no response. 'Because Mikki Dragusha had agreed to underwrite it.'

'There was nothing illegal about that,' Bland retorted.

'Illegal, possibly not, but it has unethical written all over it,' said Ottey. 'Not a great image for a company like this.'

'To be fair to Mr Bland I can see that even he is surprised by this development,' said Cross, indicating the photo of Justin's beaten face.

'I know nothing about this,' Bland protested.

'You should perhaps be a little more circumspect in the people you choose to do business with then. Even if they are family. Or, in your case, particularly if they're family.'

'I don't understand what's going on here. Are you suggesting that Mikki Dragusha—' Chapel began.

'One of your major investors,' Cross helpfully pointed out.

'—is behind this beating?'

'And kidnap. Justin Frampton is currently missing.'

Chapel began thinking on his feet. 'As I've said, I know nothing of this. But it occurs to me, and I know how dreadful this sounds, but what would Mikki Dragusha have to gain from this now that Peggy is dead? I'm assuming you're saying this is all wrapped up in the harbourside development.'

'You're asking the right question, but of the wrong Dragusha,' said Cross. 'The question is, what would his father have to gain?'

'Andi Dragusha's twenty-nine-year-old daughter is having an affair with Luke Frampton. It's fair to say he's not happy about it,' said Ottey.

'You're kidding. What is it with that man? He just can't keep his dick in his trousers. So where does this leave us?' asked Chapel.

Cross turned to Bland. 'Once you alerted Mikki to Justin's financial predicament, as it were, you left the door wide open for his father.'

'You'll have to explain. I'm not as well versed in the activities of organised crime families as it appears some of us are,' Chapel said, looking directly at Bland.

'People like Dragusha see the problems of people like Justin as opportunities. This one just happened to fall into the old man's lap. Mikki bought Justin's debt as his father had seen how to turn it to his advantage. They have no interest in the money. They see that as a small price to pay to get Agnesha away from Frampton,' Cross said.

'That's what this is now all about. Pure and simple,' added Ottey.

'So, talk to Frampton,' said Chapel.

'The reason we're here is that we have no lines of communication with Justin's abductors,' said Ottey.

'Wait a minute. How do you know that Mikki's definitely involved?' asked Bland.

'They've made no attempt to conceal their identity,' Cross replied.

'They're sending Frampton a message,' added Ottey.

Chapel turned to Bland.

'Clive, what are you waiting for? Get hold of your cousin immediately,' he said with disdain. 'Find out what he wants and put an end to this. Now.' His face was firm and unflinchingly unfriendly. He'd practically spat out the word 'cousin' as if it were giving him mouth ulcers. Bland was taken aback to be spoken to in this way by a man who was normally so equably polite. He left the office quickly, taking his phone out of his jacket pocket as he did so.

'I have to ask you one question,' Chapel continued, making sure that Bland was far enough away. 'It makes me shake just thinking about it. But is there any possibility that these people had anything to do with Peggy Frampton's murder?'

Cross was about to answer in the negative when Ottey got in first. 'It's possible,' she replied.

'Oh my god,' Chapel muttered quietly and turned away from them.

★ ★ ★

'Why did you say that?' Cross asked Ottey when they got back into her car.

'I just wanted to keep the pressure on them both.'

'Because travelling in the lift had annoyed you,' he said.

She thought for a moment. 'Yes,' she replied.

Her phone rang through the car speaker system.

'Ottey,' she answered.

'It's Clive Bland,' the disembodied voice said, filling the car.

'You want us to come back in? We're still outside.'

'That won't be necessary.'

'Okay, well you're on speaker.'

'Mikki Dragusha knows nothing of this abduction, and hasn't bought Justin's debt.'

'Of course not,' said Ottey ironically. 'But let me guess. He wants to help.'

'He does. As you know, he and his father have a long reach and are much respected—'

'Look, Bland, I'm not going to dance to your bullshit tune. You sound about as genuine as a Politburo spokesperson with a drink problem. So cut the crap and tell me what they want.'

48

Luke Frampton was pale and drawn as he sat in the drawing room with Ottey and Frampton's daughter Sasha. He'd looked exactly like this once before, Cross reflected. It was when he'd seen his wife coming out of the house in a body bag. Was this situation comparable, in his mind? He looked shocked to his core, bereft, and at a loss what to think.

'Does Aggy know about this?' he asked.

'No one knows where she is,' replied Ottey.

'What the hell has that got to do with anything, Dad?' exclaimed Sasha.

'I just need time to think about this,' came the barely inaudible reply.

'Are you serious?' asked Sasha, almost laughing in disbelief. 'What is there to think about? Look at him!' She brandished his phone in front of him with Justin's swollen face on it.

'You might want to consider what could happen to your son if you don't agree to this. Your girlfriend's family think nothing of killing someone to solve a problem,' said Cross.

'Then why haven't they come after me?' he asked.

'Give them time,' said Ottey.

The solution was as simple as it was predictable. If Frampton agreed to end his relationship with Agnesha, Justin would not only be returned to the family, but his debt would be magically erased.

'This is blackmail. Can't you do something about it?' Frampton wailed with an outrageous sense of indignation, Ottey thought.

'According to them, they don't have your son, but are willing in the circumstances to broker his release, and write off his debt in exchange for your holding up your end of the bargain.'

'And you believe them?'

'It's irrelevant what I believe or don't believe. The fact is you have till five,' Cross said and left.

'I wouldn't leave it much longer to decide, if I were you,' Ottey advised the barrister before she, too, left.

Frampton capitulated within sixty minutes. Justin was then picked up a few hours later by an ambulance that was called to a lay-by on the A38 south of Taunton. He was taken to the Musgrove Park Hospital emergency department, where he was treated. His father and sister drove down to collect him. He would need surgery for a fractured eye socket and dental work to fix some broken teeth. But he was alive and debt-free. Even so, this family's main tragedy had yet to be solved. Who had killed Peggy Frampton?

49

That night, Cross was at home reading when an email pinged through to him from his friend Oliver Black, in Cambridge. He studied its contents carefully. It was just as he thought. The text exchange between Janette Coombes and her husband, and her text exchanges with Peggy Frampton when she'd been working for her, had been written by two completely different people. This, together with the fact that Mark Coombes's phone records showed no international calls of any kind, neither outgoing or incoming, in the last six months, was enough for Cross.

Heather Matthews's phone rang beside her bed. She was half-awake anyway. It was 3.45 a.m. Her husband slept soundly through it, as always. He'd got used to calls at all hours of the night over the decades of being married to her. It annoyed her slightly. Not that she wanted to disturb him. It was just that she was such a light sleeper and was envious.

'Matthews,' she said, answering the call.

'It's DS Cross,' came the reply.

It was still dark when Cross and Matthews sat in her car together, in the quiet Knowle West residential estate. There

TIM SULLIVAN

were a couple of lights on in some houses, where early risers were getting ready for work or school. They were waiting for a custody van. When it arrived, they drove slowly through the estate until they were parked outside the Coombes's house. Along with them was another police van with six uniformed policemen in protective vests. Matthews hadn't questioned Cross's decision to arrest Mark Coombes that morning, once he'd told her all the evidence he had. Cross himself had been reflecting in the car how refreshing her response had been. Had he called Carson, there would have been a long conversation on the phone, followed by a tedious meeting at the MCU. The decision-making process would have taken a further twenty-four hours. In the normal course of events Cross wouldn't have called either of them but Ottey had told him fifteen minutes before he called Matthews that Carla had a follow-up at the hospital at ten, and her daughter was going to be her main priority that morning. It was Ottey who'd suggested that he called Matthews, rather than Carson, for all the reasons Cross had just been reflecting on.

They generally carried out arrests this early in the morning, not just because they knew their suspect would be in, but also because it gave the officers an element of surprise. This often rendered the suspect vulnerable and, after being cautioned, they would sometimes just open up.

One of the officers smashed Coombes's front door with a small battering ram, known as an enforcer. The others ran past him into the property with shouts of 'POLICE!' Mark Coombes was fast asleep. Matthews and Cross allowed him to get dressed, then took him to the kitchen, as the rest of the officers searched the property.

'You're being arrested for the murder of Peggy Frampton

on February the seventh of this year,' Cross informed him, then went on to caution him. Coombes laughed nervously and looked shocked.

'This is so wrong. All I've tried to do throughout this investigation is help you. I've put you in touch with Janette. Why on earth would I want to kill my wife's boss?'

Neither Matthews nor Cross answered. He'd told his senior officer of his preference to interview suspects under caution, back at the MCU. She'd heard of his skills across an interview table, and the truth was, she was looking forward to witnessing it first-hand. So she was very happy to follow his lead and say nothing.

Michael Swift arrived to obtain some of Coombes's DNA from the house. He was really pleased to see Cross again and couldn't help muttering to him as he passed him in the corridor.

'The assistant's husband? Awesome! Didn't see that coming. Any chance you can talk me through it later?'

'Certainly not,' Cross replied, instantly regretting it, as nothing would have given him more pleasure. The request just struck him as inappropriate in the circumstances.

They left Swift and the other officers searching the property and took Coombes back to the MCU. Cross was given a couple of laptop computers in evidence bags, which he took with him. Coombes was processed and put into a cell while they waited for his solicitor to arrive. He seemed so baffled and smiley that Matthews began to wonder if they had in fact got their man. She wasn't halfway across the open area when she heard a familiar plaintive cry of 'Ma'am?' cross the floor.

'My office,' she said to Carson, who was already in pursuit.

* * *

'Have you quite finished?' Matthews asked Carson after his five-minute-long self-indulgent whine about being the deputy SIO, and not being kept in the loop.

'I have,' he said with the absurd confidence of the righteous.

'I don't know you very well, but I think you would be much happier in your job if you didn't see everything that goes on in this department as some sort of well-orchestrated conspiracy against you, and stopped interpreting what anyone says as a personal criticism or demonstration of a lack of respect. As far as I can see, everyone respects you, except for when you try to take a lead where there is no lead to be taken. It just irritates people. I am the SIO on this case and I know that you saw that as an insult initially. But I am senior to you, and it was deemed necessary to have someone of my rank running the case. That had nothing to do with you personally. Having said that, things moved very quickly this morning and as SIO I am under no obligation whatsoever to keep you informed of all developments or my movements. So, instead of wallowing in self-pity, why don't you go and announce to the team that we've made an arrest, and you can even pretend you had something to do with it.'

He was about to reply when she stopped him.

'Go!'

What he couldn't tell her was that he'd already made such a song and dance about them not being in the office to the entire unit an hour earlier. Asking where the hell they were. So he couldn't really go back in there and pretend he was in on it from the start. Or could he? he wondered, as he went back to his desk.

50

Mark Coombes seemed bemused by the situation he found himself in. He sat in one of the interview rooms with a duty solicitor beside him. This particular lawyer seemed very young, to Cross, no more than twenty-six, he estimated. He gave off a distinct air of nervousness and anxiety, which Cross managed to read easily. It was a behaviour that was exhibited to him in that room on a regular basis; although normally on the part of the suspect, not their lawyer, it had to be said. He wondered whether Coombes had also picked up on it. Ottey arrived as Cross was organising his files symmetrically on the table.

'Good morning, DS Ottey,' Coombes said brightly.

'Mr Coombes,' came the polite reply.

'Mark, please. I certainly wasn't expecting to see you again under these circumstances,' he said, as if there had been some daft misunderstanding which they would shortly clear up. Ottey didn't reply. 'Measuring you up for a new conservatory perhaps, but not this. Being arrested! Did you manage to have a look at the brochure I gave you the other day?'

'I haven't, no.'

'Oh well, plenty of time. If you do find something you like, I can pop round and advise you in situ, if that works.'

Cross decided to bring this conversation to an end. 'Mr Coombes—'

'Mark, please.'

'Mr Coombes,' Cross insisted. 'Where were you on seventh of February this year?'

'That was the night Peggy was murdered?'

'It was.'

'I was at home. Watching football.'

'What did you eat?'

'A pizza.'

'Did you order in?'

'No, supermarket jobby.'

'You remember the evening well?'

'Of course I do. I remember thinking the next day that, while I was doing that, someone was doing Peggy, if you'll excuse the pun.' Cross noted this was a favoured expression of Coombes's.

'Was anyone with you?'

'No.'

'So, you don't have anyone who can prove you were home that night? Maybe a neighbour calling round, or a delivery of some sort?' Cross suggested helpfully.

'I do not.'

'What was your relationship with Peggy Frampton like?'

'Fine. She was a good woman. Driven, mind you.'

'How did she behave towards you?' Cross asked.

'Me?' he said, as if it were something he'd never given much thought to before. 'Fine, mostly apologetic, if I'm honest. We only ever spoke when I answered the phone and she apologised for disturbing us.'

'She felt the need to apologise.'

'Probably, but it wasn't at all necessary. J enjoyed working for her.'

'Enjoyed?' Cross repeated.

'Yes.'

'I was referring to the tense.'

'Oh, I see. Well she's not going to be working for her when she returns, to put it bluntly. Is she?'

'How would you describe your marriage?'

'Um, all right.'

'Ever thought of separating?'

'Not seriously, no.'

'What does that mean?' asked Cross.

'Well, everyone has their ups and downs, don't they? We've had our share. I mean we've been together a long while.'

'No children,' Cross observed.

'Correct.'

'Choice or circumstance?'

'That's personal, if you don't mind.'

'I do mind.'

Coombes's lawyer leant over and whispered in his client's ear.

'We couldn't,' Coombes said.

'Did you seek medical advice?'

'We did.'

'Was any cause determined?'

'Yes. It was me. My fault. A low count.'

'And how did your wife feel about that?'

'She was great. Said it made no difference to her. She didn't mind. But I knew that wasn't true. She'd always wanted a family. We both had.'

'Were you upset?'

'Wouldn't you be?'

Cross ignored the question. 'Was it a source of tension in your marriage?' he went on.

'It was for me. Her not so much.'

'But you didn't think she was being entirely honest?'

'No.'

'Did you seek help?'

'You mean therapy, couples' counselling?'

'Either.'

'No.'

'Not even online?' Cross asked. He noticed a slight hesitation in Coombes.

'No.'

'Does the online name glassman86 mean anything to you?'

'No comment.'

Cross consulted his notes and ticked a question. He turned a page, then looked up.

'Did your wife ever discuss your marriage, your lack of children with Peggy?'

'I have no idea.'

'Did they discuss Peggy's marriage at all?'

'They did, but J's very discreet.'

'Glassman86 went on Peggy Frampton's website quite frequently in the last twelve months. Why did you do that?'

'No comment.'

'But it was you?'

'No comment.'

'We have all of the correspondence and the responses you received from her other followers. Such a strange word that, in this context, don't you find? "Followers"?

Redolent of a cult with a revered leader. But anyway, some of the responses you received were quite brutal, were they not? People do say the most dreadful things on the internet. Do you think they really believe what they say, or is it all for show? To me it's like a modern Colosseum, with digital gladiators dealing out verbal barbs instead of steel.'

No response.

'I'm not going to go into enormous detail about this, Mr Wilson,' Cross said, addressing the lawyer. 'But suffice to say, if glassman86 isn't your client then he has a strikingly similar, to the point of identical, life story to tell. Married for twenty years. No children. His fault. Worried his wife might leave him because he's unable to provide her with a family and find someone to impregnate her.'

Coombes visibly winced at this.

'Or possibly, someone who could give her stepchildren, an instant family if you like. Then he seemed to build up an all-consuming resentment towards her. Seems unfair to me. What do you think, DS Ottey?'

'It wouldn't be the first time a man blamed a woman for everything that was wrong in his life, whether she had anything to do with it or not,' Ottey replied.

'Did your wife know you were communicating with Peggy Frampton on the website?'

'No comment.'

'Really? Did you know that Janette and Peggy often discussed people's problems that cropped up on the site? Peggy would ask her advice and more often than not act on it. In fact, over the years she worked for her, she increasingly came to run the website and respond to people's problems in Peggy's absence. According to Peggy's daughter, Janette was such a success that the number of visitors and followers increased. Peggy was going to introduce her officially as another consultant on the website.'

'She never mentioned that to me.'

'You should ask her. I'm surprised she never mentioned it. But let's get back to the forum. You became quite angry. Belligerent. You had rows with so many people. That must've been difficult.'

Again Coombes didn't reply. So Cross looked at his notes, as if that line of questioning wasn't going anywhere, and maybe he should try a new one.

'When was the year off, the sabbatical, first mooted?' he asked.

'What?'

'When was it first mentioned?' Ottey translated.

'About a year ago.'

'And whose idea was it?' Cross asked.

'Janette's, obviously.'

'That's not actually true, is it? It was Peggy's initially.'

'If you say so.'

'What did you think about it?'

'I was all for it.'

'Why?'

'It made a lot of sense. She needed a break and so did I.'

'From the marriage?'

'From everything.'

'From Peggy Frampton?'

'From work, definitely. It was full-on, twenty-four seven. The poor woman needed a break.'

'So you were supportive?'

'Very much so.'

'Mr Coombes, did you kill Peggy Frampton on February the seventh of this year?'

'I did not,' Coombes said, laughing at the absurdity of this suggestion.

'Does the online name glassman86 mean anything to you?' Cross asked again.

'You've already asked me that question,' replied Coombes.

'I'm giving you another opportunity to answer it,' said Cross. There was no response. Cross looked at the lawyer. 'Mr Wilson, you might want to remind your client that we are in possession of both his laptop and his home computer.'

The lawyer leant over and whispered something to Coombes who then looked up at Cross.

'It may have been a username I used in the past. I use a lot of different ones,' he explained.

'Yes or no, Mr Coombes? I have no use for "may",' said Cross, looking straight at him.

'Yes,' came the answer.

'So, this means your last exchanges with Peggy's website were in October of last year,' Cross continued.

'I haven't said I had any exchanges,' Coombes said.

'I'd like to speak to my client,' said the solicitor, speaking to the detectives for the first time. Cross said nothing, but just picked up his file and left the room.

Matthews was watching a feed of the interview with Carson. 'He takes his time, doesn't he?' she said.

'Oh yes, he can go on like this for days,' Carson replied.

'I bet he can.'

'It's all completely scripted, you know. Nothing

spontaneous, well, hardly ever. But he plans for any eventuality and if an answer goes a certain way, he'll take a different route in his notes. It's like an interactive play.'

51

'My client acknowledges the use of glassman86 in this thread, on this particular website,' said Wilson.

'And also in the online forum?' Cross asked. Wilson looked at Coombes who nodded his assent.

'And also in the online forum,' the lawyer confirmed.

Ottey then pushed a piece of paper across the desk to Coombes. It was something Mackenzie had found a few days before. It was a breakthrough at the time. A breakthrough they couldn't confirm till they got hold of Coombes's computers.

'This is the last piece of advice given to you on that forum. You never visited it again,' she said.

'Under that pseudonym,' Cross clarified.

'Yes, this was your last interaction as glassman86. Do you recognise it?'

Coombes didn't even look at it. This small act of defiance was a significant development in the interview for Cross. They were possibly getting somewhere.

'Would you like to read it out for your lawyer's benefit?' Ottey asked. Coombes didn't reply, but just stared at the female officer. All pretence at jocularity had left the room. There wasn't a trace of it left.

'Then let me,' she said, before Cross interrupted.

'To put what you're about to hear in context, Mr Wilson, it comes at the end of a quite cantankerous, from Mr Coombes's side, exchange with Peggy Frampton. In this exchange he was being advised to let his wife have a little more freedom in their relationship. That he had her on a tight leash and maybe needed to let go a little. She had no room to breathe, was another observation made. He was stifling their relationship with possessiveness and resentment. Resentment of a curiously inverted nature. Resentment, it would seem, of the fact that his wife was ostensibly so accepting of the childless state of their marriage. Which he repeatedly points out is his fault. As if to somehow explain his behaviour away.'

'So, this is what was said,' Ottey continued. '"You are suffocating your wife emotionally and crushing the life out of your marriage… you may as well just put a plastic bag over her head."'

There was a moment's silence, broken by Wilson. 'I fail to see the relevance.'

'And you are alone in that. Mr Coombes, together with DS Ottey and myself, are well aware of the chilling relevance, are we not?'

Coombes didn't reply. He just looked at Cross fixedly.

'Then perhaps you could explain?' asked the lawyer.

'Certainly. Peggy Frampton was asphyxiated with a plastic bag,' Cross said, matter-of-factly. The young lawyer did his level best not to look shocked.

'It must've been agonising for her. When she was found her head was arched back, her mouth stretched open in extremis, struggling for a last gasp of air, but just sucking the plastic into her mouth.' Cross gave a grotesque impression of Peggy

Frampton's head post-mortem, staring at the ceiling, mouth wide open.

'Do you want to respond to this, Mark?' asked Ottey.

'No comment.'

'Maybe it was an accident. Was it an accident?' she asked.

'Of course it wasn't an accident,' said Cross, contradicting her immediately, as planned. 'He took a bag with him. It was premeditated. Poetic justice, perhaps, Mr Coombes? I wouldn't have had you down as the sort for dramatic gestures, but it just goes to show you can never be sure about people.'

'Did you kill Peggy Frampton on the seventh of February this year, Mark?' asked Ottey.

'No comment.'

'There's actually a tragic irony in all of this,' Cross continued. 'The fact is, you weren't talking to Peggy Coombes at all, that day in the forum. Their log shows that you were actually talking to your wife. It was Janette who told you that you were suffocating the life out of her emotionally. Your wife who said you might as well put a bag over her head. I wonder if she knew?'

Coombes looked momentarily confused at this. It was as if he didn't know how he felt about this piece of information, or what to do with it.

'You didn't tell us you'd done some work on the Framptons' conservatory.'

'You didn't ask.'

'Is that how you had the alarm code? Or was it Janette who told you?'

'No comment.'

'Well let's move on, as we have a lot of other things to cover.'

'What other things?' asked the lawyer, not able to completely mask a sense of unease in his voice.

'We'll come to it in due course. DS Ottey?'

'We know you were there, in the Frampton house, Mark, and we know you killed her. Do you want to talk to your lawyer before we go any further? You must remember this interview will be used by the prosecution. The jury will get to hear how you conducted yourself in this interview. How long you refused to admit your role in the victim's death.'

'No comment.'

'You thought you were being careful. Marks on the bedroom carpet show that you were wearing shoe covers to prevent us from identifying your shoes by their soles. Presumably the same foot protectors you wear in your work when visiting people's homes. You waited for Peggy in her bedroom, behind the door. She walked straight past you into the bathroom, which you weren't expecting, to run a bath. She came back into the bedroom to change and saw you. You were face to face with her. Again, something you hadn't anticipated. You'd thought you'd attack her from behind as you imagined she'd go to her dressing table or maybe the near side of the bed to get undressed. But here she was, looking straight at you. Quite unnerving, I should imagine. Did she speak to you? Ask you what you were doing? Or didn't she have time, before you grabbed the nearest thing you could see? A glass paperweight, which you smashed into the side of her head. Then, as she fell to the floor, you suffocated her with the bag from behind, making sure you couldn't see the fear and terror on her face.'

She paused. No one said a word.

'You were careful not to leave any trace of yourself. Or

so you thought. You rummaged through a drawer to make it look like a burglary. How could we possibly deduce a cause of death like asphyxiation from a plastic bag? But you inadvertently ripped one of Peggy's earrings out of her ear when you tore the bag off, possibly in a bit of a panic, as the reality of what you'd just done sank in. In the earring was a fragment of the bag. But of course that doesn't prove it was you. Nor, before your lawyer points it out, does the DNA trace, your DNA from the saliva that dropped out of your mouth, from the sheer effort of suffocating her, onto the bag once we'd found it. It doesn't place you at the scene.' Cross was convinced the lawyer actually looked a little grateful she'd said this, as it clearly hadn't occurred to him as yet. He wondered if this was the young man's first murder interview. If it was, it would be one he'd never forget. People tended to remember their first.

'But you did make a mistake in the heat of the moment. The bath was still running. You couldn't leave it like that. It'd flood the whole place. So you turned it off. Very considerate but also very incriminating as you left a fingerprint on the tap. The taps which had been cleaned only that morning by their cleaner. Only the one print but enough to place you at the scene. You'd been careful enough to wear gloves, but after you hit her with the paperweight – not part of the plan – you had her blood on the gloves. You still needed to disrupt the drawers to make us think she was killed in the commission of a burglary. But you couldn't leave blood traces in the drawer as we'd realise she was murdered before the killer was "interrupted." Your mistake was to then turn off the taps. Could be thought to be considerate, not wanting to cause a flood. Had you not already killed the homeowner who was now beyond caring about such a domestic inconvenience.'

As no one said a word Cross suggested, 'Perhaps another conference with your client, Mr Wilson?' A suggestion that was gratefully taken up.

Carson, Matthews and Ottey were watching Cross as he made himself a cup of tea.

'Why bring the print up? We can't use it in court,' Carson began.

'We don't need to use it in court,' Cross replied.

'Leverage,' answered Ottey.

'But we can't prove it's his,' Carson protested, puzzled that they couldn't see the point he was making.

'Is there a fingerprint on the bathroom taps?' Cross asked.

'A partial which is of no use to anyone,' Carson replied.

'Do you believe it to be the killer's?'

'Yes, but like I said. We can't prove it.'

'Do you believe that all the other evidence we have proves that Coombes is Peggy Frampton's killer?'

'Yes,' Carson conceded, still not knowing where this was leading.

'Ergo the print has to be Coombes's. He doesn't know it's useless, but he knows he turned the taps off without his gloves and so he believes that it places him at the scene.'

'So, you lied to him.'

'I did no such thing. I told him we had a print which we all, you included, genuinely believe to be his, which places him at the scene. That, together with all the other evidence we have, will lead to his solicitor encouraging him to confess,' Cross concluded.

★ ★ ★

When they returned from their conference Mark Coombes immediately confessed to killing Peggy Frampton, but claimed it had been an accident. He wanted to frighten her off. She was ruining his marriage, and now his wife had left him for a year which he saw as the beginning of the end of their marriage. His argument was flawed, but Cross was perfectly happy to leave it to a prosecution barrister to pull it apart.

'Result!' proclaimed Carson.

'Oh, he's not finished yet. Not by a long chalk,' replied Matthews. But what she was really thinking, was how quickly Carson had got from his questioning Cross's methods to celebrating the confession as victoriously as if he'd elicited it from the suspect himself.

52

'Are you going to charge my client?' asked Wilson.

'All in good time,' Cross assured him, as he leafed through his folder in his measured fashion, before finding the document he was after. He pushed it across the table to Coombes.

'This is the transcript of your text conversation with your wife that you provided us with. Do you recognise it?' Cross asked.

Coombes gave it the briefest of glances.

'Yes.'

'All right. So, here are a few pages of Janette's work notes about Clive Bland that you yourself gave us a couple of weeks ago,' Cross went on. 'I'm no linguistics expert, but on closer inspection even I noticed some differences in style. In her conversation with you the sentences are quite short. The punctuation is somewhat perfunctory. Your wife was a librarian for much of her working life and, judging by the number of books in your house, was quite a reader; obviously literate.'

'They could be my client's books,' Wilson pointed out.

'Fair point, but even if we accept they are shared, it still indicates a great interest in literature.'

'And your point is?' asked the lawyer, who Cross thought was either getting progressively more confident, or bored and wanting to go home.

'My point is that Janette's notes are written in a quite different style. Longer sentences with subclauses and a preponderance of commas.'

'One is a text conversation, the other written notes. Both requiring differing styles,' the lawyer pointed out.

'I thought you might say that, as it also occurred to me. So, I found some other digital exchanges between Janette and Peggy. They too are quite different to the text conversation you provided us with. The other thing that struck me was the use of acronyms in that conversation; you'll see I've highlighted them – TBH, CTTOI, LMK, etc. Yet in all of her other correspondence, emails, notes, she doesn't make use of them at all.'

'Again, it's a modern conversational convention,' Wilson pointed out.

'Quite so, though not used by everyone. But we also have the email that Janette wrote for us about Clive Bland and all of Peggy's dealings with him and his attempted intimidation of her to compare to other documents we know she wrote. Anyway, as I've already said, I'm no expert, but I do happen to know one at Cambridge University. Clever man, completely obsessed with language, like no one else I know, and he confirmed it for me. That the text conversation you claim to have had with your wife is, when compared to other texts of hers in our possession, not actually written by her. Nor the email you provided. They were all written by someone else.'

Coombes's face had set into an expressionless neutrality. It was a defence mechanism usually employed by suspects when they felt the evidence had started to stack up irrevocably against them. In this case, though, it was maybe simple resignation of the fact that he would be going to prison, in that he'd already confessed to the murder of Peggy Frampton.

'They were written by you, were they not?' Cross asked.

Coombes said nothing.

'Care to comment, Mark?' said Ottey.

'Mr Coombes, where is your wife currently?'

He thought for a moment. 'She's working her way down the coast of Malaysia.'

'East or west?' asked Cross.

'East.'

Cross thought about this then looked up. 'Really? Why not the west? Much more interesting, by all accounts.'

'You'd have to ask her.'

'It's also odd because it's right in the middle of the monsoon season,' said Cross.

'Can't be helped.'

'On the contrary, it most certainly can. Is she not aware that there are two separate monsoons in Malaysia? The south-western and the north-eastern? They take place at completely different times of year. So, she could have avoided it by going down the west coast. Maybe she didn't know that. Or was it you who didn't know this particular Malaysian meteorological idiosyncrasy?'

Coombes didn't answer.

'Your wife isn't in the Far East at all, is she, Mark?' Ottey asked.

'No comment.'

'Why was her passport in your bedroom?' she went on.

'No comment.'

'And why did we find her laptop in your house?'

'It's her work laptop. She has another.'

'Is there anything you'd like to tell us at this point, Mark?' Ottey asked.

'No comment.'

Cross started to go through his folder again till he came to the right page.

'I called in on some of your neighbours last night – they all know you, of course, although in my experience it isn't always that way. Modern society has become so fragmented, so disparate, don't you think? Everyone's quite content to text or WhatsApp and follow one another's lives on Instagram, so there's no actual need to see friends. But the neighbours told me you've been doing a bit of work on the house – specifically the conservatory. Is that true?'

'No comment.'

'But the conservatory is quite new, you told us. So what exactly needed doing? Something to do with the floor, perhaps?'

'No comment.'

'That's strange. You normally seem so keen to discuss conservatories. You're like me, I imagine – your work is your hobby.'

'No comment.'

'I wouldn't have thought a conservatory would be in need of underfloor heating, but according to your neighbour, yours did. She saw the cardboard packaging put out for the bin men,' Cross continued.

'It might be useful in the winter months,' suggested Ottey.

TIM SULLIVAN

'I suppose that is possible.'

'You could sit in there with the Sunday papers, a cup of tea and nice toasty feet. Is that what you installed in October, Mark? Underfloor heating?' Ottey asked.

'No comment.'

'Very well,' said Cross, extracting another piece of paper from his folder. 'Let me show you something else which I think will bring our conversation to a quick conclusion.'

He pushed the sheet of paper across the table. It had a picture of a wave pattern on it.

'This is a wave pattern taken by a ground-penetrating radar of your conservatory floor. GPR sends electromagnetic wave energy through the concrete floor and it shows up any anomalies underneath. It's all perfectly normal until we get to this bit.'

He indicated a part of the picture where the waves became much more pronounced.

'This is the interesting bit. Right there.'

Michael Swift had been gathering DNA samples in the Coombes house when the GPR machine and operator arrived. He'd been impressed not just by the fact that George Cross had managed to get his hands on one so quickly – he had in fact requested it two days earlier, in anticipation of when and where it would be needed – but that this case had taken an unexpected twist. They had surveyed the floor of the conservatory as requested. The GPR technician then examined the read-out, as well as emailing it to his superior for confirmation. It was obvious to Michael Swift, looking over the man's shoulder, what they were looking at, but he held back and waited to be told. There was definitely something under the conservatory floor and it was big enough to be a body.

A forensic archaeologist was summoned and the excavation began. Her job was to remove any human remains from the site without causing any damage and possible loss of forensic evidence. After a couple of hours they came across what Cross presumed was Janette Coombes's body, wrapped in a dust sheet. She was fully dressed, which meant that together with being entombed in concrete the rate of decomposition had been slightly arrested. Having said that, the pathologist insisted on pointing out that the underfloor heating complicated the post-mortem interval calculation. But he was fairly confident that the body had been buried around October of the previous year. Exactly the time that Janette had started her 'trip abroad'.

'We can wait for a positive identification of the body, but I'm not entirely sure that's necessary, is it, Mr Coombes?' Cross asked back in the interview room. The young lawyer couldn't help but give the man sitting next to him, his client, a look of barely concealed shock.

Mark Coombes was then charged not only with the murder of Peggy Frampton, but also that of his wife. He claimed that his wife's death was another accident, which resulted after a drunken argument about her plans to leave for a year. Coombes thought it was the end of their marriage. She disagreed. They fought and he ended up strangling her. Months of guilt, grief and anger boiled up into a rage against the woman he blamed for the unexpected turn his life had taken, Peggy Frampton.

How quickly – in a space of just months – one life could change completely, and two end, ruminated Cross. There had been nothing remarkable about this conservatory salesman. Seemingly happily married, though childless, he had managed to destroy it all.

53

Heather Matthews was clearing her desk a few days later. There wasn't in actual fact much to pack up, but she took what there was and walked into the open area.

'You can have your office back now,' she said to Carson.

'Thank you, ma'am, it's been a privilege,' he replied.

She looked at him, weighing up whether to say what she was really thinking. What might help him at the MCU. She thought whatever she said would inevitably be taken as a criticism, so decided not to.

'You have a great team here.'

'I know,' he replied.

'Do you, though?'

'I like to think so.'

'Okay.' She looked at him, hoping to imply that she wasn't so sure. But nothing came back from him, so she walked over to Cross's office, where Ottey was sitting across his desk from him.

'Right, I'm off. It really has been a pleasure working with you – both,' she said in Ottey's direction. 'I now know why the chief rates you so highly.'

'You mean puts up with us, more like,' Ottey replied.

Cross looked at Ottey for a moment and then turned to Matthews and said helpfully, 'That was a joke, ma'am.'

Matthews and Ottey smiled at each other, as Cross went back to his file, thinking it was lucky for Ottey that he'd been there.

'Thank you, George. Good to know.'

She left and found herself hoping that it wasn't the last time their paths crossed.

Over the next few weeks Cross and Ottey put together all their documents and evidence for the prosecution in the case against Coombes, while it was all still fresh in their minds. At the outset of the investigation, no one could have foreseen that they were dealing with a double murder. But nothing like this ever surprised Cross in a case. He just looked at things as they came along, as an investigation progressed, and took them in his stride. The most shocking of things were just facts or pieces of evidence to him, that fitted into the jigsaw of events they were examining.

Sasha Connor had been in touch a couple of times. Despite her feelings about her brother she wanted to know whether any action would be taken against the Dragushas. Ottey had advised her to walk away. Leave well alone and move on. It was almost impossible to prove. She felt Sasha's time was better spent keeping her brother in check and making sure he had the help he so obviously needed. There had been distant rumblings about the Bar association conducting an enquiry into Luke Frampton's behaviour, both in terms of his impropriety in his relationship with Agnesha and, it emerged, other clients over the years, and his attempted fraud over the 'stolen' jewellery. But Luke retired quietly and quickly. Presumably in some deal brokered with the Bar designed not to attract too much bad publicity to itself. As for Peggy's jewellery, it was never seen again.

Clive Bland left Chapel's company by 'mutual agreement' and was thanked for his time there. Cross read, some months later in the *Financial Times*, which he had the occasional desire to buy, that Chapel had 'significantly scaled down the ambitions of the company going forward.' They would no longer be going public. A new deal with a Chinese bank meant that he could buy out all of his new investors with a modest return for them. In a small sign of rapprochement, he appointed Mike Rowbottom as a non-executive director. 'To keep my artistic and moral focus closer to the ideals we both embraced when we started out,' was Chapel's official statement. Cross reflected how much the pandemic had changed the world with Zoom and Teams apps, meaning that Rowbottom could fulfil this function effectively from the other side of the world.

54

Something else was preoccupying Cross outside of work. He had looked further into his father's life after his mother had left them and pieced it all together. He was surprised by what he discovered. He wasn't expecting it at all. The sitting room in his flat now looked like the incident room at the MCU, in the middle of a case. On one wall was a map of the UK on which he'd placed coloured pins, with dates, for his and Raymond's visits to famous Brunel engineering landmarks, together with various amusement parks. There had been occasional trips abroad, but Cross had never gone, as he wasn't entirely convinced of the safety of flying as a means of travel. There were so many imponderables, so many factors over which no passenger had any control, that he'd decided from an early age not to fly. There was the airline to consider first. What was its safety record like? What was its annual budget for maintenance and how did that work out per aircraft? Did the airline buy its planes new or second-hand? If second-hand, all the above questions applied from the start again, plus – why did they sell? This was before you even got onto the pilot's flying hours and individual personality. So, Ron had accompanied Raymond on the infrequent trips abroad, leaving the young Cross in the care of Raymond's

THE POLITICIAN

late sister. Cross gave these trips their own coloured pins with
dates.

Ron came on a lot of their trips throughout the UK too.
More pins on the map. They had all three at one time or
another shared a room to save money, with Cross on what
was referred to in those days as a camp bed or, if he was
particularly unlucky, a zed bed. These always seemed to have
a thin concrete mattress on them, with rock-hard buttons
at regular intervals across, that would invariably find a
way to stick in his back and wake him up. The more Cross
investigated, he came to realise Ron had spent a long time
with them, before his death at the age of forty-three in 1998.
As he painstakingly put their lives together with ticket stubs,
restaurant bills, theatre bills, Cross began to see a pattern.
Raymond had kept virtually everything, so Cross was able to
construct quite a detailed narrative of the years immediately
after his mother left them. But so many of the bills were for
three; three train tickets; three cinema stubs.

He then discovered a pair of photographs, individual
portraits of Raymond and Ron taken in a professional
photographer's studio. They were black and white and the
two young men looked like romantic matinée idols from a
bygone era. Thick gelled black hair, wrinkle free, they looked
in their prime, which of course they were. Raymond was
looking out of the right-hand side of his photograph, Ron
looking out of the left of his. So if you placed them together
they were looking at each other. On the back of Ron's picture
were the words 'To R from R' in his father's handwriting. The
same inscription was on the back of Raymond's portrait but
in a different hand. The date was 5th June, 1979. It brought
back another memory for Cross. Raymond always used to

tell him that he and Ron were collectively called Rolls Royce, or the two R's, at work, as they were in the same department.

It didn't take a detective to figure out what Cross was looking at. It made sense of everything. It had to. His father and Ron were more than just friends. They were lovers.

He wanted to talk to his father about this but knew that it was a delicate, sensitive discovery. Delicacy and sensitivity were not things that he excelled at. This he knew. He had no idea how to go about it. He also knew that there was a risk of him upsetting his father deeply, by bringing this all up. But he also knew it wasn't something he could ignore. He didn't work like that. It was something that would gnaw away at him, until it was resolved.

Stephen and Cross sat in the sitting room of the parsonage. Cross had declined the offer of tea, despite the fact that, a couple of years before, he had schooled the priest in the art of making a proper cup of tea with loose leaves.

'If you're going to insist on offering me cups of tea, then it's best you know how to make them satisfactorily. Otherwise my constant refusal of such offers will only lead to you taking increasing offence,' he had told him.

Stephen had sensed as soon as Cross arrived that morning he had something weighing on his mind. After all, the only reason he normally came to the church was to practise or maintain the organ; never to talk.

'I know there is no priest–worshipper obligation for confidentiality on your part with me, as I have no faith. But I'd like to ask you to treat what I'm about to tell you as confidential, between two friends,' Cross began.

'Of course, and may I just say thank you, George.'

'What for?' asked Cross, puzzled.

'For considering me to be a friend.'

'I'm not entirely sure I do. It was the only noun I could think of that was vaguely descriptive of our association.'

'I'll take that,' said Stephen.

Cross then described what he had discovered about his life, after his mother's desertion of them.

'A very emotive word, "desertion", George,' observed the priest.

'But not inaccurate, although in the light of what I'm about to tell you, perhaps perfectly understandable.'

He then told the priest how he and his father had gone away together, often accompanied by Raymond's best friend Ron. He showed Stephen the studio photographs of the two young men, which made Stephen smile. He looked at the inscription on the back.

'What happened to Ron? Was he married?' he asked.

'No. He never married. He died suddenly. My father had his death certificate among his papers. Myocardial infarction. He was in his early forties.'

'What do you remember about him?'

'Very much the soul of the party. Very dynamic. Different to my father.'

'They complemented each other.'

'His will,' Cross said, handing it over to Stephen, ignoring the observation. 'He left everything to my father. All he had, and if they died together, everything was to come to me.'

Stephen looked at it.

'I think they were in a relationship,' said Cross.

'It would certainly seem so,' Stephen agreed.

'A homosexual relationship.'

'George, I think while that it is strictly true linguistically, nowadays we would be more inclined to say a romantic relationship. That is the expression I would use with Raymond, which is why I assume you're here.'

'It is, and thank you for that distinction. It's well noted. But this all makes sense of my mother's letter.' He then showed Stephen a photograph he'd taken of it on his phone. 'She wasn't talking about me. She was talking about Ron. It was him she couldn't accept in the way my father must have asked.'

'Definitely.'

'Did you know? Did she tell you?' Cross asked as it suddenly occurred to him.

'No, she didn't. She's far too discreet.'

Cross sat there for a moment in deep thought.

'It must have been so difficult for them, George. People were still so intolerant in the seventies. These men worked together every day. They could never have let people know, especially in the factory. It just wouldn't have been accepted. The strain must have been awful. And your mother was obviously incredibly considerate. She must've been hurt and angry but didn't out them, as it were. Good for her.'

Cross nodded as he thought about this.

'If attitudes had been different back then, your father would probably never have married. He probably did it because it was expected of him. Or maybe he was in denial, confused about his sexuality. It was the thing to do. But thank goodness he did, as we wouldn't have you. What is it you want to tell your father?'

'Just that I know.'

'Is that all?'

'What else is there to say?'

'Are you angry?'

Cross gave this some thought, as if it hadn't occurred to him. But it was best he gave it some thought now. 'No. Not at all. As you say, different times. He couldn't, can't help, who he is.'

'But it meant your mother left. Doesn't that anger you?'

'No, it all makes sense. Well, most of it. I do wonder why she didn't take me with her.'

'I'm sure it was because she felt you were better off with Raymond and Ron. Which you could say was very enlightened of her.'

'In that case, why not share custody of the child?' Cross asked.

'You'd have to ask Christine that. But maybe it was too painful. Her husband had left her for another man. Maybe it was something she didn't want to be regularly reminded of. When you think about it, they all had to live lives of great self-sacrifice. Her, by leaving the child she loved. Your father and Ron could never have lived together in those times and brought up a child. They had to live separately and under a hideous cloud of enforced pretence.'

'I imagine there would have been a certain amount of stigma.'

'Are you kidding? Raymond had a child. People would have accused him of leaving his wife for another man.'

'Of course. But he didn't.'

'That's not how people would have seen it then. I'm not even sure the authorities would have left the care of a child to the care of two men living together. So they couldn't live together. Raymond and Ron put you first, George.'

Cross stood and walked to the door.

'I'll say a prayer for you both,' Stephen said.

Cross looked at him, incredulous.

'Well it can't do any harm now, can it?' said the man of faith with a twinkle in his eye.

Phase one of Raymond's model railway project had been completed. It was fairly rudimentary and looked a bit like a snowscape, as it was all made from plaster of Paris. But it had a track, some templates of buildings and, by the look of it, some prototype trees. The pride of Raymond's achievement, though, was the long tunnel he'd constructed, which ran almost the entire length of the back wall. This had mystified Cross the second he saw it.

'Why such a long tunnel? You can't see the trains for such a long time. Doesn't that defeat the whole object of the exercise?' he'd asked. But Raymond was chuffed to bits. Simple as.

Raymond recognised the look on his son's face the moment he came into the flat. He'd known this day would come. He'd always wanted to tell him about Ron. It wasn't in any way something he was ashamed about, why should he be? It had been a very important part of his life. But he'd never found the right moment. As soon as George mentioned meeting his mother, Raymond knew he would have questions, and it was only a matter of time before he looked into it and found answers. He was, after all, an accomplished detective. He was impressed that Christine hadn't just told him outright.

Good for her. She'd always had a good soul. In a way, this situation was preferable to Raymond. He felt it had enabled his son to work his way through what had happened, before they actually spoke. Why his mother really left them. Having said that, he wasn't sure how to speak to his son about it. They so rarely discussed personal things, as George had such an aversion to it. Any father in this situation would find the prospect of such a conversation with his son daunting. But with George it was different. He would have certain things he wanted to get from the conversation, and nothing more. It had always been Raymond's role to work out what this was, in any given situation, and navigate his way round his son's needs.

George told him what he'd discovered and Raymond acknowledged it without any hesitation. He apologised for never having told him, and that it had always been a source of great regret. He was also ashamed of the fact that he had let George blame his mother for her leaving them for all these years. But telling him the truth about his mother would have involved telling George the truth about his relationship with Ron, and the timing just never seemed right. Before he knew it, it was just too late. George said he understood and had no need of apologies. He was simply glad to know the truth, and could see why it would have been awkward for his father to bring it up. It was something that had niggled away at George for years, but now he had his answers and it all made sense. He wasn't angry with his mother, and wasn't in the least bit judgemental of his father. Raymond wanted to tell him how fond Ron had been of him. How he was almost like a second father, but adjudged the moment wasn't right. This was simply about acknowledging what had gone before. In a way he found himself hugely relieved to have it all out in the open. He looked forward to telling George, sometime in the future, about Ron and the many happy times they'd had together, the three of them, albeit under a shroud of secrecy. It had been a forbidden chapter in the story of their lives up until now, but no more. Raymond apologised again, instinctively. Again, George told him it was unnecessary. He relayed what Stephen had said about how impossibly difficult it must've been for him and Ron. His father smiled in silent gratitude. Not for what Stephen had said to his son, but the fact that he'd become someone George felt he could talk to. He simply didn't have many of these people in his life, and it still worried Raymond that, when he died, his son would have no one to talk to at all. But maybe things were changing.

The conversation came to a natural end, mainly because George had nothing further to add, and so said nothing. He then made them tea, and they sat there for a long time in their familiar pocket of silence. After half an hour George stood up to leave. He'd achieved what he'd set out to do, and it had gone better than he expected, with no drama or outbursts. If only other people could conduct their lives in this way, the MCU would probably find itself out of work. As he stood up, Raymond said to him, 'I really loved him, you know. I loved him very much.'

George nodded as he took this in, then walked to the door. He stopped for a moment as he remembered something, then turned, looked at his father.

'I'm so sorry for your loss,' he said, and left.

Raymond looked at the studio portrait of Ron that George had brought with him and burst into tears.

ACKNOWLEDGEMENTS

I'd like to thank my editor Laura Palmer for her guidance, patience and invaluable encouragement together with Peyton Stableford. All the team at Head of Zeus, Andrew Knowles for his marketing expertise, Ben Prior for his cover design, Christian Duck for production and Nikky Ward for digital sales. My literary agent Jason Bartholomew for putting this all together and his passionate belief in my writing. Joanna Kaliszewska at BKS for foreign rights sales and Angela McMahon for managing my PR. This book is dedicated to Derek Granger, who is 101 this year. He took a chance on a twenty-two-year-old wannabe screenwriter and enlisted me to co-write the screenplay for *A Handful of Dust* and then *Where Angels Fear to Tread*. He is now, literally, my oldest friend. All power to those with experience in the creative world who encourage and mentor younger talent rather than looking over their shoulder and resenting its approach. Finally my wife, Rachel, and two girls, Bella and Sophia, for all their love and support.

ABOUT THE AUTHOR

TIM SULLIVAN is a crime writer, screenwriter and director, whose film credits include *Shrek, Flushed Away* and *Jack and Sarah*. His crime series featuring the socially awkward but brilliantly persistent DS George Cross has topped the book charts and been widely acclaimed. Tim lives in North London with his wife Rachel, the Emmy Award-winning producer of *The Barefoot Contessa* and *Pioneer Woman*. To find out more about the author, please visit TimSullivan.co.uk.

Did you love *The Politician*?

Then don't miss DS George Cross's next case.

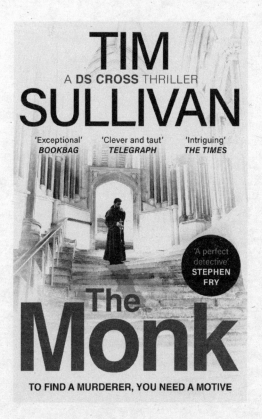

TIM
A **DS CROSS** THRILLER
SULLIVAN

'Exceptional'
BOOKBAG

'Clever and taut'
TELEGRAPH

'Intriguing'
THE TIMES

'A perfect
detective'
**STEPHEN
FRY**

The
Monk

TO FIND A MURDERER, YOU NEED A MOTIVE

A man with no past.
A case with no leads.
A crime with no motive.

COMING APRIL 2023